A FIERCE RADIANCE

ALSO BY LAUREN BELFER

City of Light

A FIERCE RADIANCE

A NOVEL

LAUREN BELFER

HARPER PERENNIAL

NEW YORK • LONDON • TORONTO • SYDNEY • NEW DELHI • AUCKLAND

HARPER PERENNIAL

P.S. is a trademark of HarperCollins Publishers.

A hardcover edition of this book was published in 2010 by Harper, an imprint of HarperCollins Publishers.

A FIERCE RADIANCE. Copyright © 2010 by Lauren Belfer. All rights reserved. Printed in the United States of America. No part of this book may be used or reproduced in any manner whatsoever without written permission except in the case of brief quotations embodied in critical articles and reviews. For information address HarperCollins Publishers, 10 East 53rd Street, New York, NY 10022.

HarperCollins books may be purchased for educational, business, or sales promotional use. For information please write: Special Markets Department, HarperCollins Publishers, 10 East 53rd Street, New York, NY 10022.

FIRST HARPER PERENNIAL EDITION PUBLISHED 2011.

Title-page photograph copyright © by Corbis.

Designed by William Ruoto

Library of Congress Cataloging-in-Publication Data is available on request.

ISBN 978-0-06-125252-5

11 12 13 14 15 ID/BVG 10 9 8 7 6 5 4 3 2

FOR TRISTAN,
AND FOR MICHAEL

The Lord hath created medicines out of the earth; and he that is wise will not abhor them.

—Sirach (Ecclesiasticus) 38:4

When thou dost ask me blessing, I'll kneel down,
And ask of thee forgiveness.

—King Lear, V, iii, 10–11

A FIERCE RADIANCE

CHAPTER ONE

~

Claire Shipley was no doctor, but even she could see that the man on the stretcher was dying. His lips were blue from lack of oxygen. His cheeks were hollow, his skin leathery and tight against his bones. His eyes were open but unfocused, like the glass eyes in a box at a doll factory she'd once photographed. Although his hair was full and dark brown, not gray, Claire pegged him at over eighty. His head swayed from side to side as the orderlies slid the stretcher out of the ambulance and onto the gurney. Beneath the once-white blanket, his right leg was grotesquely swollen.

Making a split-second appraisal of the scene, guided by intuition, Claire crouched and pivoted until she found the best angle. Using the 35 mm lens, she stopped down on the Leica to increase the depth of field. She took a quick series of photos, bracketing to guarantee the exposure: the patient in profile and a half-dozen nurses, doctors, and orderlies gathered around him, like a group portrait by Rembrandt, their faces saying their thoughts. They knew he was dying, too. Out here in the cold without their coats on, with the man looking dead already and nobody else nearby but Claire, they dispensed with their usual cheery and encouraging expressions.

The group proceeded into the hospital. Claire followed, the others oblivious to her. She was like a spy, paid to fit in, to hide in plain sight, her identity and her loyalties concealed. Her ability to hide in plain sight was a paradox, even to herself, because she was physically striking. Had the others taken the time to notice her, they would have seen a thirty-six-year-old woman filled with the confidence and glamour of success, tall, slender, strong, her arms and shoulders shaped from carrying heavy photographic equipment. Her thick dark hair fell in waves to her shoulders. Her face was broad, her features well defined. She wore her usual winter uniform of loose navy blue trousers, cashmere sweater over silk blouse, and a beige fleece-lined jacket with eight pockets. It was a hunter's jacket, and she'd ordered it from a specialty store. Claire Shipley *was* a hunter: searching and waiting for the proper angle, the telling moment, for a narrative to give sense to the jumble of existence.

Upstairs, the group crowded into a private room. In one coordinated heave the orderlies shifted the patient from the gurney to a bed. The man moaned. At least the orderlies were quick. The staff bustled around the bed, taking the patient's pulse, drawing blood, rearranging his useless limbs. In the enclosed space, the rotting stench he gave off assaulted Claire. She felt a constriction of revulsion and forced herself to ignore it, because the man's eyes were alive now. Golden brown eyes, shifting slowly, their movement consuming his energy. His eyes followed the voices of the nurses. When Claire's daughter, Emily, was a newborn, her delicate face peering from a wrap of pink blankets, her eyes had followed Claire's voice around the room just so while Claire's husband held her.

Claire felt a piercing ache. Her daughter had died seven and a half years ago. June 13 would mark eight years. Rationally, Claire knew that seven and a half years was a long time. Nonetheless sudden, intense memories jarred her, bringing Emily back with painful clarity. Claire's husband was gone, too, although by now she could usually keep a mental door closed on the anger and despondency that had followed his departure. Automatically Claire did a maternal check-in: her younger child, Charlie, was safe at school. Later he would be at home following his usual routine with Maritza, their housekeeper, who was like a grandmother to him.

At the recollection of tucking a wool scarf into Charlie's coat this morning, Claire confronted the dying man before her. Outside, he'd been easy to objectify. Here, with the movement of his eyes, he became an individual. Someone's husband, dad, son, brother. His fate became personal. Focusing on his eyes, Claire opened the camera's aperture to narrow the depth of field. She wanted to portray the staff and equipment as blurry and ominous, the way he must be experiencing them.

Claire couldn't help herself: there was Emily, lying on her bed at home, too weak to fight on, lost to infection, strands of her curly, light brown hair sticking to her cheeks. The well-meaning doctor who visited each day couldn't help her. Claire held Emily's hand long past the moment when Emily's spirit or soul or spark—whatever constituted *life*—slipped away. In a wave of delayed recognition, Claire understood that Emily was no longer simply resting after her terrible, twisting struggle, but was lifeless. Without life. Dead. After a moment Emily's eyes opened, staring at the ceiling without seeing it. Her pale blue eyes seemed to turn white while Claire watched. Screams of torment consumed Claire in waves, even though someone else seemed to Claire to be screaming, a kind of ghost self within her.

Charlie woke from his nap in the next room. "Mama," he called. "Mama."

Whom did he want? Claire wondered as she heard his cries. She was immobilized by a dense weight within her chest. Then Claire realized with a start that *she* was his mother. The "mama" Charlie called for was her. She heard footsteps in the hallway. A voice hushed Charlie. Comforted him. Took him from his crib. Claire's own mother, here to care for them.

Ever so softly, with a lifetime's worth of gentleness, Claire pressed

Emily's eyelids shut. She kept her hand in place for long minutes. Beneath her fingers, she felt Emily's brow, the tickle of her eyelashes, the tender perfection of her eyelids, the softness of her eyebrows. Emily's eyebrows were darker than her hair, and Claire's mother had predicted that Emily's hair would turn dark as she grew older. Now they would never know. Claire tried to collect within her hand a generation of caresses, from the moment of Emily's birth to the point far in the future, past Claire's own death, that should have been the natural course of Emily's life. Emily's skin was still warm beneath Claire's palm.

Seven and a half years ago. Like yesterday. A cliché that was always true. Claire picked up the chart from the end of the hospital bed and read the history of the man lying helpless before her. *Edward R. Reese Jr. Age: 37. Height: 5'11". Weight: 175. Marital status: Married. Two children. Address: 1020 Park Avenue, New York, N.Y. Profession: Banker.*

Claire shuddered. He was only one year older than she was. She imagined him holding his children on his lap to read them a story at bedtime, the way she held Emily and Charlie. She saw him advising clients in a wood-paneled office.

He began to breathe in quick, choked gasps, as if the air were a knife cutting his lungs.

Claire read on. *Fever upon arrival at the Presbyterian Hospital on Monday, December 8: 104.1. Fever upon transfer to the Rockefeller Institute: 106.04. Bacterial level in his blood at 7 AM on December 10: 100 per milliliter.* Claire didn't know what that meant but assumed it was high. He'd been treated with two types of sulfa drugs, sulfadiazine and sulfapyridine. Neither had worked. He'd had three transfusions to try to clear the bacteria from his blood, to no avail. The infection had entered his bloodstream from a skin abrasion at the right knee. There were six abscesses in his right leg. His lungs were affected. *Diagnosis: Staphylococcal septicemia.*

Blood poisoning. Emily had died of blood poisoning.

In one gliding motion, a stately, straight-backed nurse took the chart from Claire's hand and reattached it to the end of the bed. CHIEF NURSE BROCKETT, her identification badge read. Beneath her regulation cap, her steel gray hair was pulled into a bun. Her aloof severity reminded Claire of her high school headmistress, the type of woman who could intimidate with a glance.

"You may not read the chart." Nurse Brockett enunciated each word with precision, as if she suspected that English were not Claire's native language.

"That's fine." Claire pushed her memories of her daughter out of her mind and attacked the problem at hand. Nurse Brockett. Well, Claire wasn't subject to this hierarchy, and Nurse Brockett didn't intimidate her. Through her years of work she'd learned to agree with everyone in charge and then, when their attention was diverted, do exactly what she needed to do to get the story. Bravado was a trait Claire put on each morning with her silk blouse and tailored trousers. Her boss had sent her here to follow the testing of a potentially revolutionary medication, but already Claire knew that the real story, the one with emotion and power, was about saving the life of Edward Reese.

To establish her prerogatives, Claire took her equipment bags to a narrow table against the wall on the far side of the room. The table held a blue-patterned porcelain vase filled with white, billowy hothouse roses. Claire placed the vase on the floor. Sensing the nurse's glare at her back, she slowed her movements, staking her claim. She took off her jacket, folded it, and stashed it beneath the table. When Claire heard the nurse's footsteps leaving the room, she felt relieved: first skirmish won. She arranged her cameras and film on the table for easy access. In her notebook, she wrote down the details about Edward Reese. She checked the picture count on the cameras and sketched out rough captions. Claire was working alone today, without a reporter to take formal caption notes and help with the equipment. Ever since the attack on Pearl Harbor several days before, the office had been topsy-turvy. This assignment had come in unexpectedly, and with staff heading to Washington and Hawaii, editorial had no reporters to spare. Just as well. Claire preferred to work alone, without a reporter's interference.

When Claire finished what she thought of as her housekeeping chores, she looked around and was surprised to find herself alone with Edward Reese. His eyes had settled on her. She felt self-conscious and wanted to say to him, don't worry, I'll do you proud. Meeting his gaze, she said nothing, but it was the vow she made to herself. With her light meter in hand, she toured the room, taking sample readings and orienting herself. Luckily the room was bright. She wouldn't need artificial light or a tripod, at least not yet.

The setup here was a little strange for a hospital. She glanced at Reese, who continued to watch her. She wondered if he'd noticed the oddness. The spacious, high-ceilinged room looked like the reception area of a private club, with floor-to-ceiling windows facing the river and an arrangement of leather chairs and a sofa. Brilliantly colored, semiabstract seascapes decorated the walls, no doubt loans from Mrs. John D. Rockefeller Jr., who collected modern art. Sunlight reflecting from the river shimmered and trembled upon the walls and ceiling, as if the hospital room were an extension of the paintings.

"Claire Shipley?"

Claire turned. A doctor in an unbuttoned white coat stood before her. He was about six feet tall, lean, with brown hair brushed back, and steel-rimmed glasses. He wore a conservative tie, buttoned-down oxford shirt, and a dark suit beneath the white coat. A stethoscope was draped around his neck. He held a clipboard and a three-ring binder. He was in his late thirties, Claire judged from the lines around his eyes. His face had an open, boyish handsomeness, yet the hard set of his shoulders revealed his disapproval. Nurse Brockett stood like a sentinel behind him. In the light from the river, the doctor's eyes were deep blue. At five foot eight, Claire could almost look him in the eye, an advantage.

"I'm Dr. Stanton. The physician in charge of this case." As Claire evaluated him, he evaluated her, and he was surprised. She was attractive. A professional woman who paid attention to herself. He appreciated that. She wore red lipstick. Her clothes, clearly designed to be comfortable for her work, nonetheless showed off her figure.

Claire understood his look and gave him time to indulge it. She needed Dr. Stanton, because now her narrative had two protagonists: the man dying on the bed, and this doctor, who might, or might not, save his life.

"Would you kindly step outside?" he said.

"Happy to." As she followed him into the hallway, she sensed Reese studying them. Dr. Stanton walked with a certain insouciance, or maybe simply absolute confidence. Of course the confidence could be a veneer forced upon him by his position. Whichever, Claire found it stirring. The bottom of his white coat flicked backward with each step. He turned to her when they were several yards down the hall.

"Dr. Rivers told me you'd be working here today." Dr. Rivers was the director of the hospital. He was the one who'd contacted her editor about the story, following up on a casual conversation they'd had over lunch at one of their clubs. "Frankly it wasn't my idea to invite you, but he's the one in charge. We don't have time for you, and we won't be making allowances for you. I'd advise you to stay out of our way."

"Good. I'm hoping to stay out of your way, too. I'm hoping you'll forget about me completely."

Frowning, James Stanton appeared at a loss for a response. Nothing like agreement to diffuse an argument, Claire had learned long ago. By necessity, she was an expert in the manipulation of her assigned subjects. Stanton stared at her, and she stared back.

"Maybe you should tell me what you're dealing with here. So I can work harder at staying out of your way," Claire added with a flirtatious touch of irony.

Her tone surprised him, too. For one instant, he allowed this woman to take him away from the morning's pressures and responsibilities . . . to a vacation at the seashore, a hotel room filled with sunlight. He confronted her naked body on the bed.

Stop. She'd made a request for information. What was he dealing with? He couldn't easily explain the issues to an outsider. Here at the Institute, the medication had been tested only on mice, never on a human. Worldwide, the medication had been tested on only a half-dozen humans. For a variety of reasons, none had survived. Nothing about the medication was established except its unpredictability. Educated guesswork alone would provide Stanton with the proper dosage for the injections. Edward Reese might have an allergic reaction and die the moment Stanton gave him the first shot. An undiscovered impurity in this batch of the drug could kill him. Yet the patient was on the verge of death anyway. Most likely he would be dead within hours. There was also a chance that the medication would work. In that case, James Stanton and his team would save Edward Reese's life.

All this he was dealing with. To Claire Shipley he said only, "The patient will die without radical intervention. That's what makes him a suitable candidate for this experiment."

Claire detected the emotions held in check beneath Stanton's professional demeanor. She made herself sound sympathetic. "I understand, Doctor. Tell me about the medication."

To Stanton, the potential power of the medication was staggering. Its origins, however, were preposterous. "What about it?" His tone was harsher than he'd intended.

Claire heard his defensiveness, and it alerted her: here was a place where she could penetrate his inner life, his doubts, fears, and hopes. "Everything. What it is. Where it's made. How it's made." She asked a string of questions to keep him engaged, to develop a common ground between them.

"We make it in the laboratory downstairs."

"I'd like to photograph the lab later."

"Not possible." His refusal was automatic. He wouldn't let an outsider get too close.

"Think about it." Keep the conversation moving forward, don't stop to recognize rejection. "What's the medication made from?"

When his professional colleagues heard the answer to this question, they thought he was crazed. He'd learned to confront their disapproval openly rather than retreat from it. He gave her a half smile, not exactly a friendly smile, more like a dare. "Green mold. It's made from a fluid produced by a common green mold in the same family as the mold that grows on stale bread and that's used to make Roquefort cheese."

"Sounds delicious." Green-mold medicine didn't bother Claire, if it worked. She saw Emily's small and perfect hands folded upon her chest as Claire waited for the undertaker. Who had folded those delicate hands? Claire herself? She couldn't remember doing it. Her own mother, who might have remembered, was dead now, too, so this was something else Claire would never know.

"Depends on your point of view." Stanton was glad she made a joke about the mold, glad she didn't try to ingratiate herself with disingenuous acceptance. After all, maybe he *was* crazed. Recognizing the possibility steadied him. Gave him perspective. In the lab, they grew the mold in milk bottles and bedpans. The drug had worked well on mice in the lab; indeed the results had been spectacular. The medication was ready for the next step. This was an experiment like any other, he reassured himself. Just like any other.

"Jamie." Cradling a folded towel, a young woman walked down the hall toward them. Swaying on high heels, she held herself with the elegance of a movie star. Her makeup was perfect. Her dark hair was held back with a filigree barrette at the nape of her neck, a utilitarian style that she'd transformed into the height of fashion. Beneath her unbuttoned, tan-colored lab coat, she wore a stylish skirt and a white silk blouse. Claire rarely felt outdone in appearance, but this woman made her feel overweight and earthbound.

When she reached them, Stanton said, "Claire Shipley, this is Dr. Lucretia Stanton. Our resident mycologist."

Claire demanded of her memory the meaning of the word *mycologist*. A page in a high school science textbook came to mind. A mycologist studies mold.

"Please, call me Tia." Her tone was more youthful and friendly than Claire expected from her appearance, and her appearance was the opposite of what Claire would have expected from a woman who studied mold. "Jamie told me you were coming today. I wish I could shake hands, but as you see." She held forth the towel, and Claire glimpsed a glass vial of brownish yellow powder cradled within it.

Tia Stanton, James Stanton . . . were they a couple? That would make an intriguing twist, a modern-day version of Madame and Monsieur Curie, the French couple who discovered radium. In her best of-course-you-can-trust-me manner, Claire asked, "Are you two married?"

The female Dr. Stanton laughed and took a step backward, as if to escape a common accusation.

"Tia is my sister. She's younger and much more brilliant than I am," James Stanton said. "She's willing to work here at the Institute even though she has to put up with me. The job market for mycologists, let alone female mycologists, who want to do medical research is somewhat limited—a fact that is obviously an affront to our civilization."

Claire was an only child and thus not an expert in siblings, but she thought Tia looked at her brother with an unusual degree of trust and affection. Glancing between them, Claire saw that the two shared a familial link in their eyes and their coloring.

Despite its appeal, Stanton resisted the urge to continue this conversation. "Let's get started." Abruptly he turned away and walked into the hospital room. Tia followed with the vial of brownish yellow powder. Claire experienced a satisfying sense that both Dr. Stantons had forgotten her. At the long counter along the wall, the two had a quiet discussion and checked the information in Stanton's binder.

Using the Rolleiflex, Claire went to work. She knelt to make the two scientists look larger and more dramatic in the photos. The distinctive feature of the Rolleiflex was that the viewfinder was on top, and Claire held the camera close to her waist to frame the shots. Nurse Brockett brought them a sealed container of clear fluid. A Filipino orderly wheeled in a cart of sterilized glassware. James Stanton chose a beaker from the cart. Double-checking the measurements, he mixed the powder and the liquid in the beaker. Claire photographed every step. Film is the least of our costs, so use it, her photo editor always said. Better to have too much coverage than not enough, to give some choice in the layout meetings.

While Claire worked, she recalled reading in the *Times* some months before about a new medicine made from a fluid given off by green mold . . . sitting in the garden, the pale leaves feathery on the trees, her son building a model-train village across the flagstones at her feet. Yes, she'd read the article in the spring, May or June. The experimental drug was called penicillin. The drug had been discovered in the late 1920s by Dr. Alexander Fleming, a researcher in London. Although Fleming published his discovery and experimented with the mold, he'd had no success developing the fluid into a viable medication. The mold was temperamental, virtually impossible to work with. Few researchers saw any reason to pursue Fleming's discovery. Penicillin was essentially forgotten until the past few years. With the war raging in Europe, physicians and military leaders were desperate to find a cure for battlefield infections. The development of sulfa drugs in the 1930s had shifted physicians' attitudes toward systemic medications, those that could be injected into the body without harming healthy tissues. Researchers at Oxford in England, and at Columbia University here in New York, began experimenting with penicillin. According to the newspaper, penicillin was thousands of times more powerful than sulfa drugs. Unlike sulfa drugs, which were made from chemical dyes and caused a range of side effects, thus far penicillin had proven to be nontoxic and without side effects. Scientists theorized that it would prove to be useful against a wide range of infections, including pneumonia, scarlet fever, meningitis, syphilis, and blood poisoning. However, the necessary clinical testing hadn't yet been done. Given the production problems, the *Times* noted, penicillin might remain nothing more than a laboratory curiosity.

A quiet crowd gathered at the door, doctors, nurses, orderlies, and several administrators. Their presence alone showed Claire what was at stake here today for James Stanton and Lucretia Stanton. A robust, gray-haired man dressed in the white uniform of a naval captain pushed his way into the room. From his sense of entitlement, not to mention the flashy uniform, Claire pegged him as Dr. Rivers.

"All right, let's get going, I've got a luncheon meeting at noon."

The usual way of the world, even here. Rush ahead because the boss has a luncheon to get to.

"I trust you've checked this batch for impurities, Stanton."

Instead of answering the question, Stanton said, "Dr. Rivers, this is Claire Shipley."

Forgetting his schedule, Dr. Rivers turned gracious. He took Claire's hand and patted it, holding it a second too long. His skin was puffy. She suppressed the inclination to pull her hand away. "Honored to meet you. I've admired your work."

"Thank you," she replied, grateful for the recognition. If his admiration made the assignment easier, so much the better.

"I knew Harry would send me the best." He was referring to the magazine's editor, Henry Luce. "You have everything you need, Miss Shipley? Mrs. Shipley?" He had the soft trace of a southern accent and a cultivated southern charm.

"Mrs." Claire continued to use her married name, both because she'd made her reputation with it and because it felt like a protection for her son. The stigma of divorce was bad enough; she didn't want the parents of Charlie's friends to wonder if he'd been born out of wedlock.

"My staff has made you welcome?"

"Extremely." James Stanton was the one she had to work with, so she positioned herself on his side. "They've been most accommodating. In every way. Especially Dr. James Stanton."

"Good. Stanton, give Mrs. Shipley every consideration, would you?"

"I have, sir, and I will." She heard the edge in Stanton's voice. She didn't dare glance at him, for fear she would smile and give the game away.

Dr. Rivers glanced around the room. "You're alone here, Mrs. Shipley?"

Claire knew what this question meant: no *man* here with you, Mrs. Shipley? No *man* to be in charge of everything? After years of experience, the question annoyed her only a little. She didn't need to fight any personal or societal battles with him or anyone. She only needed to get the story. "Quite alone, Dr. Rivers."

"And you can manage?"

"Yes, I can manage."

"Good for you." He play-punched the air with approval. "Okay, Stanton, let's go. I've got three minutes."

Dr. Stanton ignored his boss's injunction to hurry. He stood at the porcelain sink at the end of the counter and slowly washed his hands. Nurse Brockett held a clean towel for him. He dried his hands methodically. With care, he filled a syringe with liquid penicillin measured to a precise amount.

"Thirty-five thousand units," he said to Tia, who nodded and made a note of it in the binder. The dosing was extrapolated from what they'd been giving the experimental mice. A mouse weighed x and was cured with dose y. This human subject weighed a and therefore needed dose b. A simple algebraic equation. He tried to maintain this level of detachment, to keep at bay the other variables vying for his attention by the hundreds. The leap between a mouse and a human suddenly became staggering. Yet he had to move forward. Holding the syringe upward, he pushed the plunger to make certain no air remained inside. He capped the needle. Tia watched intently, as if poised to catch any misstep. He stoppered the beaker that held the remaining penicillin. He went to the bedside. Nurse Brockett followed him.

Edward Reese appeared comatose, his head fallen to one side at an odd, twisted angle. The stench was pervasive, but Stanton didn't notice. Holding the syringe in his right hand, Stanton put his left hand over the patient's.

"Mr. Reese, I'm Dr. Stanton." He took his time. Stanton believed that reassurance and respect were part of the treatment process, too. "Everything that's happened to you in the past few hours must be a little confusing."

Mr. Reese showed no sign of hearing him.

"We've got a special medicine we want to try today. It's proven useful for the type of illness you've come down with." His voice and manner were soothing and calm. "You shouldn't feel anything when I give you the shot, possibly some stinging, but that will pass. We'll be giving you this medication every four hours. All you have to do is rest and let the medicine work. Someone will be with you all the time to make sure you're okay. If you need anything, just ask."

Mr. Reese wasn't capable of asking for anything.

"Now I'm going to inject the medicine into a muscle in your arm." Based on his research, he chose to give the medication intramuscularly instead of through an intravenous drip.

Claire positioned herself on the far side of the bed, looking across Mr. Reese to Stanton and Brockett, capturing in one shot the contrast of their faces: the intense concentration of the doctor and nurse, the skeletal emptiness of Mr. Reese, Tia gripping a pencil and frowning in concentration in the background.

Nurse Brockett pushed up the striped sleeve of the hospital gown and cleaned a spot on Mr. Reese's upper arm with an alcohol-dampened cotton ball, adding the smarting scent of alcohol to the stench of infection. Dr. Stanton removed the cap from the needle and slowly injected the medication. Those standing around angled to get a better view as they watched the brownish yellow fluid being pressed into Mr. Reese's body.

When the injection was complete, Dr. Stanton withdrew the needle and placed the syringe on the metal tray Nurse Brockett held out to him. In the silence the syringe clattered against the metal. She placed the tray on the bedside table and wiped the injection spot with a fresh alcohol-dampened cotton ball, pressing against the skin to ward off bleeding. Dr. Stanton stepped back. He felt suspended in time, waiting for a reaction. What he wanted was no reaction. Everything should remain the same. Mr. Reese continued to breathe in short, shallow gasps of pain.

After several minutes, Nurse Brockett checked Mr. Reese's pulse and blood pressure. She nodded to Dr. Stanton, then to the others. The audience relaxed into a fidgety sense of relief, the men touching their ties, the women patting their hair. Everything was normal. The patient had received the medication and was still alive. Nurse Brockett noted the pulse and blood pressure on the chart, maintaining the usual routines.

"Well done, Stanton," Dr. Rivers said as he strode out. The crowd slipped away. After a few private words with her brother, Tia left. Dr. Stanton asked Nurse Brockett to put the remainder of the liquid penicillin into the refrigerator until it was needed. Then he turned to Claire. He was surprised by how liberated he felt, how lighthearted. He even felt a touch of pride that he'd been able to show Claire Shipley this accomplishment. But work pressed against him. "Most likely we won't see any results for several hours, Mrs. Shipley. Probably not until tonight. Perhaps you'd like to return to your office? I'll have someone telephone you later."

"No, thanks," Claire said cheerfully. "I'll wait here."

"I thought you would." His face softened into a diffident smile. "I need to make some notes, so I'm afraid you're on your own."

"Exactly what I like to be."

"I suspected as much."

All at once Claire liked him, his dry humor, his hidden shyness. Retrieving his binder, he sat at the desk in the corner and began writing, his legs stretched out and crossed at the ankles. Observing him from a distance, Claire realized how attractive he was. When she took his picture, he didn't glance up.

What now? The story had just begun, yet the action had dissipated. Of course the waiting was part of the story, too, with its own rhythm, its own creeping boredom and anxiety. Claire organized and numbered the rolls of film she'd exposed and outlined the captions. She loaded the cameras with fresh film, so she wouldn't be caught changing film at a crucial moment. Sensing that she needed a few more shots of Mr. Reese at rest, she turned to him.

Then she noticed the woman standing at the far side of the bed and clutching a camel-hair coat to her chest. When had she slipped in? The woman's shoulder-length straight hair, a bright, pure blond, was pushed behind her ears uncombed. Her youthful skin was splotchy, her eyes swollen. She wore a blue cashmere twin set that was stretched down on the left side, as if she'd slept in it. Her plaid skirt had twisted so that the zipper was halfway toward the front. Her perfect pearls, glowing with a pinkish sheen, made her appearance even more bedraggled by comparison. She stared at the bed but appeared afraid to take the ten steps that would bring her to the bedside and envelop her in the reek of infection.

The patient's wife. She had to be.

Claire's renowned colleague Robert Capa said that if you didn't take sides as a photographer, you were nothing but a voyeur. Claire knew Capa, had talked to him for hours over drinks, questioning him about his experiences. He'd forthrightly said that he'd be happy to continue their conversations in a hotel room, but although Claire didn't oppose an occasional (or more than occasional) fling, she avoided men who were reputed to ask every woman who came along. Claire appreciated the perhaps naive pleasure of feeling special. Instead Claire made Capa her friend and learned what she could from him.

Now, following his precepts, she took this woman's side and photographed her staring at the bed, capturing her pathos and her tragedy. Approaching her afterward, Claire moved slowly, trying not to startle her. "Mrs. Reese?"

Like someone sleepwalking, the woman turned toward Claire. She nodded.

"My name is Claire Shipley."

"Patsy Reese." She held out her hand with instinctive courtesy. Her palm was overwarm and damp. Nevertheless Claire shook it firmly.

"I'm a photographer with *Life* magazine." Claire paused to let the name sink in. *Life* was wildly popular, the most popular magazine in the country, defining and reporting on everything that was newsworthy and exciting. "We're doing a photo essay on penicillin, the medicine they're giving your husband. We're hoping other people will learn about the drug and be helped by it."

This was exaggerating the truth, but Claire had to get Mrs. Reese's permission to do the story. Without her permission, the story would end here. *You can trust me.* This was the message underlying Claire's every professional interchange. She sensed that someone from Mrs. Reese's background, Park Avenue and pearls, would be best influenced by an appeal to charity.

"Do you mind if I follow your husband's story?"

Mrs. Reese looked confused. "I don't know."

"Dr. Rivers, the director of the hospital, thought the testing should be documented." How quickly she called upon the support of a man she hadn't liked. Claire despised this part of her job.

"Dr. Rivers was the man wearing the uniform?" Patsy Reese asked.

"Yes. Would you be willing to sign a permission form?" Claire pressed. "You can change your mind later." Theoretically this was true, although in Claire's experience people seldom felt emboldened or entitled to retract a signature on a document. "There's no problem with changing your mind later."

Patsy looked as if she couldn't wrap her mind around the option laid before her. She concentrated on it, struggling to pin it down. "I guess it's okay."

"Thank you." From a zippered compartment in her camera bag, Claire retrieved the permission form. Placing her coat on the back of a chair, using the coat as a table, Patsy signed the form without reading it.

"Again, thank you." Well, that crucial task was easier than Claire had expected.

"Ed and I read your magazine." Patsy spoke with an extreme politeness, as if she were courting Claire instead of the other way around. "We enjoy it."

"That's kind of you to say."

"I remember when *Life* first came out." Her voice turned wistful. "Ed brought home a copy. We were the only family on our elevator bank to have one." That first issue, November 23, 1936, just over five years ago, was famous for selling out within hours. "Our neighbors came over to see it."

Patsy was filling time, Claire realized. Reaching for any available triviality before she had to confront her husband on the bed.

"That must have been fun," Claire said soothingly.

"It was. I made popcorn and we sat around the living room taking turns looking at it." Suddenly Patsy grasped Claire's hand and pressed her fingernails hard into Claire's palm. Claire steeled herself and didn't move. "Claire? Your name is Claire?"

"Yes."

"May I ask you a question?"

"Of course."

Patsy glanced at Dr. Stanton, engrossed in work at the desk. "Not here." She searched the room for a safe haven. "By the windows." She dropped Claire's hand and crossed the room, Claire following. When they reached the windows, Patsy leaned toward Claire and whispered, "What did you say about the medicine they're giving my husband? What did you call it?"

"Penicillin."

"What's that?" she challenged Claire, as if Claire, not the medical staff, were responsible for it. "I never heard of that. At Presbyterian Hospital, they wouldn't tell me anything. Only that they wanted to try a new medicine, and they didn't have enough of it there so they had to bring him here. As if I didn't have a right to know anything else."

Claire said, "I'm sorry." And she was, terribly sorry, for this unfortunate young woman.

"When they asked me if it was all right to bring him here and to give him the medicine, I had to say yes. What else could I say?"

"You're right, you couldn't say anything else."

"They wouldn't even let me get into the ambulance with him. I had to search for a taxi. What if something happened to him while I was caught in traffic?"

"Thank goodness he arrived here safely," Claire said.

"Tell me what you know about the medicine," Patsy said.

"Not very much. I read an article about penicillin in the *Times*. About six months ago. That's all." Claire couldn't bring herself to tell Patsy Reese about stale bread and Roquefort cheese, and especially not about finicky mold and laboratory curiosities. "You should ask the doctor."

"Do you think he'd tell me?"

Both women looked at Dr. Stanton. He was using a ruler to plot out information on a graph. His intent concentration made him look like the smartest student in any class he'd ever attended. The resident genius. Claire understood Patsy's reluctance to approach him. When Claire's mother, Anna, was dying of cancer through increasingly tortured months, her doctors refused to share any information. The physician in charge didn't even want Anna to know that she had cancer. Anna demanded the truth, in a conversation that quickly turned hostile. The physicians' creed seemed to be that the fewer facts patients and their families knew about an illness, the better for everyone, especially the doctors. Physicians justified their approach by claiming that patients and their families lost hope when they knew the truth.

Patsy sighed and turned to look out the window. She pressed her forehead against the glass. She breathed deeply, taking control of herself. Her breath produced a circle of condensation on the windowpane. The reflected light was soft against her hair and cheeks. Exhaustion was layered onto her face in fine lines. Claire thought of Italian Renaissance paintings of women posed beside windows. Stepping back, she took Patsy's portrait in profile.

Then Claire followed Patsy's gaze out the window. The East River was green-black and roiling. Tugboats pushed barges piled with construction beams, gravel, garbage. A police boat patrolled the harbor. Ferries labored across the blustery current. Sunlight glinted off the steel trusses of the Queensboro Bridge. Welfare Island, with its maze of dilapidated public hospitals, seemed to shine in the winter light. The tide was coming in, rolling against the embankment, tossing the small delivery boats that plied the river. The East River wasn't a river at all, but a strait. Manhattan was a coastal island, and the sea was close by, surging and unforgiving.

"Do you want to know what happened to Ed?" Patsy asked.

"If you'd like to tell me."

"Okay." She seemed to drift, and when she spoke again, she might have been in a trance. "It started out as a scratch. Not even. He was playing court tennis."

Court tennis—here was a reference that gave away this family's social standing. Court tennis was a game played in the enclaves of the upper class.

"Every Thursday at lunchtime Ed plays court tennis with his brother Kip. Kip is a nickname for Christopher. Some people call him Chris or even Chip, which he hates, but we call him Kip." Her voice grew stronger, as if these meaningless details grounded her. "They play at the Racquet and Tennis Club. Well, that's the only place you can play court tennis. In Manhattan, I mean. When we're in Tuxedo, they play at the club there. Anyway, it was just a slip. He stumbled when his shoes stuck to the floor. You know how that sometimes happens, when you're racing from side to side and the floor is almost sticky from so much polishing?"

Claire nodded, although she didn't know, had never played court tennis or squash, had never been to the Racquet and Tennis Club on Park Avenue, or visited the protected enclave of Tuxedo Park northwest of the city. She felt an unexpected tinge of class resentment.

"It wasn't even a scrape. The skin was barely broken. That's what Ed said, at least. He didn't remember it when he was in the shower afterward."

Claire saw Emily, skipping joyfully outside their apartment building on West 111th Street. She tripped on an imperfection in the sidewalk, a small edge where one slab rose above the next by a quarter inch, no more. That quarter inch killed her. Emily broke her fall with her hands. She wasn't the type of child to scream and cry, but she moaned as she pushed herself up. Both knees were scraped. Brush burns covered her palms. But her face never touched the pavement. Her face remained perfect and lovely to the end . . . the full cheeks, the wide brow, her skin so smooth and soft. The day was warm for June. Emily was wearing her favorite dress, the one with smocking on the bodice. The dress was yellow with a print of green and blue merry-go-round horses. Emily didn't want to get blood on her dress. "Mommy, hold my dress," she said as they went upstairs to wash and bandage the scrapes. Claire bunched the skirt and held it above Emily's knees. Four days later Emily was dead.

Patsy continued, oblivious to Claire's anguish. "By Sunday his knee was a little swollen and stiff, but then we heard about the attack on Pearl Harbor and he put the stiffness out of his mind. It seemed so minor compared to everything else that was going on."

Patsy paused, remembering that day. Claire remembered, too. Each morning when she woke up and turned on the radio news, she felt as if she were hearing about Pearl Harbor for the first time. Each day, she felt a shock like the first shock. The attack on Pearl Harbor and the destruction of the nation's fleet were incomprehensible. Pearl Harbor was the first topic when you telephoned a friend or passed an acquaintance on the street. Where were you, what were you doing when you heard the news, people asked obsessively, as if trying to grasp that it had actually happened. Claire and her son were at home. Claire was tormenting Charlie by making him try on all his clothes so they could donate what he'd outgrown to Greenwich House, the local settlement house, before Christmas. Claire had turned on the radio, to a concert by the New York Philharmonic. She'd been looking forward to it. In the middle of the program, an announcer delivered the news.

Claire hadn't waited for her boss to telephone her. Immediately she arranged for Charlie to spend the rest of the day around the corner with the family of his best friend, Ben. Charlie was thrilled, especially because they simply left the clothes in a pile on his bed. Claire went to the office. When she arrived, she learned that Mr. Luce had ordered the week's issue remade, a tremendous expense because they'd already closed and were in production. Trying to get an overview, Mack Mahoney, the photo editor, had sent photographers around the city for shots of ordinary people and their reactions.

When Mrs. Roosevelt spoke to the nation in the early evening, Claire was outside Grand Central Station. "I have a boy at sea on a destroyer," the first lady said in her high-pitched voice, always surprising to Claire in a woman who otherwise seemed formidable. A dozen people pressed around the open doors of a Checker cab parked in front of the station, the radio turned up loud. "Many of you all over the country have boys in the service who will now be called upon to go into action. . . . You cannot escape anxiety, you cannot escape the clutch of fear at your heart."

Along Forty-second Street in the chill of early winter, cars and taxis pulled over and strangers gathered to listen to Mrs. Roosevelt. Using a tripod and a long exposure in the misty darkness, Claire captured a rhythm of headlights, streetlamps, and silhouetted figures bundled in coats and hats. Mr. Luce admired the haunting shot and ran it as a double truck, across two facing pages, in the magazine.

"By Monday morning," Patsy said, "Ed's knee was huge, and there were red streaks up and down his shin and his thigh and he could barely walk, and the pain was . . ." She inhaled sharply, fighting back tears. Claire touched her shoulder to comfort her, but Patsy pulled away, biting her lower lip and clenching her hands together. She stared fixedly at the river. "It happened so fast. By the time we arrived at the hospital, the infection was in his bloodstream and in his lungs and everywhere. The pain was so awful that Ed asked them to amputate his leg, but they said it was too late even for that."

Searching for some way to comfort her, Claire asked, "How old are your children?"

Slowly affection transformed Patsy's face. Her clenched hands relaxed.

Claire wondered how she herself looked when she talked about Emily and Charlie, wondered if she revealed the same combination of joy and love that Patsy now showed.

"Sally is eleven and Ned is nine. Sally goes to Spence and Ned goes to Collegiate," she added, replying to a standard question, heard even when it wasn't asked.

"I'd like to meet them. Take their picture."

"For the magazine?"

"Yes."

"Thank you. I'd like that. I'm hoping they can visit Ed tomorrow." She glanced at her husband in confusion. "If he's not busy with the doctors, I mean."

If he's not dead, Claire assumed Patsy must be thinking.

"Maybe when the children are here, I'll ask the doctor about the medicine. Maybe he'll explain it to them. They're only children, after all. We can say it's a science lesson."

"That sounds like a good idea."

Patsy gave Claire a grateful smile, as if they were two mothers at the playground plotting a treat that was supposed to be for their children but was actually for the grown-ups.

Patsy swayed, gripping the windowsill to steady herself.

"Are you okay, Mrs. Reese?"

"I'm a little dizzy. I haven't been sleeping or eating."

Claire gestured toward the sofa. "The doctor said he won't know anything for several hours. You should lie down."

"Yes." Retrieving her coat, Patsy made her way to the leather sofa. Claire followed, careful not to touch her but close enough to help if she stumbled. Patsy shaped her coat into a pillow, unfolded the tartan blanket draped across the sofa's armrest to cover her legs, and settled herself on her side. She closed her eyes. A lock of hair fell across her cheek. Claire pretended to busy herself with the equipment. After several minutes, Patsy's breathing took on the steadiness of sleep.

Claire used the Leica. Although she bracketed the shot, she trusted she had what she wanted on the first try: the entire scene a blur except for Patsy's now-innocent, sleeping face.

Edward R. Reese Jr. received the first injection of 35,000 units of penicillin at 12:04 PM, when his fever registered 105.9. He received the second injection at 4:00 PM, when his fever was 105.7. Claire confirmed these details when she reviewed the chart during one of Nurse Brockett's breaks. His breathing was still a harsh, tortured moan.

At 6:00 PM, Nurse Brockett ordered a junior nurse to escort Patsy Reese, who'd woken, to the dining room for dinner. An orderly brought dinner on a tray for Dr. Stanton and came back with a tray for Claire, an unexpected gift. She looked at Stanton, expecting him to ask her to join him, but he reviewed his notes while eating. Generally she shared meals with the subjects of her stories, but in this case Claire decided not to press her position by inviting herself to join him.

At 8:00 PM, at the third injection, Mr. Reese's fever registered 105.8. Stanton was troubled when Nurse Brockett told him this. She also gave him a report on the latest blood tests. The concentration of bacteria was down, but only slightly. Tia Stanton had rejoined them, accompanied by a colleague, a slight, white-haired British man whom she called David. The Stantons didn't take the time to introduce David to Claire.

"Do you think we should raise the dose?" Dr. Stanton asked them.

"Hard to say," David said. "We don't know why he isn't responding. In our experiments, the mice responded almost immediately."

"We need to keep our long-term treatment options open, too," Tia said.

Despite all that was at stake, they gave their opinions matter-of-factly. Claire was impressed.

"Several high doses short-term might be better than sustained doses long-term," Stanton said. He, too, appreciated the attitude of his colleagues. They kept him steady. There was no room for overt emotion within the confines of the experiment. There would be time, too much time most likely, for emotion afterward.

"It's a possibility," said Tia. "We'll design the protocols to test the hypothesis in mice." She noted it on her clipboard.

Stanton thought for a long moment, considering the options. The staff waited for his decision, but he took his time. Impatience was an enemy. He had to keep his mind clear, thinking ahead to the next patient and the next. "I'll continue with 35,000 units every four hours. We'll use higher doses on the next patient. Next time, I'll also use a double dose for the first injection."

"The mice will try that idea, as well," David said.

Had they already given up on Edward Reese? Claire wondered. Their attitude was part of the story, too, the professionalism reflected in the steadfast expressions and straight postures, which she duly captured on film.

Tia and David left. After writing his notes, Stanton gave Claire an appraising glance. As attractive as she was, he wasn't in the mood for small talk or flirtation. He retrieved a back issue of the *Journal of Biological Chemistry*. Might as well use the empty hours between injections to catch up on his journal reading. He didn't want to leave the room for any length of time until he had a clear understanding of the outcome of the experiment.

Midnight. The fourth injection. *Protect us now and at the hour of our death*, the prayer came to Claire's mind unbidden. Patsy dozed in one of the big leather chairs. Nurse Brockett took Mr. Reese's temperature.

"102.4."

The fever was down, dramatically. Stanton steeled himself to a pretense of calm impassivity. "Take the temperature again, would you, Nurse Brockett."

"Yes, sir." She looked as if she doubted it herself. Afterward, she went into the hall, where the light was brighter, to read it. Claire took a shot looking through the darkened doorframe, the hospital bed a shadowy presence on the left, Nurse Brockett in full light in the hall beyond as she read the thermometer. It was a design that reminded Claire of Dutch paintings: women glimpsed through doorways. Claire was risking handheld long exposures because she didn't think Dr. Stanton would take well to flashbulbs going off near his patient or to the maneuvering of the tripod. She prided herself on being able to remain absolutely still for a half second or even more to secure night shots without intrusive equipment. The photo-lab staff would push the film during development.

Claire glanced up: Stanton was watching her. Unexpectedly, she felt self-conscious, sensitive to his opinion of her.

Rejoining them, Nurse Brockett repeated, "102.4."

"Kindly draw blood for a slide, Nurse Brockett." Make no conclusions yet, Stanton cautioned himself.

"Yes, sir." She followed his instructions, taking a small amount of blood from Mr. Reese's left index finger. Stanton smeared the blood on a slide and stained it. When it was dry, he examined it through the binocular microscope on the counter. He made notes on what he saw. Even now, he didn't let himself make a definitive conclusion.

"Mrs. Shipley, take a look?"

He beckoned to her, suddenly eager to share his work. He didn't tell her what to do. He assumed she knew.

Claire hadn't looked through a microscope since she took a required biology course as a college freshman. She didn't want to disappoint the doctor or embarrass herself by making a mistake. The eyepiece was a jab of cold metal against her skin. She decided that the large black knob on the side must be the focus, and she turned it. He stood beside her, observing. His close physical presence stirred her.

"You're looking for colonies of *Staphylococci*. *Staphylo* means 'grapes' in Greek, and that's what they look like. Round and clumped together, like a bunch of grapes."

Gradually dark shapes came into view, small, clustered circles like grapes, harmless-looking shapes that could make a thirty-seven-year-old man, and a three-year-old girl, die.

"I see two groups."

"I found three, but even so, very few." He turned to Nurse Brockett. "Well, I think we're finally making some progress." All at once he felt exuberant, as if pure energy flowed through him. His years of effort suddenly became worthwhile. When Claire raised her camera to capture the joy on his face, she sensed that his defenses had dissolved and she was sharing his thoughts.

Patsy Reese slept on. Stanton decided not to wake her. Let her catch up on her sleep. Good news is welcome anytime it arrives.

"Hi, everybody." A young doctor bounded into the room with the boisterous demeanor of a man who's just gotten out of bed, had three cups of coffee, and can't wait to start the day. Dr. LIND said the name embroidered on his white coat. He was blond and had the big, pudgy appearance of a college football player who's no longer getting enough exercise. "You okay, boss?" he asked Stanton. "You look a little . . . off."

"The fever's down and he doesn't know what to do next," Nurse Brockett said smugly, as if she'd known all along that the medication would work. She prepared to turn her authority over to the night nurse, a pert middle-aged woman who looked like a Puritan and who rapped her fingers on the counter impatiently as Nurse Brockett reviewed several dozen details.

"We're not ready to break out the champagne yet," Stanton said, "but things are going well. Better than I expected. Sit down, Lind, and I'll brief you. Mrs. Shipley," he said with resigned forbearance, "Dr. Lind is covering for the night. The patient's condition has stabilized, and I'm going to get some sleep."

At least he would try to get some sleep; he felt so jazzed up he doubted he'd be able to. As a resident physician at the Institute, he was required to live at the hospital, which was both good and bad on nights like these: good because his bedroom was nearby, bad because he could have used a little distance, a quiet walk home to gather his thoughts.

"I suggest you do the same," he said.

Claire saw no reason to insist on working all night if the physician in charge, her story's co-protagonist, felt confident enough to go to bed.

"You may come back tomorrow. Around noon, shall we say?"

"That sounds a little late." Claire challenged him because presumably he would expect it, while thinking to herself, good, I'll be able to walk Charlie to school and drop off the film at the lab.

"No visitors in the morning, hospital rule. The patients have to be bathed and the rooms cleaned. Dr. Rivers made an exception for you this morning. I'll tell the guard at the gate to let you in at 11:45." He felt unexpectedly pleased at the prospect of having her around tomorrow. "Good night, Mrs. Shipley."

"Good night," she replied, putting on a bright tone.

On her way out, she captured the two doctors reviewing the chart, their faces drawn together in concentration. The angle of the light, a slanting wedge from the desk lamp, emphasized the darkness around them.

CHAPTER TWO

⌒

"L ook, Daddy's article," Charlie said the next morning.

The discovery of one of Bill Shipley's newspaper articles, which occurred almost every day, was always a cause of excitement. For Charlie, at least. He sat at the kitchen table, the *Herald Tribune* open before him. Their house, on Grove Street in Greenwich Village, had belonged to Claire's mother. Claire had grown up here, and now she was raising her son here.

Eight years old, in third grade, Charlie had narrow shoulders and a slight frame. His cheeks were round and full, his face still shaped by baby fat. His strawberry blond hair, straight and fine, was trimmed in a bowl cut.

Watching Charlie from where she stood at the stove, apron over her work clothes, Claire's yearning for him was like a stab in her chest. If anything ever happened to him . . . she couldn't finish the thought.

Emily, impish and giggling on an autumn day, gazed at Claire from a photo on the mantel. Pictures of Emily filled the house. As much as the pictures hurt Claire to see, taking the photos down would be like saying that Emily had never lived, and that would be worse. After all, what evidence did she have that Emily had, in fact, existed? A lock of her hair. Her first pair of shoes, barely worn because Emily had outgrown them so fast. Her favorite doll, stained and tattered. And these photographs.

After Emily died, Claire's mother had warned her that some parents responded to the loss of a child by turning away from their surviving children. Claire had responded the opposite way, loving Charlie with a vehemence and protectiveness that could be frightening even to her.

As a mother who'd lost a child, what was she supposed to call herself? Maybe if she could find a word to define herself, she'd be able to cope with both her suffering and her possessiveness. The English language had a word for a woman who'd lost her husband, a man who'd lost his wife, a child who'd lost parents, but why wasn't there a word, an identifier, for a parent who'd lost a child? Did other languages have such a word? Claire didn't know.

Charlie, too, had had his share of illnesses. Nature's way, the doctor told her. *Ashes to ashes*, *dust to dust*. The frailty of life greeted her along with her love each morning when she teased Charlie awake.

"Daddy says, 'The British government's reaction to the news of America's entry into the conflict . . .'" Charlie labored to sound out the long words.

From her position at the stove, Claire listened, gently correcting his pronunciation when necessary. She was making French toast. The kitchen was on the ground floor in the back of the house. Glass doors opened onto a walled garden, which looked dreary and barren under today's gray sky.

"'British naval reaction to the losses suffered by the American fleet at Pearl Harbor . . .'"

Claire hated this morning routine of searching the newspaper for Bill Shipley's dispatches from London and reading them aloud. She put up with it only because Charlie needed the contact with his father. Typically Bill wrote to him once a week, but for the past several months, Charlie had heard nothing from his father. Claire hadn't received any checks from Bill for Charlie's support, either. Claire's questioning letters and telegrams to Bill, and a series of messages sent through his office, went unanswered. Claire wanted to get on with her life without Bill's specter haunting the background of her thoughts and plans, but she found herself continually pushed into confrontation with him, not only in her imagination but also in the time-consuming chores required to force him to fulfill his obligations.

"'Prime Minister Churchill told the *Tribune* this morning'— Daddy's trying to tell me that he got to see the prime minister!" Charlie exclaimed.

"Yes, you must be right." Claire tried not to sound as grim as she felt. For want of any other explanation, she'd told Charlie that the ships carrying Bill's letters to him had been sunk by German U-boats in the North Atlantic. She had no idea whether this was true, and it was an awful excuse, but Charlie believed it. As long as Charlie had the newspaper articles to prove his father was alive, he didn't seem to notice the lack of letters. Charlie cut out the dispatches each day and pasted them in a scrapbook. He seemed to think that they'd been written for him personally and were filled with secret messages.

Before turning over the French toast, Claire added a touch of cinnamon.

"'American Special Envoy—' would you read me the rest?" Charlie pushed away the paper in frustration.

"Breakfast is almost ready. Let's have a break from Daddy's article. I'll read it to you later." In an ideal world, she'd never have to read one of Bill Shipley's dispatches again. "Let's find some maps."

Before serving, Claire reorganized the newspapers that were spread across the table and emblazoned with the war news: the Japanese bombing of the Philippines, air raid alarms in San Francisco, the horrific suffering of the men trapped on the *Arizona* at Pearl Harbor. Claire wanted to protect her son from understanding how bad the situation was for America. Protect him from the unanswerable questions that filled her own vision of tomorrow, next week, and the months to come.

Maps were the solution. The *Times* could be counted on for several maps each day. With the objectivity of a geography lesson, the maps showed the movements of enemy forces around the world. The arrows and dotted lines revealed no hint of the human slaughter that these movements represented. Claire found what she needed, then brought the plates to the table. She and Charlie examined the maps while eating. Soon their fingers were covered with black newsprint. Between bites of French toast with maple syrup, they laughed at their muddled pronunciations of Tarakan and Balikpapan, Soerabaja and Makassar. The names took on an incantatory power. A week ago Claire had never heard of these places in the Pacific. Now they were vital to the nation's future.

Claire and Charlie had begun their morning map reading in September 1939 when Germany invaded Poland. By the spring of 1940, they were monitoring the German invasion of Denmark and Norway. In May and June of 1940 they followed each day as the Germans marched across the Netherlands, Belgium, and France. They learned about North Africa through the battles fought there in 1941. Sidi Omar, Mersa Matruh, El Agheila, Soluch—the strange names became familiar. Charlie pinpointed the location of Crete when it fell to the Nazis. In June of 1941, the Germans invaded the Soviet Union, and Claire and Charlie traced the borders of the Ukraine and Belorussia. They located the Pripyat Marshes and the Dvina River.

In the beginning, their map reading had been extremely personal: Bill Shipley was reporting from Berlin in September 1939 when Germany invaded Poland. Now Bill was in London, where he'd been during the worst of the Blitz in September 1940. Claire had managed to shift Charlie's attention away from the nightly bombing raids on London by studying maps of the Italian campaigns in British Somaliland and Egypt taking place simultaneously.

The geography of war. Claire never knew how much Charlie understood or how he visualized the world in his imagination. She hoped that for Charlie *the war* meant arrows across a newspaper, not blaring

radio reports on casualties, and particularly not the whispered speculation on whether New York City would be bombed.

Charlie pursed his lips as he examined the newspapers. His hair
was like an artist's palette with half a dozen colors, blond, red, pale
brown, even shades of gray. Claire wanted to touch his cheek, caress
his hair, but she stopped herself, knowing he'd be annoyed. He liked
to think of himself as being very grown up.

Charlie claimed that he remembered his sister, but he was only six
months old when she died. He talked about her as if she grew younger
as he became older. Nowadays he imagined her as a baby. Baby Emily.
Remember when Baby Emily learned to walk? Remember the time
she took her nap in the laundry basket? Maybe Charlie was projecting
from photographs, or from stories Maritza or Claire herself had told
him. Or perhaps he was projecting memories of his own life onto her.

Emily and Charlie, her children. Claire put her hand on Charlie's
shoulder, hoping he wouldn't shrug her off, grateful when he didn't.
She was afraid that she would lose him, especially now, with the world
enflamed.

When the United States entered the Great War in 1917, Claire had
sat here at the kitchen table with her mother and studied the maps in
the newspapers. The second battle of the Marne, the movement of
Bolshevik forces during the revolution in Russia . . . together they'd
followed the events far away. Even at the breakfast table, preparing for
a day of volunteer work at the settlement house clinic, Anna had worn
a lacy shirtwaist, pearls, and a flowing skirt. She'd held herself with
the stiff elegance born of corsets. A powdery scent of perfume surrounded her. Anna wore muslin gloves to prevent the newsprint from
dirtying her fingers.

Anna had been a rebel as well as a lady, living openly with another man while awaiting her divorce from Claire's father. Of course
she was financially independent, which made all the difference in a
woman's life. She'd taught Claire not to fear the judgments of others,

to look forward, not backward, and to work toward her goals regardless of what others might say to discourage or dissuade her. She'd given Claire her first camera, a birthday present when Claire turned fourteen. When Anna died, she'd left Claire this house, virtually all that remained from an inherited fortune lost during the crash of 1929. Sitting at her mother's table, using her mother's china and silver, Claire could pretend that Anna's spirit was with her still, giving her an extra push when she faltered.

Claire sighed. The past years had been filled with death, first Emily, then Claire's stepfather, then her mother. Now the country was at war once more, her family's personal losses set in perspective against the charnel house of the world.

December. Winter pressed upon them. Claire had forgotten to fold towels against the cracks at the base of the French doors to keep out the wind. Her feet were cold in her slippers. She felt an urge to bring Charlie a blanket to wrap around his legs, even though she knew he would push it aside. Late last winter, along with a half-dozen kids in his grade, Charlie had contracted scarlet fever. He'd been out of school for six weeks, four of those weeks spent in isolation. Claire was beside herself. Simply hearing the words *scarlet fever* could strike terror in a parent. The doctor told Claire to burn Charlie's sheets and blankets, his pajamas, his books and toys. This was the treatment for scarlet fever. No medicine could fight it. Claire took a leave from her job and sat with him, night after night. In the end, Charlie was one of the lucky ones: he didn't die, and he suffered no permanent physical harm. Several of his classmates experienced severe hearing loss, and two boys developed rheumatic fever and heart damage. With help, Charlie had managed to catch up in school, and he hadn't needed to repeat the grade.

Claire and all the parents she knew defined the seasons based on the diseases that preyed upon their children. In this neighborhood, generally one child went deaf or died from meningitis each winter.

Last year it was Danny, the younger brother of Charlie's friend Ben, made deaf overnight from meningitis; his parents were grateful that he'd survived. Several children struggled with pneumonia each winter. When Charlie was in second grade, his classmate Rebecca died from pneumonia. Her wooden desk with its attached chair remained empty for the rest of the school year. Early spring was the time of septic sore throat and scarlet fever. Every summer, two or three children—in the bad years many more—were crippled or killed by infantile paralysis. Guilio down the block now walked with leg braces and crutches. Like Danny, he was considered one of the lucky ones: he was alive. As a parent, you could never let down your guard. Measles, whooping cough, diphtheria. . . . Some children survived, some didn't. The luck of the draw. Nature's way. God's will. Claire never took Charlie's life for granted.

She thought of Edward Reese and of the story she would continue today. She tried to comprehend James Stanton's hopes and ambitions, and the sense of futility he must sometimes experience. Doctors could do nothing, or next to nothing, to help their patients. Serum treatments. Several vaccines, including those to fight diphtheria, tetanus, and smallpox. Recently (too late for Emily) sulfa drugs, with their toxicity and limited effectiveness. Pneumonia could put an otherwise healthy adult in the hospital for a month. Claire's colleague Jen, one of the reporters she worked with, still hadn't returned to work after contracting double pneumonia in August. President Coolidge's son had died from a blister he developed while playing tennis in new shoes. A scratch from a rosebush could kill you. Three summers ago, a rose-thorn scratch had killed Andrew, the gardener at St. Luke's church down the block; he'd left four young children, and the church raised money to help his widow. Tuberculosis was rampant and contagious. Last May, Claire walked Charlie to school and learned from the other parents that Miss Robertson, his art teacher, had been "sent to Saranac." Claire knew what that meant; everyone knew what it meant.

Saranac was a village in the Adirondacks where TB patients received treatment in isolation from their families and friends, so they couldn't infect them. Some patients stayed for decades. A wave of fear had passed through Claire for Charlie, but the doctor said Charlie appeared to have escaped TB infection—this time, at least.

Could a medicine made from green mold fight all that? The idea was outlandish. Incomprehensible. Nonetheless Claire was determined to capture the drama of the attempt. And if the attempt succeeded? Well, penicillin would transform the nature of life itself. Imagine Emily alive, right now. Dressed for school and sitting at the kitchen table having breakfast. Teasing her younger brother. She'd be eleven years old. In sixth grade.

Abruptly Claire rose to pour herself another cup of coffee. She returned to the table and warmed her hands around the mug. Upstairs in the formal dining room, directly above the kitchen, Maritza was Hoovering, pursuing her daily, futile battle against dog fur. Meanwhile their golden retriever, Lucas, lay beneath the kitchen table stretched out on his back, four legs spread wide, tummy revealed, as he indulged his personal version of bliss. Pushing off her slippers, Claire rubbed her cold feet into Lucas's thick fur. His warm silkiness soothed her. He still gave off an uncharacteristically sweet scent from the bath Claire and Charlie had given him the previous weekend.

After breakfast, Charlie gathered his books, and he and Claire left for school. Grove Street was a narrow, tree-lined backwater, a remnant from a previous century. Public School 3 was at the corner. Charlie was old enough to walk to school by himself, yet Claire appreciated the ritual and accompanied him whenever she could. Because of her work, she never had as much time with him as she wanted.

They neared Hudson Street, and the wind gusted, the way it always did. Claire resisted the urge to tighten Charlie's scarf. She didn't want to be overprotective. He was old enough to tighten his own scarf if he was cold, or so she tried to convince herself. Charlie skipped along the sidewalk, his book bag bouncing over his shoulder, his eyes eagerly scanning the waiting crowd for his friends. A gritty, sooty odor filled the air from garbage burning in apartment-building incinerators. A ship's horn bellowed once, then again, the reverberations reaching them from the Hudson River piers three blocks away.

Claire chatted with the other parents while the kids waited to go inside. This morning, facts about the war were giving way to rumors. The parents spoke of U-boats in New York harbor and German planes over Long Island. Blackouts, air raids, antiaircraft flak—the vocabulary of war.

"When are these kids going to get gas masks?" an irate father demanded. He was an otherwise mild-mannered man in a conservative topcoat and rep tie.

Claire had seen newsreels of British children (and adults) carrying gas masks in boxes. Would poison gas be dropped over New York City? Claire studied the sky, an empty blue above them. She saw only seagulls. She saw no planes, friend or foe. But no one could predict the future.

"We've got to watch out for Fifth Columnists," said a youthful, black-haired man in a well-worn work jacket. "Fifth Columnists are everywhere." He looked too young to be a father, but a bright-faced little boy pulled at his arm. The man smiled down at his son. The man's self-assured tone made Claire think he was quoting something he'd heard on the radio. He glanced hopefully from side to side, as if waiting for people to agree with him. No one said anything or met his eyes. "Fifth Columnists" was the term for Japanese, German, and Italian-American traitors who supported their native countries and would commit acts of sabotage in wartime.

Many families at P.S. 3 were Italian or German. Looking around, Claire spotted Karl's mom, in her threadbare coat, kerchief wrapped around her head, and Maria's dad, holding his metal lunch box, the cuffs of his trousers turned up, only half-concealing grease stains.

Claire couldn't imagine them engaging in acts of sabotage. What were their thoughts as they listened to this implied threat? Karl's mom fretted over the thin braids of her four-year-old daughter. Maria's dad stared at three longshoremen crossing Hudson Street, on their way to the piers at the end of Christopher. The hooks the longshoremen used for lifting cargo were slung over their broad shoulders.

At least the children appeared oblivious to the worries of their parents. Charlie was already absorbed in a speed-walking race with Ben on a patch of sidewalk just down the block. Ben had outgrown his coat, and four inches of cold wrist were revealed between the bottom of his sleeve and the top of his gloves. Their friends cheered them on, the war far away.

CHAPTER THREE

⁓

C laire reached Edward Reese's hospital room shortly before noon and paused at the doorway. A man was sitting up in the bed, four pillows piled behind him. He read the *Tribune*. Claire studied him. The man looked freshly bathed and shaved, his hair washed, combed, and still wet. She detected the pleasant scent of Palmolive soap. The man was handsome. Attractive.

Who was he? Had Edward Reese been moved to a different room? Had he died during the night? Was his place already taken by a different patient?

"Good morning, Mrs. Shipley." Walking down the hall, Dr. Stanton joined her at the doorway. He reached out to touch her shoulder to welcome her but let his arm drop before his hand reached her. Touching her was inappropriate, he decided. At least at this point in their acquaintance. "I knew you'd be on time." She looked even better this morning. He couldn't help but savor her presence. Against the odds, he was well rested and even more in a mood to notice her. "Let me introduce you to our patient." He entered the room and beckoned Claire to follow. "Mr. Reese, Claire Shipley. Mrs. Shipley, Mr. Reese."

"Good morning, Mrs. Shipley," Mr. Reese said jovially. His handshake was firm. "My wife said you were kind to her yesterday. Thanks. I appreciate it." He paused to catch his breath, a hint of hesitancy emerging through his determined good spirits. "She went home to change and get things organized."

How could this be? Claire wondered. He seemed . . . fine. Tired, pale, extremely pale in fact, but otherwise fine. His leg, grotesquely swollen yesterday, appeared normal beneath the neatly drawn blanket.

"Do you want to take my picture? I think I'm looking pretty good." He passed his hand over his smooth chin. "All things considered."

Claire felt tears in her eyes. Keep it light, she told herself. Keep up the banter. Don't show how deeply you've been moved. "I should say you're looking pretty good. You had me scared for a minute there. I thought you must be somebody else."

He laughed. "I've noticed that everybody who walks by that door and sneaks a look at me gets a shock and runs away. It's the first time I've had that kind of power."

"Use it wisely," Claire said.

"I'll try, starting now: what about my picture?"

"You go back to reading the newspaper, the way you were before, so the picture doesn't look posed. I'll take care of everything else."

"It's okay if the picture *is* posed so long as it doesn't *look* posed?" Stanton said.

"That's exactly the sort of question he would ask," Claire said to Mr. Reese. "You were reading the newspaper before I came in, so just go back to doing what you were doing."

"Mrs. Shipley, you have five minutes," Stanton said. "My patient needs to rest."

"This won't take long."

But it did take long. Claire wouldn't settle for a snapshot. Although she wasn't free to show her emotion, her pictures could. She framed the shot with care and set up three lights, bounced off white umbrellas, to soften his profile and create a glow upon his skin. Yesterday she'd photographed the twisted face of death. Today, the ever-shifting manifestations of life. She wanted to portray a man who was beloved, and who'd survived to do good in the world.

When she finished and was taking down the equipment, Mr. Reese said, "Astonishing news in the paper. I feel like I dropped out of time for a few days and the entire world changed. Going to take me a while to catch up."

"You'll have plenty of time to catch up," Stanton said. "We won't be releasing you for a month at least."

"A *month*? I can't stay here a month. There's probably a ton of work piled up for me at the office already."

"You've been seriously ill. You'll be here four weeks at the minimum."

"I told Patsy to phone my secretary, have her bring over the mail and the dictation pad."

"Tell your wife to cancel. Your secretary can visit in a week or so."

"That's not acceptable."

"It's my decision."

"Dr. Stanton is tough," Claire said. "Very strict."

Mr. Reese burst out laughing. "That's what I'll tell my boss. I've got one helluva tough, strict doctor. Please forgive my language, Mrs. Shipley."

"You can use any kind of language you like around me. In my line of work, I hear everything."

"I'm sure that's true," Stanton said. Claire felt an unexpected pleasure in his response.

Reese smiled broadly, as if this banter were among the most enjoyable conversations of his life. "My children are stopping by after school, Mrs. Shipley. My helluva strict doctor here told Patsy they could tour the laboratory. Special treat. Science lesson and all that. Nurse Brockett promised us a party afterward. Chocolate éclairs. Hope you can attend. Patsy said you wanted to take the kids' picture."

"I'll be here," Claire said.

"Wonderful." Mr. Reese coughed. Suddenly he was wheezing, the sound raw and harsh, as he struggled to control his breathing.

At last he succeeded. Weakened, he leaned back against the pillows. He breathed in short gasps, eyes closed, as if the slightest movement brought pain. Quietly he said, "I guess I'm more tired than I thought."

"I know," Dr. Stanton said gently. "You should rest now. Build up your strength for your children's visit this afternoon."

Reese nodded without opening his eyes, as if determined to contain himself.

"All right, Mrs. Shipley," Stanton said, "time to go."

She gathered her bags, and Stanton followed her into the hallway. Claire walked toward the nurses' station. The hospital was busy, groups of doctors consulting outside patient rooms and orderlies pushing racks of lunch trays. When Claire felt certain they were out of Mr. Reese's hearing, she said, "What happened? It's like a miracle."

"No miracle. The medication worked. Fact, not miracle." Stanton insisted on this. Doctors and scientists didn't talk in terms of miracles, even though he felt he'd witnessed a miracle of gigantic proportions. A dozen bleak scenarios about Reese's future filled his mind, but he wanted to pause now to recognize what had been accomplished. He planned to express his gratitude to the team when they met for rounds later.

"A miraculous fact," Claire said.

"I'm sure the newspapers and magazines will call it a miracle. But we don't have to debate it." Miracles were the last thing he wanted to debate with her. He wished he could ask her to lunch, but he had other patients to attend to, an endless stream of paperwork, meetings to attend, other research projects to review. "Why don't you go along when the kids tour the lab this afternoon?" He was in a mood to be generous.

"That's good of you." She'd been girding herself for a fight about this. From Claire's point of view, the presence of the kids in the lab would give the photos a more emotional and inviting perspective.

"Well, you've proven yourself fairly harmless, no offense meant."

He imagined himself putting his hands on, or better yet under, her soft cashmere sweater.

"None taken." He was charming, she had to admit. Like Reese, he was well shaven this morning, his skin smooth, his hair soft, although instead of Palmolive soap, he gave off a fleeting scent of Old Spice aftershave, one of her favorites.

A set of double doors opened ahead of them, and a white-coated doctor strode through. He was blond and lanky, stethoscope around his neck, clipboard in hand.

"Ah, Stanton, I hear you're having some good luck today." He slowed his pace but didn't stop. DR. CATALANO was embroidered on his coat, although he appeared more Scandinavian than Italian, except for his dark eyes. Blond hair and brown eyes, an arresting combination.

"Yes, thank you. Exactly what I expected."

Catalano laughed. "Always good to fulfill your expectations."

"I agree. And you?"

Claire pegged these two as friends.

"The long slog, as usual."

"You'll be having some good luck one of these days, too, I'm sure."

"No doubt." Catalano disappeared into a nearby office. Dr. Stanton looked pleased with himself.

"You seem happy," Claire said.

"I am happy."

"May I ask why?"

"Nick's a close friend, but we also have a friendly rivalry. He's expressed the opinion more than once at staff meetings that antibacterials from mold don't have a chance at success. He works in vaccine development, and that's where he puts his faith." He didn't like to lecture, but he wanted her to understand. "Just in case you didn't know, vaccines create immunity to disease by using infectious material to boost the body's own defenses. With antibacterials like penicillin, we're introducing natural substances into the body to kill harmful bacteria while leaving healthy cells alone. No one knows how or why it works. Catalano's not alone in his skepticism—I'm challenged regularly at meetings—but I'm still committed to the idea."

"In that case, I hope you're right."

"I know I'm right. And being right, I need to get back to work. I'm afraid you're on your own once more."

"Good. I need to get back to work, too."

He liked this response, a sign of her spirit. "Well, then, we're in agreement. I'll see you sometime later."

"I'll look forward to it." She turned and walked down the hall toward the elevator, sensing his gaze upon her. She stood straight and measured her steps accordingly, managing to look fairly come-hither, she thought, given that she carried about thirty pounds of equipment and had to dodge a stout nurse helping an elderly man stagger to his room.

When she reached the elevator, she turned to look back at Stanton, but he was gone.

Leaving the hospital, Claire burst into a brilliant winter's day. She felt exhilarated. Switching to the long lens, she roamed the Institute grounds, searching for scenes to photograph. This morning when she dropped yesterday's exposed film at the office, Mack, the photo editor, barked two orders: don't take any photos of scientists holding test tubes up to the light (clichéd, in his opinion) and get some shots of the place itself, because nobody ever gets into the Rockefeller Institute, and now that we've been invited, make the most of it. Fill up the file when we've got the chance. She liked Mack and told him that she would do her best.

The Institute covered fifteen acres on a bluff overlooking the East River. It was a bucolic setting of trees, gardens, and hidden pathways, enclosed and protected by a high wrought iron fence. In the distance, the guard at the stone-pillared gate refused entry to unauthorized visitors. The Institute was a refuge from the shrilling car horns and hurrying pedestrians on the streets outside. Gradually Claire found the images she wanted: blue jays rummaging for treats in the basin of a leaf-laden marble fountain. Sunlight shimmering on the far side of a stone archway, creating the impression of a passageway into a secluded cloister. The staid laboratory buildings appeared alluring and mysterious through the rhythmic texture of rows of London plane trees. As Claire made her way along the tree-lined paths, the quiet touched her, an unexpected pause in the rush of her day. A sense of peace enveloped her. She stopped working and stood still, letting the silence fill her.

In 1901, after his first grandchild died of scarlet fever, John D. Rockefeller had used part of his immense Standard Oil fortune to establish the Institute. His grandson's doctors could do nothing to help the boy, and Rockefeller wanted to change that, for his own and other people's children and grandchildren. The Institute was now the most important and advanced medical research center in America. The staff members worked for less money than they would have earned at pharmaceutical companies or in private medical practice, but they were at the forefront of innovation. The Institute was structured around a group of relatively independent laboratories or departments, each one headed by a senior physician/scientist. Within this system, researchers pursued their hunches, tested their hypotheses, and tried to develop new treatments for a broad range of human ailments.

Claire knew this history from a belated report prepared by the magazine's research department. She'd picked up the report at the office this morning and read it in the taxi on her way over. In exchange for permission to eliminate the city streets within the Institute's grounds, the Rockefeller family had donated much of Fort Tryon Park to the city. The family funded the Institute in full, with the stipulation that neither the Institute nor the scientists and physicians working here profited from their discoveries. *Pro Bono Humani Generis*, For the Good of Humankind—that was the motto.

If you were rich enough, Claire reflected, you could do a lot for humankind, enough that your fellow citizens might forget how you'd become so wealthy. In the case of the Rockefellers, their riches were the product of collusion and bribery, of the ruthless, often violent suppression of competition and of unions. This was common knowledge, taught to Claire in school. The muckraking journalist Ida Tarbell had reported . . . Claire stopped herself. Cynicism wasn't part of today's story. She'd save the cynicism for another story. Today's story would show respect for what the family had accomplished here at the Institute, which was only one of the family's many philanthropic endeavors.

The Rockefeller grandson was three when he died. Emily was— Claire felt drained. Weak. She found a bench and sat down. Her shoulders ached from the equipment bags; normally she didn't notice. She remembered Emily running with joy across the playground. Remembered her sliding down the slide six, twelve, two dozen times on one visit. She remembered—

Enough. Claire stood, determined to move on, to get her work done, to resist the incessant tug of her memories. Okay, the Institute was on a bluff overlooking the East River, but so far she'd glimpsed the river only from a hospital window. She needed to do more with this story, do better. Challenge herself. Finding her way among the laboratory buildings, she reached the corner of Founder's Hall and walked around it.

Abruptly she was at the edge of the cliff. The river spread before her. A narrow dirt path followed the bluff. The wind was fierce, whipping around her, stabbing her face with bits of ice. Gulls soared. The wind carried the scent of the sea and a hint of its ferocity. She licked her lips and tasted salt. The view opened for miles up and down the river.

All at once she had a sense of Manhattan hundreds of years before, when it was a forested wilderness. She visualized the original Indian settlers on hunting expeditions, walking this path single file, using the bluff as a lookout and concealing themselves in the thick, ancient forest. During the Revolutionary War, scouts would have peered through the trees, searching for enemy ships. Just to the south, the Queensboro Bridge loomed with monstrous glory.

Shielding her eyes from the sun, Claire looked down. The height was dizzying. The new East River Drive, completed only in sections, was virtually empty of cars. Construction had begun about six or seven years ago. The new highway had put an end to much of the East Side river trade and to the docks and swimming holes that had once lined the waterfront. A few hardy souls walked along the river on the pedestrian footpath on the far side of the highway. At the base of the cliff, drifts of leaves mingled with garbage and newspapers.

Claire realized that if she went to the bottom of the cliff and photographed the Institute rising above her, she could capture a powerful image that would evoke the drama of the research being done here.

But how to get there? She spotted an entrance to the highway a few blocks to the south; that would have to do. Hurrying back the way she'd come, past the fountains and bowers and imposing buildings, she finally reached the Institute's York Avenue gate. With a wave to the guard, she reentered the bustle of the city streets. After the silence of the Institute grounds, she felt buffeted by the common city sounds that usually she didn't even hear: the honking of car horns, the shouts of kids on their way home from school, the rumbling of buses and trucks. She turned left onto York and walked several blocks south. Diagonally across the street, a gigantic gas tank glinted in the sun. It filled the entire block. If New York City were bombed and the gas tank were hit . . . she shook off a vision of horror.

At Sixty-third Street, Claire turned left, toward the river. Here the cliff dissipated, creating the effect of a mountain pass. The East Sixty-third Street entrance to the highway curved beside her. Instead of taking the pedestrian footbridge that crossed the highway and led to the promenade along the water, Claire climbed over a low fence and walked along the base of the cliff. The highway was about thirty feet from her. The stark cliff was punctured by wide doorways cut through the stone, most likely used to receive shipping from the river before the highway was built. Now the doorways were closed up, grass and weeds growing against them, creating an eerie, disturbing image: abandoned doorways cut into a cliff at the edge of a river. The Institute's buildings, spread across the top of the bluff, appeared monumental and strange, like a series of castles along the cliffs of the Rhine.

She stopped beneath Founder's Hall. From her camera bag, she removed the towel she used to cushion the cameras and spread it upon the garbage and newspapers at the bottom of the cliff. She knew the shot she needed, and she didn't examine the garbage too closely. A quick glance revealed chicken bones and apple cores.

About a hundred yards upriver, four drifters had built a fire in a barrel. They passed around a bottle in a brown paper bag. So far, they hadn't noticed her. This would be a secluded landing spot for boats carrying contraband, or a safe refuge for ne'er-do-wells hiding from the police. A gang probably controlled the area and required payment from anyone seeking shelter. In places like this, the Depression lingered, hopelessness endured. Her equipment was valuable, a lure for any thief. She owned it, not the magazine. On the other hand, Mack would replace it without question. If someone really wants it, he'd told her more than once, hand it over. Never fight for it.

Even so, best to get on with things before the men spotted her. To accentuate the drifting clouds, she put the K-2, the yellow filter, on the Leica. She stretched out on her back. Through the camera, the Institute looked ancient and isolated, an appropriate place for medical experiments with green mold. As she lost herself in her work, a joy flowed through her. She'd solved the problem, and the results would be precisely what she wanted.

"Are you quite all right? Do you need help?"

Startled, she gripped the Leica to her chest. A man stood beside her. He'd spoken with a British accent. He wore a dark overcoat and a gray muffler. Thin and long-faced, he'd taken off his hat in the gusting wind. His hair was white. She read his appearance and manner as unthreatening. Next to the cliff, however, they were in shadow. With the sky brilliant behind him, his face was unreadable.

Even while preparing to defend herself, she thought, best to behave as if everything was normal. "I'm fine, thank you."

"Good." He didn't move. "May I be so bold as to ask why you're lying down on garbage?"

"The view upward is very dramatic." Then she recognized him: David, the man who'd come to the lab with Tia the evening before.

"Is it?" He looked up. "Yes, I see what you mean. Castles."

"Exactly."

"Forgive me for prying," he said. "We haven't been introduced. David Hoskins, mycologist." He bowed slightly. "Gainfully, or not so gainfully, depending on one's perspective, employed up above. Partner in research to Dr. Lucretia Stanton. And I know who you are, the famous photographer in our midst. The talk of the town. Of course not much happens in our little town, so being the talk of it is easier than elsewhere."

"I photographed you last night."

"I suspected as much, but I tried not to pay attention."

"Thank you."

"Well then, since you have no need of my assistance, I'll be moving along. I don't want to interfere with your work."

She'd taken two dozen shots at various exposures, so her job was more than done, and in fact she'd been indulging herself. "I'm finished at this location." She sat up. She wanted to get to know David Hoskins.

Taking off his glove, he extended his hand. "May I help you?"

Claire wore gloves with the fingers cut off halfway so she could operate the cameras in the cold. The gloves were a nuisance to get on and off, so she didn't bother, but she appreciated his graciousness in taking off his own gloves. She allowed herself to be pulled up to standing. She stepped into the light and saw him more plainly now, the thick white hair, the dark blue eyes, the wrinkled, pasty-looking skin that made him look as if he hadn't eaten a healthy meal in months.

"What are *you* doing here?" she asked.

He looked around at the water. "I like to walk up and down the river. Watch the boats and the gulls. The path goes to Eighty-first Street. There's a sense of freedom here by the water, cut off from the city. How did you find this spot?"

"I saw it from the path above, along the precipice."

"Yes, I've walked there, too. I don't get out much. Constantly looking for diversions."

Claire appreciated his tone and his British gift for using language. For her story's sake, she wanted to gain his trust. Sometimes the most obvious question did the trick: "You enjoy your work?" she asked.

"Apart from the patients, who display the most appalling tendency to die, yes, I do enjoy my work."

"Edward Reese seems to be doing well."

Instead of responding, Hoskins gazed across the river, following the progress of a tugboat. Claire thought perhaps he hadn't heard her. Finally he said, "And you? Do you enjoy your work? Lying here amidst frozen garbage in the middle of December?"

His question surprised her. She wasn't accustomed to being questioned in the same manner that she questioned others. She considered for a moment before replying. She remembered the joy she'd felt a few minutes ago as she fulfilled her vision of the Institute. She thought of Charlie, too. "I have an eight-year-old son. My job supports us. That said, yes, absolutely, I'm doing exactly what I want to do. Lying on garbage is just one of those pleasant variations in my usual daily routine. I take it you're from England originally?"

"Excellent induction."

"Thank you. When did you come to America?"

"I came over in June with a group from Oxford. Brought our penicillin samples to the safety of the New World to avoid the mass destruction of the Old."

"And you decided to stay?"

"America, land of opportunity and all that."

A movement over his shoulder caught her eye.

"What's that man doing?" On the far side of the highway, about twenty yards downstream, a man wearing an unbuttoned coat over a suit and tie was leaning over the balustrade toward the water. Claire shielded her eyes from the sun to watch him more easily. He was pudgy, but from this angle, Claire mostly saw his balding head. After leaning over to examine several sites, he lowered a bucket on a rope into the river.

"Ah. My colleague Sergei Oretsky. There's a sewage outlet there, into the river."

"A sewage outlet?"

"Indeed. He's collecting the outflow."

"You two work together?"

"Oh, no. I work with the Stantons. Oretsky's in a different department. His *own* department. But I assure you, he's a charming man."

"Don't tell me, he's trying to find new medicines in the sewage?"

"Precisely. He's searching for bacteriophages. Viruses that kill infectious bacteria."

"Is he having any success?"

"Some, I believe. He's from Russia originally. His family managed to escape to Paris after the Revolution. In '39, he came here on a fellowship for a year's work. Then the Germans conquered France and he ended up staying for the duration." The *duration* meant however long the war went on. "His family is in Tours at the moment, he believes. A wife, two daughters, an elderly mother. He hasn't heard from them directly since the Occupation."

Claire watched Sergei Oretsky shift the rope back and forth to adjust the now-invisible bucket.

"The point is, bacteriophage research has a history in Russia, as you may not know. Troops on the battlefield use phages to fight dysentery. But Americans and Brits don't do much phage research. Too sensitive to the fact that most bacteriophages come from raw sewage."

"You believe Americans and Brits will be less sensitive about a medicine produced by green mold?"

"Absolutely." His amusement held a trace of shyness. "No doubt about it."

Oretsky's bucket of sewage was safe now on the promenade. Spotting them, Oretsky waved. "Hoskins," he called. "Come, have a look."

"Shall we?" Hoskins asked.

"Why not." Claire gathered her equipment, leaving the towel for passing vagrants. After waiting for a lone car to pass, they crossed the highway.

"Look, Hoskins, you see—the color, brilliant," Oretsky said when they reached him. The water in the bucket was a sludgy brown, with a few soft brown pieces floating on the top. It smelled like what it was, sewage. "Ha, ha, wonderful." He smacked his lips. "Perfect."

"Mmm," Hoskins agreed. "I see what you mean."

"You wait and you'll really see what I mean—when I discover a cure for meningitis and you're still growing mold in milk bottles and bedpans. Who is this lovely lady?" Oretsky half-bowed to Claire. He reached to take her hand, even to kiss her hand, but with his own hands wet with sludge, Claire made a quick move to rearrange the cameras.

"This is Claire Shipley."

"Ah—the famous photographer! Very pleased to meet you."

"And you." Alas, Claire wasn't as invisible at the Institute as she'd hoped.

"You would like to photograph me and my bucket?"

How could she refuse? And the picture might prove valuable somewhere down the road. "Of course."

"I knew it." He lifted the bucket and posed like a fisherman on a pier with a giant catch.

"A beautiful shot," Claire said.

"You send me?"

"Certainly."

"This is the future, this bucket." He shook it, and brown water splashed onto his shabby shoes. He didn't notice. On his right shoe, the cracked leather had separated from the sole. Water seeped in. "You tell your children someday, you saw the future. In this bucket."

"I will," Claire said.

"Yes, yes, you never know what you find or where you find it. No stone unturned, no bucket untested. I collect effluence from everywhere, Madame Shipley. My friends bring me jars of sewage from across the world. Or at least they did, until our current situation. *Alors*!" He shook off the Russian Revolution, the Nazis, the torment of his family. "Excuse me, excuse me, I must conduct my tests while the little creatures are fresh and frolicky. I hope to meet you again, Madame Shipley."

Off he went, humming a tune that sounded like Gershwin, crossing the highway and heading toward a small door that was open now in the cliff. His body swayed from the weight of the bucket.

"Well," Claire said, astonished.

"My thoughts exactly," Hoskins replied.

"But if it works, it works." Mold, sewage, who was she to doubt any of it, as Emily's laughter sounded within her? "I'm photographing the laboratory this afternoon. Shall we go back?"

"No, no—I came out here expressly to escape. Children in a laboratory. What was Stanton thinking?" The muscles tightened around his mouth, as if he were working hard to make his words sound mellifluous and amusing. "I don't care for children, I must confess."

"That issue is irrelevant." Claire tried to match his tone. "I'm giving you the opportunity to be featured in *Life* magazine. Can't let a few children keep you away from a chance like that." In Claire's experience most people begged to have their stories told in *Life*. Those who refused often had the most interesting stories to tell. "Don't you want to show off the history-changing work you're doing?"

"Very kind of you to express it that way, but alas I must send my regrets." He looked away from her. A slight squinting came and went across his eyes, as if grit had blown into them.

"At least you should come to the party in Mr. Reese's room. Chocolate éclairs are promised."

"Absolutely not. I dislike patients intensely. Even more than children. Always dying, as I noted earlier. No matter what you do for them. Terribly ungrateful."

"You were in Mr. Reese's room last night."

"An aberration. I had to attend the impromptu conference." Again Claire saw the expressiveness around his mouth. She had an impression of him as an actor struggling to make the best of imperfect lines. "I do appreciate your asking, however. Very kind, indeed."

They said good-bye, and he continued his walk, heading south, a silhouette in the sunlight.

Yuck!" Nine-year-old Ned Reese grimaced as he examined a milk bottle filled with fluffy green mold. Then he removed the cotton wool stopper and tried to maneuver his fingers inside.

"Don't touch!" Tia knew she spoke too angrily, but there was no taking it back and she didn't regret it anyway. "The mold doesn't like touching," she added with what she hoped sounded like equanimity. Children in the lab: one of her brother's worst ideas. She had to play along because Claire Shipley was photographing them. Patsy Reese had brought the kids down and simply left them here, presumably so she could enjoy the time alone with her husband. Tia didn't appreciate being treated like a babysitter. David Hoskins had known better: he'd made himself scarce after Jamie arranged the visit.

Ned's brown eyes were large and wide, like his father's. His nose was covered with freckles. In his school uniform of blazer, tie, and knee-length gray trousers, Ned looked very proper, at least from the front. From the rear, his shirttail was hanging out and not as clean as it might have been. Ned's dark hair was cut short on the sides, but wayward locks fell across his forehead and into his eyes, a sophisticated haircut gone astray. In short, he was a mess.

"It's disgusting!" Ned said. Clearly this realization made him want to touch the mold more, not less.

Tia took a deep breath and steeled herself to patience. "You're right. There's a very high 'yuck' level in my kind of work." In theory Tia liked children. She wanted to have children of her own. At least she'd always thought she did. Faced now with two actual children, she wasn't so sure. Before their arrival, she'd had a vision of herself presenting her scientific investigations to two receptive and respectful youngsters and thereby changing their lives forever. Instead she'd become a police officer standing guard so they didn't destroy anything.

Claire worked around them, staying out of their way. Tia tried to imagine what the lab must look like to an outsider like Claire: a high table in the middle of the room held a typical array of scientific equipment, including microscopes, beakers, and a Bunsen burner. Everything else was atypical. In the extreme. In racks from floor to ceiling, hundreds of milk bottles were stacked on their sides. Each bottle, stoppered with cotton wool, contained a thick layer of green mold growing on the bottom. Yellow droplets dotted the surface of the mold and pooled underneath. The droplets were the fluid that became the medicine called penicillin. Covered bedpans were piled upon the floor in stacks four feet high; *Penicillium* mold grew in these, too. The mold grew best on flat, covered surfaces. Bedpans and milk bottles were the most practical containers Tia and David could find.

In the corner was the big counter-current machine, rows of turning, glimmering tubes that purified the fluid before it could be used.

Eleven-year-old Sally Reese said, "Look at these cute little mice." Sally was broad faced and resolute, her thick curly hair overwhelming the barrettes at her temples, the tie of her school uniform askew. Her pleated skirt was too short for her, showing how much she'd grown since the start of the school year. She peered into the two cages on the table. Each cage held about a dozen white mice. Sally pressed her fingers against the bars of the cage, and a few mice hopped over to sniff, their investigation duly photographed by Claire.

"Be careful, the mice could bite you," Tia said.

"I love baby mice. They would never bite *me*," Sally insisted, trying to push her fingertips into the cage.

Tia wondered, Had *she* been so willful when she was young? Probably.

"You're not going to kill them, are you?" Sally asked.

The mice would be dead within a day or two, as Tia and David tested the questions they'd discussed with her brother yesterday. If you wanted to help humans, you couldn't let yourself worry about mice. Tia treated them as humanely as possible, even as she recognized the contradiction of the term *humane* in a world in which humans were slaughtering fellow humans in the war every day.

"Let me show you something," Tia said, ignoring Sally's question. "Come over here and watch." Her tone was harsh, an order rather than an invitation. But every minute away from work had to be chosen wisely. The mold was unreliable. Finicky in every way. The slightest change in temperature, the slightest jarring movement, could destroy the fluid's usefulness. Yes, her patience was frayed. Often she lost hope and wanted to give up. Yet she'd force herself to keep going just as she always had. But she hated that her anxieties made her snap at these children. Luckily they seemed quite capable of fighting back.

Removing the cotton wool from one of the milk bottles, Tia put a pipette to her lips and drew out the yellowish fluid from the bottom of the bottle. She closed off the tube with her fingertip, then released the fluid into a test tube, which she stoppered.

"This is the medicine that's helping your dad. I have to clean it up a little after I harvest it, but basically, this is it. The mold likes to grow on flat surfaces, the reason for the bedpans and milk bottles. As the mold grows, it produces the fluid as a kind of waste product." She decided to explain all this whether they cared or not. It was their father, after all, whose life was being saved. Or not saved. If they were too young to understand now, maybe someday they'd look back and be grateful. "We siphon off the fluid, purify it, and eventually end up with penicillin powder. Some strains of *Penicillium* produce more fluid than others. Sometimes I think I'm doing everything right, but the fluid turns out to be useless, with no antibacterial effect at all. Temperature affects the mold, and movement, and the type of food I give it."

"Food?" Ned said with sudden interest. "What kind of food? Cauliflower? Lima beans?"

Tia laughed. Ned was funny, he really was. If she could approach this visit as enjoyable, it would become a relaxing break instead of a draining distraction. "Basically the mold likes to eat sugar. Molasses, chocolate, Bosco, Ovaltine." She tried to meet the kids on their own level: "So you see, the mold has candy for every meal. What would your mom say, if you wanted candy for every meal?"

"I do want candy for every meal," Ned said.

"But you don't get it!" Sally said.

Tia didn't think that she and her brother had ever bickered this way. Ned strode off, unmistakably looking for mischief. "Did you really eat all this jam?" he called from the doorway leading into the next room.

Tia joined Ned at the doorway. In the second room, jam jars filled with soil crowded the floor-to-ceiling shelves. Each jar was labeled with the place and date of collection. The wide windows faced north, overlooking the Institute gardens. Open petri dishes lined the windowsill, as if waiting to receive whatever organisms happened to blow in.

"Although jam happens to be my favorite food," Tia said, "my friends had to help me collect the soil to fill this many jars."

"It smells good in here," Sally said.

And the room did smell good, Tia realized. Like a field of hay. Like a walk in the woods in spring after a rainstorm, the scent moist and fertile. She was so accustomed to it, she'd stopped noticing. She was grateful for Sally's bringing it to her attention.

"The soil is filled with life-forms, and they create the distinctive scent," Tia said. "I'm searching for other substances that are as effective and nontoxic as penicillin but with any luck easier to produce. Penicillin can't be the only one. We know that, because when you put infectious bacteria into the soil, something in the soil kills it." The kids seemed to warm to her words, or maybe they were too bored now to rebel. "Otherwise infectious bacteria would overrun the earth. But they don't. Something in the soil kills them. My friends bring me soil samples from everywhere. A few years ago I called the Explorers Club, and they were willing to alert their members to what I needed. A friend of mine is married to an airline pilot, and he got his fellow pilots involved. Look, this sample is from Australia." She showed them a jar containing a sandy-looking sample. "And this one is from the banks of the Mississippi River." The soil was dark and dense. "Every sample is different. I contacted Girl Scout headquarters, and the scouts are helping me, all around the country. Do you have a backyard? You could bring me a sample."

"We have a country house," Sally said. "In Tuxedo. I could bring you a sample from there."

"Perfect."

"Would you like it from my petunia garden?" asked Sally. "That's my favorite spot."

"Or from where our dog Louie does his poop?" Ned said glee-fully.

"Ned, you just better watch out," Sally said. "I'll tell Mom. You know Mom doesn't want you talking about poop."

"In fact," Tia said, "a sample from the poop place would be perfect. Filled with fascinating bacteria and mold."

Ned gave his sister a smug look of victory. "So what do you do with all this dirt?" he said.

"I take small amounts and put them on petri dishes lined with agar. Agar is a kind of food, usually made from seaweed or algae. Then I wait to see what grows. Look." Tia showed them petri dishes filled with tufts of thriving orange, green, and purple mold.

"I'm hungry," Ned said. "Do you have anything that humans can eat?"

Suppressing a smile, Claire said, "I think it's time for the party."

Tia felt she'd been rescued.

Upstairs Ned and Sally ran into their father's room. They threw themselves on the bed, talking about mold and dirt samples and how much jam Dr. Tia must have eaten to collect so many jars, even if her friends helped. Spreading his arms, Mr. Reese tried to corral them. "Ned, Sally." He mussed their hair. Claire rushed forward to catch the details.

Patsy stood at the head of the bed, her hands on the metal head-board. She looked luminous in a pink sweater set, her hair perfectly waved. She rubbed the metal as if it were a substitute for her husband's shoulders.

On the counter, Nurse Brockett had arranged a selection of min-iature apple tarts, two-inch-square chocolate cakes, and bite-size éclairs. She'd prepared hot chocolate in a porcelain pot and laid out gold-banded white china.

Tia studied the dessert selections. She put four miniature éclairs on a plate and went to the windows on the far side of the room. As she sampled her first éclair, she closed her eyes in pleasure. To Claire, Tia was a striking image: lab coat, high heels, tight skirt, the bliss of éclairs in a hospital room.

Nurse Brockett brought Mr. Reese a cup of chicken broth. When he finished it, he said, "I'd enjoy one of those apple tarts."

"Nothin' doin,' as my nephew would say." The slang was unexpected from Nurse Brockett, an opening into another part of her life. "I'll bring you more broth. You've been extremely ill, and don't you forget it. Maybe I'll give you an apple tart later. After dinner. If you're deserving."

"Oh, I'll be deserving," he assured her. Patsy leaned over the headboard and squeezed his shoulders.

Sally and Ned sat on the end of the bed, licking chocolate frosting from their fingers. Both looked pure-skinned and well fed, at ease with themselves and the world.

After shooting two rolls of film, Claire took a break, joining Tia in the corner with her own plate of éclairs. "I met a very odd man this afternoon. He was collecting sewage."

"Sergei," Tia said with a smile. "Once you understand the principle behind it, his research isn't as strange as it seems at first."

"David Hoskins told me about it. Hoskins introduced us."

"Sergei's work makes him a bit of a loner, but he's always been very kind to me—although I've refused several invitations to go sewage collecting with him."

Claire sensed Tia's underlying warmth and good humor.

"David has no sympathy for sewage research, but I say, whatever works."

"I agree with you on that," Claire said. "I invited David Hoskins to this party, but he wouldn't come."

Tia turned serious. "Of course not."

"Why do you say that?"

"He's in mourning. His wife and son died in Coventry during the bombing."

Coventry, November of 1940. Claire remembered the newsreels. The city was virtually destroyed, the medieval cathedral reduced to ruins.

"His family was visiting Coventry for his in-laws' fiftieth wedding anniversary."

Now Claire understood the effort Hoskins made to be amusing. To pretend that all was well with his very British self.

"We've been lucky in America, haven't we," Tia said. It wasn't a question.

How long would their luck last? Claire wondered but didn't say.

"My brother and I try to make David feel welcome." Tia sighed. "I guess my brother's not coming to this party, either."

Claire wouldn't have asked, but she'd been hoping to see him.

"I suspected he wouldn't be here," Tia said.

"Why?"

"He doesn't want to get close to the family. Emotionally, I mean. I don't want to get close to them, either, but he's the physician." She paused. "He's decided not to tell them. I don't know if it's the right decision or not. I'm just glad it's not my decision."

"Decided not to tell them what?"

"That we're running out of medication." Tia spoke with the same matter-of-factness that Claire had admired during the night. "Mr. Reese might relapse, and we won't be able to help him. It took David and me six months to make the medication we've given Mr. Reese so far. He might not live long enough for us to make more."

Claire studied Mr. Reese, obediently sipping his second cup of chicken broth and teasing his children for overeating. "He seems to be doing very well to me. A little pale, but basically okay."

"What you see is a lie." Tia looked at Claire in sudden anger, a torrent of words couched in a whisper. Claire realized that Tia's beautiful clothes, the perfect makeup, the objective attitude, were nothing but a front. Tia was in torment. "You can use all that equipment of yours to take pictures of the outside of him, but you can't see the inside. The bacteria can hide for days or even weeks and then come back like the far side of a hurricane. I don't know if his immune system is strong enough to fight back. I can't figure out how to produce the medication faster, no matter how many experiments I run. Forgive me. This isn't your concern, but—" Cutting off her own thought, she strode across the room, put her plate on the counter, and left.

Claire stared at the family before her. Ned and Sally were splitting another chocolate cake, negotiating who would cut it in half and who would choose the first piece. Mr. Reese studied their every move, and Patsy Reese studied him. The scene was completely transformed. Ineffably sad. Ned and Sally could be her children. She could be Patsy, in love with this handsome, kind-hearted man who had been brought back from the dead. Claire resumed her job, her only choice, grasping other people's lives and portraying their stories.

"All right." Patsy came to the side of the bed and clapped her hands to get Ned and Sally's attention. "Homework."

Without complaint, more agreeable than Charlie would have been, the children retrieved their work from their book bags and reclined upon their father's bed with pencils, books, and notebooks.

Mr. Reese gazed at his children and smiled. With effort, he raised his hand to touch Sally's hair, but he couldn't reach her. Absorbed by her homework, she didn't notice. That was the image Claire caught: Sally's bursting health and independence, and her father's adoring face, his hand reaching across the hospital bed but never able to touch her, she was growing up so fast.

With the faith of experience, Claire knew it was the perfect shot, because the entire story was there.

By noon on Friday, Edward Reese's fever was 102.8. Tia and David had no more medication to give him. They hoped to have enough for one injection by Saturday morning, if he lived that long. Nurse Brockett told Patsy to cancel Friday's planned visit with the children.

By four, his fever was 103.5. At 4:30, the winter sun was beginning to set, turning the windows of Queens across the river a flaming orange. Mr. Reese began to shiver and call for blankets. His hands shook from cold. Nurse Brockett piled blankets on him, but they didn't make him warm. His body trembled. Without asking permission from the doctor or the nurse, Patsy got into bed with him. Dr. Stanton and Nurse Brockett observed her impassively, as if her action were part of the experiment. She placed her body over his, careful not to touch his leg, swollen huge once more. But even the warmth of her body couldn't calm his shivering.

Without warning Mr. Reese became hot. "Off, off," he cried to Patsy, tossing himself back and forth to dislodge her, thrashing to rid himself of the blankets. The bacterial level in his blood was up to 20 per milliliter.

Patsy slipped out of the bed and faced the wall. From the stooped curve of Patsy's shoulders, from the way she hugged her arms around herself, Claire sensed her humiliation and despair. Claire turned away.

After five minutes, Patsy was at Claire's side. "Why doesn't the doctor give him more medicine?" Her whispered words came fast, her fear barely held in check. She gripped Claire's wrist and squeezed it, as if this would compel Claire to grant her an answer. "He was fine yesterday. Why did the doctor stop giving him the medicine?"

Claire stared into Patsy's pleading eyes. How could this be, that Claire knew more than the man's family? Was James Stanton, was the hospital, entitled to do this experiment? Was a human being really no different from the mice in the cages downstairs? Who was to decide? The patient? His family? The doctors? The researchers? Would Patsy have chosen this treatment, if she'd been told the limitations?

What would I have chosen, Claire wondered, if Emily had been lying upon the bed?

To try the medicine, no matter the result. Claire knew this beyond doubt.

"You need to ask the doctor." That was all Claire could tell Patsy. She was here to record the story, not to shape it. She needed to be close, and to follow Capa's injunction to take sides, but she wasn't a friend. She was here to do her job. Claire felt like an opportunist, pursuing her own agenda while a man lay dying. Patsy kneaded her hands together and stared at James Stanton.

The doctor sat at the desk, reading the afternoon newspaper. He held the paper open to catch the light. The headlines blared. Yesterday, Germany and Italy declared war on the United States and the United States declared war on them. The death toll at Pearl Harbor was now reported as over 2,700. The Japanese were sweeping through Asia, continuing the massive bombardment of the Philippines, invading Burma. Guam had fallen. Wake and Hong Kong were hard-pressed. The West Coast of the United States prepared for a Japanese attack.

"You're right," Patsy said. "I'll ask him." She made no move to approach him.

What the two women didn't know was that James Stanton immersed himself in the newspaper in order to maintain his distance from them, as well as from Nurse Brockett and the orderlies, even from Tia, who would soon be upstairs to confirm that no, there wouldn't be enough medication for an injection tonight, despite their best efforts.

Stanton's worst fears had been realized. Yet he couldn't let himself wallow in failure. He had to look ahead. Next time, they'd do better. They'd increase the dose, double the first dose, somehow they'd have more medication to work with. The experiment was a success, even though the patient was going to die. They'd proven that penicillin could suppress staphylococcal blood infections. Some of his colleagues might say he was free to leave the battlefield now, to let Nurse Brockett take over for these final hours. He disagreed. The experiment was his, and he possessed the courage and honor to follow through to the end.

Once again he reassured himself: the experimental subject would have died anyway, would have been dead by now, if they hadn't tried the medication. This was the justification that he clung to as he read about the destruction of the United States fleet at Pearl Harbor, and about the dozens of United States aircraft lined up wing to wing at Luzon in the Philippines, destroyed in a single raid.

He thought of the first patient he'd lost, years ago. It must have been 1927 or '28, the heady years before the Crash. He'd had a girlfriend who'd fancied herself a flapper, complete with short skirts and bobbed hair. It was a different era. The patient's name was Natalia. He could no longer remember her family name, he was ashamed to realize. She was nineteen years old, born in Latvia, flaxen hair spread across the pillow. From Latvia to Philadelphia. Bacterial meningitis. He'd become an infectious disease expert to save people. To save Natalia. In those days, the wealthy most often received medical treatment at home. Hospitals were for those who weren't wealthy, like Natalia. When he faced her parents across the hospital bed, he didn't know what to say. He could do nothing to help her. Even so he held himself responsible for her death. Shockingly, her parents didn't blame him. "Thank you, Doctor," her father said. Her father was a low-level shipyard worker; he'd come to the hospital directly from the docks. His clothes were stained from sweat, and he gave off the sour odor of hard work. "Thank you." He tried to say more, but his English wasn't good, and the words eluded him. "Thank you," he repeated. The mother said nothing. Too abruptly, Stanton had left the room, to save himself from breaking down.

Would Patsy Reese ever tell him "thank you"? Despite the years, what a short line it was from Natalia to Edward Reese. Waiting for death. Stanton remembered the first time he'd waited for death. His own mother. During the influenza epidemic of 1918. He was fourteen. That was the moment he'd decided to become a physician. To bring his mother back, by rescuing others. Almost twenty-five years later, he was still trying.

At 5:15, the darkness was complete. Looking out the window,

Claire saw a cityscape of lights more brilliant than stars. The newspapers were speculating that soon the lights would be dimmed to protect the city from enemy bombers and from attacks by German U-boats off the coast. Claire thought how beautiful the city would look tonight to a U-boat crew surfacing in the outer harbor. How glorious, the glowing, misty lights of New York City, an arc of radiance against the horizon. She stared at the Queensboro Bridge. It wasn't the most beautiful bridge she'd ever seen. In fact it was hulking and awkward. But the enemy would be delighted to destroy it.

James Stanton joined her at the window. He, too, stared at the starscape of city lights. He'd given up on the newspapers, and he could no longer bear the weight of his memories. She wore a scent that drew him. Standing close beside her, while they spoke privately, the scent enveloped him. His residence rooms were close by. He imagined pushing her down sideways across the bed. Edward Reese would die before midnight, but he and Claire Shipley were alive. The more time he spent with the dying, the stronger his compulsion to cleave to the living.

"You must be concerned about your husband signing on with the military," he said as a polite way to begin a conversation.

"No." Belatedly she realized she sounded callous. Now she would have to explain. "We haven't been together in a long time." This circumlocution was easier than using the word that represented the truth. *Divorced* was a word that generally brought Claire looks of pity and condemnation. She wondered how much of this reaction came from people who'd decided to remain in loveless marriages to avoid the societal judgments that she now absorbed.

Stanton was surprised by her revelation. He'd noticed that she didn't wear a wedding ring, but he'd assumed this was because of the equipment she worked with. He passed no judgments, but the information changed his perception of her. Opened an unexpected line of possibility. A leap from imagination to reality.

"What about you? Are you married?" Claire asked. He didn't wear a wedding ring, but most men didn't.

"No." He laughed with a slight embarrassment. Thirty-eight years old and never married. He didn't want to appear abnormal, or like a guy who wasn't interested in women. Far from it. So he had to tell her something, and her manner encouraged confession. "I was engaged once, but it didn't work out."

He said nothing more. She sensed his awkwardness but couldn't tell if he was still upset about the engagement. She waited for him to continue, and when he didn't, she let the issue drop, feeling that she didn't know him well enough to have the right to press him.

Meanwhile he was reminiscing to himself. Ellen, his fiancée. He had met her after he stopped dating the flapper. His friends had teased that he'd managed to find the only attractive physician-in-training at the Women's Medical College of Philadelphia. Ellen caught tuberculosis from a cadaver during an autopsy. A common enough story. Three of his colleagues at Penn had caught TB from conducting autopsies. Ellen went to Saranac to recover. He visited her there steadfastly—until, on a walk during a glorious autumn afternoon, the sugar maples flashing yellow and orange in the sun all around them, he realized that she had recovered. In fact Ellen had recovered months earlier and yet remained there. And she would remain indefinitely, treating others, conducting research, drawn in by the seduction of tuberculosis in that self-contained village that constituted a world unto itself. Likewise, a story that was common enough. Ellen didn't have to explain. He understood from her contentment and from her refusal to return either his gaze or his touch.

Since then he'd found physical fulfillment, at least, through the tried-and-true method practiced among his peers: lighthearted affairs with otherwise happily married women. He wasn't proud or ashamed of this; it was standard procedure. He'd let his work absorb him, taking the place of wife and children. Nonetheless, as he reached his late thirties, and with the war putting into even higher relief the close boundary of death, he'd found himself yearning for love and for family. Yearning was not an emotion he was accustomed to.

He decided that when this experiment was complete and the notes were compiled, he would ask Claire Shipley to dinner. Despite death looming before them, life continued. Love, hate, friendship, all of it continued. Countless other patients would arrive here by ambulance. Someday, one of them would be cured. Despite all the evidence to the contrary, he knew this was true. One of them would be cured and would walk out the hospital doorway, onto the path under the arching trees, past the fountains and the birdbaths, through the stone gates and into the city's teeming, rushing splendor.

"You have children?" he asked, thinking as he was of the future, of the life that pulsed around them even as one man reached and crossed the edge of death.

"I have a son. He's eight."

"I like children."

"My daughter died of a blood infection when she was three." Her tone carried a trace of accusation, which she regretted but couldn't control, as if all doctors bore the blame for her loss.

Stanton closed his eyes. He breathed deeply. Once he'd had a very young patient who'd died of septicemia. By then he'd stopped counting the number of his patients who'd died; he could no longer even remember each one. But this one he remembered because she was so young. Eighteen months old. He reached for her name. It was something simple. Common. Beth. Betsy. Bonnie, that was it. Dead in her crib. The mark of the Catholic last rites upon her forehead. Life will go on. He couldn't remember the faces of her parents; they were shadows across the crib.

"I'm sorry for your loss," he said to Claire, a denseness in his voice as if he were speaking to Bonnie's parents also.

Easy words, in her experience, offered with little or no thought:

I'm sorry for your loss. Yet Claire sensed that James Stanton truly was sorry and wished that he could make amends, too late though it was. "What about you," she said more kindly. "You waiting to be called into the military?"

He felt grateful for the change of subject. "In a sense, I am in the military: Dr. Rivers had us sign up for the naval reserve months ago. He thought it was the best way to keep the staff together, when and if America entered the war. Plus he loves his uniform and already thinks of himself as a commanding officer." The staff joke was that Rivers had arranged for them to sign up solely so he could be their commander. But as of December 7 and Pearl Harbor, being in the reserve was more than a joke.

"Dr. Stanton?" Nurse Brockett held a report for him to review, calling his attention back to the battle in this room.

At 6:00 PM, Mr. Reese's fever was 104.2. Bacterial colonies in his blood were over 50 per milliliter.

Dr. Stanton asked Patsy if she wanted a priest or a minister to be present. She shook her head no. He told her that "it might be best" if she asked a friend or family member to join her. Without emotion, numb, she made a telephone call. Soon a woman arrived. This woman resembled Patsy in her style and demeanor, in her pearls and cashmere twin set. When she reached the door and saw the man withered on the bed, his lips blue, she hesitated, taking a step backward. Claire sensed her talking to herself, steeling herself to do her duty. She came in. She hugged Patsy firmly. She introduced herself. She was Cindy, Patsy's older sister. She carried herself with a forthright bearing that said, we will not show these strangers our fear.

Mr. Reese had calmed. Only his eyes were wild, glaring with a vehemence that seemed to Claire like madness. At 7:30 PM, the children telephoned to say good night. Still alert enough to be self-conscious, he struggled to control his voice. "Good night." He wheezed the words. "Good night. Good night," his voice escalated. "Good *night*," he shouted.

Nurse Brockett wrenched the receiver from his hand and gave it to Patsy.

"Daddy was playing a game," she told her children.

At eight o'clock, the fever was 104.9. Mr. Reese's breathing turned raspy. He sank heavily into the pillows, weak, defeated, drifting in and out of consciousness.

Claire waited for Patsy or Cindy, or even James Stanton, to tell her to leave, but no one noticed her. She'd achieved her professional goal: she was invisible. No doubt later, Patsy and Cindy would regret that they'd allowed her to stay, would demand to review her photos before they ran, would question the permission form that Patsy had signed. In the meantime, Claire shared Edward Reese's death. Patsy sat on a stool at the bedside, holding her husband's hand, resting her forehead against his arm. Cindy stood in the corner, her face an impassive mask. Claire tried to maintain an emotional distance, to narrow her concern only to the technical work at hand, but she felt a dread within her chest.

Blood tests revealed a surge in the bacterial level, over 100 colonies per milliliter. At 8:30, the fever was 105.3. Dr. Stanton tracked the vital signs every fifteen minutes. He ordered more blood tests, and when he received the results, he put the sideways figure 8 in the chart, the sign for bacterial levels at infinity. He'd made his peace with himself. He was supervising an experiment. Soon he would supervise another experiment. He would double the first dose, he would raise the other doses, somehow Tia and David would provide the medication—over and over he told himself this, and the repetition brought him comfort and hope.

Mr. Reese looked both sunken and swollen, glowing with the heat and force of the fever, at the mercy of the infection. Gradually he became delirious. "Lights, lights, turn off the lights," he called. The room was dim. Frantically he thrashed his head and shoulders back and forth, back and forth, to escape the nonexistent lights that cut into his eyes. His back arched. His breathing was a tortured rattle. Patsy tried to grab his hand, his shoulders, to calm him, but he twisted away from her.

At 9:51 PM, Edward R. Reese Jr. age thirty-seven, died. His brown eyes stared at the ceiling in a vacant, frozen gaze.

Dr. Stanton wrote on the chart and in his notes that the cause of death was staphylococcal septicemia, resistant to sulfa drugs but responsive to penicillin. He left the room to get a death certificate.

This was Claire's final shot: Nurse Brockett leaning across the bed, pressing Edward Reese's eyelids firmly closed with her businesslike palms.

CHAPTER FOUR

~

"Claire, it's Mack." From the gruff voice, she knew it was Mack the moment he said her name on the phone. "I already told them it was a go," he said to someone else. She heard animated voices in the background at his end. It was Saturday afternoon, a week after Edward Reese's death. Claire sat at her desk at home, writing out checks to pay bills. The magazine closed on Saturday nights, and the final hours before each issue was put to bed were frantic. She wasn't surprised Mack was at the office. "Claire. Just found out—you made the cover with the army wives story."

"No, I didn't." The cover closed several days before the rest of the magazine, so when she hadn't heard anything on Thursday, she'd assumed the editors had gone with something else.

"Would I kid you?" From his good-humored banter, she understood that he wasn't kidding. With the rush of developments in the war, Mr. Luce must have delayed his decision on the cover until the last possible moment.

"This is a surprise, Mack." After four years on staff, it was her first cover.

"Doesn't it make you happy? I only called because I figured it would make you happy. If it doesn't make you happy, I can hang up."

"Yes, it makes me happy. Of course it does." She raised her voice in anger and impatience, because the news made her happier than she could let him know or suspect. A cover story represented not simply professional recognition but also job security, a little leeway in the grinding competition to hold on to her staff position. She had to conceal the tears that smarted in her eyes. She was a woman in a man's profession, and she'd learned to keep any emotions her peers might consider feminine, like joy or sorrow, strictly to herself. Her renowned colleague Margaret Bourke-White had a reputation for using strategic weeping fits to get what she wanted from both her bosses and her subjects, but that wasn't Claire's way.

The day after Reese's death, she'd gone directly into a story about the army officers' wives living with their children on Governor's Island in New York harbor. This was the nature of her job: overpowering emotion, and then straight into the next story with no break to recover. Claire was supposed to keep herself distant and objective, but she couldn't. She suspected that her work would lose its impact if she tried.

A short ferry ride from lower Manhattan, Governor's Island was a military base that had become a town unto itself, with acres of barracks, public schools, grocery stores, and an enclave of old mansions. The husbands of most of the women in Claire's story were posted with the Army Signal Corps on Wake Island, under relentless attack by the Japanese. Each day, with increasingly stiff, silent despair, the wives waited for news from the Pacific.

"Billings especially liked the shot of the wives and kids walking home after school and staring at the new recruits waiting in line to get processed at the fort." John Billings was the managing editor. "That old innocence-versus-experience perspective. Always brings tears to my eyes."

"That's what keeps you fresh, Mack. All that crying." She was crying, too, even as she teased and bantered.

"I don't deny it. My personal favorite was the mom sitting in her dark living room clutching her three little kids and listening to the radio news like some kind of goddamned Madonna. How'd you get her face to glow like that?"

"Professional secret." She'd bounced the light off three umbrellas, including one behind the woman's head to create a halo effect, but she wasn't going to tell Mack. He might share the idea with her rivals.

"However you did it, that one got a full page."

That shot was her favorite, too. The kids leaning against their mother's skirt, reaching up to touch her shoulders . . . the composition reminded her of paintings of the Holy Family by Raphael. The woman, Rosemary Connor, was from Canton, Ohio. She'd never been to New York when she found her family transferred to Governor's Island and a small house with a magnificent view of Manhattan. Before her children were born, she'd taught first grade. She and her husband were high school sweethearts. Most likely he was now dead, or soon would be, on the far side of the world. Of course none of this information was in the picture itself, but knowing it helped Claire to create an image that evoked something of the woman's character. "Which shot did Luce pick for the cover?"

"The pretty young mom standing at the railing by the harbor, holding her kid's hand and staring at the Statue of Liberty in the distance. Sunlight sparkling on the sea, ocean breeze whipping her hair, her back straight and stalwart against the enemy, Lady Liberty leading the way. America the Brave."

"That's a great shot, I have to admit." She'd taken about forty exposures to get one that worked. The glare off the water was awful that day.

"You're on the A-list now, Shipley."

"That's nice to hear, Mack, since I'm sitting here doing the bills."

"I didn't say you were up for a raise, I said you're on the A-list. There's a difference."

"I'm positive I heard you say I was up for a raise."

"Don't worry, when you are up for a raise, I'll be the first to let you know. I already said I don't want that," he told someone else. "Don't come to me with the same question twice." She heard him shuffling papers. "Oh, Claire, by the way, the higher-ups killed the penicillin story."

"Now that really isn't true." She'd seen the final layout the day before. "Check with production. You're mistaken, Mack."

"No mistake. I got official word this morning. 'Too dispiriting for these difficult times,' I think is how they phrased it. In other words, the guy dies at the end. No patriotic uplift, no consolation, no moral justice."

"That's ridiculous." The layout was terrific, the story flowed smoothly from the arrival of the ambulance to Nurse Brockett's final gesture, closing Edward Reese's eyes. "It's the best story I've ever done."

"I agree. It *is* the best story you've ever done. Next week you'll have another chance to do the best story you've ever done."

"You have to fight for it." Suddenly she felt enraged. Not for the loss of her story, but for the loss of Edward Reese's life. She owed Reese this, at least: that his story would be told. His death, and his life, would be commemorated. She owed it to him, and to Patsy and their children. To James Stanton and Tia Stanton, even to Nurse Brockett. She couldn't simply accept the fact that this thirty-seven-year-old man was dead from a scratch on the knee. She needed to believe that he'd died a hero in the battle to develop a medication that would save the next man and the next. A medication that would save the next Emily.

"Look, Claire, I happen to know that the old man"—their code for Mr. Luce—"loved it, too. But in the end he said to pull it, and we're pulling it."

"Don't you think that's a little strange? First he loved it and then he didn't? Don't you think that deserves an explanation?" She knew she was overreacting, but she couldn't help herself. The story cut too close.

"This happens all the time, Claire. You know that. Besides, you got the cover with the army wives, so forget it."

"The penicillin story is important." Publicity would get more scientists involved, get more money devoted to the cause. "Lives are at stake."

"Claire, the world's exploding. I've got more lives-are-at-stake stories than I know what to do with. Ending with a shot of a dead man when the nation's at war isn't the most cheery note to go out on."

"Tell Mr. Luce to reconsider."

"For God's sake, Claire, his closest friend died of blood poisoning."

She remembered. Briton Hadden. They'd established Time, Inc., together. Hadden died in 1929 from septicemia brought on by a scratch from a pet cat. According to company rumor, Luce and Hadden had a complicated friendship. Hadden was charming and fun loving, Luce serious and businesslike. When he died from the cat scratch, Hadden had just turned thirty-one.

"Story must hit too close to home," Mack said. "That's probably the reason Luce got interested in it and the reason he got uninterested. Thought he could save Hadden, instead Hadden died all over again."

"Hadden's death makes the story even more important. Okay, penicillin didn't save a life this time, but it almost did. If the scientists can figure out a better way to produce it, it'll save the next Hadden." She didn't mention Emily. Her daughter's death was too painful for Claire to discuss in the context of work, where she had to appear forever confident and forthright. "I'll fight for the story myself."

"Do what you need to do, Claire"—a warning came into his voice— "but you'll be on your own. And don't think the old man will be happy debating this with you when he's just given you the cover. And I hate to be blunt, my dear, but your opinion on this doesn't count."

She took a deep breath and steadied herself. She was becoming too emotional, too *female*.

"Okay, enough of that," Mack said, holding no grudge. "I've got something new for you. A complete change of pace. I can tell you need it. Just in time for the holidays, a new Rockette."

"Pardon?" Claire didn't understand him.

"Rockefeller Center at the holidays . . . a beautiful Christmas tree, beautiful ice-skaters, beautiful tourists, and a beautiful new Rockette. Just when you thought everything is going to hell, here's something nice and snazzy. Dance shots, girls in tights, star-spangled costumes, guaranteed to cheer everybody up. This girl we're doing, you'll like her. She's nineteen years old, five foot eight, and I won't mention her measurements except to say—unforgettable. Born in Waterloo, New York, of all the godforsaken places. 'From Waterloo to Radio City,' that's how we'll headline it. Her name is Aurora Rasmussen. I'm thinking she must have changed it from Audrey, but we won't mention that. Maybe you can get another cover, a row of Rockettes with their legs up, Christmas lights shimmering behind them. Our beloved Managing Editor Mr. Billings is excited already. Research has a packet for you, explains everything. You start Monday."

There was no use fighting him. *Life* was popular in part because of its mix of stories, from army wives to Rockettes, and Claire covered whatever came her way. Her job was to use her artistry and technical knowledge to give even the most mundane stories a flair and an impact. Her only proviso was that she didn't travel unless absolutely necessary, because of Charlie. This limited her assignments and made some of her colleagues regard her as a lightweight instead of a committed professional, but she didn't care. She trusted she would have a long career, whereas Charlie would grow up too fast.

"All right, Mack," she said, resigning herself to it. "I'll see you Monday."

"That's my girl."

They hung up. She leaned back in her chair, frustrated and exhausted. She felt as if she'd betrayed Edward and Patsy Reese, James Stanton and Tia Stanton. They'd trusted her, opened their lives to her, and she'd taken advantage of them.

James Stanton had phoned her twice since she finished the story.

The first call was strictly business: he reported that a writer and re-searcher from the magazine had contacted him, and he wanted to make certain that the factual information he'd given them matched the photographs she'd taken. She'd appreciated his attention to this, and she'd corrected a few minor errors.

In the second call, he'd surprised her by asking her out to dinner. This call had been brief and awkward, as if the invitation meant more to them both than was superficially apparent. They dealt with their discomfort by cutting the conversation short. She remembered their terse phrases, almost comically clipped, as if they were angry at each other: "How about next Friday?" "Good." "In the Village?" "Fine."

What could she say to him now? "The story hasn't been scheduled, it's out of my hands, thanks so much for your time and effort, someone will let you know"? These were the usual excuses, and in this case, they were insufficient. She hoped the news wouldn't destroy the tenu-ous bond they'd formed. Once again she remembered Edward Reese sitting up in bed, reading the *Herald Tribune*.

An idea flitted into her mind. She would quit the magazine in pro-test. Turn freelance. Choose what she worked on. No more Christmas trees at Rockefeller Center. No more dancing girls. She would still accept assignments from *Life*, but she could also refuse if the proposal didn't pass muster. She would do documentary photography, social justice commentary, like Lewis Hine and Dorothea Lange, two of her heroes. Pursue assignments from the new magazine *PM*, with its commitment to social change. Margaret Bourke-White was already there.

Even as she played out this fantasy, Claire knew that she wouldn't quit. Couldn't quit. She had friends who were freelancers. Either they had more work than they could handle, or they went for weeks with no assignments. She herself had worked freelance before *Life* was es-tablished. She'd managed to build up a good-size group of newspaper and magazine clients, but she'd been only too aware that her clients could drop her without warning. She couldn't risk it again. She needed a regular paycheck. Charlie couldn't skip dinner for a week or a month because her phone hadn't rung. She couldn't pretend the roof wasn't leaking because she was having a slow season. She couldn't expect any boss but Mack, with his own four children, to sympathize with her desire to work close to home.

And the truth was, she loved working for *Life*. She had a voracious curiosity about people, about the tumultuous world and everything in it. She could indulge that curiosity at *Life* as nowhere else. Every assignment, even Aurora Rasmussen, presented a new challenge, required its own vision, and she wouldn't give that up.

She checked her watch. Three o'clock. She was meeting Charlie at four. He'd spent last night with her father. This morning they'd gone to the Bronx Zoo, arriving early to beat the crowds.

She put the checkbook and the rest of the bills in the top drawer of her desk. She stood. Lucas, who'd been curled by her feet under the desk, stood, too, pushing his head against her leg.

"Hello, boy." With her knuckles, she rubbed the velvety hill from his muzzle to his forehead. He liked that, closing his eyes, pressing his head against her leg to tell her to do it again. On some days, this caress of Lucas's head was the only warmth and consolation she felt. Remembering her last conversation with James Stanton, as stilted as it was, Claire felt a longing for companionship.

In her line of work, she could find more than enough sexual partners, if that was what she wanted. In the six years since she and Bill separated in 1935, she'd received more offers than she could even recall, from married and single men both. She'd had flings with several of her photographer colleagues, with an upper-level editor at another publication, with an attorney at the firm that handled her divorce . . . after Bill left, these were all she could manage. She couldn't begin to feel the trust required for a deeper attachment. Now she felt an aching emptiness inside herself, in the place where the giving and receiving of love should be. She wanted a partner in the fullest sense. She wanted passion, yet more than passion. Passion as part of a love that was emotional, intellectual, physical.

From her desk at the back window, she had a view of the garden. The sky had cleared, and the sun glimmered against the morning's dusting of snow. The branches of the maple tree were rimmed in white, exactly at her eye level, creating a complex abstraction. Her cameras were downstairs. She could get them. She checked her watch again. Alas, no time for abstractions now. She had to pick up Charlie.

She made her way down the steep, narrow staircase, Lucas following. Here in the stairwell, the vine-patterned wallpaper was peeling. A telltale swelling revealed the dampness seeping through the roof. The wet plaster smelled sour. The house dated from the 1840s. Each of the floors had only two rooms, but the cycle of repairs was endless. The house needed a new boiler, a new roof, new pipes. During the worst years of the Depression, Claire's mother couldn't raise the cash to undertake even the minimum of maintenance.

Sometimes Claire thought about selling the house. The neighborhood was generally considered a slum, however, and the house was in such bad condition that she wouldn't receive anywhere near a decent price for it, the price she'd need to secure a good home for Charlie elsewhere. Besides, she owned the house outright. She remembered the bank failures, unemployment, foreclosures, and bread lines of the 1930s. It could happen again. Automatically, an echo of past anxiety, she experienced the constriction in her stomach that she'd felt after Bill left, when she woke up day after day worried about whether he'd follow through on his promised support payments, and if he didn't, whether she could earn enough money to keep the apartment she and Charlie shared. *Life* magazine didn't exist. Her mother rescued them by inviting Claire and Charlie to move in with her. Anna, too, was struggling financially after her husband, Claire's stepfather, died, but together, they'd managed to get by.

The house now belonged to Claire. Not simply legally or financially. It was part of her spirit, filled with memories: Her mother holding women's suffrage meetings in the parlor. Margaret Sanger, the
birth control advocate, drinking coffee in the kitchen while debating
strategy with her stepfather, who was a physician. Max Eastman and
other political radicals enjoying a formal luncheon in the garden while
Jack Reed told stories of his days in Russia. Claire had spent hundreds
of hours in the darkroom she set up in the basement, pursuing her love
of photography, learning her craft before she realized it would become
her career. The house was her refuge, the place she felt safest, the place
where no one could tell her to leave. In the spring, crab apple blossoms filled the view from the front windows, the sweet scent drifting
through the rooms on every breeze.

Downstairs, Lucas went to a patch of dappling sunlight near the
long back windows and stretched out to sleep. Tom, a local high school
boy earning money for college, walked him twice a day, every day, and
Claire and Maritza managed the early morning and late night walks.
Seeing him settled, Claire put on her coat and set out into the day,
locking the front door behind her.

The sudden sweep of winter against her skin jolted her, making her
feel as if she'd just now woken up. The street itself was in shadow, but
the rooftops of the neighborhood's tenements and town houses glowed
with a precise clarity in the afternoon sunlight. Even though Claire
was running late, she paused to study the light. Often Charlie teased
her on their walks along the cobblestone streets for stopping to study
the shifting angles of the light. She laughed with him but continued
to stop, whether they were on their way to buy coffee at McNulty's or
chocolates at Li-Lac; heading to his favorite playground, on Downing
Street; or enjoying hot chocolate with whipped cream at a MacDougal
Street café. The ever-changing effects of sunlight upon the streets and
rooftops of her city always pleased her. Some photographers she knew
found inspiration in nature, in the effects of light on mountain ranges

and forests. Claire found her greatest inspiration here, amid the man-made cityscape.

When she was younger, Claire had considered herself a radical. But after Emily was born in 1931, Claire's radicalism ended in an instant. Charlie's birth two and a half years later confirmed the shift. In 1936, she'd had no desire to go to Spain to cover the Civil War—although she'd learned not to admit this, because among her peers it was an article of faith that a committed professional wanted to report on the horrors in Spain. Charlie gave her an excuse, or at least a better excuse than admitting she was temperamentally unsuited to running ahead of a ragtag platoon of bone-weary soldiers to grab shots of battlefield heroism and death. Bill loved that life. He seemed most truly alive when arguing about politics or racing after a hard-hitting story.

During this new war, Claire wanted to tell the stories of the families struggling to cope at home, rather than their sons and daughters dying abroad. She hoped she would have the choice. Mack might insist that she was needed overseas, or more likely, that with so many of her colleagues at the front, she had to take on a photojournalist's more typical burden of constant domestic travel. She felt a pang of anxiety about the looming questions of the future.

The camera her mother gave her on her fourteenth birthday was a Brownie, a gift commonly received among her friends, but it had changed Claire's perceptions of the world. Shaping and framing, capturing space and time, telling stories through pictures . . . the camera gave her a purpose, and also gave her a license, an excuse, to approach people and learn about their lives. Once her darkroom was set up in the basement, she earned money doing inexpensive portraits of neighborhood families. She put up flyers in the local grocery stores and on the lampposts. She met potential clients at their homes. Payment was upon delivery of the photos, and only if you liked them. To her surprise, everyone paid, even from the first. She remembered a few special families: Julio, Angelo, and Maria, ages seven, six, and five, who lived on Carmine Street. Every six months for two years, Claire took photos of them to send to their grandmothers in Naples. She remembered a baby, Kathleen, with bright red hair. Claire photographed her in her baptismal gown. Kathleen and her family lived on Jones Street. Claire spotted Kathleen's mother a year later on Third Street, under the El. The woman said that Kathleen had died before her first birthday, and Claire's photos were the only ones they had. Claire's view of the city, and of the frailty and rewards of life, were shaped by these chance encounters. For Claire, this neighborhood truly was a village.

During college, she had studied photography with Clarence White at the Art Students League. In those days, she'd modeled her work on the art photography of Stieglitz and Kasebier. By her twenties, however, during the worst years of the Depression, Claire became committed to the new genre of the documentary picture story. Her style moved away from art photography into realism and journalism. Nonetheless she'd spent more than a few Depression years surviving with society weddings and, when she could get it, more lucrative advertising work. She made automobile fenders gleam and refrigerators look reliably cold. *Life*, when it came along in 1936, was perfect for her. Mack had seen her newspaper work and phoned out of the blue to give her a try. Her first story for him, about jazz clubs in Harlem, never ran, but she was in the door.

She continued to love the mystery of working in the darkroom, the sharp touch of the film edge against her fingertips as she rolled the film onto the reel in the dark, the recurring sense of magic when an image appeared on paper in the tray of developer. She loved the bitter scent of the chemicals that lingered afterward on her hands and in her hair, reminding her of her hours at work and of the vision she sought to create of the world outside herself.

New York, December 1941. A black-and-white photograph of sunlight on rooftops in a city at war. From the date, the viewer would fill in the meaning beyond the intricate architecture and the geometric planes of light and shadow. The viewer would fill in the questions, doubts, and fears. The ancient Greek derivation of the word *photography* was "to write with light," the truest description she'd ever heard.

Centering and purpose. Passion and obsession. Nothing but an escape, Bill Shipley once said derisively toward the end of their marriage (although he never complained about the salary her escape provided), as she gave up the hard-hitting documentary work he believed in for easier work that she could manage around Emily's and Charlie's schedules. When her children were young, Claire was bound at home while Bill had more and more assignments coming his way. She slipped into a daze during those years, when one or the other of the kids woke her up every night. She no longer had the energy or, she had to admit, the interest to discuss politics at the breakfast table. Those were tumultuous years . . . the Depression, the rise of Hitler, the election of FDR. Claire couldn't focus her attention on the outside world. At 7:00 AM, as she held Charlie in her arms and cooked his rice cereal while, from the table, Emily demanded more applesauce, the ins and outs of the latest piece of New Deal legislation made little sense to her. For his part, Bill found her home-centered concerns irrelevant. Bill became impatient with her, for myriad reasons. After Emily died, their crisscrossing guilt pushed them still farther apart. When the *Herald Tribune* offered Bill the opportunity to report from Europe, they both knew he had to accept, and that Claire and Charlie wouldn't be going with him.

When would these memories of Bill stop pushing into her mind? The memories were visceral in the way they assaulted her, shaking her into hesitation and self-doubt even though they'd separated six years ago and she hadn't even seen him since the war began in Europe in 1939. Sometimes she felt as if he were still beside her, watching her, passing judgment upon her.

Resisting him, she firmly turned right and began walking the few blocks to Seventh Avenue. Her house was at the western end of

Grove Street, where it gently curved toward Hudson Street. The Village streets, laid out on pathways among farms and along meandering streams, intersected at odd angles and sometimes turned back on themselves. West Fourth Street intersected with West Tenth, West Eleventh, and West Twelfth. Charlie and his friends loved to meet at the corner where Waverly Place met Waverly Place. Another favorite was the junction of Minetta Street and Minetta Lane, two small thoroughfares that looked identical. What made one a street and one a lane? This was a continual source of debate for Charlie and his friends. Grove Street, with its trees and hundred-year-old town houses, with its hidden courtyard entered through a narrow gate, was among the loveliest in the neighborhood. Even so, Claire's house wasn't especially desirable, too close to the bars and waterfront commerce of Hudson Street.

In the nineteenth century, the Village had been affluent and elegant, but for decades now, immigrants and youthful newcomers to the city had gravitated in the Village to take advantage of the inexpensive rents. Radicals of one sort or another had settled here for generations. The neighborhood boasted a gritty avant-garde culture that was separate from Claire's sedate way of life. It was a culture of late-night, boozy parties and impromptu jazz concerts, art openings, shoestring theatrical productions, and political zeal. The Republic of Bohemia, tourists sometimes called the Village, coming here to search for the artists of every stripe (many of them *artistes*, in Claire's opinion) presumed to be holding court at every corner.

Claire's mother had been in the thick of the radical movements of the teens and twenties. She was friends with Mabel Dodge, Jack Reed, Louise Bryant. She was a patron of the Provincetown Playhouse. The playwright Eugene O'Neill had once come to dinner.

One family, with three generations in the Village: Anna, the radical sympathizer and activist, part of the seething cultural ferment of her time. Claire, the bourgeois seeking a staid and conservative life with her children. And Charlie . . . he knew nothing of radicalism. For him the Village was a place from fairy tales. He loved to search the streets for the narrow alleyways, the width and height of a horse, that led into hidden gardens with small houses and old stables. He loved Grove Court, to him a secret street behind his street. He liked to take friends to Charles Street, between Perry and West Tenth, and to the restaurant that shared his name. The Charles restaurant, at Sixth Avenue and Eleventh Street, was too expensive for a family dinner and anyway served French food, which Charlie didn't care for, but nonetheless, seeing his name on street signs and restaurant windows added to his sense of enchantment.

As Claire passed the cast-iron gates and small front gardens of her neighbors, she noticed that the street was surprisingly quiet. The sweet scent of wood burning in fireplaces filled the air. She felt close-knit into the fabric of the neighborhood. And she felt a sudden, surging happiness, that she was lucky to be here, alive, at this moment, on her way to pick up her smart, healthy son, with a steady job that she loved waiting for her on Monday, and an actual dinner date, not simply a quick mutual seduction, in the days ahead.

On Seventh Avenue, across from the subway station, stands of Christmas trees gave off the aching, memory-laden fragrance of pine and balsam. On Christmas Eve morning, Claire and Charlie would choose their tree. As always, they'd search for a Douglas fir. Claire loved its silky needles and deep scent. Artie, the handyman who worked at the tenement down the block and did small projects at Claire's house for extra cash, would help them carry the tree home and set it up in the living room. These were the comforting rituals of years. After dinner, Claire and Charlie would pull out the box of decorations kept in the closet under the stairs. Claire's favorites were the collection of iridescent ornaments given to her by her grandparents. Charlie had a collection of carefully detailed ships inside glass globes. Charlie loved Christmas Eve, and Emily . . . at three years old, bursting with energy, Emily had spent her final Christmas Eve running around the sofa chasing Hughie, Lucas's predecessor.

Claire went down the stairs to the subway. She changed trains twice to travel uptown to her father's. After a lifetime of subway riding, she made the transfers almost without conscious thought. Her mind wandered back to James Stanton, to the flick of his lab coat behind him as he walked, to the magnetic presence of his body near her as she looked into the microscope. She imagined herself unbuttoning his shirt, placing her hands upon his chest, feeling their bare skin touching, their bodies entwined.

Long-distance phone call for you, Dr. Stanton," said Nurse Brockett, coming into the hospital ward. It was midafternoon on a typically busy Saturday. The ward faced the Institute gardens, dusted with snow. "The switchboard can put it through wherever you like."

Phone call? Long-distance? Whatever it was, it could wait until he finished with this patient. "Thank you." He wasn't going to interrupt his work for a telephone call. Stanton sat at the bedside of Gino Puccio, fifty-one years old. He examined the festering wound in Mr. Puccio's calf. The wound wasn't life-threatening, so the radical step of amputation was certainly not called for, but the wound refused to heal.

This ward had three patients being treated for inflamed, suppurating skin infections. The wounds were extremely painful, although contained, somehow cordoned off within the body. None had sparked blood infections, so the body was fighting back. How? Why did one person die within days from a seemingly trivial abrasion, while another fought back for months or years? Stanton didn't know.

He was experimenting with gauze bandages soaked in a diluted penicillin solution. For topical application, on the surface of the skin, much less penicillin was needed than for injections. Even so, three patients were the most he could manage. He'd told several doctors at area hospitals about the experiment, and these three patients had been

referred to him. Although they weren't bedridden, they were staying here at the Institute for two weeks to receive the treatment in a
controlled environment, with the Institute paying their salaries and
a stipend. That, Stanton reflected, was what it meant to say that the
Institute was funded in full by the Rockefeller family.

The patients had been in residence for four days, with little progress. Mr. Puccio, a butcher, weighed upward of two hundred pounds.
His calf had been sliced open in a freak accident at work, and the
wound had become infected about a week later. After three months,
despite debridement, the removal of damaged tissue, his infection still
hadn't resolved. The wound was six inches long, raw, swollen, and
oozing. Stanton used a pocket flashlight to examine it closely.

"Hurts a little less today, Doc," Mr. Puccio said. "I think it's getting better. Hasn't throbbed since last night."

"That's good," Stanton said. "It looks maybe three percent better."
He felt frustrated by the slow progress.

"I don't care how it looks, I just want it to stop hurting."

"Then I'm glad for you," Stanton said. "What time is your daughter
bringing her fiancé?" He'd already met Mr. Puccio's wife and three
daughters.

Mr. Puccio shrugged dramatically. "Five-thirty. But like I told you
before, I don't like him."

"You haven't even met him," said Mr. Kutner on the far side of the
room. Bandages were wrapped around his head and covered his left
eye. Mr. Kutner was a retired sewing machine operator in the garment
district. Four weeks earlier, he'd taken a tumble on the subway stairs
and gotten a bad scrape on the brow, along with a lot of bruises. The
bruises had healed, but the scrape had turned into an ugly abscess.
Kutner was seventy-six, which didn't stop his ward-mates from speculating that he'd been drunk at the time of the tumble. Initially Mr.
Kutner was irate about the teasing, but recently he'd begun giving back
as good as he got.

"That's the point," said Mr. Puccio. "What kind of guy can he be, if the first time you meet him is when he's already engaged to your daughter? Aren't you supposed to meet him *before* the engagement?"

"Maybe he was afraid you'd take a butcher knife to him," said Mr. Kutner. "Meeting here at the hospital, at least he's safe."

"No guarantees," Mr. Puccio said. "I still got a lot of fight in me, with or without a knife. Hey, Doc, don't you wonder who's calling you long-distance? Could be something serious." The words *long-distance* often evoked an edge of anxiety.

"Everybody I care about is either in New York or dead, so what the hell." Nonetheless Stanton was touched by the concern. "Can't be too important." He placed several sheets of gauze freshly soaked in penicillin solution upon Mr. Puccio's wound.

"You take the call before you get to me," said Mr. Dunleavy, whose turn was next. He was a longshoreman, thirty-one years old, physically fit, with a deep gash on the left shoulder. He'd been injured six weeks before. "I want your complete attention."

"Since it's the only attention he's getting these days," said Mr. Kutner. "His wife hasn't been here in forty-eight hours and counting."

Nurse Brockett said, "Let me finish up with Mr. Puccio, Doctor. I can do the bandaging."

"She does better bandaging than you anyway," said Mr. Dunleavy.

"Thank you for the compliment," Stanton said, getting up. He gave the tray of supplies to Nurse Brockett. Exiting the ward to the voices of his patients teasing Nurse Brockett, he walked down the hall to the semiprivate office behind the nurses' station and called the switchboard. "Dr. Stanton here. I understand you've got a long-distance call for me."

"Hold on, Doctor, I'll connect you," the operator said. "The call is from Washington, D.C."

While he listened to the static and clicks on the line, he looked out the window at the river. Two dozen police boats and Coast Guard vessels were massed together in some kind of exercise or patrol. The boats were too well ordered to be responding to an actual emergency. He stretched his back and neck. Oh, boy, he was tired. As usual. Later, he had a meeting scheduled with his sister and David Hoskins. He needed to increase the dose of penicillin in the solution he was using for the current research. Edward Reese came into his mind. He'd written a condolence note to Patsy Reese and received a very kind reply, thanking him for his efforts on her husband's behalf. They'd been so close to saving him. If only, what if . . . so many unanswerable questions.

"Is it Dr. Stanton?" a woman's voice asked.

"Yes."

"Please hold for Dr. Bush."

Dr. Bush—who was that? The Washington operator was off the line before he could ask for details. Although Stanton was frequently asked to consult on cases, he didn't recall a Dr. Bush working in infectious diseases in Washington.

"Stanton!" A hale-and-hearty male voice.

"Yes."

"Vannevar Bush here."

Now he remembered. Vannevar Bush was the head of the government's Office of Scientific Research and Development. He was a Ph.D., not a medical doctor. This call, unexpected, made Stanton wary.

"I've got some news for you. I've decided to do something for our troops." Bush's tone was strangely glib. "I'm starting a program to supply the entire military with penicillin within the next year or two. Got millions of dollars budgeted for it. Top priority on supplies. Researchers lined up around the country, ready to get to work on mass production. What do you think of that?"

Why should Vannevar Bush care what I think? Stanton wondered. But apparently he did, or he wouldn't be asking. "It'll never work.

Penicillin's not ready. It may never be ready. We're producing it in milk bottles and bedpans. So far its greatest success is in treating mice. Don't go forward, that's my advice."

Bush laughed. "Good answer. I appreciate honesty—bear that in mind down the road, Dr. Stanton. I need somebody to be the national coordinator of scientific research. Keep the milk bottles full and stop the pharmaceutical companies from killing one another on the road to mass production."

Bush wanted his advice on personnel? "Even though you're making a mistake, I'll try to think of somebody and phone you back."

Raucous laughter. Stanton wasn't happy about the amusement he seemed to be providing Vannevar Bush. "The person I'm thinking of is *you*. I already spoke to Dr. Rivers. Looks like you're a perfect fit. You're not beholden to anyone—especially not to the commercial companies. You're in the research trenches already. Your work at the Institute flows right into the government's work. Come to Washington on Monday and we'll discuss it."

Stanton couldn't keep up with this. Was Bush offering him a job, or was he calling him for an interview? What exactly was the job? Did he want it? He tried to delay, to give his thoughts a chance to catch up. "I'm in the middle of a project here. Monday isn't good."

"Turn the project over to one of your assistants."

Okay, Dr. Lind was already involved, Stanton thought. Lind could take over.

"By the way," Bush continued, "the interview is pro forma. Unless we turn up something in the security check, the job is yours."

What had Bush called the job? *Scientific coordinator?* That sounded bureaucratic. Stanton didn't want to be a cog in a bureaucracy. "Why me?"

"Any reason to say *not* you? You're not a Communist, are you? A sympathizer, fellow traveler, hanger-on?"

Now Stanton laughed. Imagining himself involved with politics was ludicrous. He was lucky if he found time even to vote. "None of the above. But I am in the middle of a penicillin project here."

Bush lost patience with him. "*Your* project is now officially *my* project. Anything to do with penicillin is under my jurisdiction. Part of the cause. There's a war on, as you possibly recall. Penicillin's going to be a weapon in this war. Get our wounded and sick troops back in the field while the other guy's troops are still sick or better yet dying in the hospital. I'm calling you up for active duty in the navy starting today. Consider yourself to be following orders."

Stanton said nothing for a moment, then, "Why are you doing this? Penicillin's never even saved a life."

"Sulfa drugs have too many problems, they're too limited," Bush said dismissively. "My docs tell me penicillin's the best we've got. So let's make the most of it. Now then, my girl will get on the line and give you the details, train, hotel, expense account. I'll see you at 10:00 AM on Monday at my office. Welcome aboard!" He finished with the same flourish he'd begun.

Stanton took notes from *the girl*, who gave her name as Tracey. After hanging up, he stared out the window, although he no longer noticed the police and Coast Guard patrols. What had Bush called penicillin? A "weapon of war"? Well, Stanton supposed it was a weapon of war. In the Civil War, 50 percent of the wounded died from infections. In the Great War, 30 percent. Venereal disease was rampant in the military during any war. Streptococcal infections spread like wildfire when thousands of men were transported on troop ships. Theoretically, penicillin worked against gangrene, syphilis, meningitis, pneumonia, blood infections, scarlet fever, and more. These diseases were caused by the so-called gram-positive bacteria, which stained violet or blue in the standard test. The hypothesis was that penicillin worked against all gram-positive bacteria, but no one knew for certain. The necessary clinical tests hadn't been conducted. The supply of the drug was too small for large-scale testing.

But if Bush's project succeeded and penicillin was indeed mass produced? Presumably the medication would be available for civilians, too—and that would mean a world transformed. No more hospital wards filled with victims of chronic, suppurating infections. No more thirty-seven-year-old men, and three-year-old girls, dying from scratches on the knee.

Stanton rubbed his neck. He was sweating. Bush's goal was intimidating and inspiring both. If it succeeded, being part of it would be the accomplishment of a lifetime. And yet . . . being drawn into the military, governed by military regulations. This was hard to fathom. Called to active duty. Following orders.

Without preamble, he'd been pulled into the war.

When Claire came out of the subway at Lexington and Seventy-seventh Street, she was forced to stop daydreaming and pay attention to her surroundings. On the Upper East Side, she felt as if she were in a different country. Her father's country. Here, the shop windows and apartment entryways gleamed with ostentatious cleanliness. The Christmas trees in the regimented stands along Lexington Avenue cost twice as much as those downtown. As if passing judgment on each passerby, the strictly uniformed doormen regarded the street severely. Even the newsboys, shouting reports of Japanese triumphs far away, looked better groomed than those in the Village. The standardized buildings cut and recut the sky, as if forcing it into the city's Uptown grid. Christmas shoppers bedecked in mink coats streamed around one another in a graceful dance. As Claire crossed Park Avenue, the wind blew hard against her, the monolithic wall of apartment buildings transforming the street into a wind tunnel.

Claire shivered. She crossed her arms, making herself into a fortress against the wind. By the time she reached her father's building at Fifth Avenue and Eighty-first Street, across from the Metropolitan Museum, she felt numb from the cold. The building was renowned for its monumental entryway, a glass and steel marquee that made anyone who walked beneath it look and feel small.

"Good afternoon, ma'am," the white-gloved doorman greeted her. He called upstairs on the house phone to announce her. His similarly white-gloved colleague operated the elevator and nodded at her with detached formality. Charlie knew their names, knew the names of everyone who worked here. He had serious discussions with them about topics of concern to him alone, such as the relative speeds of the passenger elevator upon ascent and descent. He used his grandfather's stopwatch to make the comparison.

Claire felt like too much of a stranger to memorize the names of the staff. By committing their names to memory, she'd be committing herself to her father, when she still didn't trust him. At any moment, he might disappear for another thirty years. Her visits here might turn out to be only a temporary aberration in her life.

Edward Rutherford, her father. In the appearance-bound era before the Great War, Claire's mother, Anna Rutherford, née Reed, daughter of a family that summered in Newport, deserted him to run off with Dr. Daniel Lukins. Unlike the self-made Rutherford, Lukins was a man of Anna Reed's own background: the Lukins family of Portland, Maine, with a tradition of Groton, Harvard, and the Johns Hopkins Medical School. Sometime during his medical training, his family lost its money. Daniel (so the rumor went) was so shocked by this turn of fortune that he decided to use his high-flown education to labor in the settlement houses on the Lower East Side and in Greenwich Village. He willingly served immigrants and the poor when the finest families would have welcomed him as their physician. He lived off the dwindling personal fortune of his mistress, then wife, Anna Reed Rutherford.

Making this scandal even worse, Anna Rutherford took young Claire with her on her escapade from Fifth Avenue comfort to Greenwich Village Bohemianism. She refused to let her estranged husband see their daughter. Instead of fighting for her, Claire's father gave her up. Dr. Lukins adopted her. His surname became hers.

How and why did this happen? Whenever Claire asked her mother, Anna smiled wanly with a turn of her head that indicated the topic was inappropriate. For all her Bohemianism, Anna remained oddly bound by propriety, especially in regard to her daughter. She even sent Claire uptown to Brearley for high school.

By the time she was eleven, Claire had learned to stop asking for explanations. Nowadays she wondered if a child could ever reach a full understanding of a divorce. Something always remained incomprehensible. What did Charlie think about his parents' divorce? He wasn't asking questions about it. But if tomorrow Charlie began asking, what would she say? She wasn't prepared to answer him honestly, to share with him the anguish she'd experienced. She didn't want to destroy whatever love Charlie had for his father.

Not surprisingly, Anna's silence transformed Edward Rutherford into an intriguing figure for Claire, a man of mystery and glamour. As she reached adulthood, she searched the business pages of newspapers and magazines, looking for references to him. In the early 1930s, she'd come across a profile of him in *Fortune*. She learned that his specialty was taking over unknown companies, backing new ideas that were on the cusp of the possible, and providing the necessary infusion of cash (his own and that of his investors) to make these companies and their innovations successful. He followed his hunches wherever they led, from fisheries to adding machines, from railroads to farm implements. He sounded brilliant and gutsy. Claire nurtured a stockpile of impressions and facts about the fantasy figure she'd made of him.

For Claire, the 1930s was a decade of death—Emily, her marriage, her stepfather, and finally her mother. Soon after Anna's death, Claire felt a compelling desire to contact Edward Rutherford. With her mother and stepfather both dead, her husband gone, she yearned for a family, not just for herself but for Charlie, too. She debated the proper approach and opted for the most straightforward. She'd written him a letter: *Dear Mr. Rutherford, I am your daughter, Claire. Perhaps you remember me.*

Within a few days, he'd invited her and Charlie to dine with him. That first evening, as she studied his gestures across the dining table and saw herself in him, Claire was taken aback by the anger she felt. She'd come prepared to admire him, but instead, faced with the reality of him, she felt wounded by the decision he'd made years before, cut to the quick by the years they'd lost. Several times, she'd been on the verge of asking him why he'd given her up, but—as she watched him laughing at something on the radio, enjoying seconds on dessert, playing checkers with Charlie—she couldn't summon the courage.

Charlie became the buffer between father and daughter. He regarded the apartment as a wonderland and investigated every room. Watching him rush through the hallways and up and down the stairs, Claire realized that Charlie found nothing odd about meeting a grandfather he'd never known. Charlie lived in the here and now. He demanded explanations of the present, not of the past. After the losses of the past years, Charlie needed a grandfather even more than she needed a father. Bill's parents were both dead, and his sister lived in Nebraska and was seldom in touch. For Charlie's sake, Claire struggled to pretend that she'd outgrown her distress.

That first dinner led to more invitations, as Rutherford embraced Claire and Charlie. He'd been married and divorced again. Claire was his only child. She sensed in him a need for family that was similar to her own. Charlie became his future. They'd be together for Christmas this year. And yet . . . unasked and unanswered questions charged the interactions between father and daughter, a subtext they both expended energy avoiding.

The elevator opened directly into the apartment. Claire thanked the elevator operator, stepped out, and listened to the elevator door closing behind her. The pseudo-Gothic front hall, with its wood paneling and vaulted ceiling, was silent. Tapestries decorated the walls, scenes of youths and maidens frolicking in sylvan glades. The apartment was a combination of museum and mausoleum. The silence pressed against her ears. She remembered standing in this hallway when she was four or five, her nanny adjusting her hat and scarf as she waited for her father to take her for a walk in Central Park.

Claire took off her coat and folded it over a carved, medieval-style chair. She rubbed her hands together, trying to warm them. "Charlie?" She didn't call for her father. "MaryLee?"

There was no response. Maybe Charlie and her father weren't back from the zoo yet. MaryLee, the housekeeper, would have answered the doorman's call, but the apartment was rambling, and she could be working anywhere.

Because she was alone, Claire began to explore, searching for memories. At the far end, the hallway opened into the dining room. Here the curtains were drawn, the dining room kept dark to protect the drawings by Watteau and Fragonard that covered almost every inch of wall space, in the style of an artist's salon. In someone else's house, she'd consider herself privileged to see such exquisite drawings so intimately displayed, but here she felt outrage. These drawings should be in museums, not decorating a rich man's dining room.

In frustration, she moved on to the arched entryway of the room her father called "the parlor," his idea of a joke. The archway opened onto a balcony, eight steps leading down to the vast space below. The so-called parlor was done up in stonework like the banqueting hall of a castle. The six windows were double-height and double-width, as if the apartment's owner had invited the sky in as a guest. Paintings by Claude Lorrain covered the walls, wide vistas of seductive lakes and valleys. The flamboyant marble mantelpiece, with its baroque carving, had been brought from a castle in Bohemia. The painted coffered ceiling was from an Italian palazzo.

Suddenly Claire remembered . . . playing hide-and-seek in the bare fireplace on a summer afternoon, her father pretending to search for her when surely he could see her hiding behind the fire screen. With the eyes of an adult, she saw that the fireplace wasn't much beyond normal size, but to her child self, it had been enormous. A tunnel, a cave. Her father had swept her up and hugged her when he found her, and she'd buried her face against his linen jacket. His shoulder was solid and curved perfectly to fit her cheek. She breathed deeply the scent of his cigars. She'd been scared, within her hiding place, and he'd rescued her.

Claire tried to conjure what her father looked like at that moment. His eyes, his chin, the curve of his brow . . . she couldn't re-create his face. She remembered him in disconnected details: his wide hands. His firm stride. His beautiful shoes, the leather buffed and tender to her touch.

The memories brought a wave of sadness for all they had missed. He wasn't with her on her first day of school, or when she graduated from high school or college. He wasn't with her when she got married. He'd never met her husband. He'd never met Emily. He and Emily had the same eye color, a dark greenish blue.

She turned away from her memories. The entrance to her father's bedroom was on the opposite side of the hall. Stepping out, revealing a glimpse of French provincial décor as she opened the door, was MaryLee. She'd been the housekeeper here when Claire was a girl, in her thirties then, in her sixties now. She was a petite black woman, slender to the point of frailty. Her white apron was clean and starched, but the red sweater she wore beneath it was threadbare at the elbows— "It's my favorite," she maintained—revealing the sleeves of her calico-print dress. She never wore a uniform. She held a bucket crammed with cleaning supplies, the handle of a toilet scrubber sticking out above the rest.

"Good afternoon, Miss Claire." Her voice was lilting. She'd come to New York from South Carolina many years ago. She lived in. On her days off, she visited her sister in Brooklyn.

"And good afternoon to you, MaryLee. You're looking well."

"Thank you. Seeing that boy of yours always perks me up. He's a charmer, that one. Brings the house to life."

"That's kind of you to say."

"First thing this morning, before leaving for the zoo, he comes right into the kitchen and says, 'Would you make a fudge cake for *me*, Mary*Lee*?' Making it rhyme like a poem. So of course I did. But I told him we couldn't eat it until you were here. Make a little party."

"You're very generous."

"Thank you indeed." Graciously she nodded her head in acknowledgment.

"Are they back yet?"

"For sure they're upstairs on the terrace waiting for you." With her bucket, she urged Claire up the staircase.

"Thank you."

The stairwell was lined with early Italian Renaissance paintings of the Holy Family, Cimabue, Duccio, Giotto, a line of golden halos accompanying Claire up the stairs. A stained-glass window graced the landing, a Tiffany scene of a river meandering into an emerald landscape. Claire turned at the landing and glimpsed MaryLee below opening a door camouflaged to blend into the wall. The hall lavatory. It was papered with hand-painted reproductions of the murals of Pompeii. In this apartment, time had slowed and then stopped. The apartment bore no relation to the fraught and throbbing city outside.

At the top of the stairs, she entered the penthouse solarium. Willowy trees filled the room, a tamed bamboo forest reaching toward the ceiling. The solarium's marble floor was laid in the intricate pattern of a Renaissance maze. Small Roman sculptures of charioteers were perched on the ornate mantelpiece. The French doors leading to the terrace were stuck, as usual, and she pulled hard to open them, the glass trembling within its lead squares. Outside, a warmth radiated from the flagstones after their day baking in the sunlight. Before her rose the gleaming spires of Midtown. The skyscrapers had transformed the staid New York of Claire's childhood into a futuristic fantasy that brimmed with energy. A sense of hope and possibility washed over her. Upon the Empire State Building, vertical lines of metallic decoration glowed golden in the lowering sun.

On the Fifth Avenue side of the terrace, facing Central Park, a boy in a long navy blue winter coat stood on a crate next to the five-foot-high stone balustrade. Reaching up, he rested his elbows on the balustrade's wide upper railing to steady himself as he used large, cumbersome binoculars to study three birds circling above the park's Belvedere Castle.

Charlie.

Had her father actually left him out here alone on the terrace, fifteen stories above the street? She hurried forward, rage mixing with fear. "Charlie," she called as calmly as she could, willing him to get down from the crate.

He turned, happiness lighting his face. "Mom! Grandpa gave me binoculars for Christmas."

"Step down from the crate, Charlie."

"Ah, Claire. Welcome." Her father was sitting in a window embrasure, out of the wind, but right next to Charlie. How quickly she'd assumed the worst about him. Charlie was safe, she realized as she reached him. Her father rose, and she accepted his awkward embrace. Even bundled against the cold, he was suave and sophisticated.

"Mom, look." Charlie's head was at the height of her chin. He held out the binoculars. From their size alone, she knew they were expensive, more than she could afford. She wished her father had waited until Christmas to give them to him. "He got me this pad, too, see, with a pencil attached to it, so I can make notes about the birds." He held up the pad.

"That's terrific, Charlie. What are you looking at?"

"Hawks." The wind tousled Charlie's hair. As usual, he refused to wear a hat. The long coat made him appear younger than eight. "Did you know that the buildings in New York City remind hawks and falcons of mountains?"

"No, I didn't know that."

"I learned about it at the zoo. When they build their nests on tall buildings and bridges, they think they're building them on cliffs and mountainsides. I'm trying to think the way a hawk would think, that the skyscrapers are mountains, and we're living in a mountain range."

How she loved him.

"Time to go inside and warm up, if you ask me," Rutherford said.

"No," Charlie insisted, "the hawks aren't done for today. We can't go in yet."

Claire was about to correct him for his tone, but her father said smoothly, "Okay, boy, leave the crate where it is and go to the other side of the terrace, and stay away from the railing. We'll keep an eye on you from the sofa. Your mother and I will be nice and warm inside, and you can be out here freezing."

Without protest, Charlie did as his grandfather asked. Once he was safely situated, Claire and Rutherford went inside. Rutherford threw his jacket and hat on a chair. He sat down on the white sofa facing the French doors, sinking into the cushions. He wore a blue button-down oxford shirt with a paisley silk ascot at his neck. His baggy corduroy trousers looked, on him, like the height of casual elegance. His steel gray hair was brushed back from his forehead. Rather than sit beside him on the sofa, Claire chose a hard-backed chair and adjusted its position so she had a full view of her son.

When they were settled, Claire could no longer restrain herself. "Why did you give Charlie his present before Christmas?" She didn't want her visit to start out this way. She wanted to maintain a veneer of appreciation and respect, but she couldn't, her pain using the Christmas present as a way to slip through her defenses.

"But, sweetheart, the hawks are here today. They may not be here on Christmas. You've got to take things as they come, words to live by." He gave her a mischievous grin. "Let me tell you, this morning we go up to the zoo, he wants to spend the whole time in the birdhouse. What am I supposed to do in a birdhouse? I want to look at the lions, the tigers. All he wants to do is look at a bunch of birds."

How charming her father was.

"But okay, he's the star of the show, I pretend I like birds. The magenta bunting, maybe it was the scarlet bunting, if he likes it, I like it. On the way home, we make a little detour to Hammacher Schlemmer and I get him the binoculars. He's busy for the rest of the afternoon, and I get a little rest, which by then I needed, I can tell you."

He made her laugh, in spite of herself.

"In conclusion, Charlie had a good day. So what's going on with my best girl?"

"Nothing much." This was her standard answer to him. She tried to keep the conversation centered on Charlie so she wouldn't be tempted to ask him questions that she might regret. She didn't come here to argue with him or confront him, and she certainly wouldn't provoke an argument in Charlie's presence. "The usual."

"How's your work?"

"Okay."

"What are you working on?" he pressed.

"I've got a story coming out this week about a group of army wives on Governor's Island. Very brave and inspiring. At least that's how they come across in the layout. In person they're pretty much tired and worn down, struggling to keep up their spirits and pretend to their children that everything's fine. Most of their husbands are on Wake Island. Army Signal Corps."

"That's hard going."

"Yes." She didn't want to tell him about the cover, didn't want to have to accept his compliments or his enthusiasm.

"Sounds like a good story for you."

"Yes."

"Well." He hesitated. "I've been wanting to talk to you about something." Again the hesitation, unusual for him. "I've been hearing about the newspaper and magazine fellas, and the women, too, getting ready to go overseas, to cover the war. You think the magazine'll make you do something like that? Send you overseas with the others?"

She didn't want to admit her own concern until she knew his intentions. "Hard to know."

"Well, what I wanted to say was, there's plenty of room here. More space than I need. Why don't you rent out the house downtown, or even sell it, and you and Charlie move in with me? It'd be the best thing for the boy. We can put him in school up here, a good prep school, not like the public school he goes to now. Set him up for life. MaryLee and I would take good care of him, you wouldn't have to worry when you're traveling. Your housekeeper can come, too. MaryLee's getting old and could use the help."

No, never. That was Claire's first thought. The house downtown was her home, even if maintaining it was costly. This apartment was impressive, but how well did she really know the man who owned it? Not very well. She wouldn't sacrifice her independence and security so easily.

Then she saw something in her father's face, in the instant when her anger flared. The mask of charm was gone, the sparkle in his eyes at his own cleverness, the elegance and élan, gone. Loneliness and need took their place. He was a man in his midsixties, alone with his housekeeper, filled with love for his newfound daughter and his grandson. He was begging her to give him a family. Begging her to allow him to redeem the years that they'd lost. For the first time she noticed the wrinkled pallor of his skin, the flatness of his expression, the bags under his eyes. He was turning into an old man, and it was the old man she answered, as best as she could.

"I'll think about it."

He nodded his head gravely, as if she'd granted him a concession larger than he'd anticipated. "Thank you. I appreciate it." He sounded choked up. Claire realized that she was the one who should be thanking him for his generous offer. Yet she said nothing. She couldn't bring herself to offer her gratitude, or her trust. He glanced around the room. He seemed to be searching for something to talk about, a topic that she, not he, would enjoy. When he found it, his usual mask of charm still wasn't in place. "Whatever happened with that medical story you mentioned? That sounded interesting."

"Yes, it was." And because she'd seen, or thought she'd seen, the depth of feeling within him, she said, "I got a call today that the editors killed it."

"What? Why?" Outrage filled his voice. He was her father, defending her.

"Said it was too bleak."

"Idiots."

"It was the best work I've ever done."

"Tell me more about it."

After she shared the details, Rutherford leaned forward speculatively.

"So this penicillin stuff really worked? You saw it work?"

"I saw it work. Not only that, the scientists are investigating similar substances that might be easier to produce. Other molds, even bacteria that fight other bacteria. They're looking at hundreds of possibilities."

"If Charlie ever got sick . . ." He let the sentence go. Father and daughter exchanged glances, and Rutherford looked away before Claire did, thoughts of Emily flitting between them. Finally Rutherford took refuge in the arena that made him most comfortable: business. "The point is, Claire, the person who figures out how to mass-produce this stuff is going to make a fortune."

"That doesn't seem likely. Right now, they're making penicillin in bedpans and milk bottles. The other medications are still waiting to be discovered in soil samples they're storing in jam jars."

"Remarkable." He laughed, shaking his head in disbelief. He seemed more sure of himself now. "However, never underestimate American ingenuity, I always say. Maybe I should make some selective investments in milk bottles."

"That's probably where the biggest profit lies," Claire agreed, enjoying their repartee. "Or in a medical supply company that manufactures bedpans."

He gave a mock grimace. "I'll stick with milk bottles."

"Don't forget the jam jars."

"You're right. Extraordinary. Can't you fight for this story, Claire? The story runs, it gives my milk-bottle and jam-jar investments a tremendous boost."

All at once she felt worn out from the effort of maintaining her professional front of self-assurance and high spirits. She wanted to confide in someone. She wanted to confide in her father. She told him about her argument with Mack.

Rutherford thought through the options. "Well, Claire, I see Harry Luce here and there around town, over lunch at the Cloud Club, that sort of thing. Want me to say something to him, put in a good word for my girl?"

"No, of course not!" After a moment's pause, they both burst into laughter at the absurdity of his suggestion. "That's not the kind of help I need."

"I suppose not." He shrugged, the playful glint back in this eyes. "Outraged fathers don't have the influence they used to have. Especially in relation to their very professional and successful daughters. Why don't you make an appointment to see Luce yourself to talk about it?"

She'd never heard of anyone in her position making an appointment to see Mr. Luce.

"He's a tough customer," her father continued, "but when you work for someone, you have the right to see him. That's how I run my business, at least."

"I don't think that's how he runs his business."

"No, more like a dictator, from what I've heard."

She didn't respond. She felt loyalty to the company, and she wouldn't be drawn into gossip about Mr. Luce.

"The point is, Claire, you've got to keep on top of this. Maybe next week they'll come up with a patient who lives—now there's a twist—and you're in a whole new ball game. Money pouring in from all over to manufacture this medicine, families frantic to buy it. Magazines all over town, all over the world, begging you for pictures of penicillin, or some similar stuff made from dirt in jam jars, everybody hailing a miracle, and old Harry Luce giving you a bonus to keep you on his side. At the very least you should claim this as your territory. He should know that you've got the inside track on it for him, if anything happens down the road. My girl doesn't give up."

Yes, Claire thought, this is what a father is for, to make you believe in yourself. She'd been right to confide in him. She felt a stirring that she now had someone to back her up. She was no longer alone. "You're right. I'll make an appointment to see him."

"Good."

MaryLee came upstairs. From the dumbwaiter in the hall, she brought an embossed silver tray with the fudge cake and a pot of hot chocolate, cups, plates, and silver. She placed the tray on the coffee table and then opened the French doors, hugging her arms around herself in the cold. The breeze blew her calico-print dress against her thin legs. "Come on in, Charlie, your cocoa and cake are ready."

Charlie bounded in to join them, his hair ruffled, the binoculars swaying around his neck, his left hand clutching the steno pad and pencil. He brought with him the pure, sharp scent of a winter's afternoon.

"Get over here, boy." Rutherford spread his arms wide for him. Charlie threw himself at his grandfather and in a wave of giggles pushed him over.

For Claire, the entire visit was worth that moment.

W ill you have to move to Washington?" asked Tia. Her tone was so surprised and forlorn that Stanton couldn't help but laugh. He'd just told her about his conversation with Vannevar Bush.

They sat at dinner in the hospital's dining room, a formal place with high ceilings and long windows overlooking the river. Atypical for a Saturday night, the dining room was bustling. A few weeks after Pearl Harbor, Stanton's colleagues seemed to be working nonstop to complete projects before the war pulled them elsewhere. His friend Nick Catalano sat with the vaccine group. He'd never known Nick *not* to have a date on a Saturday night; probably Nick was heading out later. Sergei Oretsky had joined a table of young nurses-in-training. From his wild gesticulations, he appeared to be entertaining them with extravagant stories. At the beverage table, Jake Lind filled multiple cups of coffee on a tray. Even Dr. Rivers was here, holding a meeting with administrators. David Hoskins was absent: he'd slipped away to his monthly dinner with British friends residing in New York.

"I don't know. Nothing is certain yet."

"Well, it's very exciting," Tia said, clearly believing the opposite, but steeling herself to a positive attitude. "It's a great honor. I'm proud of you."

He read her so well. He knew she relied on him. After their parents died in the influenza epidemic in 1918, they'd become closer than many siblings. In most respects she was an independent, successful woman; but still, deep within, she was a four-year-old orphan gripping his hand.

"Don't worry," he said. "My guess is that nothing will change for a while. Now tell me if I can do anything to help you and David produce more medicine for my three patients upstairs."

With that, she was on solid ground again. Lind joined them with his cups of coffee, and they had a familiar discussion about the quirks of penicillin production.

Stanton wasn't on call this evening, so after dinner he walked Tia to the lab and spent some time reviewing her notes. Afterward, he went to his residence rooms, which passed for home. He had some correspondence to catch up on, a letter of recommendation for a young colleague, a note to his college roommate to congratulate him and his wife on the birth of their third child. After an hour or so, he began thinking about Claire Shipley. He felt a compulsion to share his news with her. He wanted to talk about his new job frankly, with someone on the outside, to gain some perspective. With Tia, he was so accustomed to playing the role of older brother that he couldn't reveal his doubts or his worries.

He dialed Claire's number. No answer. He organized his mail, paid some bills. He called Claire again. He was about to hang up when, on the fourth ring, she answered.

"Hello?"

She sounded tired. Half asleep. Damn. Probably his persistence had taken him too far into the evening. He checked his watch. For him, it was still early. Just after 10:00 PM. But for her, who knew? Was he being foolish? Even though he'd worked with her for days and asked her to dinner, suddenly he was afraid that she might not remember him, especially if she was half asleep.

"Mrs. Shipley, it's James Stanton. At the Rockefeller Institute." He felt a peculiar self-consciousness with Claire, and it threw him off his stride. He was accustomed to being in charge, both of himself and others. But with her . . . at least he hadn't added the "doctor" title to his name.

"Oh. Dr. Stanton."

Well, she hadn't forgotten him. "Please, call me Jamie."

"Yes. Jamie. And do please call me Claire." She tried to push the sleep from her mind, to wake herself up for him—the very man she'd been thinking about in empty moments.

"Thank you for calling." What made her say that, she chastised

herself. There was no reason to thank him for calling. She was react-
ing to him in unfamiliar ways.

"I hope I didn't wake you."

"Not exactly." She and Charlie had returned home from her father's
around nine. She'd made a fire in the living room, and they'd sat in the
upholstered chairs on either side of her small fireplace, with its plain
mantelpiece, to begin their evening ritual of reading aloud, alternat-
ing chapters. They were making their way through Arthur Ransome's
Swallows and Amazons. After three pages, Charlie had fallen asleep,
a testament to his mother's reading-aloud skills. He was curled in his
chair, a blanket over his legs. Claire had drifted into semisleep herself,
even as she contemplated taking Lucas for a final walk and getting
Charlie upstairs to bed. "I just put my son, and nearly myself, to sleep
by reading aloud."

He appreciated her self-deprecating humor.

Then she remembered: she had to tell him about the cancellation
of the story. Best to get it over with, before she started worrying about
the proper way to tell him. "I'm glad you called. I got word this afternoon that my penicillin story was canceled. I'm sorry. Sometimes this
happens, and no explanations make it okay."

So, he thought, the war had caught up with them both. He paused
to find the proper reply for news that must have upset her. "I'm not
surprised."

"You're not? Why?"

"The government must have intervened. The director of the Office
of Scientific Research and Development must have contacted the editor of your magazine and stopped publication."

To Claire, this seemed a little too high level, a little too cloak-and-
dagger, to be true. "Why would he do that?"

"The government's created a project for the mass production of
penicillin for the military."

"For the military? Bedpans and milk bottles?"

"I know it sounds crazy, but, well, it's all we've got." He heard himself echoing Vannevar Bush. "In any war, more troops die or are incapacitated from infection than from actual wounds on the battlefield. Hundreds of thousands of troops jammed together on ships and at makeshift military camps, syphilis and gonorrhea rampant, men living in muck as they fight their way across foreign soil. Wounds gaping on the battlefield, hemorrhaging flesh pressed against dirt and shredded clothing, gangrene and staph and all the rest seeping in despite the best efforts of battlefield medics."

He realized he was lecturing her. He didn't want to, but he couldn't stop himself. These were the facts he was mulling over in his mind and sharing them with her, hearing them said aloud, brought him a sense of perspective.

"At Pearl Harbor, the burn victims numbered in the thousands. Infection is the greatest threat to their survival. With penicillin we'll be able to save lives and get those men back onto the battlefield while the enemy's hospitals are overflowing."

She knew next to nothing about these issues, and she was grateful for the lecture. "How come you know so much?" she asked, as a way to urge him to keep talking.

"I'm being called to Washington to interview for a job with them— which apparently I'll get. Unless I turn out to be a Communist."

"Will you turn out to be a Communist?" Was he saying that he'd be leaving town before they had a chance to get to know each other?

"I'd be surprised if I did."

"Well, that's a relief, I suppose." Following the code, she kept her tone light, not revealing her disappointment. "What's the job?"

"I've been named the national scientific coordinator."

She caught an edge in his voice that revealed his doubts. "Sounds important. Congratulations. Are you happy about it?"

"Yes, of course . . ." With his sister, he was always the strong one. With his peers, he always maintained a professional objectivity, wry, ironic, cynical, the guilty-until-proven-innocent tone that he and his colleagues cultivated among themselves to survive the constant presence of death in their lives. But here was a secret: he wished someone who loved him would say, don't worry, you can do this. You'll face this problem and wrench success from it. How long was it since he'd experienced, or needed, such reassurance? How long since he'd allowed himself to be vulnerable around another person, to feel the combination of friendship, attraction, and mutual support that he defined as love? For reasons he didn't understand, he felt vulnerable around Claire Shipley. This feeling was simply an instinct. In fact, they barely knew each other. He recognized that he shouldn't let his emotions jump ahead too quickly. "The job's a great honor, I'll put it that way."

Claire sensed his insecurity. "I feel positive, well, almost positive, that whoever made this decision didn't put all the possible names in a hat and just happen by chance to come up with you as the best person for the job." She stopped, waiting for him to reply. When he didn't, she added, "I'm pretty sure it wasn't a lottery."

How did she do it? he wondered. How did she reach exactly the right tone to reassure him without patronizing him? He had no choice but to take the job, yet discussing it with her made him feel more settled inside himself. More in control. "Thank you for your vote of confidence."

"When the story was canceled, I was afraid I'd let you and your sister down. And Patsy Reese and her children. I thought the story would redeem his death. That sounds self-serving now that I say it, but even so."

"We've all been let down. But officially the test was a success. The medication worked. There were no side effects. We simply didn't have enough of it to save the patient's life. Anyway, there's no redemption for that kind of death, except for the work we do to prevent the next death and the one after that." He paused. "I'm sure you still miss your daughter." He wanted to know this. In fact, he wanted to know everything there was to know about Claire.

"Yes." Although Claire was often shocked by memories of Emily, she rarely talked about her. She'd learned to stop talking about Emily because of the looks of pity she'd begun to receive from her friends. Not pity for Emily, but rather pity for her, Claire, because seven years had passed and still she hadn't been able to separate herself from Emily's memory. "She'd be almost eleven now."

"What was she like?"

So Claire talked about Emily. About simple scenes captured like snapshots: Emily on the sofa, paging through a book; at the beach, building sandcastles. Claire spoke also of her own guilt, of what she could have done, might have done, to stop Emily from tripping on the sidewalk, to better wash her injuries, to save her life . . . if only, if only, alternatives pressing into her thoughts over and over, too late.

"I think the same, too, sometimes. For the patients I've lost."

"But you shouldn't," she said. "This is your work."

"I mention this only to say that the guilt is both natural and unnecessary."

She was grateful for that. Grateful for once to be understood, rather than be told she was being obsessive, those friends who didn't have children shaking their heads as if to say, why can't you just move on?

They were both of them too familiar with death, Stanton thought.

"So," Claire said resolutely, to bring them back to the present, "our dinner next week will be a celebration of your new job. Or at least a chance to take note of it."

An idea came to him. "No need to wait. I happen to be free right now." Nothing wrong with asking, he figured. He felt awash with desire for her. "I can be there in, say, half an hour."

She knew what he was proposing. She also knew how easy it would be: get Charlie situated in his bedroom upstairs, and when Jamie arrived, take his hand and lead him to the guest room downstairs. She'd make sure he was gone by morning. Charlie, who usually slept late on Sundays, would never know. She glanced at her son, curled up and asleep in the living room. Yes, she'd be very happy for Jamie to come over. She longed to be close to him, to caress her fingertips across his back.

But no, she wasn't going to invite him tonight. Step by step, that's how she wanted to play this. She wanted to give them a chance, at least, to build more than a series of meaningless trysts.

"That's a terrific idea," she said. "You keep on with ideas like that, and you'll go far. I'm sure of it. But tonight's not good. Feel free to ask me again, however."

"I will." The postponement only increased his desire for her. "It's not an idea I'm likely to forget."

"I should hope not."

I t was 10:30 PM, and Edward Rutherford was alone. He was a multi-millionaire enjoying, to all appearances, a quiet evening at home, relaxing in his library with the *Wall Street Journal*, sipping a cognac. The library was silent. The sound of Fifth Avenue traffic never intruded, not even during rush hour. His library . . . wood paneling, drinks cart, leather-bound books kept dust free within their glass-doored cabinets, and over the mantel a Constable landscape of sheep and shepherds with an endless horizon. Here he could relax. He could never relax in the parlor with its Bavarian-castle atmosphere, although it was a terrific place for entertaining men as rich or richer than himself, especially when he was trying ever-so-subtly to convince them to invest their money with him.

The clock on the mantel was ticking. Was he really listening to the sound of the clock ticking? Yes, he was. At least he'd convinced Claire and Charlie to stay for an early dinner. Ever the trooper, MaryLee had managed to add to the meal she'd planned for him alone, and they'd brought the dining room to life with jokes and teasing. How he loved the sound of their voices in the apartment, the thump of Charlie's feet as he raced up and down the stairs, Claire helping MaryLee with the dishes.

Claire and Charlie had changed his life, no doubt about it. Once even the dog, Lucas, had come for a visit, much to Charlie's pleasure. Rutherford hadn't encouraged a repeat of the dog visit: with his exuberant rolling around on his back, Lucas had left tufts of fur imbedded in the parlor's Persian carpets. MaryLee was still vacuuming up dog fur weeks later. Nonetheless, the annoyance was more than worth the sight of Lucas chasing Charlie around the apartment and vice versa. If Claire and Charlie came to live here, he'd get accustomed to dog fur. He'd buy MaryLee a new vacuum cleaner or better yet commission an inventor to design a better one. A specialty vacuum, with a dog-fur attachment and an artist's rendering, Norman Rockwell-style, of Charlie and Lucas side by side. A boy and his dog, in profile. No dog-owning prospective vacuum-cleaner purchaser would be able to resist, not after Rutherford's sales experts got on board.

He sighed. He felt his loneliness most keenly at the end of their visits, this evening more than ever, since he'd confessed to Claire his hope that they would move here for the duration. At least she hadn't rejected the idea outright. He'd try again at the next appropriate moment.

What to do with the hours before bed? He could fill his now-empty evening by going to one of his clubs and drinking too much. Then he'd feel even worse in the morning. He could go to a different kind of club, for a woman. But he wasn't in the mood. He'd received a few dinner party invitations for tonight, formal events where, as an unattached man, he'd no doubt have been seated between two eligible ladies, but he'd turned down the invitations on the chance that he'd have Charlie for a second night.

When Charlie and Claire left early, he'd decided to use the time productively to catch up on his reading. For his work, he regularly reviewed at least fifteen technical journals, as well as dozens of newspapers and magazines. This was a great time to be in business. New industries were being developed overnight for the war effort. Hundreds of previously unforeseen needs had to be met, and new companies were being established to meet those needs. He was already doing deals with the navy for new types of refrigeration. The navy was building a lot of ships, and every one of those ships needed refrigeration. He was investigating a small company that was poised to become a big company by manufacturing quartz crystal oscillators, which were a breakthrough in radio transmission. On the back burner he had—

Ah, it was useless, he couldn't concentrate. His thoughts kept getting invaded by images of Claire and Charlie, and poor little Emily, whom he'd never known. In photographs, Emily looked like Claire at that age; once at the house downtown, he'd been looking through a photo album and had actually mistaken Claire for Emily playing in the snow in Central Park. "Look at Emily in the snow," he said. Claire came over and glanced at the photo. "That's *me*," she said, laughing, maybe even a little proud that she and her daughter looked so much alike, but he'd been embarrassed.

He stared at the small Turner watercolor framed and propped on the end table beside his chair. A ruined castle with three cows staring at their reflections in a lake. Very serene.

He didn't feel serene. He regretted that he hadn't fought for Claire years ago. He could have, should have fought for her. Now his guilt made him nervous around her. He stumbled over his words, repeated himself. He was desperate for her approval, or at least her acceptance. He found himself second-guessing just about everything he said to her—everything important, that is. Sure, he could joke about the smaller stuff, binoculars and bird watching. But he wanted to share more than that. He was glad he'd been able to advise her on Luce and the penicillin story.

He wanted her forgiveness. How could he earn it? What could he give her? She wasn't the type to value diamond necklaces or sable coats. He could pay to fix her leaking roof, but that didn't seem dramatic enough; he resolved to do it anyway, because Charlie (and Claire, too, naturally) shouldn't be living in a damp house with a leaky roof. If there was no direct gift he could give her, maybe he could do some charitable work in her name. Who wouldn't like that? Yes, maybe he was on to something with the charity idea. The point was, he needed Claire and Charlie so very much.

How far he'd come. He'd been born and had grown up in Bethlehem, Pennsylvania, on the wrong side of the river. If anyone asked, he said he was from nearby Allentown. He hinted that his people were in trade. They were actually immigrants from Croatia. He didn't want to link himself with Bethlehem in the eyes of the world. Bethlehem meant steel. It meant hard factory labor and a way of life he'd turned his back on. Yes, his father had been a steelworker, and he'd died too young, in a mill accident. A cable slipped, snapped, and five men— five fathers—were dead. No compensation. In those days steel was a miserable, dangerous, low-paying immigrant job. Maybe it still was; he didn't have anything to do with it, didn't even want to know about it. He'd done well in school, and his teachers pushed him. Even when he was ten years old, he was always tinkering, taking apart pulleys and door handles, figuring out how things worked.

After graduating high school, he'd gotten himself out of Bethlehem. Shifted his immigrant name around to something more pronounceable. He went from Rugovac to Rutherford, from evocations of the Balkans to British country estates in one stroke of an official's pen. He found the name *Rutherford* in the Allentown telephone directory. A common enough story. After he got rich, he sent his widowed mother money, bought her a house. Did the same for his ne'er-do-well brother. They were both gone now, but he hadn't neglected them, even though he never went back.

In his new life, he watched, he listened, he learned. College had been out of the question: he didn't have the tuition, and he didn't want to waste the time. He got hold of books on engineering, chemistry, finance, even Shakespeare, and educated himself. His first real job was with a company that manufactured locks. He could have made a career there, designing new and better locks, but after a few years he got restless. He wanted to do more, see more. He spent some time in West Virginia working for a coal mining company, trying to figure out better methods of ventilation. Went to Texas, trying to develop new ways of searching for crude. He had a gift for technical problems, a kind of special insight. When he was young, he thought everybody had that gift. When he got older, he realized that nobody else, at least nobody he knew, could do what he did.

He came to realize that inventors needed cash to do their work. They needed someone to say, I'll back that new-fangled lock, I'll support your research on that new chemical process, I'll pay your room and board while you're designing a revolutionary airplane engine. I'll believe in you—for a share of the profits. A hefty share. He realized he could do even more if he brought in other investors. He wanted to be the guy making money from the tinkering instead of the guy doing the tinkering.

So he made himself into the kind of man he needed to be, to secure the trust of others. In those days, he was the only one doing this type of investing. Nowadays, others were in on it, giving him some competition, especially Laurance Rockefeller, the old man's grandson. Sure, Rutherford drove a hard bargain with the people and the companies he supported. He was ruthless when necessary. Sure, he skirted the line of legality, but never so much as the big boys did, old man Rockefeller, Flagler, Carnegie, Frick, and the rest of them, lying, cheating, and exploiting their way to the top and then giving away millions (while keeping still more millions) and being hailed as heroes. He could never be as ruthless as they were, and so he'd never made himself as rich as they were.

He was already a millionaire, however, when he set himself up in New York. Once he'd married Claire's mother, every New York door opened to him. He had to admit it, her position in society attracted him. It was a sign that he'd arrived. What a rebel Anna was, to choose him instead of a man of her own background. They had a few happy years. Then her idealism began to get in the way. The very thing she'd professed to like about him—that he was a self-made striver—she turned against. She had a drive to rebel. As time passed, he became exactly what she was rebelling against. She objected that he devoted himself to making money instead of fighting for the poor—easy to say, when you've been born to wealth, when you've been fortunate enough to enjoy the Newport mansion of your childhood and the Fifth Avenue duplex penthouse of your marriage, all paid for by somebody else's hard labor.

But maybe these were just excuses. His life and his love both were his work, and she was bored and lonely. She was tired of coming in second, with little Claire third. She rebelled again. When she left him for Lukins, moving to Greenwich Village, she was the one condemned by society. Her own mother called her reckless, selfish, and immoral. He was judged the wronged party, which opened even more doors to him. For several months Anna's mother urged him to fight for Claire, but once the shock wore off, Anna and her mother reconciled, at least for Thanksgiving and Christmas. They became just another family, muddling along.

When Anna left with Claire, he felt—what? Some anger, of course. But truthfully, he hadn't really noticed, at least not then. He was traveling constantly, looking ahead, not simply planning for the future but creating the future. This was his obsession, then and now: to create the future. Except in those days he was still on the trajectory upward. His life hadn't yet plateaued. It had plateaued now, he knew, if only from the way he panted when he reached the top of the stairs.

He needed some coffee, had to get himself back on track with his reading. Couldn't allow himself to waste time. He set himself an immediate goal to fulfill before bed: *Scientific American*, *American Scientist*, and the *Journal of the American Chemical Society*. He prided himself on staying engaged, on thinking ahead. Couldn't let himself wallow in the past, in might-have-been or should-have-done. Today and tomorrow were what counted. If he kept his eyes open as usual, he'd figure out what to do to gain Claire's trust.

He pushed himself out of the chair and picked up his empty cognac glass (after all these years, he still wasn't habituated to MaryLee cleaning up after him). As he made his way through the Gothic entryway toward the kitchen, he glanced into the parlor in admiration. In his business, surface impressions counted for a lot. That was the reason he bought this apartment and filled it with art. He made certain he projected an image of measured, self-assured, highly solvent discretion. This image helped get him through the bad times. He'd steeled himself to turn the Depression to his advantage. He'd made educated guesses and invested when everybody else was running the other way. He had an iron stomach, as the cliché went. Even so, he didn't want to repeat the experience. He didn't relish that walking-along-the-edge-of-a-cliff feeling.

In the kitchen, he turned on the table lamp rather than the overhead light. He could think better in the half-light. He made himself a pot of coffee in the percolator. While he waited for it to brew, he looked out the long kitchen windows toward the apartment building across the side street. He watched lights being turned on and off, and figures, silhouetted against the curtains, moving from room to room. He was fascinated by these hints of his neighbors' lives.

When the coffee was ready, he went to the refrigerator to get the milk. This new business opportunity with the navy, improving refrigeration on ships heading to the Pacific Ocean—Lord, his job was fun. No matter what was going on in his private life, he had fun every day, just doing his job.

How would he describe his job, if ever some young guy looking for a career asked him about it? He'd describe it like this: imagine that every newspaper or magazine you saw at a newsstand, every radio program you happened to tune in to, every snippet of conversation over-heard on an elevator or at the next table in a restaurant—every single one—had the potential to earn you a million bucks. That was his job, and there was no job on God's good earth more exciting.

As he reached for the half-full milk bottle, he remembered what Claire had told him about scientists growing mold in milk bottles to make medicine. Searching the soil for cures for disease.

Incredible.

CHAPTER FIVE

~

egs. Mack didn't need to specify legs for Claire to know what he
and Managing Editor Billings wanted. After all, virtually every
issue of *Life* featured a starlet posing in her underwear. What they
wanted was a line of legs clad in flesh-colored tights, seams straight,
heels high, legs topped by well-endowed female torsos clad in identical, curve-hugging, red, white, and blue costumes. Thirty-six girls,
seventy-two legs—a glittering, giggling gathering of Rockettes.

"Perfect!" Claire called to them. They were outside at Rockefeller
Center, skyscrapers soaring around them. She'd arranged the Rockettes
in the lower plaza, around the golden statue of Prometheus, pretty girls
draped over the statue's arms and shoulders, the poses outrageous and
charming at once. The Rockefeller Center Christmas tree rose on the
upper plaza behind them, lush and colorful. Claire was shooting both
black and white and Kodachrome, with three Leicas around her neck.
On one, she put a filter with a crisscross of thin white lines to make the
Christmas tree lights sparkle in starbursts of blue and green, red and yellow. The scene was guaranteed to make *Life* readers in Indiana and Iowa
smile despite the awful war news in the front sections of the magazine.

The temperature hovered just below the freezing mark, but the
girls chose not to notice. Today's assignment was a major shoot, and
Claire had two assistants to handle crowd control, another to deal with
captions, and three more to maneuver lights to fill in the shadows and
to position ladders for the girls to climb into position.

"How's this?" asked Aurora, in the middle of the group, draping her arm around the statue's shoulders. At least Claire assumed it was Aurora. After four days of shooting, Claire still had trouble recognizing her from a distance. With her dark hair pulled up, Aurora was lithe and lovely and looked like . . . a Rockette. Especially when they were in costume, the Rockettes looked alike. Variations in their hair and facial features retreated into the background. They were hired specifically to look alike. Winsome expressions, high cheekbones, long legs. Sweet kids, one and all—at least that was the impression they were required to create. No room for cynicism here. Each girl was the girl next door, having fun acting glamorous but never a glamour girl, never crossing the line from innocent-attractive to experienced-seductive.

"Wonderful!" Claire said, encouraging Aurora, keeping up her spirits in the cold. "Everyone else, move into line," she directed. She motioned to her assistants for what she wanted, and they helped guide the group into place.

Rockefeller Center: twelve buildings on twelve acres, decorated with modern art, filled with shops, theaters, restaurants, cafés, gardens on skyscraper terraces. The complex was still new. John D. Rockefeller Jr. had driven in the final rivet only three years before. To Claire, the atmosphere was startling and exhilarating. This was the center of New York, and New York was the most glorious city in history. She felt the wind upon her, heard the conversations of tourists around her, the click of their cameras as they took their own photos of the Rockettes. She inhaled the scent of roasting chestnuts.

In the past four days, Claire had photographed Aurora and her fellow Rockettes being fitted in the wardrobe department, resting between shows in their dormitory, putting on makeup in the dressing rooms. She'd followed them home, in this case to the one-bedroom apartment Aurora shared with two other Rockettes. She'd photographed Aurora and her parents visiting the top of the Empire State

Building. Watching today's shoot from the sidelines, Mr. and Mrs. Rasmussen took photos of Claire taking photos of Aurora.

"Okay, next, let's try a kick line in front of the statue," Claire called. The girls arranged themselves. They set the rhythm and began the dance they were best known for: legs kicking high, in perfect unison.

Claire thought, this story is pure showmanship. Mack was right, when he said she needed a change. This was fun, this was star-spangled glamour, and it did make a difference to daily life, it did cheer you up, especially after her stories about Edward Reese, and the army wives. A magazine required balance, so that it became a complete book of, well, *life* each week. No one could survive long dealing with gloom and doom every moment of the day. There had to be room for dancing girls, too. She knew it sounded hokey, but Claire's faith in the magazine and her place in it was renewed.

The Rockettes gave several performances a day, and they needed to get back to the theater. Claire had to work fast. She saw that the two forklifts she'd ordered (*Life* had that kind of power and budget) were being moved into position: she wanted a shot of Aurora placing a crystal star, donated by Waterford, atop the Christmas tree.

At that moment, three young sailors approached the girls, their naval uniforms no doubt giving them courage. "Hey, ladies, what're ya doin'?" one called. He was short and stocky. Claire couldn't see his face.

In their own uniforms of red, white, and blue spangles, the girls had courage, too. "Hey, sailors, want your pictures in *Life* magazine?"

"You bet!" the man said. He pulled his buddies along. One was taller and so thin he looked unhealthy, the other was blond and looked lost, a farm boy dropped into Manhattan.

Three girls matched themselves to three sailors, climbing the ladders to join them on the balustrade of the upper plaza. The girls took the sailors' hats and put them on their own heads, sexily covering one eye. Three and three, they posed themselves as couples across the balustrade, Claire working fast to capture the evolving scene. Finding their own choreography, they moved from pose to pose. The scene came alive in front of the cameras. All six stretched out across the balustrade. The girls each lifted a leg into the air, and the three sailors followed their lead—lissome legs in tights contrasted with white Naval uniform trousers falling to reveal socks and a few inches of hairy shin. They all looked eighteen, nineteen at the most.

Which they probably were. They were just kids, playing around. Any *Life* reader looking at the photos would know that the three sailors would soon be on ships bound for the Pacific. They might never come home.

Claire turned and saw Mr. Luce, surrounded by a phalanx of dark-suited men, staring at the scene. The sailors and the girls were teasing one another now, laughing, relaxed, the girls refusing to give the sailors back their hats. Perhaps Luce was on his way to lunch in the private Rockefeller Center Club, part of the Rainbow Room complex in the RCA building across the plaza. Luce was a big man, clad in a warm, well-tailored overcoat, hat, and leather gloves. From his somber expression, Claire thought he caught the underlying sadness of the scene. He shifted his gaze to Claire, and their eyes met. Luce nodded, tersely, and he strode away before she could nod in return.

"All right, finished here," Claire called. "Aurora, we'll do the crystal star next. Everyone else, thank you very much. Let's take five minutes."

During the break, Aurora joined her parents on the side of the plaza. Mrs. Rasmussen reached up to wrap a blue coat over Aurora's shoulders, holding the coat tightly closed in front to keep her daughter warm. Claire photographed them through the long lens. Mr. and Mrs. Rasmussen were both overweight, bundled up in thick wool coats and hats that made them look even rounder. In her high heels, Aurora was a foot taller at least than her mother and almost as tall as her father. She was a magical, otherworldly creature who'd somehow been bred by these two graying, ordinary-looking Americans.

Her lovely face filled with gratitude, Aurora leaned down to kiss her mother's cheek.

Another smoke-filled room, this one with a clattering of coffee cups.

While Claire organized the Rockettes in the cold, Jamie began a fourth day of meetings in Washington, D.C. Today's was a mass meeting with the heads of the pharmaceutical companies as well as noncommercial research groups from around the country. Merck, Pfizer, Lederle, Hanover, Wyeth, Squibb, Lilly, they were all here.

His friend Nick Catalano was also here. On Tuesday, Bush had decided that Jamie needed an associate coordinator. David Hoskins would have been the ideal choice in terms of knowledge, but he was a British citizen and this was an American project, so Dr. Bush declared Hoskins out of the running. Dr. Rivers recommended Nick, even though Nick had expressed doubts about the entire line of research. Rivers said this was an advantage: Nick would be objective.

Jamie didn't care about the reason Nick was chosen; he was simply glad to be working with his friend, someone he could trust and share ideas with. He also appreciated that in this particular setup, Jamie was definitely the one in charge, since Nick had no penicillin experience. However, Nick had a Ph.D. in chemistry as well as a medical degree, so he understood those niceties. Furthermore, bureaucratic work didn't drive Nick crazy. And Nick was always thinking ahead: he'd already picked out a bar for them to visit later, one where young government secretaries, filling the city en masse to serve the new bureaucracies of the war, were rumored to gather, on the lookout for naval officers. Nick and Jamie were naval officers, so they'd have the inside track with these young ladies, Nick said. Nick claimed he was looking for someone to fall in love with; he said the war had made him realize what was important in life. Picking women up in bars didn't seem, to Jamie, the best way to go about finding someone to fall in love with, but he was happy to accompany Nick on his escapades, if only for the pleasure of seeing him in action. Jamie could simultaneously relax with a drink. Jamie's own, still private romantic thoughts were more focused on Claire Shipley than on twenty-year-old secretaries. He suspected, however, that Nick didn't know any other way. Nick had become a victim of his own reputation.

"We've got factories already under construction, preparing for mass production," Vannevar Bush said from the head of the table. Bush was slim, and he wore a suit with a bow tie. His gray hair spiked upward. He cultivated a New England Yankee bluntness, which apparently he came by honestly: he'd grown up in Massachusetts and spent much of his career at MIT. "In Indiana, Wisconsin, Missouri—away from the coasts, I'm sure you can figure out why."

Jamie already knew. In case of bombing raids and invasion, the factories would be safer inland.

"Nothing to fill them with, however. Nothing yet, that is."

They'd gathered at the opulent Hay-Adams Hotel, across from Lafayette Park and the White House. Not surprisingly, Bush had positioned himself so that the White House was visible through the long window behind him. In four days of working together, Jamie had learned that Vannevar Bush left little to chance.

"As you know," Bush was saying, "we have two options here: mass production from chemical synthesis of the penicillin molecule, and mass production using the living mold. Let's go around the table and you'll tell me the progress you're making. By the way, kindly remember that whatever we discuss here is top secret."

Was that supposed to impress everyone? Jamie wondered. Within the scientific community, the push for penicillin production was no secret at all, judging from the number of old friends and acquaintances who'd contacted him about job opportunities in the past week. His own so-called security check had been cursory. Here at the Hay-Adams, secretaries and assistants entered and departed freely, delivering whispered messages, offering carefully folded notes. Waiters circulated, refilling coffee cups, distributing platters of cookies, emptying ashtrays, and refolding the starched napkins of anyone who slipped out to the restroom.

"Chemical synthesis first."

If penicillin could be synthesized in a laboratory, it would be simple to mass-produce and distribute. No one would have to deal with the notoriously uncooperative *Penicillium* mold.

"You start," Bush nodded to the man on his left. The Squibb representative, according to the wooden plaque on the table before him.

The Squibb man was stoop-shouldered, balding, and nervous. His ashtray was overflowing. He looked everywhere around the room except at Dr. Bush. "We've got ten chemists on this problem. The difficulty is . . ." He slipped into chemistry terminology. Jamie couldn't follow the details. But although he wasn't a chemist, Jamie understood the problem. Penicillin had an unusual chemical structure, which, so far, no one had been able to replicate.

Somewhere in the hotel, bacon was being cooked. The scent had to be coming in through the air vents. If he were given the choice, Jamie would order a bacon, lettuce, and tomato sandwich on dark toast for lunch. Probably he wouldn't be given a choice. Dr. Bush held working lunches, and all week chicken salad sandwiches had been the only option.

The synthesis review made its way around the table, finishing with the Eli Lilly company representative on Bush's right.

"Thank you," Bush said to the table at large. He paused for a moment, sucking on his pipe. Then, "On to our second option: naturally occurring penicillin."

Jamie reflected that because he was staying into next week, he was going to have to do laundry and locate some extra elements of his uniform. Trousers, jackets . . . was there a depot where naval lieutenants bought such things? Was he allotted a certain number for free? If so, how many pairs of trousers? How many jackets? These questions were becoming crucial matters.

"Let's start with Pfizer. Mr. Smith?"

John L. Smith, senior vice president of Pfizer, was big and bluff, the phrase "hale and hearty" made for him. "As you may know, Dr. Bush, Pfizer has been at the forefront of this research, helped by our vast experience in fermentation. We are the leader in American production of citric acid, and therefore reasonably expect to be the leader in penicillin production." He made this bluster sound generous and gracious.

"Mr. Smith, your progress?" Dr. Bush pressed.

"None," Mr. Smith said.

And so it went, along the table. Of course the pharmaceutical companies could be concealing their progress, protecting their discoveries in order to achieve commercial gain. This industry was ferociously competitive. The word *cutthroat* could have been invented for it. For example, Lederle could work on a new product for years, but if Squibb stole the product before Lederle had received a patent on it, Lederle was left with nothing. Even if Lederle had a patent, Squibb could change the product slightly, get its own patent, and undercut Lederle's price in the marketplace. The companies operated on a basis of secrecy, and they weren't about to change their approach now.

At any rate, John Smith was right about this: the mass production of penicillin was essentially a fermentation problem. Like making beer, Jamie thought. He'd love a beer with lunch, but probably that was too much to hope for.

On the far side of the room, a shy voice spoke up. "Excuse me, Dr. Bush. I'm John O'Donnell, from Peoria, sir." Jamie turned to read the man's identification plaque, as did everyone else in the room. The Northern Regional Research Laboratory of the United States Department of Agriculture, Peoria, Illinois. This was a branch of the government, so the philosophy of research would be different from that of the pharmaceutical industry. It would be more like that of the Rockefeller Institute. O'Donnell wouldn't be focused on protecting commercial secrets. On the contrary, he'd feel a responsibility to share his discoveries. "Through trial and error, we've landed on an exceptionally successful new food for *Penicillium*. It's called corn steep liquor."

"Corn steep liquor?" Bush asked skeptically.

"It's not a beverage, sir."

Minor laughter from around the table. Probably Jamie wasn't the only one who wanted a drink, even though it was only 11:00 AM.

"Corn steep liquor is what's left over from the process of making corn starch. The purpose of the agricultural lab in Peoria is to investigate alternate uses for the products of corn, so this is our area of expertise."

What a remarkable lab that must be, thought Jamie. It was probably fully staffed with obsessives like Tia.

"We've had another breakthrough, too, from one of our girls."

Not for the first time, Jamie wondered about the definition of *girl*. Even though she was a brilliant scientist, Tia would probably be referred to as *a girl* by the men gathered around this table.

"Our girl went to a local food market and found a rotten cantaloupe. This cantaloupe was covered with a strain of mold that turned out to be *Penicillium crysogenum*. This strain of mold loves to eat corn steep liquor. As a result, our production levels for penicillin fluid have gone way up, far surpassing our expectations."

Corn steep liquor, rotten cantaloupes. How serendipitous scientific research could be, Jamie reflected. Tia could work with *Penicillium* for years and never chance upon its favorite food, corn steep liquor.

"We're having a problem, though. Corn steep liquor used to be cheap. In fact, it was considered almost worthless. Now the manufacturers are wising up, and the cost is going through the roof."

"We'll get you price controls." Bush turned to his secretary, who sat directly behind him. Tracey Dodd was nearer to sixty than sixteen.

Dressed in a utilitarian wool suit, her thinning gray hair fashioned in a simple, straight cut, she was as far from "a girl" as anyone could be.

"Price controls will certainly keep the idea secret," said Nick Catalano. The group turned to him. Jamie envied Nick's ability to state unpleasant facts in humorous ways that made others pay attention without becoming defensive.

"I'm sure there are many uses for corn steep liquor," Dr. Bush said. Sheepishly O'Donnell said, "No, there aren't."

"Then we'll create some." Bush flashed a grin. "We'll put out some false information. Have a little fun." He turned to whisper to Andrew Barnett, the security man. Barnett was youthful and dapper, and like his boss, he wore bow ties.

Jamie looked at Nick, to gauge his opinion on the false information issue, but Nick was taking notes. Typical of Nick, to take notes instead of letting the meeting wash over him the way Jamie did. Jamie could spend hours taking notes on every detail in a patient's reaction to an experiment, but he couldn't keep his mind on meetings. He was bored the moment he sat down at a conference table.

Nick took his notes, however, not because he enjoyed writing things down, but because it was the only way he knew to keep up. Although he didn't talk much about his background—what was the point? He'd been an adult for over twenty years now, responsible for himself—he wasn't born into the world of the Hay-Adams Hotel or the Rockefeller Institute. On the surface, yes, people might think he was born to it: Cornell for undergraduate work, Harvard for medical and graduate school. All done on scholarships, so through the beneficence of others. Sometimes, a voice inside him said, at the mercy of others. The scholarships had covered only tuition. He'd worked hard, in college cafeterias and medical school animal labs, to earn his room and board. His parents would have felt blessed to be able to help him, but they were getting by on factory jobs. Receiving this assignment to be associate coordinator of scientific research on the government's penicillin project was an honor Nick didn't want to lose.

"More coffee, sir?" said a waiter at Nick's elbow. Nick looked up at the man. EBENEZER, his name tag said. A white-haired black man, impeccable in his uniform.

"Yes." Nick moved the cup closer to the edge of the table for easier access. "Thank you." Ebenezer poured and gave a half-bow before moving on to the next man.

"Does corn steep liquor travel?" asked Mr. Smith of Pfizer. "Not on its own, I mean." The wisecrack elicited brief laughter from the executives. "Is it easy to work with? Maybe one of my fellas can pay you a visit in Peoria and find out about it."

Mr. O'Donnell looked to Dr. Bush for approval.

"Smith will send one of his men from Pfizer out to Peoria to take a look at what you're up to. And O'Donnell, you'll go to Brooklyn tomorrow to take a look at what Pfizer's up to."

Smith appeared less than pleased at this turn of events.

Inwardly Nick laughed as he imagined O'Donnell's upcoming tour of Pfizer: no doubt Smith would figure out a way to show his visitor the cafeteria, the mailroom, maybe even the citric acid production facility, but never, ever, anything relating to penicillin. Meanwhile when the Pfizer representative went out to Peoria, O'Donnell would show him everything they had.

George Merck ostentatiously stacked his papers on the polished table and cleared his throat. "One question, if I may, Dr. Bush. Sorry to interrupt." George Merck was over six feet tall, blond and blue-eyed. Something stolid and overprosperous about him prevented Nick from landing on the word *handsome* to describe him. "Each of us at this table is putting time and resources into penicillin development, with almost nothing to show for it. In this context, I must bring up, on behalf of my colleagues in the industry, the question of patent protection."

"Glad you mentioned it, George." Bush's use of Merck's first name was not a friendly gesture. It was patronizing, a bid to show who was in charge. "This topic is next on my list. First I remind all of you that penicillin is a naturally occurring substance."

Bush's voice turned soft. The others had to lean forward, straining to hear. Nick had to admire Dr. Bush's ability to take charge; something he could learn from.

"You and your colleagues know very well that you can't patent a naturally occurring substance. You're not making a new airplane engine here. Penicillin isn't a new type of radio transmitter. So I presume what you're hoping to patent are your individually developed means of production. Which leads me to a small announcement."

Bush paused. "Don't let my apparent . . . jocularity fool you, gentlemen. These issues are of the utmost urgency. Our troops need penicillin *now*. Immediately. They're dying without it. Therefore, for the duration, I expect you to share your discoveries with one another, pool your data, and in general behave like upstanding citizens in a nation at war. I will arrange for the Department of Justice to waive all applicable antitrust laws. To codify the formula, the government will take the patents on penicillin's means of production, when you've got some means of production to be patented. This way, I'm glad to remind you, no company will profit from them. I'll cover your production costs, and the military will buy your penicillin at a fair price when it's ready. Now that must make you boys happy, doesn't it?" He leaned back, smoking his pipe, a self-satisfied look on his face.

Jamie thought, Bush can order them to pool their data, he can tell them there won't be any commercial patents, but they'll try to find a way around his edicts. In the long run, they'd get what they wanted. Sure, they might make some wartime concessions, but overall the companies would do exactly as they pleased, as they always had. Bush had little or no real enforcement power over them.

After perhaps thirty seconds, George Merck continued in a perfectly reasonable tone. "Let me assure you, Dr. Bush, that we in the pharmaceutical industry know our duty to the nation and intend to do our duty. Even though penicillin has never actually saved a life. Even though clinical trials have been extremely limited. Even though we have no actual proof that penicillin will cure the wide range of diseases that we hope it will cure."

Merck let this sink in for a moment. "At the same time, some of us are investigating other antibacterial substances. This research remains extremely preliminary. In fact, I would say that we, as an industry, have had no success at all with this line of inquiry into penicillin's cousins, although we continue to pursue this humanitarian effort, expending resources on the cousins with no guarantee of return."

Enthusiastic assents circled the table among the executives to confirm their utter lack of success and their implacable devotion to research that held no hope of monetary reward.

The cousins. Neither Nick nor Jamie had ever heard the name applied to nonpenicillin antibacterial substances, and they exchanged a glance.

Merck continued, "On behalf of the group, I wish to confirm that the suspension of antitrust regulations, and the government's control on patent protection on means of production, applies *only* to penicillin and not to any other related antibacterial substances—which other substances, as I say, do not now exist and may or may not come into existence at any point in the future."

Jamie felt sure that Merck was reading a statement provided by an attorney.

"I also wish to confirm that the possibility exists for full patent protection on these other substances, which I refer to as 'the cousins,' even though under current patent law, they would be considered natural products. This would seem to us to be a just reward for the extensive sacrifices which we as an industry are prepared to make in the area of penicillin production."

For an instant Bush glared at Merck. Then, Bush slammed his

hand on the table and guffawed with laughter. "You got me there, Georgie, you got me there," Bush said, as if this were a game. But it was far from a game, Jamie knew, for any of them. "Now look here, gentlemen, if I get a hint—even a hint—that you're slacking off on penicillin work to focus on your own projects, or that you're using the government's money for private purposes, I won't be very happy with you. And the president won't be very happy, either. Very close we are, the president and me. Very close and getting closer."

He shrugged over his shoulder in the direction of the White House, visible through the window.

"Once you're mass-producing penicillin, you'll have plenty of free time to work on your so-called cousins. Meanwhile, you can be sure that I'll be spending every moment of my day thinking about patent issues." Dr. Bush leaned back in his chair, regarding them with a self-satisfied grin.

CHAPTER SIX

I n mid-January, Claire stood at the doorway of Chumley's restaurant at the corner of Barrow and Bedford streets. The reek of soot and garbage from the entry courtyard surrounded her. Chumley's was a former speakeasy, without a sign to mark the entrance. If you didn't know where it was, you didn't belong. Pushing her way around three heavyset men on their way out, she peered into the restaurant, trying to find Jamie through the cigarette-smoke haze. Broad wooden columns divided the dining room beyond the bar, columns that were most definitely holding up the ceiling. The building was decrepit, the floor dramatically uneven, and Claire teased the bartender about how long the place could remain standing. Jamie had asked her to choose their meeting place. Chumley's had a reputation for literary gatherings, but more important to Claire, it was informal and close to home, only a block away. She'd debated going to the Blue Mill, at the corner of Barrow and Commerce, but Chumley's was livelier and had a history that she enjoyed sharing.

Naturally she was running late, and when she didn't see Jamie with the crowd at the bar, she was afraid he'd misunderstood her directions, or given up on her and left. She waved to Chris, the bartender, who motioned to show her that her cover shot of Aurora Rasmussen placing a star atop the Rockefeller Center Christmas tree was framed and hanging in a place of honor on the wall among the book jackets and theatrical posters of the other regular patrons. Claire's Rockette story had created a splash, newsstand sales among the highest ever. Pretty girls, brave or adorable animals, anything about the navy but not the army, no one could figure out why—these were *Life*'s best-selling covers. Two covers in one month and don't even think of asking for a raise, Mack had said when he called to tell her, but he'd said it with such uncharacteristic resignation that she'd sensed his resolve crumbling.

Jamie had phoned to say that he'd walked over to a newsstand on First Avenue to buy the issue. He'd questioned her about how she'd gotten the cover shot, the forklifts, the lenses she'd used. The questions surprised her. He wasn't surreptitiously planning to become a photographer and exploiting her for her knowledge and connections. He wasn't simply trying to get into her bed. Instead he wanted to share in her experiences. To understand her thought processes. The men she'd known before had never asked for that.

Between her long hours at work, and Jamie's continuing duties at the hospital and more than one trip to Washington as the government's penicillin project gradually took shape, they'd been forced to cancel several dates in the past month. Instead of seeing each other, they'd had a string of late-night telephone conversations that left Claire feeling restless and overalert, attuned to every detail. The more she learned about him, the more she wanted to know. The more they spoke, the more she wanted to protect the connection that was building between them. This connection felt more and more precious to her as the time passed.

And yet . . . during these weeks apart she'd lost the sense of his physical presence. As she searched for him in the restaurant, her expectation mixed with a gnawing anxiety at the prospect of finally seeing him. Would she recognize him? She couldn't reconstruct what he looked like, couldn't re-create his image in her mind, even though she knew so well the timbre of his voice, deep, gentle, encouraging. The fact that they'd actually gotten to know each other made this encounter too important to take lightly. Passing flings she knew how to handle, only too well. James Stanton was new territory.

Finally she spotted him at a table against the back wall, a beer three-quarters finished in front of him. Yes, it was Jamie, no doubt about it. In the dim light, he read what appeared to be a medical journal. As she made her way toward him, maneuvering around the restaurant's crowded tables, she was taken aback: he was in uniform. Even though he'd explained on the phone that he'd been called to active duty in the navy, the uniform made his words starkly real. He'd been drawn into the vortex pulling men away from home every day. The idea filled her with protest and regret. At the moment she'd found him, he could be gone. At the moment when she realized with a jolt just how handsome and attractive he was, the light brown hair, strong features, the confidence and diffidence combined, he could be on the verge of leaving her. She ached for him. So very handsome and accomplished and waiting for *her*? Claire didn't typically feel undeserving, but at this moment she did.

"Forgive me for being late." She slipped into the chair across from him.

"I just arrived myself." Obviously not true (with the almost-empty glass to prove it), but he didn't care about her lateness. She was worth waiting for. Even in the restaurant's half-light, she was more beautiful than he remembered, with a combination of wayward sexiness and demure elegance that he hadn't registered before. She was dressed simply, in tailored trousers and a close-fitting sweater. Without her ubiquitous cameras and equipment bags, she was more vulnerable and feminine than he recalled. He wanted to reach across the table and caress her hair. Actually he wanted to do much more than that—making love with her flashed through his mind—but he held back. He didn't want to make her uncomfortable by moving too close too fast. He was willing to wait for her. "Drink?" he asked, preparing to call over the waiter.

Sitting here in the overheated restaurant filled with cigarette smoke, Claire felt her yearning become unbearable. That soft smile of his. She wanted to reach across the table and touch his lips, capture his smile on her fingertips.

"Are you all right?" He placed his hand lightly over hers. He didn't yet know how to read her. He didn't know how to decipher the underpinnings of gesture and expression, the private language beneath the words. After their extended phone calls, as surprising to him as they were to her, he was willing to be patient enough to find out.

"It's a little close in here, isn't it?" she asked. What's wrong with me? she wondered. She wanted to surrender herself to him. Collapse into his arms so that he could make her exhaustion and frustration disappear. Instead she was expected to order a drink, then dinner, and follow through on pleasant conversation in a convivial restaurant. She'd had a productive day, and she was worn out. She'd started with an early lunch with her father at the elegant Cloud Club near the top of the Chrysler Building. Her father had regaled her with whispered gossip about the many business titans dining around them. She'd enjoyed their time together, just the two of them, truly getting to know each other at last. In the afternoon, she'd gone to the Pennsylvania Station rail yards to follow newly hired female mechanics on their rounds. A cold rain had fallen as the female mechanics, old and young, pretty and not, were trained to inspect axles and brakes. She admired their gumption. They were filling in for men who were leaving for the war, just as the man before her might soon leave for the war.

"You sure you're feeling all right?" Even as he sensed her essential vitality and attractiveness, Jamie recognized that she'd become pale and fragile. He did a physician's quick evaluation. Her wrist felt cool to his touch. He was relieved that she wasn't feverish. He felt her pulse. A bit high, but close enough to normal.

"Shall we go?" she said abruptly.

"Of course." He was surprised, but he was happy to do whatever she liked. He didn't imagine that he'd done or said anything to offend her. He settled the bill. When he helped her on with her coat, he wanted to wrap his arms around her but settled for turning down her collar.

Claire headed toward the back door, the former speakeasy's escape door, opening onto Bedford Street. During Prohibition, a speakeasy needed a back door if the police showed up at the front, something she would have enjoyed explaining to him if she'd been feeling more herself.

They stepped outside, and they entered a snowstorm. Thick flakes, soft and caressing, landed on Claire's face and hat, enveloping her. The temperature had fallen and the wind had died down since her hours at the rail yards. The snow drifted as it did in a child's snow globe. The air smelled clear and pure. Her lungs cleared. She could breathe again. Because of the war, weather reports had been banned. The Germans and Japanese could exploit weather forecasts to plan bombing raids. So the snow caught Claire and Jamie by surprise. The street beckoned. The sidewalk was a white pathway into a city transformed. A city of wonder and enchantment.

Claire wanted to say, "I live just down the street, would you like to come home with me?" But Charlie was home with Maritza, halting any lingering urge toward a quick fling. She'd tried halfheartedly to arrange a sleepover for Charlie, but a bad cold was circulating among the third graders. Most likely her father would have been happy to host Charlie for the evening, but going uptown on a school night seemed like too much. So there would be no quick fling. Instead she said, "Would you like a tour of the neighborhood?"

"Sure." She seemed more steady now, he thought. More like the woman he was acquainted with. He longed to kiss away the snowflakes that had landed on her nose. "Show me where you grew up. Your favorite places."

Was he always so calm? He made her feel comfortable. They crossed Bedford Street and headed down Barrow Street, beneath the snow-covered trees. They walked to the turning where Barrow met

Commerce Street. She showed him the Cherry Lane Theatre, in a building that was once a factory, and before that, a warehouse, and before that, a brewery. Now it was a center of avant-garde theater productions. They walked past nineteenth-century town houses and tenements. On Hudson Street, she headed north, turning again on quiet Perry Street. Then Perry to Bleecker and onto Bank . . . cobblestone streets of homes with snow-laden wrought iron balustrades. When the sidewalk narrowed, Jamie followed behind her; when it widened, he was at her side once more. The snow brought them close. Claire's neighborhood . . . wrapped in mystery, alive with the expectation that around the next corner some secret—a hidden shop or a concealed courtyard—would be revealed.

The parents of Claire's classmates at Brearley thought the Village was dangerous. It was risky to go west of Seventh Avenue in the Village, their mothers said, and her friends were seldom permitted to visit her. Nonetheless they came downtown to see her without permission, to prove their daring or perhaps simply because they liked her, Claire Lukins, who lived in the wrong part of town and had a scandalous mother.

James Stanton had no sense of being in the wrong part of town. He appreciated seeing the neighborhood through Claire's eyes. He enjoyed conjuring an image of her when she was young. The unpredictable pattern of the narrow, intersecting streets disoriented him. He gave up trying to trace the route of their walk on a mental map. He felt a soothing pleasure in walking the snow-covered streets with this lovely woman, far from his usual haunts—away from the stench of infection and disinfectant, away from death and exhaustion and his continuing professional setbacks, away from the pressures of the war, and from always having to be strong and in control. It was a relief, sometimes, not to be in charge. To defer to the wishes of another.

She led him to St. Luke's Place with its perfectly preserved town houses, the front lanterns lit by gaslight. Undisturbed snow covered the wide, steep front stoops. They crossed Seventh Avenue South and made their way to Bleecker once more. They entered the northern reaches of Little Italy, passing butcher shops and bakeries. Claire paused beneath the exhaust vent of Zito's. Eyes closed, she breathed deeply the scent of warm, freshly baked bread. She'd come to this spot since childhood. She loved the aroma of baking bread. Zito's seemed to bake bread twenty-four hours a day, the fragrance wafting through the gritty street.

For dinner, Claire chose Grand Ticino on Thompson Street. They sat at the window. The snow was falling more heavily, and Claire was glad now to be inside. Jamie ordered a bottle of wine. From the kitchen came the staticky sound of a radio reporting the war news. They listened while the waiter went through the theatrics of showing them the wine, opening the bottle, giving Jamie a sample. Lately the urgent, grating noise of radios was becoming more and more pervasive as the war news became worse and worse. A few days ago, the British had pulled out of Kuala Lumpur. Wake had fallen before Christmas. Hong Kong surrendered on Christmas Day. Manila was occupied on New Year's Eve.

America would lose the war. This was the whisper in the shops, and even in the magazine bullpen. New York City, at least, would go down fighting, defended by its citizens block by block, according to the bravado at the butcher shop. Claire remembered the news photos she'd seen of Rotterdam after the German bombing in 1940. Of London during the Blitz, September 1940 through the spring of 1941, block after block of destruction. How long could America withstand an attack? The war in Europe had been going on for two and a half years already. New York was a coastal city, and so New York was particularly vulnerable. Claire knew that she would not be among those defending Manhattan by fighting for her neighborhood, from Houston Street north to Fourteenth Street. Her battle would be to keep Charlie alive and safe.

And if the Germans conquered the city, what then? Would the

magazine continue publishing? Would Charlie's school stay open? Would the grocery stores have food? Would there be water and electricity? Jamie was in the military and doing government work. If he wasn't captured, he'd probably go into hiding. Or the military would retreat to the center of the country and continue fighting.

Her father . . . he'd know what to do. He had the money and the savvy to keep them safe. How quickly idealism ended when confronted with enemy soldiers patrolling the streets.

"Let's leave the war behind this evening, shall we?" Jamie said when the wine was poured, calling her attention back to him. He understood that despite her strength and ambition, a part of her, a side she kept well hidden, was skittish and shy. Perhaps this was from the wounds of her divorce, or maybe her daughter's death had given her a constant fear about the safety of her son. He wondered about her life during the worst years of the Depression, how she'd gotten by, what compromises she'd had to make. During the early 1930s, he'd been sheltered, almost cloistered, within the confines of hospitals and research labs. He'd experienced the Depression mostly on the faces of his undernourished hospital patients. Claire Shipley had been struggling with divorce and death while he'd been protected. Now he felt an urge to protect her, to create a refuge for her. "Let's have a toast. To the future."

"To the future." The toast made her feel like crying. The future existed on so many levels. The war, Charlie, this man across from her. Gradually something shifted inside her. They drank the wine, spoke freely, and she lost herself in the moment, something she rarely allowed herself to do. As the hours passed, she realized that she'd forgotten the joy of simply being with someone, the pure pleasure of talking, for hours, with ease and grace, sharing opinions on the books they'd read, the movies they'd seen, re-creating their past lives for each other, finding common ground.

In an abrupt confession, Jamie said, "Another penicillin patient died today."

Initially he'd resolved not to darken their evening by discussing this. Now he needed to trust her with it. "This morning."

Instinctively she reached across the table and took his hand. "Tell me."

He squeezed her hand in return. The case was different from Edward Reese in every way, and yet it was the same. "A teenage girl. Sophia Metaxas. Osteomyelitis. That's a bone infection. For three days, she was better. She was even knitting a sweater in bed, as a way to pass the time. The sweater was dark red. Burgundy, I think, was the name of the color."

Claire knew the talk of sweater colors was only a way to divert attention from his sorrow.

"She was going to give the sweater to Tia when it was done. Her immigrant mother made a fuss of taking Tia's measurements. Then the medication ran out, and she died." He rubbed Claire's palm with his thumb.

"How do you go on?"

He paused before responding. "It's my job, I suppose that's the reason. What would I do with my time otherwise? It's the only job I know," he added with a touch of humor that he regretted. Humor was his usual armor against tough questions. He didn't want to armor himself against her.

Claire sensed that he hadn't yet found a way to reveal himself more fully. She didn't speak, to give him time to consider, and after a moment, he said, "To tell you the truth, I don't know."

The waiter arrived, breaking into their conversation. "Finished?"

Each nodded assent.

After the waiter cleared the table and left them, Jamie added with a genuine laugh, "I'll try to think of a better answer to your question for next time." She wrapped both her hands around his across the table. He turned his hands so that their fingers intertwined.

They ordered coffee and cannoli for dessert. Claire savored hers.

For a few moments the tangy sweetness of the cannoli pushed aside issues of life and death and even the blare of war news on the kitchen radio.

Watching her, Jamie had trouble resisting the urge to press his palm against her gorgeous face. Only one other table in the restaurant was occupied, by two couples in the far corner calling for a second bottle of wine. Would they notice or care if he got up and kissed the place where her jaw met her ear?

Through his mind, an image flashed of Ellen, his great love—or so he'd thought. When their engagement ended, he'd felt lost. He'd had their future mapped out, the work they'd do together, the goals they'd achieve, the children they'd raise. All that, suddenly wiped out. He'd left Saranac on the train knowing that most likely he'd never see her again. Over the years, occasionally her name appeared on journal articles. She'd never married, but now and again the long trail of gossip brought him news of her affairs with this or that colleague. Somewhere in his mind he'd still thought that someday, somehow, they would marry. He'd used her as an excuse for avoiding the risk of committing himself to anyone else.

He understood this now as he sat across a dinner table from Claire Shipley at the window of an Italian restaurant in Greenwich Village, snow silencing the street outside. His feelings for Ellen were gone. He reached across the table and placed his hand upon Claire's cheek, and she leaned into his palm.

After dinner, they walked through Washington Square beneath the lacy, interlocking branches of the snow-covered trees. The cool air steadied him after the wine. He let her lead the way. They turned west onto Washington Place. Lights glowed behind the curtains of the town houses. Debate continued in the press about a blackout or dim-out for New York City, but so far the authorities had reached no decision. Claire was glad to see the hints of life through the windows, the intimations of warmth and family. Washington Place led to Sheri-

dan Square, which led to Grove Street. They crossed Seventh Avenue
and continued on Grove. The snow was three inches deep, the sidewalk was slick, an excuse for her to take his arm. He pressed his hand
against hers, securing her arm in place.

Claire realized that she'd lost track of these intricacies of affection,
the initial wariness in the smallest gesture, the flicker of happiness
when each small gamble was rewarded with an equal gamble by the
person beside you. Each move brought them closer. The street looked
like the snow photographs of Alfred Stieglitz. Not a car passed, no
plows lumbered by, the sidewalks weren't shoveled. No one was out
but them. Snow had conquered the neighborhood. Jamie and Claire
walked in silence, and the silence felt like a cocoon.

How unlike her former husband Jamie was. Bill Shipley was always
taut, eyes stripping bare everything he saw. To him conversation was
argument. A casual comment, such as that they needed more milk for
Emily and Charlie, elicited a cataloging of where in a twenty-block ra-
dius milk was freshest at any given hour. When they met in college, he
at Columbia, she at Barnard, the intensity of his attention convinced
her that they could build a professional life together that would serve
and help others. They thought of themselves as a team, Claire taking
the pictures, Bill doing the writing, covering stories of injustice and
poverty across the nation. Together they'd change the world. Despite
their extravagant idealism, their plan worked until they had children.
A child, Claire learned, needs time simply to be, to gaze, to do nothing in particular. Bill couldn't tolerate hours filled with nothing in
particular.

Compared to Bill, the man walking beside her seemed at peace
with himself. He had nothing to prove, or perhaps he'd already proven
whatever he needed to prove to himself. She sensed his calling as a
physician; he could soothe even those screaming in pain, emotional or
physical. Instead of feeling challenged and too often found inadequate,
as she had with Bill, she felt calmed and safe.

"Look at that dog," he said.

She gazed down the street. Lucas was sitting on the front stoop, holding his leash in his mouth, which he wasn't strictly allowed to do. Snowflakes covered his muzzle and his floppy ears. Turning his big head from side to side, ears poised, he searched eagerly through the snow.

"That's my dog. That's my front stoop, where he's sitting. His name is Lucas." Charlie must by asleep by now, so Claire didn't have to worry about him peering out the upstairs window and wondering who this man was, accompanying his mother home. "Lucas loves the snow. He's hoping for a walk."

"He knew when to expect us?"

"He'd wait outside for hours like that, knowing that eventually I'd turn up. My housekeeper is looking after Charlie tonight, so she must be keeping an eye on Lucas from the parlor."

Jamie felt an ache of yearning in his chest. The dog waiting on the front stoop. The two empty milk bottles on the top step, ready for exchange by the milkman in the morning. The lights beckoning within. These meant home. For too long, his home had been a hospital, sickness and death all around him. For months, the only milk bottles he'd focused on were filled with green mold. He wanted to be able to walk into that house and take her upstairs and make love with her, for the rest of his life. He felt tears welling in his eyes, from the cold, from the night, from his desires.

Lucas greeted Claire by bounding down the steps and running toward her, snow flying off his fanlike tail. When he reached her, he leapt up and placed his paws on her shoulders, not strictly allowed either, but she gave him a hug, which was what he wanted, before she pushed him down.

A wave of sadness came over her: Pets were forbidden in air raid shelters. Last week she'd done the illustrations for a story on what to do with pets during bombing raids. Lucas had been the story's featured dog. In the event of an air raid, *Life* explained, dogs should be chained to the firmest fixture in the house, such as a bathtub foot. A blanket, a bowl of water, and a chew toy should be left with them while their owners went to the shelter. Lucas, freshly groomed for the occasion, had been quite game for his star turn, posing with his blanket, bowl, and stuffed duck while leashed with a heavy chain (provided by the research department) to the bathtub foot. The prospect of leaving Lucas alone in the bathroom while bombs fell on the city filled her with a grasping love for him.

Jamie's thoughts were elsewhere as he did a quick calculation: spying housekeeper, easily awoken child, wet excitable dog. Probably not the best setting for what he had in mind. Nor could he easily take her to his rooms at the hospital: lots of prying eyes in the corridors, as well as a distinctly unromantic atmosphere, reeking of disinfectant. He should have thought ahead, secured a hotel room. He'd do that next time, or with luck she'd arrange for the child to stay with a friend.

"Shall we take the dog for a walk?" Jamie asked, both to prolong the evening and to show her that he wasn't the type to pressure her. "If you're not cold, I mean." Taking off his glove, gently he rubbed the back of his hand against her cheek.

She stepped toward him. Moved her face against his fingers. How warm his skin felt. She rued the fact that she hadn't planned better for the end of their evening. She'd imagined making love with him, but hadn't planned for it. Or perhaps this was her true planning, to be able to move ahead only so far but no further; to set up the circumstances that made a fling impossible.

"No, I'm not cold." In fact she was freezing, her toes and fingertips numb, but the touch of his hand was warm upon her face, and she no longer cared about the cold. "Let's walk to the churchyard at St. Luke's."

"You walk a dog in a churchyard?" he asked.

"He's a very religious dog." She snapped the leash onto the dog's collar. Climbing the front steps, she opened the door and greeted Maritza, who was indeed waiting in the parlor.

"I'll take Lucas for his walk," she said. "Thanks for looking after Charlie. Good night."

He couldn't hear the housekeeper's response. Claire and the dog rejoined him, and she walked ahead.

"You have to see Grove Court," she said, beckoning to him. They stood at the gate, which opened onto a cobblestone courtyard. A row of small houses lined the far side of the courtyard, houses otherwise hidden from the street. Their lights seemed to flicker through the snow. This wasn't the New York he knew. Claire was introducing him to an alternate city, a place outside normal time, where she lived her daily life. In the light from the streetlamps, her face was eager with the expectation of his appreciation. Because his appreciation went far beyond Grove Court, he could find nothing adequate to say. He squeezed her hand instead, which for some reason made her laugh. She took his arm, and they continued down the street.

St. Luke's Chapel was a simple church, consecrated in 1822 as a country parish when this part of New York City was still farmland, a place where people escaped from the noise, crowds, and recurring epidemics of cholera and yellow fever in lower Manhattan. Claire related this history to Jamie, who enjoyed hearing it because she so clearly enjoyed telling it. The church had a plain tower, suited to an English village. The gate to the churchyard was kept latched but not locked. Claire led the way down the path, around the back of the church and into the garden on the opposite side. The garden, protected by a tall wrought-iron fence, was lit by a streetlamp, a golden-yellow orb glowing through the snow. In the spring, Claire came here often with Lucas (despite the signs prohibiting dogs) to sit and read upon the wooden benches beneath the flowering apple trees. She'd come here almost every day after Emily died, even though she lived uptown then, because she discovered consolation here, a tiny, precious kernel of peace.

Jamie wiped the snow off a bench, and they sat close beside each other. Claire was aware of every aspect of his presence, alert to how easily and naturally she could slip her hand onto his leg and stroke his ankle, his calf, his inner thigh. But she didn't. She waited for him.

She was breathtaking, he thought, with snow covering her hat and the curled hair that flowed around her shoulders. He sensed that she waited for him, and the thought filled him with pleasure. His pleasure made him move even more slowly, because he wanted to prolong it.

"Look at you, you're covered with snow." Gently and carefully, caressingly, he brushed the snow away. He wrapped his arms around her and felt her turn to move closer against him. He kissed her eyelids and she responded by kissing the line of his jaw and his neck, and finally he found her lips upon his own.

CHAPTER SEVEN

Y"ou have four minutes." Henry Luce spoke without looking up from his hunched-over examination of the page proofs on his desk. He didn't need to set a stopwatch; he seemed to have one running relentlessly in his brain. He had a cigarette going, and the ashtray was already full at 9:20 AM. The room was stuffy from the smoke. His penthouse office, on the thirty-third floor of the Time & Life Building at Rockefeller Center, was a palazzo in the sky, with ornate furniture, wood paneling, thick rugs, and double-height windows. The morning sun glittered upon the windowpanes of the surrounding buildings. Luce, however, didn't waste time staring out of windows. "What do you want?"

Claire burst out laughing. Her laughter must have startled him, because now he did look up. He evaluated her. Carefully he reviewed her legs, her clothes, her hair, her face, the front of her low-cut silk blouse. His blue eyes were sharp and intense. He was known to appreciate a good-looking woman, and this morning Claire had made certain she fell into that category, with a tight skirt instead of her usual trousers, high heels, her hair in a Veronica Lake wave. She sat at the end of the chair, legs crossed, skirt pulled above her knees.

For his part, Luce was not particularly attractive. He was only forty-three, but his scowling, weighty demeanor made him seem older. Generations older than Claire. He was tall, but with a round-ness that suggested short. His dark hair was thinning, his eyebrows bushy, his suit rumpled and frayed at the cuffs. Cigarette ash dusted his tie. His accomplishments were astonishing. He was the founder, publisher, and editor of the most important magazines in the country. He and Brit Hadden had invented the weekly newsmagazine. His empire included the phenomenally successful radio and newsreel series *The March of Time*. Raised in China, the child of missionaries, Luce was said to be inspired and motivated by the Christian teachings of his father and to believe that America had a God-given duty to lead the world.

As far as Claire knew, none of his employees had ever seen him smile. Much of the staff was terrified of him. Claire had heard a rumor that at high-level meetings, the top editors of his various publications maneuvered to take the seats farthest away from him, praying that he would overlook them. She resolved to stand up to him. She was one of his star photographers, or so she told herself. She'd had two recent cover stories. He wouldn't fire her, if only because he wouldn't want her to take her work to *Look* or *PM*. She was entitled to speak to him the same way he spoke to her.

"I have an idea for you." Good. She sounded focused, objective, and professional.

This appointment had taken weeks to set up. Luce had been away over the holidays, then traveling, then absorbed with work. They were already into February. His secretary made certain Claire understood how lucky she was to get the appointment. Claire didn't tell Jamie or her father that she was meeting with Luce; there'd be plenty of time to tell them if she accomplished anything.

"Yes?"

"We both know that you killed the medical story I did because penicillin came under government jurisdiction."

"That's a supposition." He returned to his reading, correcting and querying the proofs with a sharp pencil. At his elbow rested a cup stuffed with similarly sharp pencils, at the ready for quick comments.

She imagined him knocking the cup to the floor, pencils rolling across the carpet. The image fed her determination.

"I presume you know also that the government is devoting a fortune to the research and mass production of this drug. From reviewing my story, you know that similar drugs are being developed. They're made from substances in the soil. From the earth itself. The entire philosophy behind these drugs is revolutionary. You'll want to tell the full story in your magazines when it's no longer a secret. A story of American technological achievement transforming human life. You'll want to be the one to document it from beginning to end. To present the American heroes who made it happen."

He looked up from the page proofs and squinted at her. "What's this to you?"

She hesitated. She didn't want to be too personal with him, too *female*. But she also knew that to be taken seriously, she had to tell him why it mattered. Her father had told her to claim this territory as her own, and now she did. "I don't generally discuss personal matters at work." She hoped he would respect her years of professional forbearance. "I had a daughter who died when she was three. Of blood poisoning." Emily, lying on her bed, lifeless, hands crossed. Claire felt a constriction in her throat. She paused to let it pass, to stop her voice from quivering. "Penicillin might have saved her life. *Would* have saved her life. I already know the scientists involved with this story. I understand the issues. I only ask that I be the one to follow the story, wherever it leads."

Impassive, Luce stared at her for a long moment. Was he remembering Briton Hadden, his dear friend and business partner who died from a cat scratch? "How's your son?" he asked, surprising her.

In the welter of contradictions that was Henry Luce, he could be generous and considerate. Last year when Charlie was ill with scarlet fever and out of school for a month, Luce had arranged and paid for a tutor to help Charlie keep up with his schoolwork. Luce was known for his unpredictable generosity, which his detractors labeled paternalism.

"He's well, thank you. And thank you again for sending the tutor for him last year. That was kind. It made a difference in his life." She'd written Luce a note at the time, but she'd never thanked him personally. Staff members weren't supposed to speak to him informally, weren't supposed to ride the elevator with him or initiate a conversation in the hallways. Nonetheless he seemed to know everything that went on at the magazines. She never learned how he found out about Charlie's illness; at the time, she'd been so distracted with caring for Charlie that she'd never pursued it.

He waved off the personal thanks as if it were an embarrassment. He flicked his cigarette, spreading ashes on the proofs across his desk. "Terrific story on the military wives. Ditto the Rockette girl. Excellent newsstand sales."

He always kept track of the money. Yet Claire knew enough about his courageous positions on controversial issues to recognize that money was not his primary motivation. "Thank you."

"Military wives. Brave. Moving. Showed America that the families in the trenches know how to behave. Know how to do the right thing. The right thing." He tripped over his words. He'd had a bad stutter when he was young, and he still fought to overcome it. Often he repeated himself or spoke in machine-gun outbursts. "Exactly what I expected. The families of our military men—exactly what I expected." Perhaps because of his childhood in China, he had a straightforward idealism about what America stood for and what the country could achieve.

"Yes."

"My wife liked it, too. She's noticed your work. She wants to do a story with you."

Oh, no, here it was: Claire's punishment for daring to come to see him. His wife, Clare Boothe Luce, was a successful playwright, journalist, and editor. The staff considered her a holy terror, snobbish, condescending, and mean-spirited. She was notoriously charming to men in power whom she wished to court. Her play *The Women* had been hugely successful on Broadway and made into a film. "She'll write the story. You'll take the pictures."

Traditionally, any Time, Inc., employee who crossed Clare Boothe Luce was in trouble. "I'd be honored, Mr. Luce."

"Knew you would be," he said without a trace of irony. "She'll decide what she wants to do. She'll be in touch."

Claire could only hope that Mrs. Luce's idea wouldn't involve traipsing through a jungle somewhere during the rainy season; or that she wouldn't decide that this was the perfect moment, with the Japanese rampaging across the Pacific, to visit China and lend some Time, Inc., support and prestige to Generalissimo and Madame Chiang Kaishek, a couple much beloved by the Luces.

"I'll look forward to it, Mr. Luce." Claire's photographer buddies, especially those who'd had a special story or two killed over the years, were going to get a good laugh out of this.

"Excellent. I'll tell her tonight. Now you can go."

She'd accomplished nothing. She made one more attempt, with flourishes, what the hell: "You're missing out on the most important medical story of our era."

He glared at her, thick brows drawn together in a frown. "You're just like my wife. You never know when to stop. When to leave well enough alone."

This she had to interpret as a compliment. After all, he'd left his first wife and their two children to marry the divorced Clare Boothe Brokaw. Rumor was that he'd proposed after only three, some gossips said two, meetings. "Thank you, Mr. Luce."

The frown eased. He looked almost relaxed. "Mrs. Shipley. I cannot discuss the penicillin matter with you. It touches on official secrets. As you know. But you can trust me to do what's best. For the magazines. For the nation. Not for you."

She couldn't help but smile. His meager concession felt like a victory. "Thank you, Mr. Luce."

"I look forward to seeing what my wife decides on for you."

Was there the merest twinkle in his eye, to say that he understood his wife, knew what Claire would be up against? No, there wasn't. He returned to his page proofs, showing that good-byes or even good mornings certainly were not in order.

CHAPTER EIGHT

———

D ear Claire, I'm writing to you from New Haven. I arrived yesterday afternoon.

At 3:25 AM, Sunday morning, March 15, 1942, at the Yale University Hospital, James Stanton was writing a love letter to Claire Shipley. He sat in the corner of a hospital room observing the penicillin treatment of a patient who was approaching death. He wrote the love letter to fill the hours. He also wrote it to grasp at the future while another life came to an end far too soon.

The patient was a female, thirty-three years old, suffering from hemolytic streptococcal septicemia acquired after a miscarriage. Her fever was spiking to 107. She was delirious. She'd received her first dose of penicillin on Saturday afternoon. Yesterday.

A description of the facts, nothing more. Only what was necessary to know for the purposes of the experiment. This was Jamie's defense.

But of course he did know more, the Yale staff providing detail upon detail. She was one of their own, after all. The staff took this test personally. Her name was Anne Miller. She had young children. Her husband, Ogden Miller, was the director of the athletic department at Yale. She was a trained nurse. She was slender, blond, lovely. At thirty-three, she was in the glory of her days. She was dying.

I'm here to observe a medical test. Jamie was learning to pay more respect to the government's code of secrecy regarding penicillin development. He kept the letter in his notebook, so anyone observing him would think he was simply writing a report on the experiment. Which he was also doing, on pauses from the love letter.

I hope you are well. He certainly did hope she was well; he didn't know what he would do if she wasn't. Suddenly the polite, throwaway cliché—*I hope you are well*—became fraught with anxiety. How easily she could become the woman on the bed before him. Like this woman, she could miscarry a child, their child, their hope turned to despair. *I miss you.* Another easy euphemism, charged with meaning. *I wish I could see you soon.* This morning at breakfast, for example. And at lunch and at dinner for the rest of his life.

At any moment, without warning, Claire could contract an incurable infection. At any moment and without warning, he, too, could contract an incurable infection. He wanted to pray that it wouldn't happen. *I'd like to see you as soon as possible.* He felt like praying although he couldn't imagine a God. Even the small amount of human suffering he'd seen as a doctor had made him doubtful about religious faith. And yet his love for Claire felt sacred, a blessing upon them both, a gift of grace they'd been granted beyond deserving or comprehension.

4:00 AM. Time for the next injection. A medical student, covering for the night, came in to give the shot. The student looked young, so smooth-cheeked that Jamie wondered if he'd even started shaving. And the student look scared. His hand shook as he prepared the syringe. Jamie looked away. He didn't want to make the young man more nervous than he already was.

The physicians in charge here were guessing with the doses, Jamie knew. They preferred their own guesses to his recommendations. Well, it was their experiment, and he didn't have authority over them. This was their territory, and he respected professional boundaries. Nonetheless he had to be here. He was the government and military representative. The penicillin had been manufactured by the Merck company. The Merck representative, sporting a dashing black mustache that contrasted with his conservative tweeds, was also observing, pacing the room as his company's product was put to the test. Jamie found the man's pacing irritating. He wished the man would sit down and find something to occupy himself, such as writing a love letter.

I'm glad I've been able to spend so much time with Charlie. Several weeks before, they'd taken Charlie and his friend Ben ice-skating at Prospect Park in Brooklyn. That was Sunday afternoon, February 15, the day that the supposedly invincible British outpost of Singapore fell to the Japanese. When he and Claire heard the news, the shock was as great as the bombing of Pearl Harbor.

Jamie remembered, could still almost feel, the fragility of Charlie's hand within his own as they ventured onto the ice. Ben, more experienced, skated on the other side of Jamie with his hand touching Jamie's arm—touch and away, touch and away, as Ben recaptured his skills. Within ten minutes, Ben and Charlie both were circling with abandon, sprays of ice sparkling off their skates in the sunshine. Watching Charlie, proud of him for overcoming his initial fear, Jamie realized that he felt a growing affection for the boy. He saw Claire in Charlie's wide cheekbones and curious gaze and, most of all, in his endearing combination of vulnerability and courage. As he fell in love with Claire, he was also coming to love her son.

After Charlie and Ben were safely occupied, Jamie was able to turn his attention where he preferred it to be, on Claire. She stood at the side of the rink, bundled against the wind, hat low, thick scarf covering her mouth and nose. The expression around her eyes revealed that she was hiding a smile beneath her scarf as she welcomed him to her side. He wished he could sweep her up and carry her away to a deserted cabin somewhere in the mountains. But he couldn't. Not right then, at least. He'd have to be satisfied with teaching her to skate. He suspected she was pretending to a lack of knowledge, but he didn't mind, because pretending or not, she pulled his arm around her, leaned close to him, and let him guide them across the ice. They stayed near the railing, and more than once, she slipped or feigned slipping and they fell against the wall in a laughing embrace.

A week later, on the night of the twenty-third, they were together for the president's fireside chat. This was a momentous occasion, not simply for the speech, which didn't begin until 10:00 PM: Tia came to dinner at Claire's. He wanted his sister to feel part of this new life he was creating. The evening was informal and relaxed. Tia brought an apple pie she'd baked from their grandmother's recipe, and it was a great success. Tia reviewed Charlie's homework, played a game of tug with Lucas (Tia had loved dogs when they were kids). There was much laughter at the dinner table—exactly as he'd hoped, as if they'd all known one another for years. He'd urged Claire to invite her father to dinner also, so they could finally meet, but on this Claire refused. She wasn't ready, she said, explaining that her hesitation was entirely about her father, not about him. She'd told Jamie a few details about her father, but he sensed she was holding back painful memories, and he didn't press her for more information.

Charlie asked to stay up late to hear the president's speech. Despite her concern for his reaction, Claire allowed him to. Obeying the president's widely publicized instructions, Claire bought a map of the world, and after dinner she spread it on the kitchen table. Before the speech began, Charlie showed Jamie and Tia the places in Europe where his father had been posted. Jamie was pleased that Charlie freely talked about his father, as if Charlie considered Jamie and Tia to be part of his family already.

At ten, the president began. First FDR talked about the early days of the Revolutionary War, when the patriots were close to defeat. He spoke about the struggles at Valley Forge. Then he turned to the present. He knew that they, all the Americans listening to him, could hear the worst without flinching.

"What does *without flinching* mean?" Charlie asked.

Claire explained it to him. At that moment, Jamie loved her more than he imagined possible. She was brilliant, beautiful, self-possessed, yet helpless as they all were against the forces of the world. Calmly she explained to her curious eight-year-old the meaning of "without flinching."

The explanation meant that they missed the president's first several sentences about how bad the situation was around the world. Maybe that was for the best, because Claire, Jamie, and Tia already knew. No need to frighten Charlie with every detail. The Japanese controlled the Pacific. Europe had been conquered. The enemy was getting closer. A Japanese submarine attacked an oilfield near Santa Barbara, California. Off the coast of New Jersey, a Standard Oil tanker was sunk by a U-boat. Even *Life* magazine was presenting educational maps on the most likely ways for the enemy to invade the United States, the Japanese coming through Alaska and down the western coast, the Germans through the Gulf of Mexico and up the Mississippi.

A noise startled him. Jamie checked his watch. 6:00 AM. He must have drifted off. The corridor outside the room had begun to stir, orderlies wheeling carts, nurses chastising underlings. Jamie had spent most of his adult life in hospitals.

A nurse came in, checked the patient's temperature and vital signs, took blood. On her way out, she looked at him and saw he was awake.

"Mrs. Miller's temperature is normal."

Jamie said nothing. Her tone was like an accusation. The Merck rep had finally stopped pacing and fallen asleep in a chair. His soft snoring provided a rhythm to the silence.

"What do you think about that?" she asked, a challenge. She looked about seventeen, soft and pretty. Of course she had to be older.

"Too soon to tell," he answered. Don't be fooled. Don't hope. Keep your perspective. He wanted to tell her this, but her steady, questioning gaze disarmed him. She wore an engagement ring. The diamond

was small but bright in the half-light of early morning. She had a com-
plexion that he could only describe as rosy. She wanted answers that
he couldn't give her.

"Her fever's been over 104 for days. Yesterday morning it was
107."

Most likely the young nurse wouldn't dare to speak to a resident
physician this way. Because he was from the outside, she risked bar-
raging him with questions.

"What happens next?" she insisted.

He heard laughter in the hallway, early morning greetings exchanged. He smelled coffee and cigarettes. He wanted to reenter the
stream of daily life outside the door. Instead he was bound here, out of
time, waiting for death. "I don't know."

Jamie realized he sounded impatient, even condescending, which
he didn't feel. Yet he had no comforting answer to give her. He needed
to keep comforting answers away from himself, because they were always proven false.

"She lives next door to my sister. I looked after her children once on
New Year's Eve. Is she going to be okay?"

"Just take the blood to the lab." That impatient tone again. He
wished . . . in equal measure he wished he could pat her shoulder and
tell her everything would be fine, and he wished she would go away
and leave him alone. The nurse supervisor would tell her to buck up
and get a grip on herself, which is what he would have said to a junior
physician at the Institute. Instead he forced himself to show her that
she, too, was part of the forward process. "The results of the blood
work will provide good information."

This at least he knew, the step-by-step requirements of medical
routine, this he could cope with for himself and recommend to others
as they searched for reassurance.

She turned and walked out. He was alone again. Well, not actually alone, for the Merck man slept on, and the patient . . . he allowed

himself to glance at the patient, the disheveled blond hair, the ghostly pallor, lips tinged with blue, thin arms, skin hanging loose. She'd been ill for over a month, and she'd lost a good deal of weight. On the bedside table was an informal photograph of her with her husband and children, all of them laughing. Once she'd been a beauty.

Claire Shipley. He had to center his thoughts away from here, and he centered them on Claire. He pulled out his letter once more. Found his pen. Where had he left off? Ice-skating with the boys in Prospect Park. Wasn't that where he was?

I'm even more pleased to spend so much time with you. How far could he let himself go in a love letter? He didn't feel he could write, *I wish I was* (actually, "were" was probably the correct form) *lying on your bed right now, waking from sleep naked beside you and turning to you and entering you, feeling your breasts beneath my chest, both of us still half in dreams.* Or maybe he could say that. Maybe that was exactly what he should say. Be honest and forthright about his passion, about his craving for her. But it wasn't simply passion he was feeling. He wanted her to know that he was feeling much more than passion. Not to dismiss passion, though.

The woman on the bed moaned. No doubt her husband would arrive soon, after he'd made breakfast for their children and situated them with relatives or a neighbor for the day. Maybe he'd take them to church before he came here to visit his dying wife. Jamie put up a roadblock in his mind: he wouldn't let himself think about the husband, the children, the miscarriage. Wouldn't let himself think about Claire suffering a miscarriage of their baby. Wouldn't think about what a child of theirs would look like, or what kind of person their child would grow up to be.

He mustn't get ahead of himself. After all, he couldn't judge Claire's feelings. Well, maybe he could. The way she'd taken his hand on the subway coming home from Prospect Park, concealing their hands under a fold of her coat so that the boys wouldn't notice. Such a simple act of tenderness. At home, she'd cooked them dinner. Afterward, when he was drying the dishes, she'd slipped her arms around him, resting her head against his shoulder, her breasts soft against his back. They'd stood that way for several minutes, until they heard the clamor of boys and dog racing down the stairs and into the kitchen. He had to tread carefully with Charlie at home. He didn't want to create for her a problem of loyalty or priority. He didn't want to force her to choose between them. Although he and Claire took advantage of the limited private moments they could find, naturally he wanted more. The presence of Charlie slowed everything down, even though he was coming to love Charlie.

No sentimentality, he cautioned himself. He couldn't allow it, not in his work, nor in his personal life. *I'm sorry I had to cancel our dinner plan for Saturday night.* Saturday night was last night. He'd come to New Haven yesterday morning, fewer than twenty-four hours ago. Remarkable. He felt as if he hadn't seen Claire in a year at least.

I'm thinking of you. Did that sound sentimental? He knew how to deal with lust, but he had little experience with love. Only Ellen, left behind in Saranac. Did Claire sense his relative inexperience? Is this why she was so gentle in her manner with him, seeming to wait for him to take the lead? Or was she somehow afraid? If so, afraid of what? He knew that he was afraid. Afraid because Claire mattered so much to him.

He felt dazed from lack of sleep. Maybe he should go to the on-call room that had been assigned to him at the end of the hall. Lie down for an hour or two, take a shower and shave afterward. The Merck man had woken up and gone off to take a shower. Certainly Jamie would try to get some sleep before sending the letter to Claire. When he was more alert, he'd review the letter and maybe rewrite it. On the other hand, maybe he should let himself be impetuous for once and mail it now.

I miss you. He'd said he missed her at the beginning of the letter, but it was worth repeating. He imagined himself cupping both her breasts in his palms and gently kissing first one, and then the other, especially that place on the side, where her breast curved around, his hand underneath. *I think about you all the time.*

"Dr. Stanton, would you mind taking a look at these lab results?" The chief physician, stout, bald, an arc of white hair around his lower skull, stood at the entry to the room. At least the man was in early this morning; Jamie had been taken aback when the physician went home last night. The man held a sheet of paper and looked skeptical.

Well, this must be something serious, if they were asking for his opinion. Jamie closed his notebook, its love letter hidden inside. He stood. He felt a little light-headed from lack of sleep, lack of coffee, lack of breakfast, and lack of Claire. Putting on an air of nonchalant self-assurance, he walked to the door and took the report that the chief physician held out for him.

He read the report. Its news did not surprise him. He'd read reports like this before.

"It's astonishing, isn't it?" the chief physician said.

Jamie absolutely couldn't remember the man's name. They'd been introduced yesterday afternoon, and Jamie had made a mental note of his name. It related to animals. Fox, Wolf, Hunter . . . no use, it was gone. During his training, he'd been able to stay up night after night and still remember every name, every diagnosis, every testing schedule. Maybe he'd bragged about this ability once too often to his colleagues, and now forgetfulness was his reward.

"I wouldn't have believed it, if I hadn't seen it myself," the nameless colleague continued. The belt buckle on the man's trousers had disappeared completely under his large abdomen. "And her fever is normal, did you know?"

"Yes." Jamie vowed that he would never allow himself to become stout. How could he confidently present his naked self to Claire if his abdomen was four feet around? She wouldn't be able to find the crucial parts.

"I caught that fellow from Merck on his way to the shower, and he says they've got enough medication stockpiled to last one patient for three weeks. He can have it up here on a day's notice, though he says we won't need it all."

"You'll need it all," Jamie said. "Tell him to send it. Now."

"All of it?"

"Yes, all of it."

The woman on the bed was stirring. She called out a name. Her husband's name. Said the name clearly, although her voice was weak. Her delirium had passed.

Anne Miller. Wife, mother, nurse. Weeks of medication, available on a day's notice. Suddenly Jamie grasped the truth. Anne Miller was different from the other critically ill penicillin patients he'd treated. Different from Edward Reese and Sophia Metaxas. Different for one reason only: Anne Miller would survive. The first human to be rescued from death by penicillin.

⸺◠⸺

CHAPTER NINE

R apture.

That's what Tia Stanton felt at midnight as she sat at her laboratory bench. She wore diamond earrings, pearls, high heels, and, under her lab coat, a low-cut midnight blue cocktail dress. Although Tia had a small apartment nearby, she hadn't wasted time going home to change. She'd returned to the lab directly from the engagement party for her college friend Evelyn.

A fake, that's what she felt like in this getup. What was she trying to prove? She went through the list: that women could be both scientists and attractive. That she, Tia Stanton, could be both a scientist and attractive. That she could find a man to marry. That she could have children and live a "normal" life despite the drive she felt to know things, the nagging curiosity that never left her alone.

She did try to maintain what her friends considered a "normal" life. For example, she'd been invited to five engagement parties in the next two months, and she planned to attend them all. Tonight's gathering had been hosted by her Bryn Mawr roommate, Beth, and Beth's husband. Determined good cheer suffused the atmosphere. On the far side of the world, Bataan had fallen. More than 70,000 Allied troops had been taken prisoner, including over 10,000 Americans—the population of a small city, as if every man, woman, and child had been ordered out of their homes, businesses, and schools and marched into oblivion. How many small cities could the Allies afford to lose?

Most of the men at tonight's party would be in uniform soon. Joe, the high school history teacher. Eric, the lawyer. Keith, the store manager. Beth's husband, Robert, who worked at an investment company. Robert wondered if he should join up, hoping for a better posting, rather than wait for the rumored end to draft deferments for married men. Who knew what the future would bring these men, or what battlefield they'd end up on. Despite their degrees and their good jobs, they were heartrendingly vulnerable. The party had an atmosphere of frenetic desperation, a sense that everyone had to pair up fast, before fate or history or simple bad luck made pairing up impossible. Life among Tia's friends was speeding ahead as if they were all hurtling toward death.

The urgency of her work centered her, taking the place of the peer pressure to bond before it was too late. Jamie had told her the dreadful statistics of the number of military men who died from infections. Trying to change that meant more to her than, say, enjoying another glass of champagne at an engagement celebration.

Nonetheless she was more than a little pleased when several appealing men at the party asked for her phone number. She'd given her number gladly, ever hopeful, while knowing that if they weren't interested in the life she led, she wasn't interested in them. By now her women friends had given up worrying about her, at least in her presence. She felt no need to defend her work. If she were a man, her dedication would be considered praiseworthy and inspiring. Even heroic.

Luckily she was developing a few romantic possibilities right here at the hospital, among men who, presumably, understood her better. Jake Lind, who assisted Jamie with the clinical trials for penicillin, had taken her to dinner. He worshipped Jamie, but although Tia adored her brother, Jake had made the conversation a little too Jamie-centric even for an admiring younger sister. She was willing, however, to give Jake another chance. Nick Catalano had been visiting the lab more often than was strictly necessary for the questions he supposedly came to ask—although since he was working with Jamie now, he did have a lot of questions to ask, trying to catch up on ideas he'd ignored (or dismissed) before. Tia would be extremely pleased if ever Nick decided to pose his questions over dinner. She'd had a crush on him since she came to the Institute. Andrew Barnett, the security officer for Vannevar Bush, had been around a few times, checking up on everyone, apparently making certain that no one on the Institute staff was a German or Japanese sympathizer. Barnett had taken her to lunch and made her laugh with his imitations of film actors, from James Cagney to Humphrey Bogart.

Maybe it was for the best, that her brother had fallen in love with Claire Shipley and had a new job that was taking him away from the Institute. Well, obviously it was best for him: at dinner she saw how contented he was with Claire, and his job seemed inherently worthwhile. Tia had met Ellen only once or twice and could barely remember her; Tia had been caught up in high school concerns when Ellen and Jamie were engaged, and then Ellen went to Saranac. Jamie's newfound happiness with Claire pleased Tia, of course. But she was realizing, too, that his increasing absence forced her to be on her own more.

Was she deluding herself, with her faith that against the odds she'd eventually marry and continue the work she loved? Was she naive, that she kept looking upon the world as if it were filled with possibilities? Probably she should know better by now.

The truth was, mold was much easier to deal with than men. Tonight she was working with soil bacteria, molds, and actinomyces (small life-forms, half-plant, half-animal). The colors of the actinomyces astonished her. Tufts of green. Squiggles of orange. Blue towers. Magenta curlicues. White tumbleweeds. They appeared delicate as they grew in the petri dishes arrayed upon the table, yet when Tia touched them with a sterilized pipette, they proved to be sturdy and strong. The life-forms didn't look like this in the soil. Tia made them look like this. Through trial and error, she discovered and fed them their favorite foods, provided them with their favorite climate, and allowed them to achieve their glory.

Tia had forced herself to accept the fact that the breakthrough penicillin research was passing her by. After the medication rescued Anne Miller, industry had been galvanized by penicillin's potential. Pharmaceutical executives who'd been dragging their feet on penicillin production before Anne Miller weren't dragging their feet now. Industry worked on a scale that Tia couldn't match here in her small lab. As national research coordinator, Jamie was traveling constantly and dealing with questions that involved thousands, tens of thousands, of milk bottles and bedpans. The first problem was how to move beyond milk bottles and bedpans to—what? Giant vats? Huge flats? Fields of mold covered with tarpaulins?

David Hoskins had already been "seconded," as he termed it, to the Hanover Company, to use his expertise there. On his days off, he came to the Institute to help produce penicillin for the continuing, small-scale research on skin infections. Jamie's three original patients had finally recovered, and they'd been replaced by three more. Jake Lind supervised this project. Tia missed David, both for his humor and his expertise. And for his friendly presence, she had to admit.

Both Merck and Pfizer had approached Tia to offer her jobs—at a lot more money—but she turned them down. Despite the high salaries the companies paid, she didn't want to be part of a commercial, profit-driven venture. Pride played into her decision, too: Tia and her colleagues from graduate school felt a patronizing resentment toward their peers who'd taken higher-paying jobs with industry. Justifying their own choices, they implied that their money-preferring peers were second-rate researchers.

In any event, Tia had a good deal of independence at the Institute, and her goal now was to concentrate on discovering a substance better than penicillin. So far, she'd tested 683 soil samples. Of these, 31 showed initial promise in fighting infectious bacteria, but none was successful in more advanced tests. She was certain that the substances were somewhere in the soil: every day strep, staph, TB, and all the rest found their way into soil, and something in the soil destroyed them. Her job was to find and harness the biological mechanism at work.

From the incubator on the counter, she brought out a rack of liquid-filled test tubes. The liquid had been cloudy when she put the test tubes into the incubator three days before. The substance used here, from soil sample number 642, had passed the first level of testing by destroying infectious bacteria in a petri dish. She held up the rack to the light. The fluid in the test tubes had a bluish tinge. It was also transparent instead of cloudy. This was surprising.

Every other time she'd done this test, the fluid had come out of the incubator the same way it went in: cloudy. The cloudiness was caused by thriving bacteria. She shook the rack to see if the cloudiness had settled at the bottom of the tubes as a sediment.

No, the tubes were still clear. She retrieved the control rack from the incubator. These test tubes had received infectious bacteria only. They had remained cloudy, which told her that the bacteria were still alive.

She placed both racks of test tubes on the table. She sat down to think this through. If the test tubes were clear, that meant the substance she'd added three days ago had killed the infectious bacteria. Closing her eyes, she reviewed the experiment in her mind, observing her actions as if watching a movie in slow motion, frame by frame. Yes . . . she'd done everything correctly.

All right, don't jump ahead of yourself, she thought. Most likely she'd made a mistake somewhere along the line. She'd repeat the test, and then repeat it again. If the results remained consistent, she'd isolate and identify the substance, purify it, and concentrate it. Then, following established protocols, she'd conduct experiments on mice. First, she'd inject the substance into healthy mice to see if they suffered adverse reactions. This way, she could determine if the substance was toxic to mammals. If it wasn't toxic, she'd infect mice with staph and strep, then treat half of them with number 642, and see what happened. If number 642 had antibacterial properties, the treated mice would recover and survive. The untreated mice would die, sacrificed, as the euphemism went, for the greater good.

She checked her lab book to review the details of number 642. Yes, she remembered now . . . she'd collected this sample last September, when she'd visited Swarthmore, the village outside Philadelphia where she'd lived with her grandparents after her parents died. She was attending the memorial service for her grandmother's closest friend. After the ceremony, she'd changed her shoes and gone for a walk in the woods. The day was warm, 94 degrees according to the thermometer at the train station. The air in the woods was heavy with humidity, but Tia didn't mind; she'd grown up with it, and it reminded her of her childhood. The leaves, ferns, and shrubs were a dense, dark green, their summer color, and they were huge and overgrown. The arching trees reflected green into the water of the creek. The air itself glowed emerald, sunlight dappling upon her. The path, narrow, hidden, haphazard, led along the creek. The Crum Creek meandered through swamps and stands of rhododendron and hanging moss.

When Tia was young, she'd walked in these woods almost every day, through every season. Then, as now, the trees were oak, hickory, beech, tulip, poplar. *Quercus palustris. Liriodendron tulipifera. Fagus grandifolia.* The rhythm of the scientific names—this was her poetry. During winter thaws, witch hazel shrubs, *Hamamelis virginiana,* bloomed. The small, yellow petals were bright against the plant's bare branches. During the droughts of summer, the creek bed revealed its mysteries. Always Tia studied the mold and fungi that lived off both the living and the dead in perfect balance.

Why? That was the question that was always in her mind. *Why, why, why,* and no one could answer all the whys, although her grandfather, who taught botany at the college, came closest. Eventually she realized she'd have to figure out the answers by herself.

When she'd taken this sample, in September of 1941, America hadn't yet entered the war—although Poland, Belgium, Holland, Denmark, and France had already been conquered. Russia had been invaded in June of 1941. Japan controlled much of China. England was fighting on despite the Blitz. And yet, last September, Pearl Harbor hadn't been bombed, Hong Kong and Singapore hadn't surrendered. Joe, Eric, Keith, and Robert weren't discussing which branch of the military they were better off joining.

How tired she was. She rested her face in the palms of her hands. Remembering her September walk in the Crum, and the many forest walks of her childhood, she remembered her parents. Their deaths played in her mind more often than she liked to acknowledge. She wondered how often Jamie thought of their parents. She never asked him, however. For years now, they'd had a kind of silent bond, an unspoken understanding that they wouldn't spend their adult lives dwelling on what had happened to them when they were children. Besides, they were among the lucky ones.

Suddenly, she was reliving those days. Philadelphia. Early November 1918. Near the end of the Great War. The influenza epidemic. Everyone called it the Spanish flu.

The influenza spread fast and killed fast. Within a week it closed schools, theaters, restaurants, churches. Telephones didn't work because the switchboard operators were ill. On Thursday afternoon, her father collapsed on the street on his way to a meeting. A passerby took him to the hospital. At breakfast, he'd been healthy, holding Tia on his lap while she finished her hot chocolate and he finished his coffee. By dinnertime, he was dead.

Tia was four years old. She couldn't remember every detail. She remembered scenes, but not the connections between them. The morning after her father died, she didn't wake until the sunlight filled her bedroom. Yesterday it was still dark outside, when her mother rubbed her shoulder, gently urging her awake. Tia rose in a rush, threw off her nightgown, and put on the same dress she'd worn yesterday, the blue muslin with the sailor collar. Everyone in the house had forgotten her, and she had to find out where they were.

She hurried down the wide staircase, gliding her hand along its carved, polished banister. The parlor was empty. Dust motes fell in shafts of sunlight over the Persian carpets. The house was large yet simple and somber. A Quaker house. Outside the long windows, nothing was somber. The outside was a riot of colors, the sugar maples brilliant with yellow and red, branches tapping against the glass, calling her. Tia wanted to go outside, wanted to run in the park beneath the red and yellow trees, but she wasn't allowed to go out to the street alone. Confused, she returned upstairs. She approached her parents' door. She knocked on the door, as she'd been taught to do. No one answered. The door was open several inches, however, and she pushed it. The hinges creaked.

Her mother lay in bed with the sunlight pouring over her. She wore the same clothes she'd had on yesterday, a lacy shirtwaist and a full, dark silk skirt, the fabric reflecting the sun as if in ribbons of light and shadow. She'd taken off her shoes and stockings, which were on the floor beside the bed. She hadn't gotten under the covers. Instead she'd pulled the far end of the quilt over her legs. Her hair had come unpinned and lay in dark blond twists around her head and neck. Her angular face was pale and still, like alabaster. Like an effigy Tia had seen in her brother's book about the Middle Ages; he'd explained to her what it was.

Tia watched her mother breathing, her chest moving up and down beneath her shirtwaist. Her breathing sounded raspy, a kind of rattling sound Tia had never heard before, as if the air were scratching her as it went in and out.

She touched her mother's shoulder. Slowly her mother turned her head toward Tia and opened her eyes. "Good morning, Lucretia." Her mother never called her *Lucretia*. Tia was named after a Quaker abolitionist and suffragist, Lucretia Mott, who was a distant relative of her mother's. "What are you doing?" Her voice was soft. Tia could barely hear her.

"Watching you breathe."

"Ah." The skin beneath her mother's eyes was dark blue.

"Why are you still in bed? It's almost lunchtime."

"I have a touch of croup. A bad headache." She brushed her hand across her forehead, as if to push the headache away. Her fingers were bruised. How do you get a bruise on your fingers? Jamie did once, playing stickball on the street. The pitch hit his hand, but he took the base, so he didn't care. Jamie's bruise had been purplish. Her mother's fingers were blue-black. "The headache is behind my eyes. Remember once when you had a headache behind your eyes? We knew you were going to get a bad cold."

"And I did!"

"Yes, you did. Look at you, how nice you look this morning." Weakly she made a twirling motion that told Tia to spin around, and she did spin.

"Let me give you a kiss," her mother whispered.

Tia leaned over her, and her mother kissed Tia's forehead. Her mother's lips were chapped and hot, so very hot. Her mother was always careful not to let her lips become chapped. Awkwardly Tia's mother repositioned herself, one foot coming out from beneath the quilt. The foot, too, was blue-black, with blue-black streaks up to the shin. The sight made Tia freeze in place.

By the following dawn, her mother was dead.

The next scene Tia remembered was in the evening, when the sky was already dark. Jamie and Tia stood together at their open front door and waited for the carts. The carts had been coming in the early evening every day for a week. Jamie and Tia waited for the cart from the Arch Street Meeting—*their* Meeting, where they went every Sunday with their parents.

"St. Joseph's, St. Joseph's," said the man driving the first cart. His words were muffled by his face mask.

No one called to stop the St. Joseph's cart, even though a Catholic family, the Baileys, lived directly across the street. Tia saw her friend Mary Bailey peering out the window of the dark house. Was Mary home alone?

"Tenth Presbyterian," called the driver of the next cart. Tia felt cold, especially her legs. She'd forgotten to put her coat on, but she didn't want to go inside for it now.

Diagonally across the street, at the McManus house, nine-year-old Christina came running out, waving a white handkerchief, as if she were surrendering. In a moment, Christina's father carried out a shape wrapped in a heavy blanket to keep it warm. He placed it on the back of the cart. Christina had three older brothers. And a mother. None of them stood at the door to watch.

"Temple Beth Zion-Beth Israel."

The Rose family down the block called to the cart driver and brought out their own shape wrapped in a blanket.

Tia's father told her that Philadelphia was a miraculous place because every religion lived here in peace. As the carts passed, Tia wondered if she were witnessing a miracle.

At last, "Arch Street Meeting."

"Stop," Jamie called. The cart was already moving on. "Arch Street Meeting! We need you!"

"Hold up," the man who stood on the back of the cart called to the driver. The driver shushed the horses. The cart man jumped off and approached them. Because the cart had moved on from them, and because it was an open cart and there was light from the streetlamps, Tia saw into the cart. She saw shapes piled up, wrapped in sheets and blankets, and stacked in neat piles like cords of wood.

"Hey, kids." The man was short and broad shouldered, like a wrestler. He wore a cap and, like all the men on all the carts, a white face mask, which muffled his voice. "Who is it?"

"Our mother," Jamie said.

"Oh, sorry, son. Sorry. Where is she? You're supposed to bring her out to us. We don't have time to go inside every house to get people."

Jamie inhaled, put his arm around Tia, and stuck his fingernails into Tia's shoulder, hurting her. They were supposed to bring her out. How could they bring her out? Jamie was fourteen. He couldn't lift her alone. Tia wasn't big enough to help.

"Hey, Mike, what's the trouble here?" A man who'd been sitting in the front of the cart next to the driver joined them. He was taller but less muscular than Mike and better dressed.

"They didn't bring her out. Their mother."

"Look, we got blocks and blocks to go. We'll get her tomorrow. Bring her out later, kids. Wrap her up good. Go slow, take your time. We'll pick her up tomorrow. She'll be all right, one day, it's not too hot, leave her on the porch, she won't start to—"

"You kids alone here?" Mike interrupted.

Jamie didn't answer.

"You don't have face masks? You should have face masks."

Again Jamie didn't answer.

"We'd give you face masks, if we had any," Harry said. "But we ran out."

"Come on, Harry, let's just go and get her," Mike said. Now Tia recognized them from Meeting. Harry and Mike were the men who took care of the lawns and flower beds around the Meetinghouse and swept the autumn leaves off the paths.

"It's getting late."

"It's their mother. They're just kids."

"All right, if it means that much to you. But you can take the blame if we get behind schedule." They came in.

"Stay here, Tia," Jamie ordered, and she obeyed. Jamie led the men upstairs. When they came back, they'd wrapped Tia's mother in the quilt. Mike held her shoulders, Harry her feet.

"Don't look," Jamie said. He turned Tia around and pushed her head against his chest. His shirt was soft flannel. He'd grown so tall so fast that his body hadn't had time to catch up with his legs, their mother said. He was skinny. Tia felt his ribs pressing against her cheek. He held her while the men went by, carrying their mother. Because Jamie told Tia not to look, she didn't. She heard the horse cart begin to pull away, the driver clucking his instructions to the horse. "Okay," Jamie said, releasing her.

She stood beside him, and he kept his arm around her. Together they watched the cart drive away. Apart from the cart, the street was empty of traffic. The only sounds were the calling of the driver, and their neighbors, one by one down the block, calling for the cart to stop. Six Quaker families lived on their block. Mr. Yard at the end of the block brought two wrapped bodies to the cart, carrying them one by one. At the top of the pile of bodies in the back, the white quilt that covered their mother seemed to Tia to glow, calling to her.

In the morning, they packed a few things in Jamie's school book bag. Jamie told Tia to dress up, to put on her Sunday Meeting clothes, and he put on his, too. He wore knickerbockers and a Norfolk jacket. Tia wore a white pinafore with eyelet lace over a blue plaid dress.

Jamie searched their parents' room for valuables. He found some paper money in the back of their father's shirt drawer and some silver in their mother's reticule. Almost ten dollars. A lot. More than enough. When they left, Jamie carefully locked the door behind them and tested it.

Only years later did Tia realize how beautiful her house was, how

exquisite her block, the loveliest in Philadelphia. Delancey Place between Eighteenth and Nineteenth Streets. An enclave of peace and
tranquillity. They walked into a gorgeous autumn day, the trees a pa-
rade of color.

Jamie led her up the block. Every house was large and well cared
for. Every house had an arched doorway, and wrought-iron grilles
at the windows for holding flowerpots. The street was quiet. Not
simply today, but any day. Every day. The week before, when Tia
and her father had walked down this block together, her father had
said, "On Delancey Place you don't even know you're in a city." And
it was true.

Jamie and Tia turned onto Nineteenth Street and walked to Rittenhouse Square. Tia was confused. The square, which she'd visited
for as long as she could remember, looked like a place she'd never seen
before. Garbage was strewn in the gutters and along the paths. The
sidewalks were sticky from pigeons and dogs. There was no traffic
around the square. No horses. No carts. No automobiles. Instead there
were kids everywhere, boys playing stickball, girls jumping rope on
the grass. Their clothes were dirty, their hair a mess. There were no
parents in the park, no nannies keeping order.

They walked across the square into the commercial district. Jamie
wanted to take the trolley to the train station because it was a long way
for Tia to walk. While they waited at the trolley stop, an old man told
them that the trolleys weren't running. All the drivers were sick. So
they had no choice but to walk. Tia held her brother's hand tightly.
She didn't want to lose him. When they reached the train station that
served the small towns around the city, Jamie bought tickets to their
grandparents' town. Although they had to wait a long time because
the schedule was off, he found the right train. They disembarked at
the right stop. He led her to their grandparents' house.

Only their grandfather was home. He was upset to see them. Because the telephone switchboards weren't operating, he'd had no idea

of their troubles. Their grandmother was nursing flu patients at the local hospital. This was safe for her, because by now everyone knew that this particular type of influenza mostly spared the children and the grandparents. It killed the people in between, the ones in their twenties and thirties. The mothers and the fathers. The ones who weren't supposed to die from influenza.

Twenty-four years later, working as a scientist in the midst of another war, Tia shook herself back to the present. She sat up and brushed tears away. Sometimes she felt she was forever in that moment, gripping her brother's hand as they walked through a city of death. In that one week in Philadelphia, four thousand people died from influenza, Tia learned years later. Tens of thousands were ill. The city ran out of coffins. The churches buried their members in mass graves. Tia and Jamie never knew for certain where their parents were buried. The newspapers were virtually silent about the influenza. At the end of the Great War, no one wanted to be unpatriotic by reporting on mass graves at home. As she grew up, Tia came to consider herself fortunate. Unlike many influenza orphans, she had a good home to go to, with grandparents who loved her. She had her brother. The influenza faded from memory.

Tia looked around the laboratory. The room grounded her. Gave her a purpose. In her mind, she saw her parents as she most often remembered them, reading in front of the parlor fireplace. Jamie was reading, too, while she sat on the floor sorting the bags of autumn-colored leaves that she'd collected in Rittenhouse Square.

No matter what happened in other parts of her life, she told herself, her existence had meaning, because of her work. Once more she examined the clear fluid in the test tubes. She turned to a blank page in her lab book and wrote down the results of this latest experiment. She reminded herself that most likely number 642 would prove toxic in mice. If it did, she would move on to the next substance, and the one after that. Soil samples filled her lab. She would test them all and gather still more, from around the world, until she found the breakthrough.

And yet Tia couldn't help but speculate . . . number 642. Maybe she'd stumbled upon the exception to her run of failures. Maybe number 642 was exactly what she'd been looking for. What she knew was there, somewhere, waiting for her.

Yes, she took it very personally.

Her thoughts moved ahead. The protocols for human testing. Successful results in humans. The Institute filing for a patent to codify the substance's formula, then abandoning the patent to the public domain, so the medication could be manufactured and sold at low prices—this was the idealism that had brought her to the Institute and kept her here.

A knock on the lab's outer entryway interrupted her reverie.

"Tia?" A man's voice, muffled by the distance. No doubt one of the physicians on call tonight. Everyone on the staff knew that she worked late and that she was always willing to discuss research questions and problems. At the Institute, colleagues shared their questions and looked to their peers for ideas. Tia had visitors several nights a week. Often more than one visitor arrived, and they had an impromptu party. She kept a bottle of gin in the cabinet and tonic in the fridge. "You still there, Tia?"

She checked her watch. 1:15 AM. Maybe it was Nick—her thoughts went to him first, although she wasn't certain he was in town. Quickly she pushed her hair into place, patted her cheeks to bring some color into her face, reapplied her lipstick. She hoped her eyes weren't red from crying.

"Come in," she called. "It's open." She heard the door opening. Footsteps through the outer rooms.

Sergei Oretsky was at the lab doorway. "Don't you ever get tired?" he asked gently.

"Not very often," she said, standing to welcome him. Well, he wasn't Nick, but he was pleasant enough. "What about you?"

"Oh, I can't sleep, always worry, worry. My children, my wife, my mother. I was walking and saw your light. What are you working on?"

"Something interesting. I'll show you. It's nothing, probably. I'm sure I made a mistake somewhere along the way. In fact, I'd like your opinion."

⟋

CHAPTER TEN

C laire stared at the dragon, and the dragon stared back. Then the dragon shrugged. If Claire had been the man inside the dragon suit, she would have shrugged, too.

For the magazine's *"Life* Goes to a Party" section, Mrs. Luce had tapped Claire to cover the gala she was hosting at the River Club on what turned out to be a lovely April evening. The River Club was exclusive even among the exclusive private clubs of New York City. The club's waterfront gardens and its dock on the East River were legendary. The event was for Mrs. Luce's favorite charity, United China Relief. Much of China was under Japanese occupation, and UCR was an amalgam of charities that provided assistance to areas still fighting back.

"Life Goes to a Party" was the most dreaded assignment a *Life* photographer could get. The party rooms were generally difficult to light, and for these sorts of parties the photographer was expected to wear evening clothes, not advantageous when you might have to climb a ladder or lie on the floor. And then there were the party guests to contend with. Once Claire's colleague Hansel Mieth was set upon by a rowdy guest at a Waldorf-Astoria stag party. She hit the guy, and from then on Mack told women photographers to strike back whenever necessary.

As much as the staff hated the feature, readers loved it. It gave them a window into celebrated places most could never hope to visit, like the Stork Club and El Morocco in New York, as well as princely mansions around the country and abroad.

Little did the readers know how lucky they were *not* to be invited, because most of the events were extravagantly dreary. Claire and her colleagues had the job of making them appear exciting and glamorous. Shooting this feature was fun only when *Life* most definitely had not been invited. In that happy case, the photographer had to sneak in and take the photos secretly with a camera concealed in her handbag or in the pocket of his suit jacket. In this way, you might even capture an indiscretion or two. If you were really lucky, you'd be discovered, and you could photograph the host or his minions throwing you out.

"Delighted to meet you at last," Mrs. Luce was saying. Her blond hair was pulled back, her smile was as fixed as a fashion model's. She was stunning, Claire had to admit, even more stunning in person than in photos. "I've admired your work in my husband's magazine." That surface charm. Maybe Claire could avoid the reputed daggers. Mrs. Luce needed something from her, which made things easier. She'd even sent a car to pick her up, which Claire appreciated.

"Thank you, Mrs. Luce. I've admired your work, too."

Mrs. Luce gave Claire a long appraisal and appeared displeased by what she found. Claire thought she'd dressed appropriately, wearing an off-the-shoulder royal blue gown with a loose, gauzy skirt for freedom of movement. She wore her mother's pearls and diamond-and-pearl earrings to match. However, Mrs. Luce had a reputation for wanting to be the best-looking woman in a room.

"Your dress is beautiful, Mrs. Luce." It was a full-length, closely cut Chinese silk gown, dark red with intricate embroidery. Mrs. Luce even had the figure for it.

"Thank you. It's called a cheongsam. Now, Claire, you must photograph the flowers. And we'll want coverage of how lovely the room looks before everyone arrives."

"Yes, Mrs. Luce." Clearly Mrs. Luce would call Claire by her first name and Claire would call her "Mrs. Luce." She led Claire on a tour of the River Club's cavernous Art Deco ballroom, its geometric decorations shimmering in silver and lapis. Mrs. Luce had already dealt with a crisis tonight, having arrived at the club to find that the decorator had inadvertently hung Japanese lanterns throughout the ballroom.

"Remove those *immediately*," Mrs. Luce had ordered, and she'd instructed Claire to edit the film accordingly.

"Now, Claire, please make certain your lights aren't blinding. Surely you can bounce them off the wall or the ceiling instead of pointing them into the eyes of my guests. And don't use flashbulbs. That's not really necessary nowadays, is it? Especially when you'll be setting up lights."

"I'll do my best, Mrs. Luce," Claire said, an edge of rancor slipping into her voice. Claire never appreciated writers, even the boss's wife, interfering with her work.

Mrs. Luce glanced at Claire sharply. "Let's hope your best is good enough."

Ah, well. One night, how bad could it be? The ballroom was indeed arranged beautifully. Apricot-colored roses overflowed from the centerpieces on each table. The dance floor was highly polished, the band was tuning up, the dragon was perfecting his gait, long tail dragging behind. In the games area, Chinese men in traditional garb were setting up dart boards and balloons. Waiters hovered with hors d'oeuvres on trays, expectantly awaiting the first arrivals. The barmen were arranging and rearranging glasses. Claire herself could have used a drink, but Mrs. Luce certainly wouldn't approve of that.

The guests began to arrive, and just to make the party even more . . . unusual than Claire had imagined possible, they were in costume. Imperial Chinese-inspired costumes, ornately beaded and brocaded, with elaborate headgear to match for both men and women.

"All right, Seth, here we go," Claire said to the young man who stood beside her, clutching a clipboard. Tonight she had an assistant helping her with the equipment and captions. His most important job was to make certain that every shot was documented, every name spelled correctly. Seth Wiley was tall and thin, with an almost concave chest, which made him appear shy. He had a boyish, questioning look. His bow tie was askew. Seth was a recent graduate of Yale, Mr. Luce's alma mater, and a favored staff recruitment center. "I want you to stand near Mrs. Luce every ten minutes or so, just quietly, not bothering her, in case she has special instructions for us."

"Yes, ma'am."

Moving around the ballroom as it grew crowded, Claire felt the raw power of the gathering. Rockefeller, Willkie, Baruch, Lamont— the evening overflowed with national leadership, financial, industrial, and political. And what did these leaders spend their time doing at the party? They continually glanced over shoulders, seeking even more influential partners for conversation. They competed in their enthusiastic support for the suffering masses of China by tossing darts at balloons.

Looking across the room, Claire had to smile when she saw Seth hovering beside Mrs. Luce. The boss's wife appeared to like him, whispering in his ear. Seth took to his job heartily, making notes and hurrying back to Claire. His sincerity and eagerness were appealing.

On a night like this, you felt the influence the Luces wielded. The guests were more than willing to appear ridiculous in their Chinese costumes if their dear friend Harry and his wife demanded it. He greeted their fawning in his usual way, with a pointed question or two, then an abrupt dismissal. People were familiar with his rudeness and ignored it. If he liked you, he might put you on the cover of one of his magazines. Run a feature or two or three about you or your company. *Fortune* might embrace you. He might make you *Time*'s Man of the Year. Claire had heard through the rumor mill that huge amounts of money had been raised for United China Relief in Hollywood from producers and actors who were dependent on the acres of free publicity that *Life*'s entertainment stories provided.

Halfway through the evening, Claire stood at the side of the ballroom, taking a break and observing the crowd. Seth had excused himself for the men's room.

"Looks like you're doing a good job. Under tough circumstances." Henry Luce stood beside her, dressed in white tie rather than Chinese robes, a sensible choice.

"Thank you. I agree."

To this, he actually laughed.

"Your wife is looking very beautiful, Mr. Luce."

"Thank you. I agree."

She hadn't seen him since their meeting in his office, when she'd pushed him to cover penicillin development. "Looks like this party is a success."

"Yes. John D. Rockefeller the Third is here. Wendell Willkie, Bernard Baruch . . ." He rattled off the list with a boy's wonder, as if he himself weren't among the famous names. As if they came here—not because of the power of his magazines—but strictly out of sympathy for China, the beloved, lost land where his missionary parents had raised him.

"I'm sure you've raised a good deal of money for China tonight."

"No matter how much we raise, the need is greater still. The horrors faced by the Chinese people . . ." He proceeded to lecture her on the starving people of China and on Generalissimo and Madame Chiang Kai-shek as their only hope. He put his faith in the Christian Chiangs to defeat China's Japanese occupiers and to resist the atheist Communist insurgents. Apparently he ignored the darkly whispered reports of the Chiangs' corruption.

"You must miss your homeland," Claire said.

Luce did not reply. He was studying the crowd, and when he spoke again, he didn't look at her. "I haven't forgotten our conversation."

She waited for him to say more.

"I'm moving forward."

She took this as an acknowledgment that he'd transformed her idea into his idea.

"I'm considering the potential."

"Thank you."

"No need to say thank you. I'm not doing it for you."

He was known to speak this way. Was he joking? She couldn't tell. "Of course not."

Seth joined them.

"Who are you?" Luce asked.

Seth appeared bewildered.

"What do you want?"

Undoubtedly recognizing Mr. Luce, Seth didn't know how to respond.

"The lady and I are talking."

Claire stepped in. "Seth, I don't believe you've been introduced to our editor. Mr. Luce, this is Seth Wiley, who recently joined our staff. A Yale graduate. He's doing a fine job tonight."

"Good to meet you, sir." Seth bowed, the Asian influence seeming to have rubbed off on him. Mr. Luce did not offer his hand to the new recruit. They had reached an impasse. Claire needed to resume work anyway.

"I think I'll go out on the terrace," she said. "I'd like to get some shots from the outside looking in."

"I'll go with you," Luce said. "Carry your camera bag."

"Thank you." This was indeed an honor. To Claire's knowledge, only Margaret Bourke-White had been so recognized.

With a triumphant look at poor Seth, Mr. Luce picked up the bag and strode across the room, parting the crowd. Claire followed, Seth trying to keep up. She sensed the crowd filling in and Seth being left behind.

Outside, the terrace was peaceful and cool after the packed crowd inside. The gardens were filled with the flowers of early spring, crocuses, daffodils, forsythia. She caught the scent of hyacinth on the breeze. A Chinese junk had moored at the Club's dock on the far side of the East River Drive. Only a few cars traversed the still-incomplete roadway. Claire turned and peered into the ballroom through the wide French doors. This was a perfect shot, romantic and intriguing. The camera on its tripod took the position of the magazine reader at home, staring through an arched doorway into a warm scene of formal evening clothes, dancing, and enchantment.

"Mr. Luce, you see how beautiful this shot is?"

"Beautiful? How?"

"Because of the composition. You see, the ballroom framed by the arched doorway? The dancers looking dazzling and alluring? The costumes romantic and mysterious?"

He looked through the camera. "I do see it." He sounded amazed. "It's a good shot," he added gruffly, a puzzled expression on his face, as if he were struggling for words that would be more poetic and would express better, or more exactly, what he meant. "I can see it. A good shot," he repeated, finally.

"Glad to see someone's earning her salary tonight." Mrs. Luce swept onto the terrace. "Harry, my dear, you mustn't let your employees monopolize your time with their problems. Your guests are waiting for you." She took her husband's arm. He allowed himself to be led away. Claire wondered if he ever regretted his headlong pursuit of this woman, or regretted the sorrow he must have caused his family. As she led her husband inside, Mrs. Luce managed to turn and whisper to Claire with a measure of privacy, "If you're searching for a man, Claire Shipley, I suggest you don't do it on *Life*'s time."

Well, there was a line worth repeating, one that sounded like it'd come right out of her famous play, *The Women*. After seeing *The Women*, Eleanor Roosevelt reputedly said that the only woman she knew who actually talked like the catty women in the play was Clare Boothe Luce herself. Claire imagined regaling her photographer buddies with the line at the staff watering hole over a gin and tonic. She tried to suppress her laughter. With luck her supposed impropriety with Mr. Luce would ensure that she'd never have to work with Mrs. Luce again.

By ten, the crowd began to thin. Mr. Luce departed, but his wife stayed, courting the guests as they said good-bye. Claire pulled the plugs on the lights, abruptly rendering the scene less glamorous. The waiters started to clear the dessert dishes. The maintenance men brought back the ladders that Claire and Seth had used to put up the lights, a sure sign that as far as they were concerned, this party was over. At an empty drinks table, Seth was organizing and numbering the film, matching it with sheets of captions. Evening gown and all, Claire climbed a ladder and began to take down the lights.

"Can I give you a hand?" she heard from below. She looked down to see her father, dressed in white tie. He looked supremely debonair, without a trace of the faux-Chinese about him.

"What are you doing here?" she asked.

"You learning manners from your boss?" he asked smoothly.

"No," she caught herself. "Sorry, you surprised me. Have you been here all evening? I didn't see you."

"Yes, I've been here, and I've seen you, but I stayed out of your way. Nobody likes a parent hanging around when they're working. Kept my eye on you, though. Very impressive."

She found herself moved by his admiration.

"Told my friends who you are. Hope you don't mind. My daughter the famous photographer. Though I swore them to secrecy."

"The fact that you're my father doesn't have to be a secret."

"Well, thank you for that." He flushed, or perhaps, Claire thought, he reddened simply from the lingering heat of the lamp she handed to him.

"You usually come to events like this?" she asked.

"Wouldn't miss this party for the world. Clare Luce draws a terrific crowd. You have to give her credit." He paused to watch as she handled the good-byes near the door. "And of course I want to do my part for the Chinese war effort. Help the starving children of Chungking, etc. You wouldn't catch me in costume, however. That embroidered silk jacket John D. Rockefeller the Third sported pretty well did me in."

"Mrs. Luce complimented him on it especially."

"Well, anything JDR-Three does, she's bound to like." Something caught his attention across the room. "Don't look now, my currently unmarried daughter, but two handsome and apparently unattached young naval officers are heading in our direction. I'd get down from that ladder if I were you. Speaking strictly as someone who has only your best interests at heart."

Gripping the ladder, she glanced over her shoulder. Jamie was heading toward her, looking exceedingly attractive in naval dress uniform. Another man in dress uniform accompanied him. As they came closer, she recognized Nick Catalano, both men, as her father said, handsome and at this moment projecting an excitement and magnetism that heretofore had been missing from the entire evening.

The River Club was only thirteen blocks from the Rockefeller Institute. She'd invited Jamie to the party as her "second assistant," to arrive at 10:00 PM. This was bending the rules, but she didn't care. Jamie was rarely in town these days, and she was determined to see him when he was. And she genuinely needed the help here. Jamie could pack and carry the equipment while Seth double-checked the captions and spellings with Mrs. Luce. One mistake in the captions, and there'd be hell to pay. She didn't think Mrs. Luce would object to Jamie's attendance, as long as she didn't realize that Claire had invited him. She wished she could have included Tia, who might have found the evening entertaining, but that would have been too much, Claire felt. Attractive men under seventy were always in demand at charity events, so most likely Jamie would be welcomed. He'd add a certain frisson to the scene. Watching Jamie cross the room, in his eagerness walking a few steps ahead of Nick, he already had, as far as Claire was concerned.

She climbed down the ladder, maneuvering her gown. She'd told Jamie about her ambivalent relationship with her father and explained that although they were slowly growing closer, she still wasn't entirely comfortable with him. She had *not*, however, discussed Jamie with her father. She wanted to keep her feelings private until she trusted that she and Jamie had a long-term future. *Whatever happened to that doctor you were seeing? Didn't he like Charlie? Didn't he like your work schedule?* These were questions she never wanted to hear from her father. Because of her reticence, she was now faced with this: Jamie giving her a quick hug (which Claire hoped Mrs. Luce didn't see) and holding her elbows to admire her dress while Rutherford observed them with speculative interest.

"Not too early, are we?" Jamie asked.

"Not at all." She moved away from him and introduced everyone.

"I'm very pleased to meet you, sir," Jamie said.

"Indeed," Rutherford replied, shaking hands firmly. He had no need for explanations. He read the situation immediately.

"I invited Nick along, thinking there might be someone here for him to meet," Jamie said.

They looked around, but the few females remaining were elderly enough to need assistance getting to their cars and drivers.

"Don't think I'm not grateful," Nick said. He had an edge of bad-boy sophistication that Claire found simultaneously intriguing and off-putting. Because Nick and Jamie were close friends, Claire focused on the off-putting aspect, resisting the attraction. Claire knew that Nick and Jamie were working together now and that Jamie relied on Nick's clear-sighted honesty, not to mention his willingness to handle bureaucratic niceties. They made a good team, Jamie had told her.

She felt Nick's gaze upon her, taking in her low-cut dress and her body beneath it. The look wasn't leering; instead it seemed a natural part of human nature—specifically the "man" part of "human nature." Nonetheless Claire didn't appreciate it. She shrugged it off, however. Jamie hoped that someday Nick would fall in love with his sister, but exposed to Nick's stripping-her-naked evaluation, Claire wondered if Tia was experienced enough to handle him.

"Sorry about that, young man," Rutherford said genially. "Such well-respected and well-preserved pillars of society as those ladies are even out of my league." The waiters were removing the tablecloths. "I think we should be moving along. Where should we go?"

Claire wasn't certain how her father had gotten himself invited on this outing. "I need to finish up here and drop the film at the office," she said, trying to put him off.

"Why, Edward Rutherford, isn't it? How good of you to come." Claire Boothe Luce approached them with Seth in tow worriedly reviewing sheets listing several hundred names. "I'm sorry I didn't see you earlier."

"Ah, Mrs. Luce, living up to your reputation as a legendary beauty. As usual."

He was wonderful, Claire thought. In fact he was gallant. He kissed Mrs. Luce's hand. She glowed under his attentions.

"The evening was spectacular. Let me introduce two friends of mine, physicians both." Names were exchanged, hands shaken.

"Thank you so much for coming. I'm afraid we're being moved out." She gestured toward the cleaning people who were bringing in vacuums. "Forgive me, but I need to review some details with the staff from my husband's magazine." Her voice revealed a small yet pointed condescension toward Claire and Seth.

"Of course," Rutherford said. "The doctors and I were just leaving. Did you know, Mrs. Luce, that Claire Shipley here is my daughter?"

For an instant she frowned and in an equal instant recovered her poise. "How lovely for you both."

"Well, well, we must be going," Rutherford said lightheartedly.

"How about coming back to my place for a drink, young fellows," he said to Jamie and Nick, placing a hand on their shoulders. "Claire will join us later."

Jamie glanced at Claire, who nodded her assent. God knew how long Mrs. Luce would keep her here, and she couldn't excuse herself to discuss a plan with Jamie. Rutherford ushered Jamie and Nick out before him.

B ack in one piece from the Chinese ball? Well done, Claire!" Tom O'Reilly, Mack's nighttime deputy, greeted her from the drinks cart when Claire reached the office at 11:30 PM. Pipe in hand, Tom opened a bottle of beer. Claire let the equipment bags slide off her shoulders. She'd already told Seth to go home, so she'd returned to the office on her own in the car Mrs. Luce had assigned to her.

With the staff keeping war hours, monitoring events and correspondents around the world, the office was bustling. The drinks cart, hidden in a coat closet during the nine-to-five daily slog, was prominently placed in the central corridor. Outside the windows were the lights of Manhattan, rooftops and skyscrapers glimpsed in a magical array, like a painting that transformed itself from office to office.

"And how was the boss's delightful consort?"

"Beautiful as usual. And very polite. Car and driver, the works." Claire wouldn't gossip about Clare Boothe Luce here in the hallowed hallways of the Time & Life Building, where the walls had ears.

"She sent a car and driver for you?" said Edith Logan, the nighttime supervisor, joining them at the cart. Edie refilled her Scotch on the rocks. She was a tough-minded woman in her fifties with short gray hair and skin wrinkled from too much smoking and too much sunburn. She wore her usual work uniform of a buttoned-down white blouse and a beige, boxy-cut suit, matched, surprisingly, with delicate navy blue high heels with a bow on the front. "In my next life, I want your job."

"I like it, I must admit."

Edie had come up through the newspaper business, but since she was a woman, the top jobs had eluded her. The night shift allowed her promotion. "Okay, Tom, the Chinese ball is scheduled to run next week, so let's get it into production with this beer rather than the next one."

"Will do," Tom said with a good-humored salute.

Duncan Daily, a staff writer, strode down the hallway toward them. He was dressed in a tuxedo, dark hair smoothed back with something that made it shine, lips pursed, chin a touch more elevated than was strictly necessary. He tossed a black-and-white-checked muffler over his shoulder. "Claire! Beautiful dress. Come to El Morocco with me. You're already ready. We'll dance until four."

Claire suspected that "Duncan Daily" wasn't his real name. "Thank you, Duncan. It's a very kind invitation, but you know I never stay out that late."

"Live a little, my dear. Before the bombs start falling, etc." Duncan had won a Pulitzer Prize for a newspaper series in his hometown of St. Louis, Missouri, about corruption in Mississippi River shipping. Duncan Daily, man of contradictions. "I'm heading over because I received a hot tip that a prominent man is out on the town with a woman not his wife."

"Same old story," said Edie, not unkindly. She took a drag on her cigarette. "Can't you come up with anything new?"

"New, old, the human saga never changes. Besides, a visit to El Morocco paid for by Mr. Billings? How could I turn that down? I tell you, I've got the best expense account in the building. Apart from the old man upstairs, that is. Claire, slip a miniature camera into your bodice and I'll make certain you capture the photo of the year. Please—I'll be so much more incognito with you on my arm."

Gus from copyediting, who was tieless, jacketless, and needed a shave, arrived with a page proof for Tom's review. "Excuse me," Gus said to Duncan with faux gruffness. Gus had been with the company since the beginning, growing old with his job, distracted from other possibilities by his appreciation for the drinks cart. "Some of us are working." Gus had a lit cigar in his hand, and with his slightly wobbly stance, the cigar tip came perilously close to setting the page proof on fire. "I'm trying to make sure the captions match the photos. As usual."

That comment was aimed at Claire, another in a stream of warnings from copy editors to photographers to take proper notes. Editorial staff considered the photographers to be too wild, unwashed, uncontrollable, and independent to work at *Life*. Alas, *Life* was a picture magazine, so the editorial staff was forced to put up with them. Claire wasn't too wild, unwashed, uncontrollable, or independent, but she enjoyed when the reputation spilled onto her, both out of loyalty to her photographer buddies and because the image made a nice counterpoint to what she considered her entirely bourgeois existence.

"So, Gus, what have you got for me," Tom said.

"Young actresses at work and play."

"One of my favorite topics," Tom said. "Let's go to my office and take a private look. What are you drinking?"

"Bourbon."

Tom poured a bourbon for Gus, grabbed another beer for himself, and they headed down the hall. "Claire," he called over his shoulder, "don't forget the film."

"I'm on my way," she said.

"Please, Claire, make my dreams come true," Duncan implored.

"Truth be told, Duncan, I'd love to, but I have a previous engagement. I just stopped by to turn in the film and drop off the lights." The cameras were hers, of course, and she'd take those with her.

"You're previously engaged?" Duncan asked with an edge of innuendo. "That sounds like fun."

"I'm sure it will be," Claire said.

Warning bells went off in the telex room down the hall. Edie exhaled the cigarette smoke she'd been holding in. "Better see what that's about before you go," she said to Duncan.

Claire followed them, curious. El Morocco temporarily forgotten, Duncan took out his reading glasses and focused on the report being typed out by the clattering telex machine. "More bad news from Burma," he said, scanning it.

The Burma Road was the only land access the Allies had to the part of China still resisting the Japanese. Claire was no expert, but she knew that Burma was the crucial link between India and China. Already the Japanese were launching attacks against the British navy in the Indian Ocean, and against Ceylon. The Japanese had conquered Rangoon, the capital of Burma, weeks before. If Burma should fall, then India and nonoccupied China. . . .

But that was someone else's news to cover. Claire had to keep some worries at bay, to protect herself. She dragged the equipment bags to Mack's office and stowed them under his desk. "Here's the exposed film," she said, putting it on the corner of the table where Tom and Gus stood, reviewing notes and copy.

"Thanks, Claire," Tom said, not looking up at her.

She slipped away without disturbing anyone's work by saying goodbye.

A t Edward Rutherford's Fifth Avenue apartment, Jamie and Nick settled themselves on either side of the parlor's big fireplace with its baroque mantelpiece. While Rutherford arranged logs and lit the fire, the two younger men exchanged looks that said, Some place, eh?

Once the fire was going, Rutherford said, "So, drinks? I've got everything and anything. Brandy? Whiskey?"

Jamie ordered brandy, and Nick followed his lead. When Jamie leaned back in his pseudomedieval chair, Nick did as well. Nick felt tossed out of his depth here, and he studied his friend (he hoped surreptitiously) to learn how to behave.

After serving the drinks, Rutherford sat down opposite the younger men. He noticed Nick's watchful concentration, and he recognized it. It was what he himself had experienced when he was making his way. Who was this man? he wondered. He found himself much more interested in Nick Catalano than in James Stanton, whatever Stanton's understanding with Claire. Stanton was secure and centered in himself, Rutherford sensed. He'd admired the apartment, indeed he'd never seen anyplace like it, but it didn't set him off his stride; he knew he could deal with it. But Catalano . . .

"So, gentlemen, how did you two make your ways to the hallowed halls of the Rockefeller Institute?"

Naturally, Stanton answered first . . . all straightforward and exactly what Rutherford would have expected, right down to the loving grandparents ready to take over when the parents died. When Stanton finished, Rutherford asked, "What about you, Catalano?"

"Oh, just the usual, especially compared to this guy here," Catalano said, indicating his friend. Falsely blasé, Rutherford could spot it a mile away. The same cultivated sense of the blasé that he himself assumed when called upon to describe his supposed youth in Allentown, his family in trade. "Born upstate. Syracuse. Big family. Never an orphan. Went to Cornell and Harvard and then straight to the Institute. That's it, all there is to tell."

Not by a long shot, Rutherford knew. Of the two young men, Rutherford pegged Catalano as the greater idealist: it was harder to accept the lower salary offered by the Rockefeller Institute when your father was a factory worker, than when your father was a banker. Mentally he reviewed the industries of Syracuse: dishes, automobiles, soda ash, typewriters, if his memory served him (and he had a good memory for matters like that). But he suspected he wouldn't be getting any more details from Nick Catalano this evening.

"Nick's got a Ph.D. in chemistry as well as a medical degree," Stanton said, with a pleasing generosity toward his friend's accomplishments. "His background's better than mine for the work we're doing now."

"Speaking of which," Rutherford said, "my daughter mentioned all those milk bottles, bedpans, and jam jars. You fellas are at the forefront. That's my kind of business. At the forefront. In every industry. Every endeavor. New things, whatever they are. Yes, I have a lot of fun."

This was as far as he would go. He was planting a seed, that was all. A seed that signaled, sure, you're idealists now, you're working for the government and for the Rockefeller Institute now, but someday you might not be, and when that someday comes, I want you to remember me.

When Claire stepped off the elevator at her father's, the multi-layered skirt of her evening gown rustled in the silence of the neo-Gothic front hall. She paused to get her bearings. As if from a great distance, she heard voices in the parlor. It was well after midnight, but she wasn't tired. Instead she felt overattuned to the middle-of-the-night quiet and to the strange shadows thrown by the statuary. A kind of density filled the air, especially striking after the raucous high spirits at the office.

She walked down the hall and stood on the balcony overlooking the parlor. A massive fire, glowing and crackling, was burning in the fireplace where she'd hidden as a child. The three men sat in medieval-looking wooden chairs arrayed near the fireplace to catch the warmth. From the shape of their glasses, Claire knew what they were drinking. Rutherford had whiskey on the rocks. Jamie and Nick, brandy. Their naval dress uniforms reflected the shifting colors of the fire.

Claire wore a cashmere sweater over her otherwise bare shoulders, and she felt a chill. In mid-April, the nights were still cool. She wanted to be by the fire. Yet she held back, watching them. Jamie and Nick seemed to sit luxuriantly, as if they were enjoying a rare and slightly illicit treat. No doubt they weren't often invited to sip brandy in the double-height living room of a duplex apartment filled with Old Master paintings and facing Central Park. Although her father generally indulged in a Cuban cigar after dinner, they weren't smoking. He'd probably offered, and when the doctors refused, he held back in deference to them, gentleman that he was.

The sounds of their voices filtered up to her, echoing off the stonework. She caught a few phrases here and there. Roosevelt, armaments, supply lines . . . they were discussing politics, business, the war. Jamie and Nick leaned forward in their chairs, seeming to enjoy a debate. Rutherford regarded them with a slight smile, taking it all in, as if he couldn't believe his luck in chancing upon these two interesting fellows and helping out his daughter to boot.

Jamie's face was bright in the firelight. She yearned to be beside him. She wanted to caress the line of his jaw, to kiss, ever so gently, his eyelids.

Finally they sensed her watching.

"Claire, there you are, at last," Jamie said. He rose to welcome her as she joined them. He put his hands on her shoulders, taking away the cold.

Leaving at 1:30 AM, they managed to find a cab on East Seventyninth Street. When they reached the Institute to drop off Nick, the guard opened the gate and the taxi drove up the hill to the hospital.

"Is that Tia's light on?" Claire said, looking up at the hospital.

Jamie bent forward to see. "Yes, it is."

"No surprise there," Nick said.

"Maybe she just leaves it on to make people think she's working all night," Claire said.

"I don't think so," Jamie said cheerfully.

"Not likely," Nick agreed. He got out, and they exchanged good nights. Nick watched the taxi drive slowly down the hill. Forsythia was blooming in the Institute gardens, the color ghostly in the shadows. He felt light-headed from the brandy. An unexpected jealousy filled him. How close those two seemed. They had an equality, a mutual support that he'd never experienced with the young women, sweet as they were, whom he typically dated. And that apartment of Rutherford's. Where had the money come from for that?

Years ago, he'd made the choice to give up money as an end in itself and do the kind of work that interested him most. He didn't want a high-paying private medical practice (even though his parents would probably have been most proud of that). He had a passion for medical research. When he was studying at Harvard, the common view was that only second-rate scientists went to pharmaceutical companies, so he wouldn't do that. The Rockefeller Institute was the most prestigious medical research center in the United States. Coming as he did from Syracuse, with parents who did factory labor, the prestige meant a lot to him, he couldn't deny it. At the Institute, he thought he'd found his true home. The only problem was the comparatively low salaries. Many of his colleagues had family money to back them up. What if he wanted to marry someday and have children? His wife and children certainly couldn't live in the hospital's residence rooms.

That look on Jamie's face when he first spotted Claire entering the room. Nick wished he had that kind of love in his own life. He didn't even know where to start, to find it. Except . . . he went inside and greeted the hospital guard, who doubled as the elevator operator at night. Nick hesitated for a moment and then gave the floor number of Tia's lab, rather than his residence rooms. Reaching the floor, he said good night to the guard. He walked down the silent hallway to her lab. He'd been to see her several times after he got his new job, with the convenient excuse—which was the truth, after all—that he needed to learn about penicillin.

Tonight seemed different. Seeing the intimacy between Jamie and Claire made some part of him open into yearning. He'd stopped

thinking of Tia as Jamie's baby sister a long time ago, but before tonight, she'd seemed too serious for him in every way. Of course he had
to be careful with Tia. Anything with her *was* serious. He shouldn't
visit her if he didn't intend to be serious. He evaluated himself: he *did*
intend to be serious.

He stood at the doorway to her lab. Often she had visitors. Impromptu parties in the middle of the night. He listened for voices. If
anyone else was there, he'd leave, go to his rooms and get some sleep.
All was quiet. He knocked on the door.

He heard her voice, beckoning him on. At once he had an almost
overwhelming feeling that this was exactly where he belonged.

I n the taxi going downtown, Claire asked the driver to head over to
Fifth Avenue. She loved Fifth Avenue late at night, when the usu-
ally bustling street was eerily deserted. They drove past the park, the
Plaza Hotel, Bergdorf Goodman and Tiffany.

"I don't recall you ever mentioning that your father is a multi-
millionaire," Jamie said.

"Well, he is," Claire said impatiently. She didn't want to spend what
could be a romantic drive downtown discussing her father.

Jamie laughed. "You're annoyed at *him* because he's a millionaire,
or at *me* because I asked?"

Jamie always laughed at the beginning of potential arguments, dif-
fusing her anger. "Both," she said, although she was laughing now,
too.

He put his arm around her, pulling her close. "Don't worry, I won't
hold it against you."

"Thank you."

"I liked him quite a bit."

"He's charming, I know." She shrugged.

"Don't want to talk about him anymore?"

"That's right."

"No need to talk." He kissed her on the lips, bringing her closer, and Claire pressed herself against him, meeting his kiss. Then Claire remembered the driver in the front seat, with his rearview mirror, and she pulled away. She rested her head on Jamie's shoulder.

Rockefeller Center . . . the Public Library . . . the department stores Arnold Constable, Lord & Taylor, B. Altman. Madison Square with its blossoming canopy of trees. The arch of Washington Square in the distance . . . her city, her home, lent a clarity and a purity by the middle-of-the-night peace. The scents of spring flowed through the car window, a hyacinth wind upon her face, relaxing her after the work and tensions of the evening. Jamie rested his lips against her forehead.

The driver turned right on West Ninth Street. Claire squeezed Jamie's hand, and he returned the pressure. Ninth to Christopher, the driver taking the turns gently on the narrow streets, and finally to Grove.

When they pulled up to the curb, the house was dark. The school play was tomorrow, and Charlie had campaigned for permission to spend the night at Ben's house so they could practice their lines. Charlie had six lines, Ben had four, and they were determined to get them right. With Charlie out, Claire had given Maritza the night off and hired Tom to take Lucas out at ten.

"No one's home." She paused, not knowing how many words she needed to say. How explicit she had to be. "Would you like to stay?"

He hadn't been expecting this. He'd assumed Charlie would be home. Now, at last, she was ready. Everything fell into place. He felt emotion choking him. He would have prepared himself better, paced himself through the evening, if he'd known this was how it would turn out. Even on a practical level, he would have planned better: he had an 8:00 AM meeting with Dr. Rivers, and it was past 2:00 now. Luckily he was accustomed to nights with little sleep, and he didn't care anyway if he was tired in the morning. He felt a sudden vulnerability. He pushed a wayward lock of her hair back into place.

"Of course I'd like to stay." This he said in a self-righteous tone that made her laugh. He laughed also, and the moment of awkwardness was gone. They got out of the cab, he paid the driver, they were alone.

When Claire opened the front door, switching on the hall light, a heavy-lidded Lucas ambled over to greet them. He sniffed their feet, pressed his head against Jamie's leg, then returned to his bed by the parlor fireplace, collapsing into sleep. Claire walked down the hall to the stairs, Jamie following her.

Now she faced a choice. Immediately upstairs to the bedroom, or downstairs to the kitchen first, to offer him a drink. She looked both ways, as if she were about to cross the street. She held the banister. She felt the downward pull of doubt. Of anxiety. She felt as if she'd never been with a man before, despite a husband and sex partners whose names and faces she couldn't, at this moment, even remember.

Coming up behind her, he wrapped his arms around her waist and pressed her against his chest. Her cashmere sweater was soft against his hands, her hair soft against his cheek. He smelled the perfume in her hair.

He was waiting for her to decide, she understood that. *This is a time for firm resolve*—the words of a wartime leader whose name she couldn't place came into her mind, Churchill probably. She smiled at this new application for the phrase, and her smile surprised him, coming, as it seemed, out of nowhere. She turned out of his embrace, took his hand, and led him up the stairs.

Upstairs . . . the peeling William Morris wallpaper, the well-worn Persian carpets, the bookcases overflowing, and the photographs covering the walls. The house had a lived-in clutter that made him feel comfortable. This could be his home, too. He only needed to bring a suitcase, and he would be home.

Once across the threshold of the bedroom, she turned to him. He slipped off her sweater. She unbuttoned his jacket.

Reaching for the zipper of her dress, fumbling with it, he said, "I've never taken off an evening gown."

"It's simpler than you might think," Claire said, guiding his hand.

The gown fell to the floor, and Jamie placed his hands upon her breasts. She unbuttoned his shirt and slipped it down his arms. He undid the cuffs, pulled the shirt off. She pressed against him, their skin touching at last. She unbuckled his belt, undid his trousers, took him in her hand and in her mouth. As much as he enjoyed it, he put a stop to that before it was too late, pulling away from her, undoing her garters, rolling down her stockings. They were kneeling now upon the Persian carpet. Two desires warred within him: the urge to be fast and the urge to be slow; to fulfill his passion, or to prolong it; to be inside her while still thinking only of her fulfillment.

She maneuvered her mouth upon him once more.

"I need a turn," he said.

"I am giving you a turn," she paused to whisper, teasing, "A turn to accept what I'm giving you."

"Then I also need time for you to accept what I want to give you."

We might never have enough time, she said, although by then she wasn't certain if she'd said it aloud. He knew her thoughts, though. Of that she was certain.

CHAPTER ELEVEN

～

On Friday, May 22, Claire took the train from Atlanta, Georgia, back to New York. She dropped her film at the office and arrived home at 11:00 PM. Maritza had left a note for her on the kitchen table, listing two telephone messages from Mack and reporting that she'd given Lucas his last walk for the day. And she'd attached a telegram. Claire's fingers trembled a bit with expectation as she opened it. It was from Jamie, as she'd hoped. *Home this weekend. Love, J.*

The surprise of his visit filled her with contentment. With luck, they'd find some time to be alone together, she thought as she made herself a drink and went out to the garden. She sat down and leaned her head against the back of the chair. The evening breeze was sweet. She was glad to have some time, even if it was after eleven, to relax and catch up with herself.

Over a month had passed since she and Jamie had first made love. A month filled with traveling for them both. For her, stories at a hog farm outside Fort Wayne, Indiana, and an aircraft factory in Ypsilanti, Michigan. Without making a conscious decision, Claire had slipped into the new role the magazine required of her. Charlie was safe at home with Maritza and sounded happy enough the few times she'd been able to get a long-distance call through to him. The calls were an extravagance, but she'd wanted to hear his voice. She and Jamie exchanged letters, which somehow felt better for them than trying to speak of their emotions down a staticky long-distance telephone line.

Claire let herself drift through the peaceful, almost-summer evening. The sound of giggling and murmured, half-serious protests reached her from a garden down the block. Teenagers in love, she decided. Somewhere a baby began crying and was gently hushed.

In the weeks that she'd been in and out of town, she'd walked Charlie to school exactly once. She remembered that day. It was May 7, and she'd woken to a concert of birdsong from the gardens along the block. As she'd walked Charlie to school, the crab apple trees bloomed like snowflakes along Grove Street, giving off a floating sweetness. The day before, the island fortress of Corregidor had fallen to the Japanese after a long, brutal siege. Many thousands of Allied troops had been taken prisoner.

Outside school that morning, the parents had been quiet. On her way to the subway, heading for the office, Claire sensed a silence on the streets. Corregidor . . . although it was on the other side of the earth, it felt as close as the Brooklyn side of New York Harbor. Claire had studied the sky. The day was magnificent, the sky clear blue, the air pure. Manhattan was an island, too, like Corregidor. In a gust of wind, crab apple blossoms blew off the trees and settled in the gutters. The morning newspapers had printed the final message telegraphed from Corregidor. *They are piling dead and wounded in our tunnel. . . . Get this to my mother. . . . Tell Mother how you heard from me. Stand by.* . . . And then nothing, the telegraph operator dead or taken prisoner.

The following morning, she'd been off again. The story: female shipyard workers in Mobile, Alabama. Then, seven days in the life of an army induction center in Atlanta. She'd profiled boys entering the military who looked more like Charlie than like grown men. Claire met their mothers and fathers, simultaneously proud and nervous. She listened to stories of the Great War from the officers supervising the boys' enlistments. How many of these boys would survive to come home again?

Claire quickly downed her gin and tonic and pushed the memory of these boys from her mind. She went in, locked the back door, turned out the lights, and went upstairs.

Before going to bed, she looked in on Charlie. Sleeping soundly, he lay on his side, clutching his teddy bear. Although he'd given up the teddy bear years before, he'd retrieved it from his closet shelf soon after Pearl Harbor. Beside Charlie's bed, Lucas sighed and turned in his sleep, revealing the almost-white fur of his chest and tummy. He barked softly, his front limbs pawing the air, as if he were chasing squirrels in his dreams.

When Charlie slept, he looked very young. As she had done since he was an infant, she checked for his breathing, watching the slight movement of the sheet up and down upon his back. In less than a decade, he would be old enough to serve in the military. The front lines were manned by boys.

When he was old enough to be drafted, maybe this war would still be raging. Or some other war would have taken its place. She'd be saying good-bye to him beneath the monumental arches and skylights of Pennsylvania Station, trying to hold back her tears until after he'd gone down to the train platform. How would she bear it? Her eyes welled with tears from imagining it. By then maybe she'd have more children, Jamie's children, and they'd be crying at the station, too, seeing their brother off.

She looked out the window. Because of the finally enforced dim-out, she could see the stars. She found Orion's belt. The lights of a plane flashed through the sky. The plane made her think of enemy bombers. In recent weeks, the Germans had been bombing British cities in retaliation for the RAF bombing of German cities. Exeter, Bath, York, Norwich . . . historic cities were the targets. The Germans called these the "*Baedeker* Three-Star Raids," professing to use the guide-book to choose which cities to bomb.

How many stars did New York have in *Baedeker*?

If New York City were bombed, Greenwich Village would never

be a target—or so Claire tried to convince herself. Because of underground streams, the buildings were low. There were no targets of strategic or psychological importance. God and nature protected the neighborhood.

The plane banked toward the east. Claire imagined herself a passenger on that plane, gazing down at the Village. From the air, the West Village was a dark emptiness. Then she remembered: the Hudson River was only a few blocks away. The docks at the end of Christopher Street were a target. Bombs could go astray. In fact, a few blocks probably didn't even qualify as "astray." A few blocks either way were most likely considered part of the target. She'd read about German bombing raids on the London docks that wiped out nearby residential neighborhoods. You could tell when a bomb was headed toward you, Claire had read, because it sucked the oxygen from the air and trapped you suffocating in a vacuum.

The air raid warden shouted at someone down the street to either turn off the light or close the blackout shades.

After Corregidor, Charlie said that he no longer wanted to take the subway. What if a bomb fell on the street above and blocked the subway stairs, and they were trapped? he'd asked her. Much better to be on a bus if a bomb fell nearby, Charlie said, because at least they could run away. Much better to take the George Washington Bridge if they needed to leave Manhattan, instead of risking the Holland Tunnel, because if a bomb fell by mistake into the Hudson River, maybe they could escape from the bridge, but they could never escape from the tunnel. The water would pour in like a tidal wave. But what if the target was the bridge? The bridge was a logical target, Charlie assured her. Then they'd be better off in the tunnel.

Charlie had explained this while he and Claire sat at the counter of their neighborhood Schrafft's at Fifth Avenue and Thirteenth Street. While he talked, he devoured a gigantic chocolate-marshmallow sundae. They'd come here after school, when the restaurant was crowded with children and their mothers, grandmothers, or nannies. It was also crowded with men in uniform on leave in New York, four army privates at one table, three sailors a few tables down, a Marine Corps officer and his girl dining in a corner.

Claire didn't share with Charlie that she harbored similar fears, had thought through similar options. The newspapers, magazines, and radio were filled with advice on what to do if New York were bombed. City authorities assured the press that thousands of municipal employees were trained to restore basic services like electricity and water. Nonetheless, Claire had stockpiled candles, matches, jugs of water, and cans of food and condensed milk in the basement, not forgetting a can opener, in case they had to survive without the daily services provided by a functioning city. She'd kept these preparations secret from Charlie.

The plane banked again and went out of her view. Worrying was futile. She'd done what she could to prepare. Now all she could do was wait. She was luckier than most: she had Jamie in her life, and her father, so she didn't face the future alone.

She pulled the blanket over Charlie's shoulders and left his room. Following the rituals that had comforted her since her childhood, she bathed and prepared for bed. After turning out the light, she reviewed her plans for the weekend. On Saturday evening, she and Charlie were planning to have dinner with her father. Now Jamie could join them. She'd invite Tia also. After their evening at the River Club, Claire had been feeling more willing to include her father in plans, more willing to bring together the disparate parts of her life. On Sunday, she'd arrange for Charlie to spend the afternoon at Ben's house, so that she and Jamie would have a few hours alone. Or better yet, she'd call Hannah, a high school girl in the neighborhood who looked after kids on the weekends. Hannah could take Charlie and Ben to a movie. They'd like that; in fact they'd consider it a treat. She'd telephone Hannah first thing in the morning. As Claire fell asleep, she imagined making love to Jamie on Sunday afternoon, their desire especially strong from their time apart. In the afterglow, the sheet lightly upon them, she'd fall asleep with his arms around her, the fragrant spring breezes enveloping them.

That same Friday evening, May 22, Jamie's train pulled into Pennsylvania Station at 11:30 PM. A minor miracle: he'd actually made it back to New York, and only three hours late. Probably too late to go to Claire's. He didn't want to wake Charlie, and Claire needed her sleep, too. He'd phone in the morning at a proper hour and invite himself over for breakfast. Besides, he wanted to shower and shave before seeing her, and change his clothes. He reeked of the cigarette smoke that filled the interior of the train.

Tonight he could visit Tia. Share a midnight snack with her, since without doubt he'd find her in the lab. They hadn't had a meal alone together in a while. He missed her.

He retrieved his small suitcase and waited his turn amid the packed crowd exiting the train. On the platform, he followed along with the others to the exit, maneuvering up the narrow staircase. The woman in front of him was gray-haired and dressed in black: an elderly widow who went slowly, gripping the handrail.

"May I carry your bag?" he asked, to quicken the pace. When he put his hand lightly on her elbow to assist her, she smiled up at him. He saw more than gratitude in that smile. He saw a kind of closeness, as if he were her son. She offered him her bag, more of a canvas grocery bag than a suitcase.

Arriving at the top of the stairs, the cavernous station opened before him. The old woman was pulled into the embrace of her waiting family. He gave the bag to her daughter.

The concourse was crowded even at this late hour: lounging officers, clutches of parents and children, lovers gripping hands . . . the whole human drama of arrival and departure. Enlisted men slept against the walls, using their duffel bags as pillows. Young draftees in civilian clothes lined up for the trains that would carry them to their induction and basic training. The Red Cross's coffee and doughnut stand welcomed anyone in uniform. A sign pointed to the USO canteen. A woman with an Irish lilt in her voice announced the trains: "Midnight to Chicago, boarding at the east gate, track twelve."

How many times had he been in Pennsylvania Station? A hundred? And still his reaction was like the first time. The soaring arches and steel girders gave him a sense of freedom. Of exhilaration and exaltation.

Suddenly in front of him was a man he knew, accompanied by an older man he didn't recognize. His mind took a moment to catch up with this unexpected situation. Someone he knew, waiting at the station. Waiting for him, or for someone else? Jamie strode forward.

"Nick! Good to see you!" He reached to shake Nick's hand, pat him on the back, greet him like who he was, his best friend.

But Nick didn't smile. Nick didn't pat his back, didn't meet his eye. Jamie stopped. Waited. Suspected. Knew. Claire. Something had happened to Claire. An accident. Her travels, and the risks she took to get the right shot. The archways, the skylights, the station's midnight bustle . . . everything faded around him. There was only the here and now, this small circle of space, these two men before him.

Nick said nothing. Seemed incapable of saying anything. The other man stepped forward.

"Lieutenant James Stanton?"

"Yes," he replied.

"Detective Marcus Kreindler. New York City Police Department." The detective was white-haired, strong rather than stocky. His face was lined with a thousand small wrinkles. "I'm afraid we've got some bad news for you. Let's find a quiet place to talk." He motioned into the distance, in the direction of the Savarin coffee shop.

"Whatever it is, you can tell me right here."

Neither Nick nor Kreindler spoke. Did he have to force them?

"Nick," he demanded. "Is it Claire?"

"Claire?" Nick seemed to wake up. He looked confused. "Claire Shipley?" Nick thought for a moment, figuring this out. "No, no, not Claire Shipley. I mean, I don't know anything about Claire. I haven't seen her. I don't know where she is. Do you know where she is?"

Kreindler intervened. Put his big, strong arm on Jamie's shoulder. "Lieutenant, it's your sister. We believe it's your sister."

Someone had combed out her hair. Jamie wondered who. He seldom saw her hair combed out, long, around her shoulders. Framing her face, as the saying went. The heavy sheeting was pulled up to her chin, with a lighter sheet covering her face. It was this lighter sheet that Detective Kreindler pulled off to reveal her.

Despite the pennies placed on her eyelids to keep them closed, and despite the scarf tied around her head to keep her jaw closed, she looked perfect. At any moment she would wake up, take off that silly scarf, climb off the table, get dressed, and walk out with them. They'd go for a walk across the Institute grounds, where the azalea were in bloom.

"Is this your sister?" Kreindler said.

"Yes."

"The injuries are bad, especially the back of the head. But the staff managed to hide it. Knowing you were coming."

"Tell them thank you. Please."

All his adult life, Jamie had been around morgues. He was now in the basement of his own hospital, where he'd spent so many years. The basement was cut right into the cliff. The windows were cut through two feet of stone. He looked out at the middle-of-the-night blackness he knew to be the river, and Queens beyond, lights flickering here and there, despite the dim-out. He was familiar with the border between life and death. He knew how porous it was. How frail.

He had a sense of observing himself from a distance. He must be in shock, he realized. He'd seen enough family members over the years to recognize the signs. He looked at the wrapped figure on the gurney. He saw. He identified. He did what the law required. He felt empty. Confused. Doubting. He didn't think, My sister is lying cold and dead on a table in a morgue.

Beside him, Nick said, "She's so beautiful."

"Yes."

"Oh, God." Nick covered his face with his hands. Nick was crying. Weeping. "Oh, God," he said again.

Jamie watched his friend weeping. He wasn't prepared to comprehend Nick's weeping. Jamie felt disconnected. Nick, this room, the figure on the table, the detective waiting and watching a discreet distance away. What was the day? What was the time? He checked his watch. 1:15 AM. He'd arrived at the station on Friday night, so this must be Saturday morning.

Why was his friend weeping?

Jamie felt as if he were living in a connect-the-dots puzzle. He didn't know what to do next. Where to go. How to take care of everything that no doubt needed to be done. Who could tell him? His weeping friend was no help. He looked at Kreindler. Met his eyes. Jamie felt like a child waiting for a grown-up to tell him what to do.

Kreindler strode forward. Covered Tia's lovely face with the sheet. "You can call the funeral home now, to come and get her."

Jamie nodded. He didn't know what Kreindler was talking about, but a nod seemed like the correct response. Later, someone, he didn't know who, maybe Nurse Brockett, would tell him what to do.

"Let's go," Kreindler said.

Jamie was grateful to have someone else take charge.

"We'll get you a cup of coffee, and then we'll sit down and have a talk."

CHAPTER TWELVE

⁓

On Saturday morning, the phone rang, startling Claire out of a deep sleep. She checked her bedside clock. 9:00 AM. The extension was on her desk in the other room. Surely Maritza would pick up downstairs, Claire thought, fighting against waking up. When the ringing continued, Claire remembered it was Saturday and she'd given Maritza the weekend off. Maritza would have left for her own home earlier this morning.

Claire forced herself out of bed. She didn't want the ringing to wake Charlie. In their house, telephone calls at odd hours weren't unusual, the office trying to reach her with a question, or an unexpected assignment needing to be pursued immediately. Besides, 9:00 AM wasn't early. Claire was surprised she'd slept so late. There was no reason that the ringing of the telephone at 9:00 AM on a weekend morning should fill her with dread. But it did.

"Claire. Good." It was Frieda, Mack's secretary. "Glad you made it back." With troops getting priority on trains, civilian delays had become standard procedure. Claire was indeed lucky to have returned home on schedule. "Hope the trip was okay." Frieda was named after her German grandmother, but she and her parents were American— born and raised American, as Frieda was quick to explain after Germany had declared war on the United States. She'd come with Mack from the United Press and was one of the few secretaries without a Seven Sisters college pedigree. "I need a favor."

"Of course, Frieda." Favors on a Saturday, prior to closing, also weren't unusual, and Frieda was a good person to have on your side. She was known for her ability to push expense reimbursements through in record time, even though accounting wasn't strictly her area. Conversely, people not on her good side could find their expense sheets mysteriously delayed.

"Thanks in advance for helping me out."

"Frieda, you know you can always call me if you need anything."

"Not the case with everyone, I can tell you that much."

Some of Claire's colleagues had reputations for being more demanding than generous.

"Mack asked me to deal with this, and I'm asking you. He's got a million things on his plate this morning. It isn't even for us. It's a photo request from *Time*. I don't have an hour to go through a hundred contact sheets looking for a gal I wouldn't recognize if I saw her. Remember when you did that shoot at the Rockefeller Institute?"

"Yes, of course."

"You take any pictures of a woman named, where is it"—she flipped through some papers—"Dr. Lucretia Mott Stanton." She said the name flatly, reading it.

"Yes."

"Could you come over here and go through the contact sheets and tell me which one is her?"

"Why?" There's been a success, Claire told herself. A breakthrough. Tia's made a terrific discovery and gotten herself in the news. In the grogginess of her interrupted sleep, Claire was prepared to be excited for Tia. Prepared to be thrilled for her.

"Because I like you."

"Pardon?"

"Because I like you, I'll let you choose your favorite shot. Aren't you photographers always complaining that you never get to choose your favorite shots?"

"No, not that. Why do you want a picture of her?"

"Got a request from *Time*. Obit photo. They don't have anything. Institute photo's not good enough." Frieda often spoke in a kind of code, dropping words that weren't essential to her meaning, especially on Saturday mornings, when she was rushed. "Somebody knew from somebody, you did something over there, so *Time* came begging. Like we need begging on a Saturday morning. They don't close until what, Monday? Tuesday? Anyhow, Mack asked me, I'm asking you. Pass the buck, how's that for a motto?"

"An obit request? Current, or for the file?" Claire was awake now. Her heart was flying. She tried to hang on to something, anything, inside herself so she wouldn't start shouting at Frieda. Newsworthy people usually had obits prepared in advance, years in advance even, so when they died the file would be ready and would need only updating for recent career moves, newborn children or grandchildren, cause of death. How much greater the pressure now, in wartime, to keep the obit files in order before they were actually needed.

"The file? I don't think so. Request's urgent. Hold on." Claire heard more papers being shuffled. "It's an AP report. Says, Miss Lucretia Mott Stanton, Ph.D., dead at twenty-eight. Born in Philadelphia, la-di-da-di-da," Frieda was skimming. "Body found at the bottom of a cliff by the East River on Friday afternoon. Police investigation, accident, la-di-da . . . reading between the lines, I think they're trying to hide suicide."

"Suicide? That's not possible. I don't believe it." Claire's mind was spinning. Tia lived for her work, more important now than ever. She wouldn't commit suicide. Would she? "Read to me exactly what it says."

"Hold your horses, Claire. This has got nothing to do with the picture."

"It's important to me."

"Why?"

"Because . . ." A sixth sense told Claire that revealing her closeness to Tia Stanton's brother would be a mistake. She'd be drawn into
the company chain of gossip. She and Jamie would be talked about,
speculated over. She liked to keep her personal life to herself. "Sorry
for the bother, Frieda, but I did a fairly powerful story with Lucretia
Stanton, even if the story got killed. Spent days with her. You get to
know people."

"I suppose so. Okay, here goes." But even now Frieda wouldn't read
the report aloud, she'd only summarize as she read. "Nationally renowned mycologist, whatever that is, awards of this and that, publications on and on . . ."

Jamie had told Claire of Tia's accomplishments, had talked about
his admiration for her, but hearing her accomplishments recited from
an Associated Press report made them seem that much greater.

" . . . pursuing research vital to the war effort, doesn't say for what.
You ask me, she's not all *that* important."

Claire heard the tinge of jealousy in Frieda's voice. What dreams,
unfulfilled, had Frieda had for herself when she was younger?

"Must be they're having a slow week for obits over at *Time*. First big
death comes in, this piece gets killed. Mark my words. We're wasting
our time, but we have to do it anyway."

"Is that all it says?"

"Let's see . . . only survivor an older brother, Naval Lieutenant James
Stanton, M.D. *Lucretia*. That's some first name, like an Italian, but it
says they're Quakers. From Philadelphia. Sound high falutin. Never met
a Quaker. Lutheran church has always been good enough for me. 'No
indication of recent despondency.' That means they're trying to claim it's
not suicide, a line like that. Wonder why she killed herself."

"She didn't kill herself."

"What makes you so sure?"

Frieda was right: how could Claire be sure? She couldn't be. "I got
the feeling she was too . . . invested in life, for that."

"Now, now, you never know. People do the strangest things. Have all kinds of secrets you'd never guess. In my experience. Hold on, Mack, I'm talking to Claire." Frieda's attention was diverted. "That paperwork went out already." Frieda became impatient. "So, Claire, can you come over and look through the contact sheets, or not? Bring Charlie if you need to. Or if I pull the sheets, can you tell me which one is her over the phone?"

"I'll come over, Frieda. I'll get Charlie organized and I'll be right over."

"Thanks, Claire. You saved me. If you have a minute to make the print and take it to *Time*, that would cut out some arguments for me."

"Sure." Frieda's resentments toward the *Time* staff were legendary and of mysterious origins. "I'd be glad to." Frieda wouldn't see anything amiss in Claire's quick agreement to print the shot. The photo staff was always complaining that they were kept so busy shooting stories, they never had a chance to work in the lab.

"Owe you one, Claire."

"After all these years, I owe you more than one, Frieda." Claire heard herself sounding normal, clinging to the sound of normal. They said good-bye and hung up.

Where was Jamie? How could she reach him? She wanted to be with him, to help him. Not knowing what else to do, she phoned the Institute. Maybe he'd left word of his exact schedule.

"I'm trying to reach Dr. James Stanton," she said.

"I can take a message for Dr. Stanton," said the switchboard operator.

"It's urgent that I reach him."

"I've been instructed to take messages for him."

Where was he? Was he even in New York yet? His telegram hadn't said when he was arriving. Did he know about his sister? Claire felt at a loss. "Is Dr. Nick Catalano available?"

"I can take a message for Dr. Catalano."

Claire wasn't accustomed to having a wall placed before her. "He knows me."

"Excuse me, ma'am. Do you want to leave a message or not?"

Claire left messages for them both. She dressed. She woke Charlie, helped him get dressed, made him breakfast. While he was eating, she took Lucas for a quick walk and gave him his breakfast. She called Ben's house. His mother, Constance, answered.

"Forgive me, Connie, I've got a problem at the office. Can Charlie come over for a few hours?"

"We were about to call you. We're organizing a picnic to Prospect Park. I was hoping you'd both be able to come, but we'll settle for Charlie." With four sons, Connie was the prime organizer of the Grove-Bedford-Barrow Street blocks, the mom who always had brownies and milk waiting and baseball gloves at the ready. Claire felt maternally inadequate by comparison.

"Thanks, Connie. I'd love to go on a picnic, but I can't."

"You sound upset. What's wrong?"

Claire was talking on the phone in the kitchen. Charlie was listening. "I'm just rushed. You know how it is." She tried to convey to Connie the urgency she felt without alarming Charlie. "Something at the office."

"Don't worry," Connie said, understanding. "Just do what you need to do. We're always happy to have Charlie."

"Thanks, I really appreciate it. We'll be over soon." She hung up the phone.

Charlie had finished eating and was staring at her. "Can I walk over to Ben's alone?"

Claire paused before responding. Charlie had been slow developing the confidence to walk a few blocks through the neighborhood on his own, the way the other kids did. The neighborhood was safe, during the day at least, in part because of the old people who sat in folding chairs along the sidewalks, two here, three there, basking in the sun and surveying the street. "Okay."

"I'll call you on the telephone when I get there," he promised, putting on a grown-up tone.

"That sounds good. I'll wait for your call."

At the front door, he set his shoulders straight, as though a cheering audience were watching him from across the street. He walked down the steps firmly and turned sharply right. Claire closed the door, to show her confidence in him. She watched from the window until he was out of sight.

She gathered her coat, hat, gloves. She put the latest issue of *The New Yorker* into her tote bag to read on the subway. Something to make her feel normal.

The phone rang. "I got here a few minutes ago," Charlie confided, "but I had to say hi to Murphy, so I forgot to call right away." Murphy was the family's chocolate Lab.

"That's fine. I knew you were safe."

"How?"

"Because I know you're old enough to walk to Ben's without a problem."

"Thanks." She heard his pride. "Love you, Mommy."

"Love you, too, sweetheart."

They hung up.

As she made her way to the Sixth Avenue subway—down Grove, across Sheridan Square, down West Fourth—Claire looked around, forcing herself to act normal. The breeze was warm against her cheeks. The afternoon would be hot. The windows of her neighbors . . . blue-star banners filled the windows, announcing that a family member was serving in the military. Here and there, she saw the silver-star banners, reporting that a family member had been wounded. And she saw two gold stars, the emblems of death.

She reached Sixth Avenue and the subway entrance. Walking down the steps, putting her nickel in the slot, making her way along the underground ramp that led to the trains, she focused on her surroundings in order to stop thinking about Tia.

The West Fourth Street station was built in three levels. She went downstairs to the middle level, and then down the stairs again, to the Sixth Avenue train. Surely this lowest level was deep enough to serve as an air raid shelter. She imagined herself explaining this to Charlie. She knew he worried that the IRT tunnel on Seventh Avenue wasn't deep enough in their neighborhood to serve as a shelter. But how did oxygen get down to this lowest level? Charlie would wonder about that. She'd never noticed any air vents or pumps. Here on the lowest level, the air was fetid. The tunnels were dank, rats scurrying over the tracks. During a bombing raid, Claire and Charlie might survive down here, but if rubble from the raid blocked the exits to the street, they'd be trapped three stories down—most likely with hundreds of their neighbors—without an adequate source of oxygen.

She boarded a train headed for Rockefeller Center. Although several seats were available, she stood. The train jolted into motion, and she gripped the vertical handrail. That precarious path along the cliff where Tia had fallen . . . Claire remembered it from the afternoon when she toured the Institute with her camera. The wind had whipped around her. What was Tia doing there, Tia in her high heels and tight skirts? No matter why she was there, most likely her fall was an accident. Not suicide, of that Claire felt certain. Tia had never sounded defeated. Frustrated, yes. But not defeated.

And yet . . . suddenly Claire realized that she didn't actually know Tia very well. Guilt overwhelmed her. Claire should have made more of an effort with Tia. She could have, should have—included Tia in more family events, whether Jamie was in town or not; set her up on dates with her colleagues at the magazine. Claire thought back to the one dinner they'd shared at home. She remembered Tia reviewing Charlie's homework; recalled the apple pie Tia had made from their grandmother's recipe, and how much Jamie had enjoyed it. The evening had been easy and relaxed, and Claire had assumed it would be the first of many. Except it wasn't.

All at once Claire imagined herself as Tia, slipping from that cliff. Not jumping. Never jumping. How does it feel, to see the land rushing up against you? Or do you fall too fast for feeling, seeing, screaming, regretting?

Claire got off the train at Rockefeller Center and walked to the lower-level concourse of the RCA Building. Shops and restaurants lined both sides of the concourse. Bustling during weekday lunch hours, they were quiet on Saturday morning. Sandbags were stacked in corners to stop fires during bombing raids. Instruction sheets for electrical blackouts were posted at regular intervals. She reached Rockefeller Center's sunken plaza with its outdoor café. Waiters cleaned the tables, preparing for tourists, and military men with their dates, to arrive for an outdoor lunch.

Claire took the escalator up to the street level. She stepped out of the RCA Building into the glory of Rockefeller Center in the springtime. The Channel Gardens were lush, green, and bedecked with multicolored flowers. The golden statue of Prometheus, where she'd posed Aurora Rasmussen and the Rockettes just six months ago, gleamed in the sunlight. Claire felt herself drowning in sunlight as she crossed the plaza to the Time & Life Building, Forty-ninth Street and Rockefeller Plaza.

Now she was upstairs in the maze of offices that constituted *Life* magazine. "Hi, Frieda." She was acting normal. Gripping on to normality as if it were the handrail on the subway. Duncan Daily might be in today. He often noticed what others didn't. She needed to move along quickly.

"Hi, Claire." Frieda was a tireless, petite woman who dressed demurely. Today she wore a plain shirtwaist dress with pearls. She was always moving, her swivel chair a command center from which she completed eight tasks at once while balancing two phones.

Mack was on the phone in his office behind Frieda. Claire waved to him. He acknowledged her with a wink. He was a small, beefy man, and he, too, could never sit still, reviewing piles of prints, filling out order forms, approving layout boards, taking calls.

"You're an angel, Claire," Frieda said. "Here's the story number."

Frieda passed Claire a slip of paper, but Claire already knew the story number. She'd unconsciously memorized it. She went to the archive room, where the negatives, contact sheets, and caption notes from the past two years were filed in rows of wooden filing cabinets, well dusted and shiny from furniture polish. The perfectly ordered files were supervised by Miss Robbins, called Admiral Robbins behind her back by the photographers because she prided herself on running what she called a tight ship.

Miss Robbins was at her desk, labeling folders. "Good morning, Miss Robbins," Claire said as cheerfully as she could manage. Miss Robbins wore a navy blue suit. Her brown hair, touched with white at her temples, was twisted into a bun at the back of her head. "Frieda's got me pulling an obit negative for *Time*."

"I've been informed." Miss Robbins didn't look up. Her glasses, which she didn't need for reading, dangled from a chain around her neck. "Put the story number and your name on the clipboard. You know the drill."

"Thank you, Miss Robbins." She completed the paperwork.

Claire searched the cabinet labels for the story number. When she found it, she was grateful the cabinet was out of Miss Robbins's vision. Claire didn't like being scrutinized. The heavy file drawer screeched on its hinges as she pulled it out. She found the folder for the Rockefeller Institute story, thick with contact sheets, negatives, and notes. She placed the folder on top of the cabinet and flipped through the contact sheets. This was how her colleagues did it. This is what Miss Robbins expected her to do. Claire felt as if she were watching herself from a distance. She used a magnifying loupe when she reached the sheets with potential. She mulled over the alternatives. She realized she had an opportunity to prove a point, to show a woman scientist both feminine and committed to her work. A fitting memorial to Tia.

She was limited in her choices, however. An obit shot couldn't be overly emotional, couldn't be part of a picture story, because there was no context to explain the emotion. An obit shot had to stand alone. She wished she'd taken a standard, clichéd photo of Tia holding up a test tube to the light, the type of shot Mack had warned her against, perfect for an obit.

Finally she found something. It wasn't ideal, but it would have to do. Roll fifty-two, photo number 7/7A. From the series of Tia showing the lab to Ned and Sally Reese. The image caught Tia just after she'd finished pipetting fluid into a test tube. She'd lowered the pipette and was smiling at Sally, who stood beyond the frame. The shot showed at a glance both Tia's work and her character.

Claire put aside the contact sheet and its attached negatives. She closed the folder and found its proper place in the drawer.

"I'll refile the negatives and contact sheet later," she called to Frieda on her way out. She took the elevator downstairs. Again she was outside, the glorious spring day hitting her in the face. The photo lab was separate from the Rockefeller Center complex, on the third floor of a honky-tonk tenement across the street at 38 West Forty-eighth Street. The Three Gs restaurant and bar, the staff hangout, was on the ground floor of the same building.

The photographers engaged in much bitter talk about why their lab wasn't in the Rockefeller Center building. We've been forgotten, was the complaint, when we're responsible for the magazine's success. Maybe the exile was simply a way to keep the smell of photographic chemicals away from the editors. The acrid, unmistakable odor of developer, fix, and hypo assaulted Claire the moment she entered the stairwell. It transported her to years before, when she'd first learned how to work in a darkroom, first learned how to put light onto paper to create an image. It was a smell that got into your clothes and your hair, like a perfume you caught whiffs of around yourself days after sampling it.

The lab was divided into two sections, one room for developing negatives, the other for printing. In the print area, twelve enlargers were set up in rows of separate cubicles so the enlarger lights wouldn't affect other stations. The chemicals were on the counter behind, each enlarger with its matching sink and counter. The room glowed from the red of safety lights. The lab was staffed in three shifts by a group of cynical guys who were brilliant at their underpaid and underappreciated work. Jerry was in charge today, and he greeted Claire from an enlarger when she came in.

"Hi, Claire. Good to see you." Jerry was sandy-haired and fit, his jaw pronounced and angular. He had the dense wrinkles of a man who spent too much time in the sun, which Claire never understood, because he worked long hours in the dark.

"Hi, Jerry. Good to see you, too." Jerry had printed her story from the hog farm outside Fort Wayne. Never had hogs been more subtly shaded, highlighted, and cropped. "I've got a rush for *Time*."

"For *Time*? They're not closing today."

"They claim they need this for their layout right away. Frieda asked me to deal with it, since it's from a story I shot a while back. Shouldn't take long. One print. Portrait of a scientist who died, don't even ask."

He laughed with understanding. Why one story became a rush and another didn't was forever incomprehensible. "Machine number six is free. Everything's set up, right temperatures for the chemicals, the works. Gene's using it, but he's at lunch."

"Thanks." Machine six, she saw, was around the corner from Jerry. Good.

"He's due back in a half hour. You'll be done by then?"

"I'd better be. Any longer and it'd be a sign that I'm losing my touch."

"And we can't have that, can we?" he said. "When the print's out of the soup, I can finish the rinsing and drying and drop it off at *Time*, so you don't have to wait around. I've got some other things going, too. And I can drop the negatives with the Admiral."

"Thanks a lot, Jerry. I appreciate it."

The guys grunted as she went by, which for them, when they were working to deadline, represented a warm acknowledgment. She said hello without recognizing them in the red shadows. But undoubtedly they knew her and her work. They knew the failings of every photographer, and they made every one look like a genius, overcoming any problems with the negatives by improving the prints until they were terrific. These guys held her career in their hands. She made sure to give them special Christmas presents every year.

Machine six. She would do a test print first. She took the negative holder out of the enlarger and inserted the strip of film that held shot 7/7A. She blew off a few specks of dust. She inserted the negative carrier into the enlarger. Turned on the lamp. There was Tia, black and white in reverse. Putting a sheet of plain white paper in the picture easel, she framed and focused the image, moving the enlarger head up and down until she had exactly what she wanted. Claire felt tears welling, and a pressure within her forehead and behind her eyes as she tried not to let herself cry.

She set the enlarger at f/11 to keep the focus sharp. She turned off the enlarger lamp. She took a sheet of photo printing paper from the light-proof holder on the shelf under the enlarger and put it in the easel in place of the plain paper. She set the timer for five seconds. Using a piece of cardboard, she exposed the test print, increasing the light exposure three times across the sheet. She put the print into the developer on the counter behind her, using tongs to agitate it. Slowly Tia's face appeared. This was the moment of magic, of rapture, when a picture emerged upon a blank sheet of paper. Even now, after all these years, it gave her a sense of awe.

When the image was complete, Claire lifted out the print with the tongs and held it sideways to let the developer solution run off. She put the print into the first stop bath, immersing it with the stop-bath tongs, and then moved it to the second stop bath. She counted to fifteen. She switched the print to the fixer, agitating once again. Since this was simply a test print, she didn't need to do a full fix or wash the print.

She turned on the small white light on the counter to study the print. The best exposure was the middle one, ten seconds. She stuffed the test print into the wastebasket under the counter.

Returning to the enlarger, she placed another sheet of photo paper into the easel. She set the automatic timer for ten seconds. With a piece of cardboard, she dodged the background a bit, to create a better unity of shading around Tia's head. The process was second nature to Claire. This time, she kept the print in the fix for a full ten minutes, so it would never fade. As she studied Tia's face, Claire realized how similar her features were to Jamie's. They shared eyes and cheekbones, and the line of the jaw. Not for the first time, Claire realized how lucky she was to have met him. Mack could easily have sent someone else to the Institute that morning. Yes, how lucky she was to have met him, and how quickly he could be taken away. After all, here before her was a lovely, brilliant woman, dead. Life was a delicate wire waiting to be snapped. Little Emily . . .

Claire began to cry. She struggled to make the crying sound like nothing more than sniffling.

"You okay over there, Claire?" Jerry asked as he picked up some prints from another cubicle.

"These spring colds," she said, trying to catch her breath despite a constriction in her throat. "Caught it from my son and now I can't shake it."

"Me, too," a deep voice said on her left, the guy at the next enlarger, shrouded in darkness. "I got a box of Kleenex here, if you need it."

Thank God for him. He saved her. Spring colds were everywhere. "I'm working with the fix, can't reach for a Kleenex now."

"Know what you mean," he said, sniffling. "Use your sleeve, that's what I do."

"His wife just loves those snot-covered sleeves," someone said in the darkness.

Laughter all around.

"Thanks for the advice," she managed. "I'll remember it."

Finally to the rinse. Claire followed her neighbor's advice and wiped her tears on her sleeve.

A full rinse took an hour, and then the print had to be dried. She could turn the print over to Jerry's supervision now. But she didn't want to leave. She wished she could develop and print her own work every day, instead of being sent on a frantic journey from one story to the next, to so many towns and villages and farmyards that she couldn't keep track of where she was, where she'd been, or where she was going. When she was in the darkroom, the rest of the world fell away.

"Hey, Claire. Good to see you." Gene emerged from the shadows, round-faced, his graying hair thick and curly. He wore his usual work uniform of plaid flannel shirt and unbuttoned vest. He was smiling, no doubt surprised and happy to find her here. He offered her a quick hug. He'd printed the Rockette story and made radiant the glittering lights of the Rockefeller Center Christmas tree. "What's cookin'?"

Now she had no choice but to leave.

When she reached home, she phoned the Institute again, and again the switchboard operator refused to put her through. She made a cup of coffee. As she sat down at the kitchen table to drink it, the phone rang.

"Claire, I've been trying to reach you."

"Oh, Jamie, I've been at the office. I—" She stopped. He didn't want to know the course of her day. "I know what happened. The magazine called me early."

"May I come downtown?"

"I'm waiting for you."

M^{ud.}
     On Saturday afternoon, Detective Marcus Kreindler stood on the cliff overlooking the East River and studied the dried mud on the path. There'd been some rain yesterday. Not a lot, but enough. Enough so that he could see the imprint of a woman's shoe. A thin heel.

In his experience, high heels slid into everything. After he and his wife put in a linoleum floor in the kitchen of their new house in Queens, her cousin, who lived in the city, came out to visit them and jammed her heels into the linoleum, not intending to do damage, but there it was, jam, jam, jam, round imprints that would last a lifetime. Or as long as they owned the house, from which they were going to take him out feet first, since he had no intention of moving. He didn't foresee replacing the linoleum, either.

He took one of the shoes out of his evidence bag and compared it to the imprint in the mud. The very same. Yesterday afternoon, Friday, he'd found Tia Stanton's high heels about ten feet away from each other in some weeds at the bottom of the cliff. They'd come off when she fell. The shoes were from Saks Fifth Avenue, according to the inside label. Presumably she cared about having nice things and could afford them.

Again he studied the mud . . . there was the imprint of a man's shoe, following along beside her. Nothing unusual about the man's shoe, and no proof that the man and woman had been together.

Kreindler looked down to the bottom of the cliff. A small crowd shifted and reshifted, people come to gape at the site of a death. Five people, then four, then six, then two. Well dressed. Young and old. Normal people. He hated the compulsion to gape at the site of a death. They didn't have enough death in their own families, they had to go searching for it? There'd been an even bigger crowd yesterday, the gawkers combined with a dozen cops and the usual investigators who danced attendance at the scene of any suspicious death; he was among them, of course. That was his job.

From his perch high above the scene, Kreindler observed the Institute guy who collected sewage walking to the river's edge with his bucket. Kreindler had already interviewed him and six or seven others, including an Englishman who worked both here and at a lab in New Jersey and seemed completely broken up about her.

Anyway, nobody he interviewed had seen a thing. A girl takes a lunchtime stroll, ends up at the bottom of a cliff, and nobody sees a thing. They came together to protect their own. They might all be geniuses, but it was still human nature to protect your own. The girl spent her days with mold. He'd inspected her lab and seen a lot of it—green, yellow, orange, purple mold. That was her profession. Multicolored mold. Who ever heard of such a thing?

Kreindler felt a little dizzy. Woozy. He had a problem with heights—not a predicament he ever wanted to admit to his buddies. Even Sean, his partner, hadn't known. Just last week, Sean had signed up for the military police and was gone in a day. From Sean's perspective, pushing thirty, no kids, his marriage not going great, it was the opportunity of a lifetime. Kreindler had had his own opportunity of a lifetime in the Great War, and he wasn't about to repeat it.

To short-circuit his vertigo, he continued walking, following the imprints of the heels in the mud and not looking over the cliff. What the hell was Lucretia Stanton doing here, walking on a path along a cliff?

Maybe if you didn't have a problem with heights, however, the path was no big deal. He tried to approach the issue this way. The view was terrific, he had to admit. The bridge, the river, the islands in the river, a being-on-top-of-the-world feeling. Even so, if she knew she was coming here, why didn't she change her shoes? Was she trying to impress someone? Was she trying to impress the man with her? If in fact he was with her?

Kreindler stopped. Here was a place where the left heel scraped into the dirt crossways. The right heel dug in, deep, as if the heel itself had been trying to hold on to the path. And then it, too, scraped out sideways. The prints of the high heels ended here. Right here, she'd lost her balance and fallen.

Where were the man's corresponding footprints?

The man had come up beside her, stepping on top of her footprints. Then he turned, to face the cliff. Then he continued his walk.

Years ago, Kreindler's doctor had taught him the phrase, "When you hear hoofbeats, think horses, not zebras." Or something like that. This was in response to Kreindler's self-diagnosis of a brain tumor when he actually had a sinus problem from a wicked cold.

Kreindler often remembered the phrase in his work, and it applied here. Girl in high heels falls off cliff, doesn't leave a note: sounds like an accident, nothing more or less—except for the man who might, or might not, have been with her.

Later today a security guy was coming up from Washington: Andrew Barnett was his name, and he was involved with a secret government project that her brother worked for. Judging from a long-distance telephone call this morning, the security guy was pushing to have the death declared an accident. Get it over with, quiet everything down, then figure out the truth later. Kreindler mistrusted the attitude.

Kreindler risked glancing down. The sewage guy, Sergei Oretsky, was dragging his bucket across the East River Drive. Three more people had come to gawk at the place of death.

Kreindler knew that the story wasn't down there, at the bottom of the cliff. What had happened down there was obvious: a beautiful, brilliant girl hit the ground and died. He'd already talked to the autopsy doctor, who went into lots of detail about fractured bones and blunt impacts. Kreindler had seen the body, so he already knew this. Her long limbs, broken. Her spine, twisted. But her face never hit the ground. So her face was perfect. Haunting him.

The solution to the problem was here on the path, in what happened before she fell. In that high heel, twisting to hold on to the cliff. The man, turning to face the direction she fell. The man, walking away.

Claire sat at the front window waiting for him, Lucas at her feet. What could she say to Jamie when he arrived? What was there to say? After Emily died, and the undertakers took her away, nothing remained to do or say. Claire and her mother sat in silence at the kitchen table drinking tea. They had family and friends to inform, chores to do, the funeral to plan, but all that could wait until tomorrow. Right then, they were utterly drained. Where was Bill? He must have been there. Without even realizing, she'd eliminated him from her memory. There was no weeping, not then, at least. Plenty of time for that later. Had she cried against Bill's shoulder? Again she couldn't remember. She did remember crying into her pillow so Charlie wouldn't hear her, but she didn't remember whether Bill was there to put his hand on her shoulder to comfort her. Or if Bill cried, and she comforted him. Bill had become invisible.

A sibling was different from a child. She didn't have a sibling, so she couldn't put herself into Jamie's shoes. She'd offer her presence to him, so he could find what he needed.

There he was. So handsome. The love of her life. He looked . . . impassive. Steeled. His eyes were partly closed, as if he were making a tremendous effort to stay awake. Had he been up all night? She opened the front door as he walked up the steps of the stoop.

"Jamie."

"Good morning, Claire."

It wasn't morning anymore, but she didn't correct him. She hugged him when he reached her and led him inside.

"Have you eaten? Would you like coffee?"

"Breakfast would be good," he said. "Something simple." He paused, confused. He saw the look on her face, which told him that he'd said something odd but she was going along with it. His watch. 2:20. So it must be the afternoon. The sun was shining. He thought maybe he was hungry. "You see, I missed breakfast," he said, to explain to her. He wanted her to understand everything he felt, even though at this moment he didn't have the strength to explain.

"Oatmeal?" she asked, taking his hand.

He nodded.

Her hand was so warm in his. He felt as if all the standard details of daily life had become huge and vitally important. The feel of her hand. The sunlight coming through the curtains. Lucas, pushing his nose against Jamie's leg, staying close as they went downstairs.

He sat at the kitchen table. She made the oatmeal. He stared at the front page of the newspaper, but he didn't fully register what the newspaper was reporting. The Japanese now controlled Burma. Where was Burma? He couldn't remember. Well, it didn't matter to him anyway. He didn't talk and Claire didn't press him to talk. For that he was grateful. No questions about what the police thought, or what happened with this or that, or what was it like, to identify Tia's—he stopped himself from remembering that.

At the stove, stirring the oatmeal, Claire waited for him to speak, if he was going to. All the details she wanted to know were pressing inside her. But she wouldn't ask. Not now, at least. He knew he could talk to her, when and if he wanted to.

She served the oatmeal. Put out the milk and cinnamon. She'd never made oatmeal for him. She didn't know how he liked it. She wished she had blueberries or strawberries to add, but the season hadn't started. Instead she brought out the peach jam. Charlie liked jam in oatmeal.

Jamie watched her do all these things. He still felt distant from himself. He knew he should eat, but actually confronted with food, he began to feel queasy. Probably if he actually ate, the queasiness would pass. And the oatmeal was mild. She was right to suggest it. What to add to it? He stared at the options. The dog was at his feet, pressing its head against his ankle.

Claire watched him. She remembered herself after Emily died, taking one step, and then the next step, and then another. Living in an absolute present. Avoiding all thought of past and future. She felt at one with him. Closer even than when they made love.

He chose the jam. One spoon only. He ate slowly and methodically.

When he finished the oatmeal, he looked up at her. From some trick of the light, he saw himself reflected in her eyes. Did that mean she saw herself in his eyes? He wished he had the strength to ask.

"Would you like anything else?" she said. "Tea? Coffee?"

"I'd like to lie down." Suddenly he was exhausted. He didn't think he'd make it to the guest room down the hall without collapsing.

Again she took his hand. She seemed to lead him down the hall, even though they were side by side. The guest room was shadowed, the shades and curtains drawn. He pushed off his shoes and lay down on the bedspread, curling on his side. He sensed her watching him. Then she cracked open the window. He breathed the pleasant scents of spring. She pulled the far side of the bedspread over him, so that he'd be warm.

CHAPTER THIRTEEN

In Prospect Park, Brooklyn, a Quaker cemetery was hidden on a hillside. Claire would never have known this, even though she'd been to the park dozens of times, but for the fact that Tia Stanton would be buried there.

On Tuesday at midday, Claire and Jamie drove to Brooklyn with George Hallowell, the head of Tia's Meeting, as the Quakers called it, for a private burial of Tia's ashes. She had left instructions that she be cremated, and Jamie didn't question her wishes. The urn that contained her ashes was inside a plain box that sat on the front seat next to Mr. Hallowell, like a passenger in the car, leaving the backseat for Claire and Jamie. Mr. Hallowell was a thin, long-legged man with white, wispy hair and a restrained smile.

Tia's memorial service would be the next day, but a Quaker burial was strictly private. The Quaker customs were foreign to Claire, and she wanted to understand them, for Jamie's sake, but without pressing him with questions. He wanted only Claire to come with him. She rubbed her palm against his leg, and he pressed his own palm against the back of her hand.

The cemetery dated from the 1840s, before the creation of the park. Quaker Hill, this area was called on the guidebook map that Claire had found at home. When Mr. Hallowell turned off the park's main roadways, leaving behind the meadows filled with visitors flying kites and tossing baseballs on this warm, bright day, Claire felt disoriented. Soon the trees closed in and the park became wild, as if they'd gone back to the days when it was a forest. Thick foliage that cut off the sunlight arched above the narrow roadway. A forbidding loneliness filled her, despite Jamie's presence at her side, as if she'd entered the dark forest of a fairy tale fraught with nameless threats, the fears of childhood magnified, not diminished, by adulthood. She looked at Jamie. He seemed preoccupied, not even noticing their surroundings. Just as well. They reached an opening cut into the trees on the left. Mr. Hallowell made the turn onto a muddy dirt road. Several dozen yards along the rutted path, they reached the cemetery's open gates.

A light was on in the cemetery office, a small stone structure just beyond the gates. Mr. Hallowell stopped, turned off the engine, and went into the office. Jamie joined him. Claire got out of the car, too.

About twenty yards in, the land rose steeply. Claire wandered for a moment while Jamie was in the office. Her heels sank into the soft earth. The scents of grass and of heavy, wet soil drifted around her. Birds were twittering, and Claire spotted the reason: a hawk sat on a high branch, surveying its kingdom. Small gravestones covered the hillside, interspersed with exotic plantings—immense copper beeches; slender tulip trees, leaves spreading at their summits; and elegant, elongated Japanese maples. The cemetery was like an arboretum.

Jamie and Mr. Hallowell came out of the office, accompanied by a black man who wore overalls and carried a shovel. This man, older, and not especially strong for the job he had, was introduced to her: Mr. Atkins.

At the sight of the shovel, Claire inwardly cringed. Claire's mother, and Emily, were buried at the Trinity Church Cemetery on West 155th Street. Claire still remembered the services at their grave sites, the prayers of the Episcopal priest, the workmen with their shovels keeping a polite distance. She now repeated those prayers in her mind, to cover the strangeness of the ceremony, or rather lack of ceremony,

before her. Mr. Hallowell retrieved the box with the urn. They walked
up the hillside to a place that had been prepared, a mound of dirt
marking the site. *In sure and certain hope of the Resurrection* . . . she
heard the other ceremonies, filling the Quaker silence. *Earth to earth,*
ashes to ashes . . .

Mr. Hallowell placed the urn into the burial place. "We may now
speak out of the silence," he said.

No one said anything. Jamie stared at the urn. Claire looked at the
sky. She glimpsed a seagull, and then another. Long minutes passed.
Claire began to feel surrounded by a kind of sacred circle of silence.

Mr. Hallowell spoke: "William Penn wrote in *Fruits of Solitude*,
'Death is but crossing the world, as friends do the seas; they live in one
another still.' This is how I remember Lucretia Stanton."

Then it was over. The silence, which had become an invisible presence
around them, dissolved. Mr. Hallowell put his hand on Jamie's shoulder.
"I'll wait down below, son," he said. "Take your time. I'm in no rush."

Mr. Atkins stepped off, also waiting.

And so they were alone together. Claire studied Jamie. He continued to stare at the urn. Claire wished she'd brought flowers for the
grave. She'd felt at such a loss, not knowing what was appropriate.
Abruptly, Jamie turned away. He began to wander through the cemetery. Claire followed him.

"Look, Claire," he finally said. "Look at these names." He motioned
to a row of the small grave markers, some so old they were sinking into
the earth, their lettering overgrown by moss and grasses. Claire made
out Mott, and Stanton. "These are probably distant relatives of mine,"
he said. "Go back far enough and we're all related, I suppose."

"A continuum," she said.

Ten yards behind them, Mr. Atkins carried out his job, burying
the urn.

"I suppose so." He wandered on, and Claire let him be. Then he
noticed something unusual. He stopped.

Thomas Reed, January 14, 1896—November 11, 1918.

Abigail Coffin, April 4, 1877—November 15, 1918.

Jonathan Thomas, August 1, 1886—November 12, 1918.

In this section of the cemetery, one grave after another gave the date of death in November or December of 1918. These were the months of the worst of the Spanish flu epidemic. Dozens of men and women in their twenties, thirties, and forties were buried across this hillside. How many orphans did they leave behind? In his mind he saw the death cart making its way down Delancey Place in Philadelphia. He saw his mother's body there, in the back of the cart. He hated that his mother and father were buried in a mass grave. In Philadelphia in November 1918 too many died too quickly for individual burial.

Claire joined him. Put her arm though his. Jamie gestured to show the story symbolized by these graves. The story of his own life.

Wednesday, May 27, 1942, 11:00 AM. Tia Stanton's memorial service at the Quaker Meetinghouse on Stuyvesant Square.

To Claire, the square was a tranquil haven of nineteenth-century gentility, a place far removed from the jazzy glitter of skyscraper New York. The square intersected with Second Avenue between East Fifteenth and East Seventeenth streets. Its central park was surrounded on three sides by town houses and churches. Next to the Quaker Meetinghouse was J. P. Morgan's church, St. George's, with its Gothic Revival brownstone tower. Exuberantly decorated Victorian-era hospitals lined the far side of the Square. The park was lush with sycamores, silver lindens, and elm trees coming into leaf. Sunlight turned the yellow-green leaves translucent.

Claire spotted her father waiting for her at the corner of Fifteenth Street, as they'd planned. Jamie would be arriving with colleagues from the Institute.

"Good morning, my darling," Rutherford said, giving her a quick hug.

"Hi," was all she could manage.

"Difficult days, I know," he said, squeezing her hand. She was grateful for his comforting presence.

They headed toward the Meetinghouse. The building was set back from the street, surrounded by a garden and a wrought-iron fence. According to the inscription over the entryway, the sanctuary had been dedicated in 1860, the year before the outbreak of the Civil War. Yet the Meetinghouse appeared far older. With its simple, classical lines, it felt like a church where George Washington might have worshipped. Passing the newspaper photographers gathered at the gates with their 4x5 Speed Graphics and flashbulbs, Claire looked carefully in case she knew any of them, but she didn't. Their editors must have scented scandal, to send them here.

Claire wasn't accustomed to visiting new places without the protective armor of her own cameras and equipment. Despite her father's presence, she felt a touch of nerves as she made her way into the sanctuary. The plain, whitewashed room was brilliant with sunlight from the long windows. Pews on four sides faced the center. Claire and her father found a place halfway back. Once seated, she focused on the light pouring through the windows. Jamie had explained to her the Quaker belief that light led you to God. That light *was* God. In the Meetinghouse the light was blinding.

The Rockefeller Institute, the Quaker Meetinghouse, the cemetery in Prospect Park . . . Jamie came from a New York unknown to her, even though she'd spent her entire life in this city.

"It's a good-size crowd," Rutherford said. "I'm glad of that, for his sake."

"Yes." Jamie had told Claire that Tia was known well here. She'd attended the Meeting each Sunday. A dozen white-haired ladies sat near the front, the stalwarts of any church. Five or six women of about Tia's age came in together. They were crying, and they comforted one another. Judging from their stylish clothes, Claire assumed they were Tia's college friends.

"Look, Claire, over there," her father whispered, pointing with his chin. With surprise, Claire saw John D. Rockefeller Jr., the richest man in the world, it was said, and the president of the board of trustees of the medical institute that bore his family's name. He sat three-quarters of the way back, an empty place on each side of him like an invisible protective cordon. He was said to be shy and self-effacing. Cushioned within his exceptionally well-made suit, his bearing was humble. Head bowed, he appeared to be praying. He devoted his life to philanthropy to redeem the sins of his father, who'd destroyed his competitors to build the Standard Oil Trust—or so the rumors went.

Finally, Jamie arrived, with a large group. He was surrounded by Nick Catalano and others Claire recognized from the Institute. Dr. Rivers. Dr. Lind. Chief Nurse Brockett. David Hoskins, Sergei Oretsky. The group included others she didn't recognize, or recalled only from passing them in the hallways. The Institute group sat together, diagonally across the sanctuary from Claire and her father. Jamie met her gaze. She wished they were side by side.

Mr. Hallowell rose and introduced himself as the leader of the Meeting. He explained how the memorial was conducted, that anyone could rise and speak if the Spirit moved them.

To be moved by the Spirit. Most of the people in the Institute group fidgeted in discomfort.

Dr. Rivers, in dress uniform, rose, unfolded papers from his pocket, cleared his throat, and began to read from a formal speech, determined to follow his preconceived role regardless of what the circumstances required. "Dr. Lucretia Mott Stanton was a brilliant scientist and a credit to her profession. I was privileged to know her . . ."

From his tone, Claire judged that he was moved not by the Spirit but by bureaucratic responsibility. As the Meetinghouse became warm, Dr. Rivers methodically reviewed Tia's life, the loss of her parents to

the Spanish influenza in 1918, her scientific training, her many accomplishments, her exceptional efforts to bring the insights of a mycologist to the field of medical research. Claire gave up trying to follow
the details of his long narrative, delivered in a monotone. Finally he
sat down.

After a moment, a small, elderly woman sitting near Claire rose. "My
Tia," she said brightly, clutching her glasses in her hand. The woman's
eyes were a shiny, watery blue. "My Tia Stanton. Every year for five
years she helped us with the clothing drive for the poor. You never saw
such beautiful uptown clothes as the clothes that Tia brought." Tia's
college friends laughed self-consciously. "The Spirit moved within her.
Gratitude fills me for her presence here." She sat down.

A full minute seemed to pass, as the sunlight covered them. Then
David Hoskins rose. "I—well, Tia was the closest friend I ever had
in science. She had an extraordinary commitment to her peers . . ."
Claire sensed the painful effort that these words required from him.
The pain of his effort became a kind of pain inside her. "Her example
gave us all the will to move forward regardless of temporary setbacks."
Abruptly he sat down, losing his battle against tears.

Now one of the college friends rose. This young woman, wearing a
hat with a face veil and a sophisticated black suit, swaying slightly on
what must have been very high heels, looked like an elongated bird.
"Tia was the friend I relied on most," she said in a surprisingly frail,
light voice. "Whenever I had a problem . . ." The young woman spoke
on through tears, making Claire realize that the bird image was all
wrong, that this girl's appearance was a facade, just as maybe Tia's appearance had been a facade.

And so it went, speaker after speaker adding another element in
the portrait of a woman Claire had never really known. The words
washed over her. Claire felt somehow separate from them, isolated and
alone.

What was left of a life, when death came? Emily left behind a dozen small dresses, three pairs of shoes, the drawings she'd made of her apartment and of her baby brother. Little else. If Tia had been able to finish her work, another Emily might have survived. Claire saw a line between Emily and Tia, a kind of immortality that Tia achieved by working to save the lives of others, even though she'd been taken before her work was complete. Claire felt an inner urge to rise and speak, to express somehow what Tia's life meant—not in terms of solving problems or testing hypotheses or donating clothes to the poor, but in terms of saving children like Emily, or fathers like Edward Reese, and all of the individuals gathered here in the Meetinghouse.

At that moment, Mr. Hallowell stood. "Thank you, all of you. Please join us now for a reception in our fellowship hall."

Claire's desire to speak dissolved. Jamie rose and walked out. He'd told her that there'd be a receiving line. John D. Rockefeller Jr. stood and joined the line of the departing congregation.

"I don't want to stand on the receiving line," she said to her father.

"That's fine, dear," he replied, looking at her closely and with concern. Rutherford was worried. Claire seemed uncharacteristically passive. "You'll be seeing Jamie later anyway, won't you?" He wanted to make certain she'd be looked after.

"Yes. I just don't want to shake his hand."

He heard the pain in her voice. "I understand." Rutherford hadn't found much consolation in the Quaker service. He was raised in Roman Catholicism with a Croatian bent, and even though he wasn't a believer, he had to hand it to the church: once you sat through a funeral mass, listened to the choir and the prayers (even if they were in Latin and you didn't understand them), with the organ soaring at the beginning and the end, you wound up feeling better. With a pang he wondered what kind of funeral his dear granddaughter Emily had. He found himself loving and missing Emily without ever knowing her, and he didn't understand how or why. As he grew older, so much of life was becoming a mystery to him, his certainties dissolving.

Walking around those waiting on line, they reached the entry gallery in time to see Rockefeller holding both of Jamie's hands within his, as a minister might, and speaking words of reassurance. The tall entry doors of the Meetinghouse were thrown open to the sweet spring breeze. Nick Catalano joined Rockefeller, and they, too, shook hands and exchanged a few words.

To the boom of photographers' flashbulbs, Rockefeller went down the path and through the wrought-iron gate, looking neither left nor right. His waiting driver opened the back door of a black car, and Rockefeller slipped in. Thus the richest man in the world was whisked away, flashbulbs popping all the while. For once Claire saw the cameras from the other side. She felt sorry for him. How awful, to be always on view, guaranteed privacy only within the confines of a closely guarded estate or apartment.

"I need to get downtown," Rutherford said. "You okay here?"

She forced herself to smile for him. "Yes, Dad, I'll be fine. Don't worry. I'm just tired." How odd it felt, to find herself reassuring him about her well-being.

"All right then, we'll talk later." Again they quickly hugged, and he left.

Claire went to the reception room, plain and bare, its dull green paint peeling. The windows overlooked the courtyard that the school next door, Friends Seminary, used for recess. The students were on break now. Shouts, taunts, and the steady beat of a jump rope reached Claire as she went to the refreshment table. Lemonade and fruit punch were ladled out by several of the kindly white-haired ladies who'd been sitting near the front. The ladies also refilled the platters of cookies, oatmeal raisin and chocolate chip, by the look of them. Claire didn't feel like eating cookies. Sergei Oretsky stood before the cookies, seeming to study them, intent on choosing the right one.

Among the men in military uniforms and business suits talking in tight groups, Claire felt an urge to escape. To take Lucas for a walk across the island of Manhattan. To visit the Metropolitan Museum and lose herself amid the paintings of Rembrandt and Vermeer. She'd say good-bye to Jamie and then she'd slip away. He had to attend a memorial luncheon at the Institute for his and Tia's colleagues, but he would be coming to Grove Street afterward.

"A sad day." Nick Catalano stood beside her. She hadn't spoken to him since the evening at her father's. She felt an instinctive, visceral attraction toward him. His lean body, the bad-boy edge to his attitude, the blond hair and brown eyes. Six months ago, before becoming involved with Jamie, she would have acted on it, taken a chance, why not. Now she felt the need to maintain a distance from him. Maybe Nick felt a similar attraction and a similar need: he stood beside her rather than in front of her, so that they were facing the crowd without obviously being together, two strangers waiting for friends to arrive.

"Yes," she said simply. And yet . . . Jamie had told her about Nick's reaction at the morgue. Maybe he'd loved Tia, or had some understanding with her. Claire owed Nick kindness today. Where to begin? "Did you think about standing up to talk?"

"No, I'm not public about things. Memories, I mean." He laughed ruefully. "Feelings."

"I understand."

"All this seems a little foreign."

"Yes, it does."

"Left me wishing for communion and the collection plate, and the incense."

Now it was Claire's turn to laugh ruefully, the Episcopal prayers for the dead still running through her mind. "I agree."

"Is your father still here? I saw him sitting next to you."

"No, he had to get to his office."

"I enjoyed meeting him, that night. After the Chinese costume party."

"He's very hospitable." Claire remembered that night, of course. Remembered dropping Nick off at the Institute, and how they'd commented on the light visible in Tia's lab. Had Nick gone to visit her? Claire paused, trying to reach for the proper words to approach him, and to console him if that was what he needed. "Look, Nick, I know you and Tia were friends. I want to say, I'm sorry for your loss."

He was silent for a few beats too long. Then he said gruffly, "Don't worry. Thank you. What I mean is . . ." He seemed on the verge of saying more, of making a confession. Claire felt an urge to touch him on the shoulder to encourage him, and simultaneously she sensed him pulling back from her. "Well, I'm trying to make sure Jamie's okay." They caught a glimpse of Jamie through the crowd. He was holding the hands of a frail, elderly woman who leaned toward him, as if she couldn't support her own weight. "I'm sure you are, too. That's what's important now. To think about the people who are still alive. Don't you agree?"

"I—" But before she could respond, Dr. Rivers came over and, ignoring Claire, pulled Nick into a private conversation. A standard photograph in wartime: men in military uniforms whispering to each other, pursuing their own priorities as they determine the fates of millions.

She was ready to leave. Yes, she would go to the Metropolitan Museum. She hadn't been in years. She longed to go. She wanted to visit her favorite Rembrandt portrait, *Woman with a Pink*. A pink was a carnation, a symbol of love and fidelity. Of marriage. Claire wanted to give a pink to Jamie. The woman in the painting seemed, to Claire, to stare at the viewer, and her gaze riveted Claire. What was the woman thinking as she held her pink carnation?

Claire slipped away, moving toward the perimeter of the crowd. Jamie was still greeting people on the receiving line, and she didn't want to push her way through to him. She couldn't leave without saying good-bye to him, but she had to get away. She'd take a walk in Stuyvesant Square, she resolved, and then return to say good-bye.

Claire didn't know that Jamie had been surreptitiously tracking her presence despite his receiving-line duties. As he spotted her moving through the crowd, he found himself yet again spellbound: she was the most striking woman he'd ever encountered. He wanted to follow her, but he couldn't: Jenny Murphy, the stout, red-haired Irishwoman who cleaned the lab according to Tia's eccentric specifications, was gripping his sleeve and reminiscing about the time Tia asked her, as a special favor. . . . He couldn't bear to listen. In the past half hour, he'd heard more stories about Tia than he could process. He craved these stories, but he was overwhelmed. He pretended to listen to Jenny, then laughed when she laughed. Her laughter was big and deep. Suddenly Jenny was crying. Now he was consoling someone who'd come here to console him. This happened over and over. Claire was lost to his view.

Claire reached the doorway and stepped outside onto the flagstone path and into the heady scent of lilacs. Breathing deeply, she walked down the path. The news photographers had departed; John D. Rockefeller Jr. had been their big catch for the day.

"Mrs. Shipley?" a man called from behind her. "Mrs. Shipley, isn't it?" the man called again.

She turned. A man pushed his way through the crowd to catch up with her. He appeared about her age and was of moderate height. His hair was dark, thick, and carefully groomed. He was well built and square shouldered, with the appearance of an athlete in top shape. He wore a finely cut, carefully pressed dark blue pinstriped suit with a red and blue bow tie. He held a panama hat. His appearance touched on the foppish. He clasped her right hand in both of his and greeted her like a long-lost friend, although she couldn't place him.

"How wonderful to see you again, even on this sad occasion. Are you heading out? Me, too." He spoke a bit too loudly, as if for the benefit of those standing nearby. "Whatever have you been doing with yourself?" Putting on his hat, he took her arm and began leading her down the path toward the front gate.

Ordinarily Claire would shake such a person off and demand an explanation, but her senses had been dulled and she could only look at this man in surprise.

"I was hoping to find you here today," he announced as they passed, just outside the front gates, a group of six men in dark suits leaning toward one another in a circle, as if sharing secrets. The group was especially noteworthy because none of the men was in uniform. What were they discussing? The stock market? This year's prospects for the New York Yankees or the Brooklyn Dodgers? The death of Tia Stanton?

Once they were on the city sidewalk, Claire gathered her strength. "You'd better explain yourself or I'm liable to make a scene."

"Forgive me." He dropped her arm. "Listeners all around, I've noticed." He glanced back at the men in their clutch. "Would you walk with me in the square for five minutes? I'd like to speak to you."

"I don't mean to sound like a prude, but I don't generally walk with men I don't know, even if they claim to know me."

"Forgive me again." He put a hand over his heart. "Andrew Barnett. Andy. Please don't shake my hand. I'd like to maintain the pretense that we've met before."

"Why?"

He laughed. "I do beg your pardon, Mrs. Shipley." He gave a half-bow. "I'm fairly new at my job, and I'm afraid I'm still not especially good at it." He said this with a full measure of self-confidence. "It's not very much like the movies, I've discovered."

"I shouldn't think so. Not much is. What's your new job?"

He evaluated the question. "I'd appreciate a few minutes of your time, without having to resort to coercion."

"You want to tell me your intentions before we contemplate coercion?"

"I understand your feelings and possibly I can assuage them by saying that your son is growing into quite a handsome boy. Seems to enjoy school, too. His teachers like him, from what I understand. Too bad about that bout with scarlet fever last year. All too common, alas.

How curious that attempts to cure scarlet fever, among other fevers, are exactly what brought us together today."

She stared at him. He looked into the distance. A car horn honked and honked again. The sound hurt her ears. She felt pressure behind her eyes, a headache coming on.

"This neighborhood is nice, isn't it?" he said.

In the park, the branches arched over to touch the grass. The cherry and crab apple trees were just past. Pink and white blossoms blown off the trees lay in a carpet upon the lawns and walkways. In the noontime sunlight, the fountains threw flashing rainbows into the air.

"I'll walk with you, Mr. Barnett."

"Thank you. Thank you very much."

And so they began to walk through an exquisite late-spring day. A light breeze blew around them. Their footsteps crushed the pink flower petals that covered their path. The petals clung to the soles of their shoes. Their shoes were slippery with flower petals. The implied threat against Charlie gave Claire a heightened sense of reality. The edges of the leaves looked razor sharp, cutting at her eyes. The birdsong exploded in her ears. She tried to stay calm.

"Are you from New York, Mr. Barnett?"

"Alas, no."

"Whereabouts, then?"

"I grew up in Chicago, but I live in California now. Or at least I did. Palo Alto."

"Stanford."

"Indeed. I was a professor of economics at Stanford until, well, until recently."

"Until you got your new job. The one which is nothing like the movies."

"Exactly." He sounded grateful for her understanding.

Claire felt far distant from him, as if she were staring at him through the opposite end of a telescope. She breathed deeply. She'd heard rumors about upper-level professors being recruited for espionage work. To Claire, professors didn't seem like the most competent or promising candidates, but apparently those in charge, products of the Ivy League and the social elite themselves, tended to trust their own.

"I'm withholding judgment on you, Mr. Barnett."

"And I on you. Since I already know a good deal about you, perhaps it's fair to tell you that until winter break, I was teaching economics at Stanford. I'm an expert in the theory of the automatic reabsorption of displaced labor, particularly in regard to issues of technological progress. Well, that seems like a long time ago," he said wistfully. "I was tapped, I suppose is the way to describe it, to go to Washington to do some government work."

Just as she suspected. "Sounds better than the infantry. Or a ship in the Pacific."

"My thoughts exactly, Mrs. Shipley. I gladly accepted this offer to do government work. I didn't think the Pacific would suit me. Too damp. Nor the deserts of North Africa. Too dry. I'm glad we understand each other. Anyway, after a pitifully small amount of training and a great deal of bureaucratic rigmarole, I wound up under the jurisdiction of the Office of Scientific Research and Development."

Jamie's department, she realized—although Jamie had never mentioned this man to her. "That must be interesting," she said blandly.

"In fact, extremely interesting. A new challenge every day. I believe that would be many people's definition of an interesting job. I've often thought that a job like yours, for example, would achieve the standard of interesting."

She said nothing. They crossed Second Avenue, which divided Stuyvesant Square. The park's gardens smelled of rich, churned-up soil. Claire imagined Tia here, gathering samples for her jam jars. Tulips burst in colors of apricot and white.

"I had lunch with Tia Stanton once, but I can't say I knew her well," he mused. "She was quite an unusual personality, that much I recognized. A counterintuitive type: vivacious, elegant, and spending her nights with mold. I'm here to look into her death from a more . . . *private* perspective than the police can manage."

He seemed to expect a reply from Claire. "Indeed."

"You see, Mrs. Shipley, her work took her into confidential areas. As you probably know from Lieutenant Stanton." This was said with a bit of a leer, an attempt to suggest that he did, in fact, know everything about her. "The death of a person working in confidential areas is a very serious matter."

This time Claire said nothing.

"It's a curious situation. No doubt the police are correct and she had an accident. But she was a rather careful person in most ways. At least according to her friends and family—although we must keep in mind that friends and family don't always know everything there is to know about a person. Sometimes friends and family are the *least* likely to know what's most important about a person. Especially when suicide, for example, is the cause of death. The suicide of someone involved in government work is taken extremely seriously."

"Tia Stanton didn't commit suicide," Claire said.

"What makes you say that?" he asked lightly.

Only her own wish, she realized. Her desire to spare Jamie and assuage her guilt.

They continued walking. Barnett didn't press her for a response, but he didn't speak for a full minute. Then: "Did you know, my dear, that Norway was overrun with Nazi spies before the invasion? They entered the country quite legally, on tourist visas. Bird-watchers, fjord-admirers, even absentminded professors, I daresay. All keeping their heads down and waiting for the proper moment to strike. Of course with the Bund so popular right here in New York City, foreign operatives are probably completely unnecessary."

Was he implying that Tia was murdered?

"Tia Stanton was almost a sister-in-law to you, wasn't she? Did she seem despondent? Did she have boyfriend troubles? Were there new people in her life, people who might have been trying to blackmail her? You must have come to know her well. And from a perspective outside her usual circle of acquaintances."

"I didn't know her well at all," Claire said, her guilt, and her anger at herself, returning in full force. Could she have stopped Tia's death, if she'd just made some effort? She'd been so wrapped up in Jamie, in Charlie, in work, she hadn't taken the time to look beyond her own interests and needs.

"Surely you have some insight."

"None."

She wanted to get away from this man. Immediately. What did she know of Andrew Barnett? Nothing. How could she know he was who he purported to be? She couldn't. He might be working for any number of people. He said he'd spoken to Tia's friends and family, but she had only his word for that.

"Mr. Barnett, I don't know who you are, you've shown me no identification, and I feel no requirement to answer your questions."

He thought about this. "Well," he said with patient resignation, "you may feel differently as time passes. In fact I'm sure you will. Do please remember that anyone, anyone at all, could be a Fifth Columnist. The person we least suspect. Henry Luce himself. That's a joke, of course." He smirked at his fine sense of humor. "At any rate, I need to be moving along. I have a train to catch. But if you change your mind and want to talk, give me a call, would you?"

"I have nothing to talk about."

"Well, well, you never know." Taking from his inside jacket pocket a silver, engraved cardholder, he gave her his card, a fine piece of vellum. It listed only his name and a phone number in Washington.

"So glad to have met you, Mrs. Shipley. Seeing as I know so much about you already. Perhaps one day soon I'll have an opportunity to

meet your fascinating father. Or take your adorable dog for a walk."
He put his hand out for her to shake, and she followed through. She
was dressed formally and wore gloves, so she didn't have to feel his
skin against hers. "I do hope we'll meet again under happier circumstances. Good-bye." He headed off, presumably to hail a taxi to Penn
Station.

Claire stood at the corner, feeling a growing sense of rage, at Barnett and at herself. Rage mixed with sorrow, for the loss of Tia, for
Emily, for Jamie's pain. Claire recalled the look on Tia's face as she
sampled the miniature chocolate éclairs, that momentary expression
of bliss.

She turned back. Hoping to catch a glimpse of Jamie, she studied
the crowd emerging from the Meetinghouse. She wanted to reassure
herself of his love, reassure herself that she had a place in his life. She
didn't see him. Her strength seemed to drain away. She needed to sit
down. She didn't want to return to the crowded, overheated reception
room until she'd steadied herself.

Out of her gaze, Nick Catalano stood just inside the Meetinghouse doorway. He'd been there for several minutes, watching her. He
hoped Barnett hadn't upset her. Nick wished he'd been more . . . what?
Forthcoming, in their earlier conversation. But Rivers had called for
his attention, and then Claire had disappeared.

Nick would never know what, if anything, might have happened
between him and Tia. In their first approaches, he'd found her a little
intimidating. He was more accustomed to girls who were just looking for fun, or who at least hid their true desires beneath a veneer
of lightheartedness. Tia was, in fact, the sort of woman he'd always
imagined spending his life with. A true equal. But when faced with
her actual self, he'd had trouble talking to her about anything besides
work. He was acutely aware that she was from a different world, her
father a banker, her grandfather a professor. The difference in their
backgrounds had made him hesitant, a feeling that was unfamiliar to

him, especially in regard to women. And yet . . . in an ideal world, he imagined a kind of perfect harmony between them. A perfect love. This fantasy was what made him break down and weep in front of Jamie at the morgue.

"Very nice cookies, Catalano." Sergei Oretsky was beside him. "Have you tried? Here, have one." Oretsky offered him a small plate of oatmeal cookies.

Nick wondered, Am I looking so forlorn, standing here alone at the doorway, that Oretsky felt compelled to provide companionship? Probably so.

"Mademoiselle Stanton adored cookies. Did you know?"

"Yes, I did know," Nick said, although he'd never had the opportunity to learn this about Tia.

Outside, another man watched Claire Shipley. This man leaned against the gates of the park, smoking a cigarette. His funeral suit was rumpled and shiny at the elbows but presentable enough. He and his suit had never yet been thrown out of a funeral. Marcus Kreindler, New York City detective. He'd spotted Claire Shipley earlier, during the memorial service. He recognized her from a photo on James Stanton's desk in his residence rooms. When he spotted the photo, he'd asked Stanton who she was. Stanton had explained with an enthusiasm that made him seem young and in love—even though he was, what, thirty-eight years old. Kreindler remembered his own young-and-in-love days, almost forty years ago. Agnes. He felt a surge just thinking about that time. They were in love still.

Anyway, he saw the photograph, and lo and behold, here was Claire Shipley in front of him, tall, slim, brown hair in a smart wave, pale and chic in a stark, working-girl sort of way.

He bore a grudge, he was the first to admit. Not against poor Claire Shipley, who seemed disoriented and had wisely chosen to return to the park and find a bench in the sun to rest on. No, his grudge was against the imbecile who'd tormented her. Andrew Barnett. He made sure Barnett noticed him in the church. Let him know that somebody was looking over his shoulder; no harm was done and possibly a lot of good. As of yesterday, Kreindler was officially off this case. The government had taken over. The government would insist on a public ruling of accidental death, to stop a police investigation that might delve into confidential areas. Then Barnett would do his own investigation to try to figure out what had really happened.

Of course a ruling of accidental death might even be correct. Except that Kreindler was haunted by those footprints on the path. He had to bide his time, he knew. Keep his eyes open, stay out of trouble. He found a bench from which he could watch the woman, far enough away so that she wouldn't particularly notice him. He took a bag of peanuts out of his jacket pocket, ate some, threw a few to the squirrels.

After about ten minutes, the woman seemed to get a grip on herself. She took out her compact, checked her makeup. Reapplied her lipstick, always a good sign in a woman who'd experienced a shock, in Kreindler's view. She stood. A striking physique, if a bit boyish for his taste, but still. She smoothed her hair. Seemed to take a deep breath. Very pretty. She walked back into the Meetinghouse.

Kreindler was curious as to why, of all the people Barnett might have approached after the funeral, she was the one he sought out.

CHAPTER FOURTEEN

I'll just bugger off for a while then, James," said David Hoskins in the lab. "Give you some time to yourself." He put his hand on Jamie's shoulder. "You need to talk, just come and find me."

David was close to tears, Jamie could see that, but David offered his support without asking for any in return. That alone felt like a gift. Jamie didn't have to confide his feelings to David to know that David understood and offered him comfort.

"Thank you, David." Jamie hoped the simple phrase expressed the extent of what he felt. Before today, they'd always been *Stanton* and *Hoskins* to each other. The switch to first names created an intimacy that Jamie appreciated. It was, he reflected, like the move from *vous* to *tu* in French, or *Sie* to *du* in German. What made him suddenly think of that? he wondered. In the past few days, strange facts had been coming into his mind, things he hadn't thought about in years.

"Lovely day, at least." David traded his lab coat for a suit jacket and hat. "She would have enjoyed that."

The Institute's memorial luncheon had ended an hour before. Jamie had wandered the grounds by himself afterward. Such a rush of events and people passing before him these past days: he needed time to catch up with himself. The gardens were in full bloom. The plane trees were coming into their glory overhead. Remembering the years they'd walked these grounds together, he'd sensed Tia all around him. He'd finally come here, to Tia's lab, the place where she'd felt most at home.

Leaving, David shut the door behind him. Jamie was alone. But Tia was still with him. Not a ghost—he didn't hold with any of that. But he continued to have a kind of spiritual sense of her, that she was in the next room, testing soil samples. He strode through the penicillin room into what he'd come to think of as the cousins' room, but of course she wasn't there. And yet, everything was in place, as if she would return in just a moment. A cut-crystal vase, their mother's, sat on the table, filled with white, fallen tulips. He remembered his mother filling that vase with daffodils for the dining table of their home on Delancey Place.

The time was going on five o'clock. The room, although facing north, was bright with natural light. Jamie stood before the long windows, to see where the light was coming from. Sunlight was reflecting off the windows of the New York Hospital, several blocks north, and flooding the lab. This light had a peculiar quality, brilliant but diffuse, without a glare. Again Jamie had the eerie sensation that Tia had simply stepped out to get a cup of coffee. She'd soon be back. He only had to wait for her.

Stop, he told himself. She wouldn't be coming back. When he forced himself to face up to this stark truth, however, he felt that he'd betrayed her: by trying to accept that she was gone, he'd be guaranteeing it.

Of course she hadn't killed herself. Suicide was out of the question. She'd had an accident. Accidents came out of nowhere. Her death was a chance event. That was the definition of an accident, wasn't it? What was the Latin derivation? He'd taken Latin in school. *Accidens*. From *accidere*, to fall. He reeled at the connection. Why was he even remembering such things?

One of his colleagues at the luncheon, he didn't know who, had indulged a doctor's trick and injected hothouse cherry tomatoes with vodka, creating portable Bloody Marys. He hadn't been eating properly, and at the luncheon, he'd had more of those cherry tomatoes than he should have. He was beginning to feel light-headed and sick. He needed some solid food.

He sat down to pull himself together. He studied the room. What would happen to these soil samples, lining the walls in floor-to-ceiling shelves that Tia had custom-designed with the Institute carpenter? At the luncheon there was talk of Jake Lind taking over here, at least for the duration of the war. David Hoskins was too knowledgeable about penicillin to be working on the so-called cousins. Hoskins was needed elsewhere. Lind had a heart murmur and had been rejected by the military, so he'd be sticking around, making him the logical choice to continue Tia's work. Jamie couldn't bear the idea of these soil samples going untested, Tia's life work consigned to a trash heap.

He'd already asked Beth, her college roommate, to take care of Tia's small apartment, have the contents appraised for taxes, keep what she and Tia's friends wanted, and give the rest to charity. This was an imposition, he knew, but Beth's husband had recently signed up for the military, and Beth was on her own. Nowadays people left behind on the home front regarded such impositions as gifts: the gift of being useful. Jamie knew he could trust Beth.

The lab, however, was his responsibility, and his duty, to keep and preserve as best he could. He got up and went to Tia's bench, as it was called by scientists, the table where she'd been doing her most recent work. The current notebook was closed, the sample jars neatly waiting. Tia was organized and methodical. He opened the notebook to see her handwriting. To read at random. To hear her voice through her words.

As he paged through, seeing the failure of this or that substance, he remembered her talking about a sample she'd been having some success with. He should have been thinking of that first, he chastised himself, not recalling it just now. He'd had so much on his mind, he hadn't focused.

In his imagination, he placed himself at what turned out to be their last lunch together. The last time he saw her. A picnic on the lawn, during one of those warm spring days before the leaves are out but when the daffodils are already blooming and you want to be basking in the warmth. So there they were, outside on the lawn with the sun glaring in his eyes and no shade anywhere because the trees were still bare of leaves. Tia was laughing at him as he explained his discomfort to her. They had to get up; he couldn't stand the glare anymore. Finally they found a bench where they could sit with their backs to the sun.

And then Tia began to talk about her hints of success with a new substance. It was produced by a mold that she'd collected in the woods near their grandparents' house. This link to their childhood was too good to be true, she admitted, but there it was, and it made her happy. They both knew that keeping track of where a sample was collected was basically a way to keep the samples organized. Granted, the location could help tell you what type of food the mold might like to eat, and what range of temperatures and sunlight it had adapted to, but once you found a substance that actually worked, you didn't need to go back to the same location and dig up an entire truckload of soil to cart to your lab. No, you simply needed to grow the mold in the lab, and then analyze and develop the antibacterial mechanisms involved.

This substance from the Crum woods, Tia said, was easy to produce. In test tubes, the substance worked against gram-positive and gram-negative bacteria. It controlled infectious agents that penicillin missed and worked better on the ones penicillin did fight. She was in the process of testing the substance on mice. Thus far, these tests had been successful. Very much so. But of course the substance could lead to a dead end, just like all the rest. It could turn out to be highly toxic, with serious side effects in humans. It could cause allergic reactions, anaphylactic shock. She'd repeated this, about the dead end, as if she were trying to convince herself. As if she were forcing herself to hold back her enthusiasm.

The substance had a number. That's how she talked about it at their lunch. By the number. Tia was meticulous in her record keeping. If he could remember the number, he'd find everything, and her work could continue.

The number. Again he placed himself at that picnic. She'd been eating a chicken salad sandwich. He couldn't tolerate chicken salad, after the daily lunches in Washington. He had ham and cheese. The number. It was in the mid-six hundreds—he remembered being struck by the fact that she'd tested well over six hundred substances. Her voice. He had to hear her voice. He was sitting there beside her, listening to her voice.

"Wait till you see it, Jamie. It's such a beautiful blue."

"Tia, you know the color doesn't matter."

She was laughing. "You're going to be very surprised."

"I guess I will be."

"I know I shouldn't say this, Jamie, but 642 could be what we've been looking for."

There it was: 642. *What we've been looking for.*

He searched through her notebook. Nothing about 642. He started again, at the first page. Leafing through more quickly now. Nothing.

Then he saw: pages had been cut out. Probably with a razor. He ran his index finger down the sharp edges.

He strode over to the shelves to find the original soil sample. Meticulous, she always was. 640, 641, 643, 644. Sample 642 was gone. He opened the incubator. The refrigerator. He went through the stack of old notebooks on the counter. His search had to be as meticulous as her work. He couldn't give up. There had to be something. Something left behind. Everything else was in perfect order. This made the absence clearer.

What he found in the end was what he started with: nothing. Someone had gotten here before him.

"Jamie, there you are."

His best friend, Nick. Come to find him. Jamie's friends and colleagues were taking too much care of him.

"We got worried that you had a few too many of those bite-size
Bloody Marys. Organized a search party to find you. Wouldn't want
you to stumble—" Nick stopped, realizing what he was about to say.

"I'm all right," Jamie said. Should he tell Nick what he'd discovered? Sound the alarm, accusations flying? He felt too tired, and too
drunk, he now realized, to know what to do. He looked around. He'd
wreaked minor havoc during his search.

"So, uh, you going to stay here for a while?" Nick asked.

Jamie caught Nick surveying the room, no doubt wondering about
the open incubator, the notebooks tossed about.

"Just a few minutes. I've got to get downtown. Dinner with Claire.
I'll be all right, Nick. Really."

"Okay." Nick held up his hands, palms outward, as if to say, I'll accept that, I'll make myself scarce. "I'm here if you need me."

"Thanks. I appreciate it."

Still Nick didn't leave, obviously debating the right course.

"I've got someplace to go, I'll be fine, Nick." Then Jamie realized:
maybe Nick was the one who needed reassurance. Maybe Jamie had
been remiss in not thinking more about his friend and probing whatever understanding Nick might have had with Tia. "Nick, you sure
you're okay?"

Nick smiled thinly. "Now is not the time for you to start worrying
about me."

"I'm happy to worry about you. Any time."

"I've got work to do," Nick said. "Fills all the empty places, doesn't
it." Nick wasn't asking a question, and Jamie understood what he
meant. Nick turned and left.

Jamie listened to Nick's footsteps retreating. Heard the outer door
open and close.

He was alone once more.

At midnight, Claire rested her head upon the curve of Jamie's shoulder after they'd made love. She stretched her legs against his and kissed the underside of his jaw. She knew he couldn't escape the pain of Tia's death, but she wanted to show him the reasons for pushing on. When he'd arrived in the early evening, she'd made dinner and served it outside, in the garden. Charlie was at Ben's for the night, a treat all-around. Finally they'd talked about the events of earlier that day, and about memories of Tia. Claire didn't tell him about Barnett's approach to her; she didn't want to burden him, and besides, she could tell him later, if Barnett bothered her again. Their lovemaking was long and quiet.

Jamie massaged the back of her neck. Smoothed his hand down her spine. Jamie loved this room. He loved the way the moonlight came through the long windows, illuminating her hair, her back, as she lay stretched out upon him. This room, this woman . . . he felt safe here, at peace, defenses unnecessary. He wanted to let himself drift into sleep.

But he couldn't. He had a mental list of pressing matters he needed to discuss with Claire. What he'd discovered at the lab. The extended trip he would embark on tomorrow, which he hadn't focused on until this evening. His thoughts about their future, his and Claire's. He didn't want their future to be an item on a list, but it was. He was having trouble summoning the energy to begin. To begin meant bringing tomorrow into this room, instead of simply being here, in the moment, the two of them alone in all the world.

"I'm going away," he said finally.

"You've been away before," she said, lifting her head from his shoulder only a little, so that he could hear her.

She sounded dreamy. He didn't want to wake her from her dream.

"We'll celebrate your return," she said, "in the usual way." She pushed more closely against him, although he'd thought she was as close as anyone could be to another. He tightened his arms around her, even though he was already holding her tight.

"This is different," he said. "I could be away for a long time." For now, he'd be traveling from lab to lab across the country. He didn't want to tell Claire that when enough penicillin was available, he'd go overseas for clinical field trials, following the front lines, wherever they were. He wanted to spare her that worry. "I'll write to you. I'll try to get an address for you to write to me. With luck, I'll be passing through New York now and then, but I just don't know. And you'll be traveling, too, I suppose."

"Yes."

Claire pushed herself up on her elbows, upon his chest. She gazed into his face.

No one had ever looked at him that way, with such frankness, with such love. Her expression was clear to him in the moonlight.

"Where are you going?" she asked.

"I can't say. I mean, I'm not allowed to say. It's classified." This was too much now, the look on her face. He couldn't tolerate it, when he might not see her again for weeks or months. He separated from her and sat at the edge of the bed. She leaned against his back, put her arms around his neck.

Their moment of seclusion from the outside world was gone. He would have no time to catch up with himself, no time to mourn, no time to learn what had actually happened to Tia. In this way, he was a soldier, too. He would have to do his mourning on airplanes and trains, at lab benches and in hospital wards and during endless meetings. His sister's death was part of the war, too, although that was no consolation. Was it a consolation for anyone, that their sisters or brothers, husbands or wives, sons or daughters, died in the cause of the war?

He had to tell Claire about the substance missing from Tia's lab. He had to tell someone, and she was the person he trusted most. But he needed time to consider. His mind was teeming with implications. Had someone, knowing Tia was dead, gone to the lab and taken this one substance and no other? Or had someone pushed Tia from that path, and then gone to take it? Not much effort would have been necessary, to push her. Surprise was all that was needed. One moment, she would be there. The next moment, she would be gone. No drama at all. He breathed in sharply.

"What is it?" Claire said, her face pressed against the back of his shoulder.

He pulled her arms around him. He didn't want to look at her while he told her. He'd lose control if he looked at her. He couldn't let that happen. Not now, not about this, not when he'd be leaving in the morning. She said nothing, waiting for him.

No, he decided. He wouldn't add his suspicion of Tia's murder to their last evening together. He had to organize his thoughts first, make certain he wasn't allowing himself to be pulled into a web of paranoia. He didn't like withholding his suspicions from Claire, but he had to be more sure of himself before he endorsed the notion by discussing it.

He disengaged from her again, removing her arms from his body as gently as he could. He stood at the windows, moonlight surrounding him. To Claire, he was silhouetted in the moonlight.

He couldn't predict the future. He could only try to make his small corner of the world secure. There was no statute of limitations on murder. That was the law, right? He needed to get one or maybe even two full nights of sleep, so that he could be certain he was being rational. He wanted the hours he and Claire had left together to be about each other.

Looking out the window, looking into the moonlight, he said, "I have something for you." He turned to the chair where he'd piled his clothes.

"What is it?"

"A gift." He rummaged among the clothes, found his shirt, took from its pocket a carefully folded handkerchief. "It's the engagement ring my father gave my mother. I want you to have it. To keep you company while I'm away. I'll feel better knowing it's safe on your finger. It'll protect you." That was a ridiculous thing to say, he realized, but he meant it. "If you ever need protection."

Had he kept the ring there, in his shirt pocket, over his aching heart, all evening? Claire wondered. Through dinner, dessert, and coffee, through Lucas's walk on Hudson Street to Morton and back on Bedford Street? She felt a pressure in her chest, what she could only describe as an ache of her own heart. Her being reached out to him. She pulled him close even though she didn't move.

He sat beside her on the bed. He made a joke, even as he tried not to cry. "This way, you won't forget me while I'm away." Now he was crying. For Tia, for Claire, for the war that was transforming their lives and the lives of everyone he knew.

"I'll never forget you."

She sounded close to tears, too, as she caressed his hair and consoled him.

He took her left hand, placed the ring upon her finger. "I can't see the future," he said. He was unhinged by a sense that he wouldn't survive the war. "But at least you'll have this." He turned and they kissed, bodies intertwined. "Someday, I hope, we'll get married." He couldn't manage to bring himself to ask a question that would have a yes or no answer. Besides, he didn't need to ask the question to know what her answer would be.

"I know we will," she said.

She placed her hand upon him, brought him to life once more.

CHAPTER FIFTEEN

⁓

A re you finished?" growled Vannevar Bush, his voice echoing against the marble rotunda of the Carnegie Institution in Washington, D.C. He wielded his pipe like a weapon, cutting it through the air to express his displeasure.

In order to endow his small frame with the classical monumentality of the space around him, Claire had posed him leaning over the balustrade of the rotunda's wide circular staircase. She stood below on the ground floor, lucky to have found an empty spot. A haphazard collection of desks, partitions, and filing cabinets filled the rotunda. Telephone and electric lines crisscrossed the marble floor. More than a dozen young men in suits, their ties loosened in the heat, worked around her. Soft light filtered through the skylight, however, and she created the illusion that Bush was alone. To capture the details, she used a large-format Linhof camera on a tripod. She was careful to avoid reflections on his thick glasses.

"No, I'm not finished," she growled back, trying to bring out his fierceness. She didn't want a smiling, unctuous, standardized portrait. She wanted to capture who he really was and reveal the force and energy driving him to achieve his goals.

"I've had enough."

"Too bad."

"I'll walk away."

"You want your backside in *Life* magazine?"

His expression became especially nasty, and she knew she had the shot she wanted. "Finished. In this location, at least."

"Good. Come up to my office, I want to talk to you," he ordered.

"Yes, I do believe your office is next on my list."

In his wood-paneled office, Vannevar (rhymed with *beaver*, according to the magazine's research department) Bush sat at the far end of a long conference table. He probably thought the long table made him look intimidating. To Claire, it made him even smaller. She had to resist the urge to make fun of his pretensions. As usual, the magazine was trying to create an American hero. Vannevar Bush, president of the Carnegie Institution. Renowned engineer from MIT. Now he led the government's innocuously named Office of Scientific Research and Development. Claire knew his concealed wartime portfolio by rumor only: radar, penicillin, new weapons of staggering force.

Reviewing and signing documents, he worked while she worked. This assignment was personal, too, because he was Jamie's boss. After she'd taken a half-dozen shots, Bush said, "Stop what you're doing and have coffee with me."

"Not a very appealing invitation."

"Mrs. Shipley, would you care to join me for coffee?"

Her assignment was simply a portrait, and she had more than enough coverage. "Why yes, thank you. How kind of you to ask."

Ordering his secretary to see to the coffee, he led Claire onto a balcony overlooking a lush garden, rhododendrons in bloom, peonies coming on, beds of snapdragon and iris in a cacophony of color. The sky was deep blue. The air smelled sweet. Closely planted trees, dense with leaves, blocked the view of the city. The buzzing of insects provided the only noise.

They sat on cushioned chairs at a glass and cast-iron table. A striped awning protected them from the sun. As Claire looked around, she suspected that Washington must be filled with such hidden gardens, the enclaves of the powerful. This garden was completely separate

from everyday life. From her everyday life, at least. Working here, seeing this classical edifice and glorious garden day after day, you could
end up with a warped view of the world. Lose sight of what life was
like for people like her and Charlie, Maritza and her family, the common citizens you were supposedly trying to aid and protect.

The secretary brought a formal coffee service and cookies on a silver tray. Bush poured. Claire added cream, took a sip. The coffee was
strong and full flavored. In the nation outside these walls, good coffee
was hard to find. Price controls were now in effect, shortages were
rampant. Claire and Charlie counted among their most prized possessions their yellow ration books, filled with coupons, issued by the
Office of Price Administration. As a gift, her father had given her a
purple suede pouch, embossed RATION BOOKS, to store and protect
them. Charlie and her father had planted a victory garden on the Fifth
Avenue terrace. They were growing tomatoes, spinach, and carrots.

"Sugar?" Bush offered, gesturing to the sugar bowl filled to the top,
almost overflowing. His gesture indicated that she could have as much
as she wanted. At home, they carefully limited the sugar they used—
when they could buy sugar. Sugarcane was used to make explosives,
and sugar was strictly rationed.

"No, thank you." Claire didn't take sugar in her coffee anyway.

"Since I'm making an effort to be polite, I'll tell you that I'm glad
Harry Luce sent you for this assignment. I wanted to meet you."

"Why?"

"You did a fine story on penicillin a while back."

"That story never ran."

"No, but I was fortunate enough to see the—what do you call it,
the mock-up? The layout?"

"Close enough." She'd never heard of an outsider seeing the layout
before a story ran.

"Impressive. So impressive I told Harry it couldn't be published.
It gave away too much. And to make matters worse, the patient dies.

How does that make the government look, backing a secret project in which the goddamned patient dies right in the pages of *Life* magazine? Even though you know and I know that with a project like this, you're bound to lose a few along the way." He gave an unpleasant laugh. Claire steeled her face to impassivity. "However, not too long ago Harry telephoned with an intriguing idea."

He waited for her to respond. She gave in. "Did he? Mr. Luce didn't mention anything to me."

"No, we decided, or rather I decided, that I was the one to do the mentioning. Once I'd had a chance to meet you. To evaluate you. Although he had every confidence that I would find you—how shall I put this?—trustworthy."

She continued to sip her coffee. She studied a white butterfly flitting through the garden. It met up with another, and they became a team, flying in tandem, one above, one below, switching places, back and forth in an airborne dance. If Bush was trying to throw her off balance, she wouldn't let him. She wouldn't give him the satisfaction. She said nothing.

"Let's not waste any more time, Mrs. Shipley." His abruptness told her that she'd played him correctly. "Harry felt, and I happen to agree, that the government's program to develop penicillin needs to be documented. At some point in the future, the brilliance and heroism of the men and women involved must be revealed and celebrated. Scientists and businessmen working together to bring this life-saving medication to our selfless troops. A credit to our great nation. At least that's how Harry sees it. And as he sees it, so will the country. You did such a terrific job with the test story," this said with heavy irony, a bid to downgrade her, "that when Harry proposed you for the job, I happily concurred. Of course the story won't be told until, well"—no one, not even Vannevar Bush, could foresee the end of the war—"until the time is right. But when the story can be told, Harry will have exclusive rights for his magazines, and everyone on the project will receive the recognition he, or she, deserves. I can't guarantee that the commercial companies will welcome you with open arms, but I wouldn't be surprised if they succumb to the temptation of *Life* magazine. At any rate, I've made similar arrangements for a number of my projects, and it works out well. When the right people are involved."

So Luce had followed through on her meeting with him. And yet she sensed something was not quite right. The attempt to bribe her with good coffee and unlimited sugar. Bush's impatience, out of proportion to the context. Something else had to be at stake.

"Of course you'll need to pass a security check before you can work for me."

"And vice versa."

"I beg your pardon?"

"You and Mr. Luce may have devised this project, but I'm not sure I'm signing on to it."

"Sounds like a damn good opportunity to me."

"Well, you would see it that way, wouldn't you?"

He sighed, showing how put-upon he was. "Have some shortbread cookies, Mrs. Shipley. A personal favorite of mine."

"Thank you." She took a cookie. It was crisp and crumbly. Freshly baked. Sweetened with plenty of sugar. She liked it.

"If I may be so bold, what gives you pause about this terrific opportunity we're giving you?"

"I have the feeling there's more to it than you've shared with me."

He chewed his cookie slowly, although he didn't appear to enjoy it. "Let me ask you something," he said, as if bringing up a different topic entirely. "I happen to know from my security man, Dr. Barnett, that you and James Stanton have become close. Has Dr. Stanton ever mentioned to you drugs that might be better than penicillin? Has he ever indicated that his rather remarkable sister might have stumbled upon something better?"

"No," she said, caught off guard. *Had* Tia found something better? And if she had, did Vannevar Bush know about it, or was he only speculating?

He said nothing for a long moment. "You see, Mrs. Shipley, and I will tell you confidentially, since we're speaking honestly with each other"— again the irony—"I'm having a bit of a problem with my erstwhile colleagues in the pharmaceutical industry, heroes though Harry Luce would have them be. I've drafted them into mass-producing penicillin and ordered them to cooperate with one another in the interest of the war effort. To facilitate this, I've suspended antitrust restrictions and patent protections on the means of production. Or to be more precise, the government will take the patents when the companies come up with some means of production, to codify their methods. No one will profit from those patents. When the companies have their penicillin ready for distribution, the military will buy it from them at a generous price, which seems to me like a good deal all-around. I happen to be giving away quite a lot of money to people doing research on this project, but recently the pharmaceutical companies have refused to take my research money, citing their patriotism. You'd almost think they don't want to be beholden to me.

"Now I happen to know they're making progress on penicillin. They'd make even more progress—a lot more—if they'd share their discoveries with one another, but that's exactly what they don't want to do. They're like children: no matter how often I tell them *no*, they still hold out the hope that someday they'll be able to patent their individual means of production and make a fortune.

"Which brings me to my next concern: what's to stop them from devoting themselves to some other, similar drug? A drug for which they might be able to gain patent protection from the beginning, and I mean patent protection for the substance itself, leaving poor penicillin behind? I daresay, if certain people thought they could get hold of an antibacterial substance they could actually patent commercially, they might even steal for it. They might even kill for it."

"I was under the impression that this class of drugs couldn't be patented because they're made from natural products." She had a faint recollection of Jamie explaining this.

"Patents on natural products. Now that is an interesting question, Mrs. Shipley. We'd need the opinion of the experts at the patent office to get to the bottom of it."

"Or your opinion."

"Yes, there is that. The jury is still out on my opinion."

"Keeping your options open?"

"I'm glad we understand each other. There are two issues at stake: the natural product itself, in this case penicillin, produced by a mold, and the means of production to turn the mold-product into a medication. There will never be a patent on the naturally occurring substance called penicillin, and as I said, the government will control the patents on the manufacturing techniques that turn that substance into a mass-produced medicine."

"Remind me why you chose to back the green mold?"

"Right now, it's the only viable antibacterial drug we have. The *only* one. It's damn difficult to produce, but it's systemic and completely nontoxic. There hasn't been a single allergic reaction reported in all the testing done thus far. Remarkable. It does have its limitations, however. So far, it's proven impossible to synthesize. And it's effective only against gram-positive bacteria, the ones that take the purple stain, as you may or may not have learned in high school. Sometimes the stain is blue, but I won't quibble about that. We've still got to do clinical trials, but we're hoping it will work against gas gangrene, syphilis, meningitis, pneumonia, the list goes on. It also works against gonorrhea, even though that's gram-negative, but I'm not complaining. Syphilis, gonorrhea, gas gangrene— those are the enemies of any military force. Penicillin doesn't work against TB, tularemia, typhus, and something called atypical pneumonia, another one of the diseases that follows along in the troop train. I tell you, I feel like I've had to get a Ph.D. in biology to do this job."

He sat forward. "So the question remains, what if the pharmaceutical companies were to stumble upon a better drug? Discover it for themselves, or locate it in some academic research lab? It would be a valuable commodity. *In*valuable. A drug that was gram-positive *and* gram-negative effective, say, and equally nontoxic, and easier to produce or chemically synthesize—although they might need years to figure out how to mass-produce it and get it to the front lines. If there were another drug, who'd want to go forward with penicillin? Despite the war and all the talk of patriotism, who'd have a vested interest in it? Why pursue penicillin when there's a chance for something better just around the corner, with the possibility of commercial patent protection to boot?"

"Why don't you just set up another team of researchers and companies to work on other antibacterials?"

"Because, Mrs. Shipley," he said impatiently, "we'd be starting from scratch. The troops need these medications now, today, this instant, not five years from now. At least with penicillin, we're moving forward. We've got some baselines. But we're still far from mass production, and the situation is desperate. Every research hour should be devoted to penicillin, not to other, pie-in-the-sky possibilities."

He poured more coffee. His silver spoon tinkled against the cup as he stirred in the sugar.

"I have a proposal for you, Mrs. Shipley: I'll let you pursue your penicillin story for Harry Luce, and you'll keep me up-to-date on what our friends at the pharmaceutical companies are doing. Our enemies, too, if you meet up with any. I wouldn't be surprised to learn that Herr Hitler and company were attempting at this very moment to crack the code of these medications, working side by side at the lab bench with our very best young men." He gave her a thin smile. "This would be your personal contribution to the war effort. Your work is a perfect cover. You must see a lot in the course of a day, Mrs. Shipley. I expect people tend to forget you're around. I expect you pride yourself on people forgetting you're right beside them."

How well he'd read her.

"Any glimmers you pick up on nonpenicillin research, any hints here and there, anything indicative of the Krauts or the Japs or a little home-grown intrigue, you pass it along to my security man, Andrew Barnett, who'll pass it along to me."

Well, at least Barnett turned out to be who he said he was. "In other words, you're exploiting Mr. Luce's trust and generosity by recruiting me to do a little spying."

"Your words, not mine."

So this was how it was done. She'd often wondered. Over the years, she'd heard rumors about various agencies of the government approaching her colleagues, asking them to take a look around here and there overseas. She didn't like the idea. And yet . . . Bush was offering her the opportunity to walk the corridors Jamie walked, to meet the people he met, possibly to work with him directly. She'd be documenting the creation of treatments that might one day save the next Emily.

Bush misinterpreted her silence. "I'm afraid you don't really have a choice in this matter, Mrs. Shipley. You photographed that story, you befriended James Stanton, you're already too deeply involved to refuse. You already know too much. And I must tell you, I could make things rather unpleasant for you and your family if you decide not to help. You may not realize—children seldom do—that your father is a very prominent businessman. You yourself have had a rather successful career, in a short period of time. In my experience, everyone has a skeleton in his, or her, professional closet."

How hard-pressed he must be, to threaten her so blatantly. A tactical error. As for her professional closet, she didn't doubt that Bush could easily fabricate a skeleton or two if he put his mind to it. Bush was trying to bully her, but he didn't succeed. She regarded him dispassionately, from a far distance, as if he were part of a chess game she was playing for reasons that had nothing to do with him. "Really, Dr.

Bush, there's no need to put it in those terms. I was prepared to offer my cooperation before you threatened me."

He laughed heartily, pleased with himself and the world. Fine. They each had an agenda and would pursue it. He stood. She stood. He put out his hand. "So we begin." They shook hands. "Welcome aboard," he said. "Andy will brief you downstairs."

Downstairs at his desk in his makeshift office, behind a partition in the rotunda of the Carnegie Institution, Andrew Barnett awaited Claire Shipley's arrival. He already knew his boss's plan for her. Barnett had made himself scarce when she was *shooting* the boss (unlike some of his colleagues, he liked Vannevar Bush, so he didn't wish him dead, but the double meaning amused him), but now he was more than prepared to greet her.

This partitioned office didn't exactly suit his image of himself. At Stanford he'd had a view across the quad. He appreciated, however, that he was luckier than his three colleagues across the way who didn't even have partitions. They worked desk to desk, no privacy at all.

He tried to stay in the narrow path of the breeze from the inadequate floor fan. No air-conditioning in this bastion of power. The damned skylight or dome, whatever it was called, made the heat worse, as did the full occupancy of the rotunda, eighteen men exactly like him perspiring in their obligatory coats and ties in pursuit of glamorous war work.

His younger brother, Mark, was in the Pacific, God alone knew where. Barnett worried about him. Not just for Mark's sake, but for their mother's. "You stay out of the military, Andy," his mother wrote to him on the day Mark's ship left San Diego. "You keep yourself safe."

How could he respond? I'll try, Mom. I'll try.

On Barnett's desk were index cards of suspects in the possible murder of Lucretia Stanton. Because he was meeting with Claire Shipley today, he felt compelled to review this problem again. He was painfully aware that he was out of his depth. Making a fool out of himself.

Getting overdramatic, the way he had with Mrs. Shipley after the memorial in New York.

The problem was that Dr. Bush, without any evidence whatsoever, was convinced that Tia Stanton had been murdered. Although Bush would never make his suspicion public, he wanted to learn the truth, so that he could deal with it privately. Barnett was supposed to "pick up the pieces, cross all the *T*s," according to the boss. The fact that Barnett wasn't trained to pick up pieces or cross *T*s in a murder case didn't seem to matter.

Patting the sweat off his forehead with his handkerchief, Barnett tried to focus on the three-by-five cards. He didn't dare tell the boss that he couldn't handle this. If he did, he might end up in the Pacific after all.

For want of any other viable approach, he'd written one name on each card, with relevant facts and suppositions. He also had a card for Tia Stanton herself. For suicide or accident, despite Dr. Bush's suspicions. Barnett pushed the cards back and forth, weighing the motives. The cards offered him no insights.

Maybe if he just gave up on it, after a few months the boss would forget about it. Thousands were dying around the world every day, what was one death more or less? Suicide, accident, murder—in the long run, what did it matter? Maybe Tia Stanton's death actually helped the Allied war effort, who could say? Morality was a tricky commodity in wartime. An indulgence.

The index cards made for an intriguing intellectual puzzle, however. He especially liked the thought of Chief Nurse Brockett as a murderer. He'd always loved puzzles. He rearranged the cards yet again. Barnett tried to put himself into the mind of New York City detective Marcus Kreindler. What would the detective think of Sergei Oretsky as a murderer? Or Dr. Jacob Lind?

Lucretia Stanton must have been half insane, in Barnett's personal opinion, but with the kind of sublimated insanity that often did a lot

of good in the world. How else could you account for somebody working seven days a week testing soil samples? The traditional economic
model of each person working toward his or her maximum utility was
not directly relevant in this case. He had an insight: the successful
development of antibacterials would provide a useful case study in
economics. Generally workers displaced by technological change were
reabsorbed into the workforce. Antibacterials, however, constituted a
technological advance that permitted workers who otherwise would
have died, and therefore left the workforce permanently, to survive.
What were their employment prospects?

Alas, no time for that question now. Maybe Patsy Reese, the widow
in the early penicillin test, did Tia Stanton in. Her husband had died
under the Stantons' care, so she had a reason for revenge. Maybe one
of Tia Stanton's suitors, jealous of her attachment to mold, had let his
passion get the better of him. Her appointment book, which Andy had
stashed in a locked desk drawer, listed an array of engagement parties,
as well as an intriguing schedule of drinks and dinner dates with Jeffs
and Neals and Joes. Sadly for Tia Stanton, no name appeared more
than once or twice.

Barnett had been engaged, years ago. His fiancée died in a car
accident three months before their wedding date. Janice. They'd met
when they were in college. Her family was upper middle class, her
father the manager (not the owner) of a neighborhood bank. The bank
failed during the Depression, but that was later, after the engagement.
After the accident. Her sister was driving. Janice was in the passenger
seat. They were going to a fitting of bridesmaids' gowns. Janice was
killed instantly. The sister walked away unscathed. Afterward Barnett
moved from the Midwest to California and took the job at Stanford to
start over, in a place with no memories.

Barnett had to be careful: in another minute he'd get choked up,
and this absolutely was not the time or the place to get teary. No privacy here. Zero. Every time the guy in the next cubicle uncrossed and

recrossed his legs, Barnett heard the creak of his chair, the brush of his trousers.

What about the Germans, the Japanese? A Soviet threat, perhaps? Russia and America were Allies now in the war, but the Communists remained enemies still. Or—and this was trickier—a spy could be English, or French. He wrote out cards for each possibility and added the cards to his collection. Espionage would make for an easy explanation, and in fact the boss favored it. Apparently a Fifth Columnist had approached Lucretia Stanton on the street a few years before the war, trying to buy yellow fever virus for a Japanese lab. Dr. Rivers had told Barnett about this at the memorial. Just thought he should know, Dr. Rivers said. The Japanese were notorious for using disease as a weapon, even dropping grain mixed with plague-infected fleas from planes flying over the starving people of China.

If only he could come up with a suspect who had a vested interest in sulfa drugs and didn't want penicillin jeopardizing his profits. Barnett wrote out a card for the disgruntled sulfa producer. Barnett liked this choice. In his experience most people were willing to do almost anything for money. The practical side of the study of economics. Okay, maybe not Lucretia Stanton, but she was the exception that proved the rule. On the other hand, he'd heard that murder was most often personal. A crime of passion. Love, revenge, greed, jealousy. Passions were harder for him than puzzles. He was a fan of Hitchcock films. He loved the circular play of trickery. The unpredictable and yet completely natural turns of plot. Most of all the sense of menace lurking behind otherwise mundane events. He thought of Claire Shipley as a dark-haired version of Madeleine Carroll in *The 39 Steps*. He himself could be Robert Donat, the Everyman enmeshed in a maze of intrigue.

Enough fantasy. Barnett said a prayer for his dead girl, Janice. He hadn't been involved with anyone since then, not in an emotional way. He also said a prayer for his brother. Their mother was a devout Catholic, but Barnett had left the church when he left home. He'd kept his Catholic heritage secret at Stanford and here in Washington. Prejudice against Catholics was strong in the Protestant bastions where he was trying to make his way. Nonetheless, after Mark shipped out to the Pacific, Barnett started going to Mass again. Started going to confession, and taking communion.

He touched the rosary in his suit jacket pocket. He said a few Hail Marys. He felt more settled after the prayers. More clearheaded. Claire Shipley would be downstairs any minute, and he had to stay alert.

"Here she is." The boss was at the entrance of Barnett's cubicle, having made the sacrifice of escorting Claire Shipley downstairs himself. A rare honor. Bush must be placing more value in Claire Shipley than he'd let on. "She's all set and ready to go."

Bush was talking about her as if she were some kind of wind-up doll. Barnett was almost offended on her behalf. She looked as if she wore a mask; she was past being offended by a mere Dr. Vannevar Bush. Barnett stacked his cards together and turned over the pile. He stood. "Mrs. Shipley, welcome. Good to see you again." They shook hands. "I've got the conference room reserved, so we can talk privately." He retrieved his file, the one with her name on it.

As to the Lucretia Stanton murder investigation . . . a murderer to be brought to justice in the spring of 1942? The entire undertaking was ridiculous.

A half hour later, outside the Carnegie Institution on Sixteenth Street, the canopy of leaves was so thick Claire thought she'd entered a tunnel. The air itself glowed green. Unexpectedly for Washington in June, the heat and humidity weren't oppressive. The breeze carried an undercurrent of coolness. Her next assignment was at 2:00 PM, with Secretary Morgenthau at the Treasury Department, near the White House. Another portrait. Her typed schedule, prepared by Frieda, called for lunch now, but she didn't feel like eating.

After her meeting with Andrew Barnett, Ph.D., she needed a walk. Barnett combined condescension and self-doubt in a way that she found irritating. She didn't relish the idea of working with him. Nonetheless, she didn't want to make an enemy of him, so she played along. At least his questions were innocuous, and he clearly knew the answers already.

Within a block, she realized that the tripod and Linhof were too heavy for a long walk. She hailed a taxi and took it to Lafayette Square, across from the White House. At least she could enjoy her break outside on this lovely day.

At the square, she entered a scene that was like a manicured garden. Claire thought of Manet's *Le Déjeuner sur l'herbe*, minus the naked woman. Office workers eating sandwiches reclined on the thick grass beneath the trees. The light filtered yellow through the leaves, outlining the greenery. She imagined Jamie walking here at lunchtime, enjoying the shade during his visits to Washington. She took pleasure in the image, even as it made her ache. She missed him so very much. Sometimes the missing of him was like a physical presence that pressed hard within her chest. A few days ago, she'd received a postcard from him, mailed from Portland, Oregon, and showing a picture of Mount Hood. The card gave no news, simply recounted that despite a long visit, he'd never seen the sun once due to relentless rain. She twisted the ring on her finger.

On the benches along the paths, men in suits read newspapers, a rhythm of headlines down the row. Big, bold typeface: Cologne, Essen, the Ruhr . . . RAF bombing raids, 1,000 planes setting cities afire. With the Leica she kept in the pocket of her vest (today, her summer-weight hunter's vest), she framed and shot a photo. How lucky she was. Jamie wasn't a crew member on one of those planes. She and Charlie didn't live in a city set aflame.

Spotting two pay phones on the far corner of the square, Claire decided to telephone her office. Wasn't that how spies communicated,

via pay phones, in the movies Andrew Barnett said his life seldom resembled? She wanted to do her own security check on Vannevar Bush,
as she'd promised him. Since the call was long-distance, she had to
wait for the operator to get a line and put the call through. She called
collect. Frieda accepted the charges.

"Hi, Claire, everything okay? Sure you can borrow it, just bring it
back. No, he needs it now." From the clipped tone of her voice, from
her simultaneous conversations, Claire knew Frieda was distracted,
others standing at her desk. Frieda saw nothing amiss in Claire's call,
a photographer checking in, standard procedure.

"Everything's fine. Morning assignment went well. I've got an hour
before the afternoon appointment. Mack have anything for me?"

"Just a sec, let me check the sheet. You can see him tomorrow," she
said to someone else. "No, nothing, Claire. Give us a call when you
wrap up in the afternoon, in case anything comes up later. No sense
coming back to New York just to get sent down there again."

"My thoughts exactly. Frieda, could you transfer me to Mr. Luce's
office?"

"To Mr. Luce?" Now Claire had Frieda's full attention. "Why do
you want to talk to him?"

"Not to him." Claire put on an exasperated tone. "To Miss
Thrasher. A question came up that I need to check with Miss
Thrasher about. Something about two guests at the United China
Relief party I photographed. They made a large donation, wore their
custom-made Chinese costumes, but somehow their picture never
made it into the magazine." Frieda might well ask how and why these
outraged Sinophiles had contacted Claire instead of Mr. Luce directly, but it was the best excuse Claire could come up with. "They're
not amused. Someone might have to apologize. I'll never hear the
end of that shoot."

"That's what happens when you get yourself on the good side of the
boss's wife." Claire could hear the satisfaction in Frieda's voice. Luckily

Miss Thrasher never participated in gossip. She and her boss made a good pair. Like him, however, Miss Thrasher probably wouldn't have accepted a collect call from Claire, thus necessitating the subterfuge with Frieda. "I'll transfer you."

"Thanks, Frieda."

Within two minutes, she heard his gruff voice. "Where are you calling from?"

"A phone booth at the corner of, let's see, Lafayette Park and Sixteenth Street in Washington, D.C. It's very secure."

"Why am I talking to you?"

"First of all, thank you for pursuing the story we discussed a few months back." All this talk of spies was making her cautious; she wouldn't mention penicillin on the long-distance line.

"Don't thank me. I'm not doing it for you. I'm pursuing it for Time Incorporated."

"A wise decision."

"Obviously." Was he laughing or even smiling? "That's the reason for your call?"

"No. At my meeting this morning, a friend of yours asked me to do a little work for him on the side. I wanted to make sure the arrangement had your approval. How's that for corporate loyalty?"

"Our country needs us."

"I guess that means okay."

"I wish it didn't have to be this way, but sometimes it does. You're not alone, I can assure you."

"I'm grateful for that, at least."

"Did he offer you money?"

"Of course not."

"Why 'of course not'?"

"I wouldn't have taken it, if he had."

"Good. For both of you. Patriotism can't be bought. It's an honor to be asked to serve our country."

"Is that what you're going to write up as next week's editorial comment?"

"Maybe so." Now a certain edge in his voice made her think that he was amused. "I'm making a note of it. I only wish I could personally do more, to serve our country."

"You're not thinking of signing up, are you? The Marine Corps?"

The idea of Mr. Luce in the military was ludicrous, unless he was drafted for the position of commander in chief, occupied by FDR at present.

"I've thought about it. However, I sincerely believe I can do more for my country where I am."

"I'm sure that's true."

"Mrs. Shipley, if you're calling from Washington," the realization dawned on him, "who's paying for this call?"

"You are, Mr. Luce. Who else?" He was generous with budgets—the *Life* staff traveled well, stayed at the best hotels, ate at the best restaurants—but the little things disturbed him.

"In that case, why don't you resume doing whatever you were doing before you bothered me."

"That sounds like a good idea. Thank you, Mr. Luce."

"Don't mention it," he said, with a slight inflection in his voice indicating that he had in fact enjoyed their conversation.

CHAPTER SIXTEEN

⁓

On a warm evening in June, Detective Marcus Kreindler happened to be driving north on the East River Drive. He was headed from Twenty-third Street to the Triborough Bridge and his home in Queens. He had the radio on, big band music, and all four windows down. A nice sea breeze came in from the river. The tide was high. The scent was, well, tidal. Salty, fresh, and sewage laden. Exactly what you'd expect from a tidal strait that functioned as a sewer at several points along its course. From heaven to hell, that was his city, and he savored it all. A police boat glided along the water. He stretched around to see if he recognized any of the guys, but he didn't.

He liked the East River Drive, because it didn't have any traffic. As of a few weeks ago, the highway was open all the way to 125th Street. This particular section, from Twenty-third Street to Thirty-fourth Street, had been constructed on landfill that was made from the rubble of the bombed-out city of Bristol, England. Bristol was bombed in March and April of 1941, and the rubble was brought over as ballast on merchant ships. Once the rubble got to New York, a bulkhead was constructed in the river, and the rubble was poured in, enough to make something like fourteen acres of new land, according to the newspaper. Lots of praise and fanfare had greeted this rubble re-use. Kreindler had even seen a picture of the plaque that was going to be put on the pedestrian bridge at Twenty-fifth Street commemorating the whole thing and praising the bravery of the people of Bristol when their homes were bombed. Kreindler didn't think they had much choice in the matter. And he didn't see anything to brag about: chunks of people's houses, churches, and shops poured into the river to make landfill for a highway. Doubtless some body parts were mixed in with the rubble to boot, not on purpose, but when death's all around, you can't keep track of every finger and toe. He tried not to think about fingers and toes in the land beneath his tires.

Instead he contemplated breweries. The river was on his right, and on his left were warehouses, factories, and yes, breweries. He caught a whiff of hops on the air. He was looking forward to enjoying a cold beer when he got home. He reached Thirty-eighth Street, and passed Consolidated Edison's gigantic generating plant, dwarfing everything else like a monster. The plant was gone in a second as he entered the Forties. Here he was assaulted by the stench from the stockyards and slaughterhouses. His buddies who worked this district said you got used to the stench after a while. Didn't even notice it anymore. The stench was accompanied by bleating, mooing, and oinking. Cattle, sheep, and hogs arrived in Manhattan on two-story barges that looked like floating paddocks. Four of these paddocks were docked right now. Because of the highway, nowadays the livestock were unloaded onto narrow, open waterside pens and then moved through tunnels that led under the highway and into the slaughterhouses. Yep, the animals were killed, processed, and eaten right here on the island of Manhattan. What a place. Once he'd had a homicide on one of those floating paddocks. It was arranged to look like an accident, guy getting trampled in a cow stampede. But hoof marks couldn't hide a bullet in the back of the head. Soon there'd be homicides in the under-the-highway tunnels, he didn't doubt.

Now he was driving alongside the Fifties, the rich folks' blocks . . . the River House and the River Club, Sutton Place and Sutton Square. The River Club actually had a dock for yachts to tie up. Once he'd seen a Chinese junk pulled up there, and it sure did look like junk. Now he was approaching the Queensboro Bridge.

Kreindler spent so much of his workday at the waterfront, he'd started to think of New York City as Venice. Venice with cliffs. He'd never been to Venice, but he'd seen pictures in *Life* magazine. Most people forgot that in New York, water was everywhere, lapping into coves and inlets that lurked unseen until they became the crossing point from life to death.

Like right here. He drove under the Queensboro Bridge into the Sixties and saw the Rockefeller Institute silhouetted in the red sunset at the top of the bluff. He signaled, pulled over, and stopped. He kept his signal light on as a warning, although it didn't much matter. There were so few cars on the East River Drive that his stopping made no difference to the flow, and he didn't care if it did. A couple of months ago he was in a squad car with an old buddy. They took a great deal of enjoyment in slowing traffic heading north on Central Park West by double-parking at Seventieth Street to eat their sandwiches. The drivers behind didn't dare honk, just slowly maneuvered themselves into a single file and passed around. Traffic backed up all the way to Columbus Circle. That fifteen-minute experience still gave him an immense sense of satisfaction.

"Happened to be driving north on the East River Drive" was incorrect. He had to face facts, because he amounted to nothing if he didn't face facts. The Queensboro Bridge was his usual route home, and unlike the Triborough, it was free. But Kreindler was willing to toss his quarter in the bin at the Triborough for this view. His eyes followed a line from the top of the cliff down to the point where the body had landed.

Only then it wasn't a body, not when it was falling. Then it was a woman in the prime of life, with everything to live for, a great job (she was the type who wanted a great job, not just a way to earn money until she got married), lots of friends, men asking for her phone number. A

future to look forward to. What did she think about while she was . . .
Kreindler hoped it happened so fast that she didn't have time to think
of anything.

Maybe it was an accident after all, like he was forced to say in his
official report and what the coroner had ruled. So much of life was
like that: one false step and it's over. This past winter, Kreindler had
slipped on the ice in front of his own house, needed twelve stitches on
his chin and the doctor said he was lucky he didn't break his jaw. He'd
never have heard the end of it from the guys if, after forty years on the
job, he'd broken his jaw on his own front stoop.

Some instinct kept telling him that Dr. Lucretia Stanton's death
was no accident. But it didn't strike him as premeditated either. Pushing a woman off a cliff—it was crude. Impulsive. Somebody with a
grudge or a hope saw an opportunity and took it. Who? Someone from
the inside, or from the outside? The day after she died he'd checked
the entry log kept at the Institute gatehouse, but standing there for ten
minutes he saw a half dozen well-dressed visitors gain entry with only
a nod and a smile. The guard insisted he knew them all, became irate
at a suggestion that maybe he didn't, but even so.

The problem was, Kreindler couldn't forget her. He'd seen her,
there at the bottom of the cliff, her full, wavy hair hiding her injuries.
He'd learned about the unusual life she led. Some of his buddies would
think her life was odd, eccentric, abnormal even. But Kreindler had
seen enough abnormality over the years that he didn't pass judgment
against Tia Stanton. Instead his heart went out to her, as if she were
his daughter. How had she ended up there, alongside the weeds and
old newspapers and crushed seashells, amid the riverbank detritus of
his city?

Who stood to gain the most from the green mold and all the other
colored mold he'd seen in her laboratory? Not a question he'd ever
asked before. And yet, in essence it was the same question he asked
in almost every case, if you replaced the word *mold* with the word

money. Even he knew enough about science and business to know that growing mold in a roomful of jam jars and bedpans didn't translate into supplying the entire nation with a life-saving medicine. A lot of middlemen had to be involved, each one taking his cut along the way. And that cut wasn't necessarily money. It could also be fame and glory, love or sex, revenge, punishment for slights real or imagined.

He didn't discount the possibility of espionage of the Kraut or Jap variety. Tomorrow he'd spend some time walking around Yorkville, calling in some chits, seeing if anybody in the Bund had heard anything. Officially, the Bund didn't exist anymore. Got themselves arrested, suppressed, banned, preaching their stupid Nazi slogans, marching around with swastika flags, strutting in their imitation SS uniforms. Bundesführer Kuhn had even gotten himself locked up for embezzlement.

Unofficially, it was a different story. Scratch the surface, and they were still there. Every now and again Kreindler found the group's hidden stalwarts useful.

Besides, he liked walking around Yorkville. The neighborhood reminded him of his mother. She spent forty-six years, ages eighteen to sixty-four, working behind the counter at Heidelberg Candies on Second Avenue at Eighty-fourth Street. She came home every day smelling of the chocolates they made in the back. When he was a boy, they'd sit side by side on the couch while she helped him with his reading. The scent of chocolate from her clothes and her hair surrounded him. Kreindler's father died young: he'd worked construction, stepped on a nail sticking out of a stack of wood, got tetanus, that was it.

Kreindler liked to hear German spoken on the streets of Yorkville. He savored the scent of German cooking. Hard to admit to German ancestry nowadays—and in previous days, too. His actual name was *Markus*, but he'd changed it to *Marcus* during the last war. The Great War. The War to End All Wars. The idiots in the Bund trusted him because of his ancestry, never putting two and two together to see he was exploiting them.

Tomorrow he'd enjoy a good meal of sauerbraten and *Kartoffelklösse* over at Hans Jaeger's at Lex and Eighty-fifth. Just sitting there having lunch, slowly sipping a beer, he'd learn more than Andrew Barnett ever could from his desk at the highfalutin Carnegie Institution in Washington. He'd have *Schwarzwälder Kirschtorte* for dessert, in honor of his mother.

Yes, it was wartime and everybody had their very important work to do. Well, this was his important work. He was sixty-five but he wouldn't be retiring anytime soon. Not with the younger guys heading off to war, a lot of them volunteering, God preserve them, especially his partner Sean. Kreindler prided himself on being a patient man. Things came up in life. Strange coincidences. Opportunities that you never foresaw. He was prepared to wait a long time on this one, moving forward with his other work while keeping this in the background. He'd take the risk of a turf war. He'd operate on his own until the truth rolled itself out like a red carpet, the kind they used when big shots visited City Hall.

It was getting dark. He turned on the headlights. Reversed the turn signal. Checked the rearview mirror. He pressed the accelerator, smoothly reentering the sparse flow of traffic. The cooling air carried the light ocean scent he loved at the end of a hot day. In the twilight, the highway looked almost beautiful in its gently curving path along the river. The river itself was smooth and black. The dimmed-out lights of the Triborough Bridge flickered in the distance like a delicate sweep of stars.

CHAPTER SEVENTEEN

⁓

Claire sat in the backseat of a big, leather-upholstered military car while an attractive young military man named Anthony Pagliaro drove. Her official driver, her official car. She couldn't help but feel pleased with herself for the small perks provided by Vannevar Bush.

It was a good assignment, all things considered, driving through the New Jersey countryside in early July, on her way to Rahway, passing peaceful farms and woodlands, sunlight sparkling through the trees. Claire was traveling to the Merck company headquarters to photograph their penicillin production. The trip took longer than expected because the speed limit had been lowered to thirty-five miles per hour to conserve gasoline and tires.

So she had plenty of time to appreciate objectively how attractive Anthony Pagliaro was, how good he'd look in an advertising photograph, say. She wasn't attracted to him herself. She felt a generation older than he was. Every now and again she saw his eyes glancing into the rearview mirror, keeping track of her as well as the road behind, as she kept track of him. He had a sleek handsomeness, dark eyes, thick hair swept back. He carried himself with an edge of class resentment that added to his attractiveness.

Claire now had security clearance, as did Anthony Pagliaro. After today's shoot, she would send the film to Andrew Barnett via military pouch, and he would have it developed and locked in a cabinet until the story could be told. Anything interesting she heard or observed along the way, she was instructed to report to Barnett for evaluation.

"So, Tony," she said, trying to get to know her partner in espionage, "what did you do before you became a military driver?"

"I drove a delivery truck for the family business." The Brooklyn accent flitted in and out of his voice as if he were trying to coach it away.

"What business?"

"Bread. In Carroll Gardens, Brooklyn."

"Pagliaro's Bakery?"

"That's the one."

"I've had that bread. So crispy. My son's favorite."

"Yeah, it's good. Brick ovens. Makes the difference."

"I'll tell my son. That's the type of thing he likes to know. Brick ovens. Interesting. So the military gave you the same job you had before."

"Except I didn't join up to be driving around hotshots and women. No offense meant."

"None taken. What did you want to do?"

"I wanted to drive a tank. And repair tanks. That's what I told them: I'm interested in tanks and I have experience repairing trucks. This is the job they gave me."

"Maybe you can request a transfer once things are moving along. Probably they don't have enough tanks manufactured yet to need someone to repair them." The slow pace of military production—endless delays, confusions, and red tape—was daily fare in the newspapers. "Meanwhile, I'll teach you about photography."

"Nothing personal, but I can't say I ever wanted to learn about photography."

"Suit yourself."

In Rahway, the guard at the company gate found their surnames on his list, called the office, and waved them in. They turned onto a tree-lined lane that meandered through thick woods and eventually opened onto a wide, manicured lawn. Deer grazed in the distance.

"What the hell is this?" Tony asked. "Some kind of Sherwood Forest?"

"More likely the opposite. I don't think we'll be meeting any Robin Hoods here."

A circular drive led them to the company headquarters and laboratories. George Merck himself was waiting at the door. This was noteworthy. What did he find so important about her visit, to require a personal greeting? The press continually referred to him as Adonis-like, and Claire knew from more than one article that he was in his late forties, six feet four, blond and blue-eyed. Seeing him up close, however, Claire thought he was chunky and staid, too tightly buttoned into his vest and suit jacket. He and his family had made a fortune in the commercial development of vitamins. He regarded her with puzzlement.

"Everything all right, Mr. Merck?"

"We were expecting . . ."

"A military man?"

He smiled winsomely, and suddenly he did look as handsome as his reputation. "You could say that."

"I've got military clearance, so we're okay on that count."

"With so many men going overseas, I understand how the magazines must be filling in with women for nonessential jobs."

"Oh, indeed. I'm even busier now than when I went on staff at *Life* four years ago."

Merck's smile wavered, and beside her Tony Pagliaro hid a snigger.

"Mrs. Shipley, welcome to Rahway." With strained heartiness, Merck reached out to shake her hand.

Between the two Adonises, blond George and dark Tony, Claire proceeded into the building.

"Let me show you our operation. We're proud of it, I don't mind telling you."

He ushered them into a ground-floor lab. The gleaming, stainless steel counters and sinks looked bright and sparkling. The wooden lab tables were highly polished, shiny beakers arrayed upon them. The shelves were lined with glimmering, empty milk bottles.

"This is our new lab for the testing and development of penicillin. I'll bring in some scientists and you can photograph them with the equipment."

"This is an impressive lab, Mr. Merck. Has it ever been used?"

"As I say, it's our new lab."

"Mr. Luce's arrangement with Dr. Bush is for me to photograph the work in progress."

"This is the work in progress."

"I need to see where you're doing the penicillin research now."

"This is where we're doing the penicillin research now."

"The bedpans and milk bottles that you're *already* using. The old lab. The lab where you're experimenting with submerged fermentation," she added, using the rather impressive phrase that Barnett had bandied about during her briefing.

"That initial work has been rendered obsolete. We want to show you only the latest developments."

"Forgive me, Mr. Merck, I believe there's been a misunderstanding." Andrew Barnett had been allowed to walk through the Merck facility the week before. He'd confirmed that extensive penicillin research was being done here. Obviously this new lab was nothing more than a display. Was Mr. Merck playing her for a fool? "Perhaps we should get Dr. Bush on the phone to discuss the situation."

"Certainly."

As luck would have it, Bush was in the process of flying to the West Coast and wouldn't be reachable until late tonight. Shall I leave a message for him at the hotel? his secretary asked. Would you like to send a telegram?

Flying to the West Coast was rare and impressive, the sort of thing Mrs. Roosevelt did. It was also time-consuming. Claire found herself with no alternatives. They returned to the lab, and two scientists joined them. The scientists wore well-pressed white lab coats over their dress shirts and ties. Their names were Dr. Frye and Dr. Rand, M.D. or Ph.D., Claire didn't know. They were like twins, youthful and light-hearted, with blue eyes and blond hair like their boss. They greeted Claire with a playful attitude, pleased at the prospect of having their pictures in *Life* sooner or later. She took out the standard permission forms, and they signed.

Pleading other obligations, George Merck turned the supervision of Claire and Tony over to the scientists and departed. With no other choice, Claire photographed the brand-new laboratory that might someday be used for penicillin or might simply be kept for show, while the real work went on elsewhere. She photographed the two jovial scientists in their starched lab coats, undoubtedly presented to them for this occasion, as they held test tubes of water up to the light and stared through microscopes at nonexistent slides. They were exceedingly cooperative, offering to pose in any way she liked, for fake shots that Claire knew could never run. The entire endeavor began to seem like a bad joke. Claire could only hope they might inadvertently reveal some useful information in the course of their performance.

"So," she said after about an hour, as she and Tony changed the lights. She trusted she'd given the scientists ample time to be lulled into complacency. "You having any luck with penicillin?"

They exchanged glances. "Slow going. Step by step."

"Yeah, that's what I hear from everybody." She took a gamble. "The cousins are so much easier, don't you find?" She focused on a lightbulb, pretending that she couldn't get it twisted in straight.

"I wouldn't say *easy*, but—"

"We don't have time for anything but penicillin," Dr. Frye told Dr. Rand in warning.

"You're right about that," Dr. Rand backtracked. "Anyway, it's the process I enjoy." He was the handsomer of the two, although his glasses were thicker.

"I understand." Was this the right approach? She was new to espionage and apparently not yet very good at it. Movies, as Andrew Barnett had correctly pointed out, weren't much help. "It seems like the process is what everyone who does this type of work enjoys most," she said. "I once did a story with Dr. James Stanton. Either of you ever meet him?"

Again the glances, the silent questioning of each other, the doubts about what was allowed and what wasn't. "I've heard that name," Dr. Frye said slowly. "He's . . . I guess you'd have to say he's above our level. I admire him, though. His reputation, I mean. What's he like?"

"He enjoys the process," Claire said, shrugging to make them think she had no particular interest. "Just like you. I guess his sister, Tia Stanton, liked the process, too."

The young doctors said nothing.

On their way to the car, Tony said, "Boy, oh boy, they must have something pretty good to hide, to build a fake lab to hide it." Tony had proven himself adept with the equipment and Claire appreciated his healthy suspicion of authority.

"Yes, very impressive." A colossal waste of time, Claire thought. No, worse: offensive. No room for hopes or dreams of saving Emily here; no idealism whatsoever.

Now that they were working together, Claire sat in the front seat with Tony. They drove to another pharmaceutical firm (New Jersey was thick with them) about twenty miles away, Hanover & Company. When they arrived, it was the same deal: the forest, the manicured lawns, the long curving drive, the company headquarters disguised as an English country house.

"Pretty fancy," Tony said as he made the curve with a fast, pleasurable sweep. "I can see you're taking me to the best places."

"Stick with me, you won't regret it." Stay cheerful, play for the laugh, that was the code, and she made herself live by it.

At Hanover, they were greeted by the high-heeled, straight-backed Miss Margery Ryan, the director of public information. Miss Ryan wore a tight, gray suit and large, gold earrings. Claire had better hopes of accomplishing something here, without the company chairman intimidating the staff. But at Hanover it was the same story, the gleaming new lab, the scrubbed, polished, and playful young scientists, Dr. Jones and Dr. Evans, with one twist: Miss Ryan never left them. Vannevar Bush had forced the companies to allow Claire through their front doors, but that was as far as they would go; they'd keep their real work secret.

Claire gave it a try anyway. "So," she said as she posed the scientists with a rack of test tubes filled with tap water, "things must really be moving along with penicillin."

"Oh, no," Miss Ryan said before they could answer, "we haven't made any progress. So discouraging. We work and work, with no progress at all." Miss Ryan was nervous, incessantly capping and uncapping her fountain pen.

"Life is tough," Tony said.

"Oh, yes, truly. I feel sorry for these poor young men, coming here with the highest hopes," Miss Ryan said.

The young men repressed smiles.

"Especially during a war," Tony said. "You want to feel you're accomplishing something during a war, not just biding your time until it's over." Tony straightened his uniform. He did look impressive. Most likely the scientists were exempt from the draft as essential workers, but even so, Tony managed to convey the idea that they were cowards. Slackers, was the term used on the streets. "I guess if we're lucky, we'll all get sent to the front and that'll be that," Tony added. "Or maybe the front will come to us. We could engage the enemy on that big lawn you've got out there."

Miss Ryan regarded him with annoyance. Claire felt that she and Tony had the makings of a great professional team.

They continued with their sham work in the sham lab, going through the motions, taking photos, moving lights, varying the angles. Claire continued to make meaningless conversation. When they had done all they could do and were repacking the equipment, she said to the scientists, "You fellows having any luck with other antibacterials? I keep hearing about them. Lots of research being done, progress being made, breakthroughs everywhere." What was a little exaggeration at a time like this?

"That, Mrs. Shipley, is an inappropriate question, if I may say so," Miss Ryan said.

"Forgive me, Miss Ryan."

"You came here to photograph our new penicillin work, which we are showing you."

"Indeed, Miss Ryan. But all part of the same family, I should think."

"Not in my opinion."

"Obviously."

The scientists kept their heads down, but Claire caught their amusement.

"Are you quite done now, Mrs. Shipley?"

"Why, yes." They finished packing, and Tony carried the bags, yet another benefit of his companionship.

In the hallway leading to the reception area, Miss Ryan abruptly strode ahead to meet two gray-haired gentlemen walking down the opposite hallway. She swayed on her heels, and the clicking of her shoes echoed in her path. "Good afternoon, Mr. Hanover," she called when she was within earshot.

Introductions were made when Miss Ryan reached the two men,

and in her fawning over them, she appeared to forget Claire and Tony.

"Come on," Tony said. "We don't need to wait around for her to kiss us good-bye. We can sneak up a back staircase, find out what's really going on."

"I appreciate your sense of intrigue, Tony, I really do, but let's wait." In her frustration, Claire wanted to see who got to visit the real labs, who Hanover & Company fawned over, since they certainly didn't fawn over her. Claire and Tony walked closer and closer. . . .

"Why, Claire, wonderful to see you!" It was her father, attired in a robin's-egg blue linen suit. The suit was custom made, she suspected from the jacket's smooth flow over his shoulders. He gave off an aura of comfortable self-assurance. "Look at you, hard at work and looking great!"

Why was he here? She felt more than taken aback. She felt shocked. What role was *he* playing in the game taking place around her?

"Hanover, meet my daughter, Mrs. Claire Shipley, famous photographer for *Life* magazine."

"How do you do, Mrs. Shipley, a pleasure." Hanover was a short man with a large middle and thinning hair gleaming with pomade. He appeared thoroughly relaxed, at ease within the confines of his fiefdom. "Sorry I didn't have time to meet you earlier. I was with your father. Who would have guessed? Well, Rutherford, we put on quite a show for her. Miss Ryan here presented everything we're doing."

Miss Ryan preened for Rutherford, giving Claire the sickening feeling that she was attempting to seduce him, great wealth being the ultimate aphrodisiac.

"This is Tony Pagliaro, my assistant."

Rutherford said, "Good to meet you, Tony. Glad you're watching out for my girl."

Claire could have lived without that, but Tony and her father shook hands on it with great seriousness, two men allied in their protection of her. "Thank you, sir," Tony said.

Hanover said to Claire, "My driver's taking your father to the station. Need a lift?"

"Thank you, but no. We have a car." She couldn't avoid it, she turned to her father. "Can we drive you back to the city?"

"Why, yes, that's terrific. Thank you. Damn gas rationing. I love to drive, but I had to take the train out."

"Happens to the best of us," Hanover agreed.

"Gas rationing's not a problem for me in the military," Tony said, a little too glibly, but she understood his feelings, listening to these rich men complain about their struggles. Pagliaro's Bakery probably had trouble getting enough gas to complete its daily deliveries.

Tony said he'd bring the car around to the front to pick up her father, and Claire went with him, using the excuse of stashing the equipment.

"I think I'd better sit in the backseat with my father," she said as they were arranging the bags in the trunk. "Please don't be offended."

"Mrs. Shipley, you can't offend me."

"Thanks."

They were back on Route 1 before Claire or Rutherford spoke.

"Nice guy, Hanover," Rutherford said.

"He seemed to be." Claire paused. "What were you doing there?" Even she heard the inappropriate level of suspicion in her voice, but her father took it in stride.

"I could ask you the same question."

She decided to play along with him: "Ask."

"What were you doing there?"

"Secret. Government work." She made it into a joke.

"I figured, with the military driver." He looked pleased, and he was. Seeing her improved his day, he couldn't deny it. Her vibrant presence, her verve, her skeptical curiosity . . . he might not have known her when she was growing up, but she was his daughter through and through, no doubt about it, and he was proud of her.

"Actually the work is for the magazine, too. But for after the war. Whenever that may be."

"Understood," Rutherford said. The Germans were pushing ahead on the Eastern Front. They'd taken Kharkov and Sevastopol. In North Africa, they were in Tobruk. For the Allies, a long slog lay ahead, and even the experts (and he had access to the experts) couldn't predict the results. In a year's time, German or Japanese tanks could be patrolling Route 1. He didn't want this to happen, but as a businessman he had a responsibility to plan ahead. Win or lose, Rutherford knew he'd be okay. Claire and Charlie, too. His strategy would be public collaboration, while in the background, behind the scenes, he'd support the resistance. He wondered what John D. Rockefeller Jr. would do if German troops took up residence in Manhattan, or how Henry Ford, with his outspoken anti-Semitism, would react if the Nazis became the managers of his Detroit factories. Well, Rutherford couldn't worry about them. He had enough to worry about, protecting his family, his employees, and, if he could, serving the country. He glanced at his lovely daughter. His job was to make certain she and Charlie were safe and had enough to eat no matter who won the war. He wouldn't talk to Claire about his concerns for the future. He wouldn't worry her with theoretical possibilities, or even with the practical considerations he confronted each day.

"Maybe you can explain this," Claire said with more anger than she'd intended to reveal. "I went to both Hanover and Merck today, and neither one of them showed me what they're really working on. Only brand-new labs, never used. Fake labs. They kept the actual work to themselves."

"That's no surprise," Rutherford said. "The companies have their proprietary rights to protect. They don't want photographers or reporters in there. Does Vannevar Bush think the companies are going to shout their business secrets from the rooftops?"

"What makes you bring Dr. Bush into it?"

"Anything to do with medical breakthroughs and the military means it's approved by Vannevar Bush. Let me share a little secret with you, sweetheart: he needs the companies a lot more than they need him, and the companies know it. His bluster doesn't scare them. I have to laugh. Penicillin production is the worst-kept secret I've ever come across. Wherever I go, men are discussing it. Could simply be the places I go," he added. "Anyway, the companies will do their duty and get their penicillin to the troops, but as soon as they can, they'll be turning their full attention to other antibacterials."

"Are they already turning their attention to other antibacterials?" she asked, trying to sound as if she didn't care.

"Not that I've heard," he lied, also trying to sound as if he didn't care, while wondering if each was actually spying on the other. Hanover had dozens of scientists working on the cousins. Rutherford, however, wouldn't reveal company secrets even to his family. When it came to business, sometimes a protective lie was necessary. Plenty of time to tell the truth later. "The fact is, whoever does crack the other medications is going to end up with quite a tidy profit."

"How much of a tidy profit?"

"My dear daughter, what's the price of a human life, do you think?"

"The *price* of a human life?" The price of Emily's life? Claire didn't like to think of herself as naive, but she would never put a price on Emily's life. Were there actually people in this world who put a price on the lives of others? "I have no idea."

"Neither do I," he said—although he was learning fast. "But you can be sure a man like George Merck has got some accountant in a back room right now figuring it out. And I'll wager it's going to be quite a lot. Enough to make one shot of a penicillin cousin cost, say, twenty dollars or even two hundred dollars, even if the drug itself costs two cents to produce, which it will, sooner or later. Never underestimate American ingenuity, I always say."

"If it costs two cents, then selling it for two hundred, or even twenty, dollars is profiteering."

"One man's profiteering is another man's rational business planning. What the market can bear, etc. We're fighting for free markets in this war among other delightful appurtenances of our society."

At two hundred dollars a dose, most people would have to steal to get these medications for their families. Could she have afforded it for Emily, in the days before she knew her father? She would have sold the house to get it—if she could have found a buyer in the three days before Emily died. To tamp down her outrage, she forced the conversation in a different direction. "And you?" she asked.

"Pardon?"

"Your turn. To tell me what you were doing at Hanover."

"Ah, yes." He turned his hands palm upward, as if happily shrugging at the obvious. "Business."

"What kind of business?"

"The moneymaking kind. The best kind. The war's been great for business, I'm not ashamed to say. We're on a roll. The Depression is over and the business class is on Roosevelt's side now." Businessmen had hated Roosevelt for what they considered the implicit socialism of his New Deal legislation. "Hanover's trying to raise capital. Looking to expand, take on the giants. A good time for it, lots of medical stuff needed for the war effort. Sulfa drugs, aspirin, antiseptics, bandages. I got an earful, I can tell you. I'm going to get involved. To tell you the truth, I'm going to buy him out."

"Really? That's exciting," she said sincerely. Here was a man who had enough money simply to buy a company if he wanted to, and one that produced useful products, too. There was something wonderful about him. She felt carried back to the days when she was younger and searched the business pages of newspapers and magazines, hoping to find her father's name.

"Yes, I made an offer old man Hanover couldn't refuse. I won't change the company name, though. The place has a reputation worth preserving. And I'll keep Hanover on as president and manager of day-to-day affairs. In my position, I don't worry about shipping labels and lightbulbs. I do my work at a different level."

In that split second, reinforcing his previous lie, Rutherford made a decision: he'd keep his cards close for now. He wouldn't reveal to her the real reason he was buying Hanover. No, he wouldn't tell Claire about the acre of soil samples in jam jars that he'd seen, the dozens of antibacterial substances making their way through the standard testing protocols. He knew that breakthroughs were just around the corner—breakthroughs that he now owned. He'd keep all that as a surprise for her. He'd share it with her when he actually had something more than dreams and expectations to show for his investment. When he actually had a medication to take to the marketplace. The truth was, his investment in Hanover was for her. And for Emily and Charlie, too. He was making an investment in their futures. A double investment. First, creating a medication that could save their lives—and the lives of all humanity. Second, guaranteeing the family's wealth for all time. This double investment would be his greatest gift to her, his beloved daughter.

"You see any penicillin?"

He gave her a slow grin. Penicillin was supposed to be a government secret, but she'd probably been fully briefed anyway, so he could talk about it. The cousins, however, were a business secret, and he wouldn't talk about them. "Wasn't I the one in the know? Hanover took me around to see the equivalent of a city block or two of milk bottles layered with green mold, and all the while I'm thinking, Sure am glad my girl got me in on this before the curve. Do you know, there's an actual shortage of milk bottles in New Jersey? They're all going to penicillin production, at a dozen different companies, at quadruple the usual price. The dairies don't know what to do."

Claire would have to report this conversation to Bush and Barnett, she realized. And she'd tell them about her father's stake in Hanover, although she suspected that with their wide sources of knowledge, they didn't need her to provide them that sort of information. Was she betraying her father? She didn't think so. Surely he wasn't doing anything illegal.

"By the way, you see much of that other young fellow who came to my house? Nick Catalano?" Rutherford proceeded gingerly here. He had a gut feeling that Catalano could be useful to him, and he was looking for an opening to get to know him better without making a big deal of it. "Seemed like an interesting fellow. Worth knowing."

"I see him now and then." Distracted by other concerns, Claire waved the question off. "There's something I don't understand. Selling antibacterials is not like selling rivets."

He'd return to Catalano some other time. "Sure it is. Exactly the same as selling rivets."

"But these drugs save lives, rivets don't."

"I imagine rivets have saved a few lives in their long history."

"You don't think there's, well, a human right for people to be able to receive an antibacterial at two cents a dose if that's what it costs to produce? Okay, at a dollar to allow for a good profit, but surely not as much as two hundred dollars for one shot?"

"Don't tell me you've turned into a socialist?" he said, mock appalled.

"We're talking about substances that scientists are finding on moldy bread and in the dirt outside their back doors."

"Sweetheart, you can't expect a company to do years of research and then sell a product at a nominal profit. You also can't expect a company to do years of research and give up commercial patent protection. These products never existed before, so new laws have to be written to govern them. That's my opinion, at least. Penicillin is a commodity, like any other—except in the case of penicillin, the government, claiming the public good in wartime, is going to take the patents on the means of mass production. The companies still hold out hope that they can change this and get at least some patents on penicillin. Meanwhile I expect other molds coming down the pike will get different treatment. Your Dr. Stanton and I had a discussion about this."

"Did you?" She stared at him, startled. "He never mentioned it."

To Rutherford, she sounded suspicious, as if she doubted him. How could she doubt him? He was hurt and offended by her lack of trust in him. He grasped at a way to appease her. "Of course he never mentioned it. It was a *secret* discussion!"

She wished he would stop that irritating compulsion of his to charm her. "What sort of secret discussion?" Despite her best efforts, she took her anger out on him—her anger over the attitude of Merck and Hanover, over the profit motive triumphant, over Jamie and her father keeping secrets from her. She still didn't entirely trust her father, so by what right did Jamie trust him?

Rutherford felt helpless against her. He'd done nothing wrong. He had nothing to apologize for. His daughter wore what looked like an emerald and diamond engagement ring, and so he might just as well confess the truth. "Stanton came to the apartment to seek my permission to ask you to marry him. Very old-fashioned. Gentlemanly. I appreciated it. I did the same with your mother's father, although considering what happened between your mother and me, I didn't recount that bit of family history to my possible future son-in-law."

"When did he do that?"

"When? I don't remember exactly when. Sometime before his sister died. I gave my permission, in case you're wondering, while assuring him that *my* permission would have no affect whatsoever on whether you gave *your* permission. We shared a laugh over that."

At her expense, Claire thought. She recognized that her anger was excessive, yet she couldn't control it.

"Then we moved on to other topics."

"What other topics?"

"His travels, my travels . . . nothing much. Stuff men talk about. I offered him a cigar, and he refused. Knowing how you hate cigars, I told him the cigar offer was a test of his appropriateness as a husband, and he passed."

She tried to calm herself. Again she changed the subject. "You work often with pharmaceutical companies?" she asked flatly.

He was taken aback. Too late, he realized how much he'd upset her. Had Stanton not followed through? She'd been wearing that emerald ring for a while now, hadn't she? Had she bought it for herself? Rutherford wished he could come right out and ask her, but he couldn't. He wasn't used to dealing with her. She had a rough and tough exterior, but underneath she was too damned sensitive for her own good. Why couldn't he remember this? He let himself get too wrapped up in his own concerns. He should never have mentioned his conversation with Stanton. Any little misstep could get him into trouble with her. Now he had to make amends. Quietly he said, "I work in everything, honey. Got to keep up. It's the only way to know what's going on. The specialist is doomed. You've got to play in every sector of the economy. My motto is, keep a finger in every pie and you'll never miss dessert."

He paused, hoping she'd smile, but she didn't. He soldiered on. "Speaking of dessert, end of next month I'm going to Hershey, Pennsylvania, for a four-day shindig at the chocolate factory. You know the drill, guys like me getting guided around and listening to lectures on how great everything is in the chocolate business and how much better it could be with a little infusion of capital and how it's patriotic, too, because our boys in uniform love their Hershey bars. Maybe Charlie could come with me. I've heard the chocolate factory tour is really something, and I can skip most of the meetings. Sounds like fun to me." A plaintive tone entered his voice. He needed so much from her. Too much for his own good.

Claire mulled this over. Charlie was looking forward to the end of the school year. He would be having a quiet summer, a few weeks at the YMCA day camp, the usual stickball with friends from the neighborhood, swimming lessons at the pool at Hudson Park (so long as there wasn't an outbreak of infantile paralysis). "That does sound like fun," she said guardedly.

"Maybe you could get assigned a story on Hershey, we could go together. I hear the air reeks with the smell of melted chocolate. Hard to show in a photograph, but even so. Or maybe you could take a couple of days off."

A family vacation. A rare occurrence. Unheard of, in fact. Part of her wanted to go. Luckily no decision was necessary: Mack had banned vacations for the duration. She could take time off if she really needed to, but the official line was useful to her now. "I won't be able to get off from work, it's not allowed, but I'm sure Charlie will enjoy it."

"I'll count on it, then, and make the arrangements. Your plans change, just let me know." He paused. "Thanks." She should be thanking him, he thought, but instead he was at her mercy.

At that hour, traffic into the city was light. Tony took the Holland Tunnel and headed downtown toward Wall Street. They dropped off Rutherford at the corner of Exchange Place and Broad, near his office. Even though it was nearing five-thirty, he had paperwork to catch up on. He hadn't been to the office all day. His secretary was staying late, waiting for him. He had to prepare for tomorrow's meetings, too.

Nonetheless Rutherford stood at the curb and watched the car holding his daughter drive on. Exchange Place was the width of a horse cart or two, skyscrapers rising straight up on both sides. The street was almost always in shadow, as it was now. Rutherford was grateful to watch his daughter's car from the shadows, because he couldn't be certain of controlling his expression. How he yearned to find the key to draw her out. To make her trust him. How he wished she and Charlie would move in with him. With his daughter and grandson safe at home, he could truly be a father, his dearest wish.

So many wishes. Such a fine line he walked. On eggshells, at his age, with his own daughter. That sick feeling in his stomach, the nervousness and second-guessing. He never should have let Lukins adopt her, although he still didn't have the courage to apologize to her outright. Was that what it would take to win her over? A full-blown apology? Apologies were hard. Maybe too hard.

Thirty years ago, he'd had a different view of the world. Assumed he'd have more children. His second wife had three miscarriages, then no more pregnancies. Last he'd heard from her, she was in the south of France with a new husband. That was seven years ago, before Vichy and the rest of the mess. God knew where she was now, and he was glad to realize that he didn't care. Besides, Charlie was as good as a son.

Standing alone on the crowded sidewalk on Exchange Place, skyscrapers rising around him, he looked like a titan of finance. Pedestrians glanced twice at him, trying to identify him, certain they'd seen his picture in a newspaper or a magazine, which undoubtedly they had. He noticed them noticing him, and he had to admit, it was gratifying. Made him feel more like himself, after the minefield of dealing with his daughter.

He watched Claire's big military car drive away until it was lost among the cars, taxis, and delivery trucks pushing uptown in the relentless current of the evening rush.

B y six-thirty, Claire was sitting with a group of colleagues at a large round table at the Three Gs, the staff's bar of choice on Forty-eighth Street, in the ground-floor level of the building that housed the photo lab. No smell of photo chemicals here, however, only the stench of cigarettes and beer. Scenes of Italy covered the walls. Claire nursed a Tom Collins. Mack had ordered two platters of oysters for the table. As usual, the air was thick with cigarette smoke. The smoke smarted her eyes, not that she cared; she was smoking, too. A celebration was going on for Mack's half-birthday. In her office, anything—birthday, belated birthday, half-birthday, three-quarters birthday, a victory or defeat in some far-flung place across the world, a marriage or a divorce—all were an excuse to go over to the Three Gs for a drink. The drinking continued back at the office for those assigned to the late shift.

Tonight the place was packed, and as she looked around, she saw that she was one of only three women in the room. The other two were secretaries. The men treated her as one of the guys, a role she tried to fill because it was good for her career. After so many years of being one of the guys, it came pretty easily, she thought ruefully as she sipped her drink and inhaled her cigarette. Tonight, however, she felt quiet and set apart, carrying with her a sadness and a frustration that had turned to regret, after the turmoil of the day.

Through the haze of cigarette smoke, she spotted Robert Darby, a writer with *Fortune*, at a far table. All at once she realized that he could be a resource for her. She wished she'd thought of Bob before. She stood, feeling the effects of the gin coursing through her body. "Excuse me, fellas, I've got to say hi to Bob Darby."

"Not Bob," Mack said with mock chagrin. "He's married. Just back from his honeymoon, in point of fact. You don't want to be bothering him."

"Jealous, Mack? Don't worry, I only need to ask him a question. I'll be back in a minute." She made her way through the crowd. Bob and Claire had met when they'd done a story together a few years ago for *Fortune*. They'd spent a week in Gary, Indiana, putting together a portrait of the city. It was a positive portrait, even though Claire's most striking shots were from the shores of Lake Michigan at dusk, long exposures with the camera on a tripod, across the lake to Chicago gleaming in the distance like a beacon, white and dazzling. "Bob, how are you?"

"Claire." He gave her a look of genuine pleasure. Bob, who'd been a wrestler at Princeton, was about five six, tough, and balding. Despite the wrestling, his manner was shy. He was also half-blind, with Coke-bottle glasses a quarter of an inch thick. "Good to see you. You know Steve and Craig?" She'd seen them, two young, highly polished Ivy Leaguers, on the elevator and in the hallways without knowing their names. They had no obvious physical defects to keep them out of the military, but who could really know. She shook their hands.

"Bob, could I talk to you for a minute?"

"He's married," Craig said, taking a pull from his beer bottle. "Just back from his honeymoon. We're available, though."

"I only like men when they're married, so you two are out of luck."

Steve and Craig laughed, but Bob, a gentle soul, blushed at the teasing.

"How about over there, Claire?" Bob motioned toward a table for two against the wall, which a couple was in the process of leaving.

When they were settled in, Claire said, "First, congratulations. I understand you're married. I didn't know."

"Thanks." He took his glasses off for close-up discussions. The heavy frame left a red mark on the bridge of his nose. His eyes were large and soft brown, like a puppy's.

"Have time for a real honeymoon?"

"Yeah, we were lucky. Her family's got a place on Cape Cod, so we went there. By train and bus. A long trip. They keep a car there, and our parents pitched in some gas coupons so we could do a little touring. Hard to go anywhere more exotic nowadays."

"You said it."

They chatted for a few minutes about the daily hardships of the home front, finishing with the obligatory recognition of how fortunate they were to be here in New York having these relatively minor difficulties instead of being elsewhere facing much worse difficulties. Then Bob said, "Hey, I saw your pictures of the Kuomintang party at the River Club. That must have been something.

I loved the shot of John D. Rockefeller the Third in costume and throwing darts."

"We all do our part. At least the old man wasn't wearing Chinese robes. The missus had on some kind of embroidered silk sheath."

"It's coming back to me."

"I know I'll never forget it. When the old man spoke to me about work, Mrs. Luce just about accused me of trying to seduce him."

"Well, we already know from your own admission that you've got a weakness for married men."

"Somehow I've been able to resist the attractions of that particular married man."

"Personally I wouldn't want to be in a cat fight with Clare Boothe Luce."

"I think it might be fun. Provided I won. Listen"—she leaned toward him, lowering her voice in case anyone at the surrounding tables was listening—"about six months ago, I did a big story on a new medicine called penicillin. Story got killed, but I keep wondering about it. You know how it is. You hear anything in your circles about penicillin?"

"The green-mold medicine?"

"That's the one."

"Military secret, that's what I hear. Not supposed to talk about it. No civilian use allowed."

"That's what I hear, too."

"Thousands of guys on the payroll. Strict government control over patents on the means of production. Suspension of antitrust regulations, share and share alike. The companies are in a real quandary, trying to make the government happy during a war while simultaneously protecting their turf. But what I'm really hearing about are the penicillin cousins. Guess those are from red, orange, and blue mold," he joked.

Truer than he knew, Claire thought. "What do you hear about them?"

"That someday they're going to be coming out like a house on fire, patent protection on the actual substances and all. Penicillin's turning into yesterday's news, at least from a business perspective. But with the cousins . . ." Now he leaned forward, speaking confidentially. "You know, Claire, in the course of my day I spend three-quarters of my time fending off rumors. Rumors designed to make the market go up, down, or sideways, based on nothing. But even discounting the rumors, it seems to me that with the cousins, we're going to see American capitalism sent back to the robber baron days in a hurry."

"Wait a minute. I thought natural products can't be patented. I thought—"

"Ah, Claire," he interrupted her. "Still the idealist, eh?" He shook his head with friendly skepticism. "Well, idealism is where we all started, isn't it? Probably none of us would be in this room if we hadn't started out as idealists. You just mark my words: it might take years, and I can't predict what rationalization they'll come up with, to earn patent protection on natural substances. But with the cousins, it'll be Rockefeller, Carnegie, and Frick, all over again. And you know what," he added, relishing the prospect, "strictly from a reporter's perspective, I can't wait."

CHAPTER EIGHTEEN

D etective Marcus Kreindler didn't like to say that the key was food, but time and again, that's what it turned out to be. Sit these guys down with a plate of *Rindergoulasch* and spaetzle, with a liter of *Pils* on the side, and they'd tell you anything. This evening he was entertaining Friedrich Geckmann, nickname Fritz, he of the blindingly blond hair and porcine face. Geckmann's thick blond eyebrows made his forehead virtually disappear in the glare. He was a walking cliché.

"So Fritz, that's some strange place, the Rockefeller Institute." Kreindler dug into his *Königsberger Klopse*. This was his third meal in Yorkville in three weeks, and on that score, he was a happy man. This evening he was at Franziskaner, on Second Avenue, a great place to take a Nazi to dinner. The restaurant was crowded but not too crowded, with a pleasant background din and empty tables on either side of theirs. Of course Kreindler had slipped the hostess a little bonus to keep the adjoining tables empty. His seat gave him a terrific view of the giant mural of the Bavarian Alps, complete with well-endowed Bavarian girls, on the opposite wall. "What's the story over there?"

"Don't worry about that place, Detective," Fritz said smugly. "We got somebody in there watching everything for us. You think we'd let a prize like that get away?" His expression turned nasty. "What kind of people do you think we are?"

Fritz's simultaneous self-righteousness and insecurity drove Kreindler crazy. Talking to Fritz was like being on a seesaw gone wild. By day, Fritz worked at a grocery. By night, he enjoyed Nazi pursuits. "I think you're the kind of people I can count on to have a contact in place over there."

"That's right." Mollified, Fritz calmed down. With his bulging stomach proving that he'd had more than a few too many beers in the past years, Fritz guzzled down the entire contents of his mug.

"You want another?" Kreindler said. "Why am I even asking?" Kreindler lifted his hand and motioned to the waitress, shapely in her dirndl. "Another for my friend here."

"Always glad to enjoy your hospitality, Detective," Fritz said.

"That makes two of us. So who is it?" Kreindler asked, putting on an offhanded yet respectful tone. Meanwhile, Kreindler was thinking, this might be his chance to get back on the case. Officially.

Fritz gave a thin, knowing grin. "The person you'd least suspect."

"Clever choice, then."

"That's right. I have to confess, though—I didn't make the choice myself. The higher-ups made the choice. The *highest*-ups, in fact. A choice I never would have dreamed of."

"Don't underestimate yourself," Kreindler replied.

"I don't, usually," Fritz said. "Hey, did I tell you that a few months back I got paid a visit by the FBI?"

"No," Kreindler said, feigning concern.

"Yes!" Fritz was excited. "Told them an hour's worth of lies and sent them on a wild goose chase."

Was Fritz already being watched? Kreindler wondered. He'd have to find out from his contacts at the FBI. "Of course you did."

Fritz nodded in agreement. "What happened was . . ." Fritz started into a long story.

Kreindler leaned back, an appreciative smile fixed in place. He had a long evening ahead. He'd bring a *Stück* of Franziskaner's marvelous *Käsekuchen* home to Agnes to make it up to her. Everything came back to food, after all.

CHAPTER NINETEEN

⌒

Rutherford was alert with expectation. Yes, at his age, and with his experience, this still meant something. He had a place at the table. A metaphor that in this case was also literally true: here he sat at the Harvard Club, in the Harvard Hall, surrounded by a stuffed elephant, the directors of the pharmaceutical industry, and various government bureaucrats. Vannevar Bush himself was at the head of the table. Tapestries covered the top part of the walls, with the bottom part taken up with carved wood paneling and two huge mantelpieces. An old ship model dangled from the ceiling on a chain. Gigantic chandeliers could cause death on impact. Old men stared at him from old paintings.

Dr. Bush was going around the table, asking each man to give a report on the current status of his group's penicillin research and production. To the left and slightly behind Bush (not actually at the table, denoting thereby a secondary position) sat a bow-tied and officious man whom Bush referred to as "Dr. Barnett." James Stanton, Rutherford's future (he hoped) son-in-law wasn't here. Must be traveling. Just as well. Rutherford didn't want to appear beholden to a younger man. Nick Catalano *was* here; they'd shaken hands coming in. Rutherford was still hoping that an opportunity would present itself for them to get to know each other better. But Rutherford wouldn't push this; he'd let his wish take its natural course. Looking around, Rutherford recognized George Merck from photographs in the newspapers. The others he didn't know, but he tried to memorize their faces with their nameplates, so that at the next meeting he could walk right in and say, "Mr. Smith, a pleasure to see you again." And, "John O'Donnell, isn't it? In from Peoria for the meeting? How's the weather out there, this time of year?"

He was also paying attention because he wanted to learn how they did it. Not so much the penicillin part—his researchers were ahead on that, he quickly realized. No, he wanted to learn their manner. Learn to put himself into this scene and become the master of it. Exactly what he'd been doing all his life. Although he'd never gone to college, by now he was accustomed to fitting in with men who had—and at the best places, too. Nobody would ever guess that Edward Rutherford wasn't formally educated.

"Mr. Edward Rutherford, on behalf of Hanover and Company," Bush's secretary, sitting slightly behind him on the right, intoned from her list.

"I'm happy to report that we've had progress on all fronts, except the elusive synthesis," he added with a touch of irony, guaranteed to make the others smile. No one had success on synthesis. "We're making exceptionally good progress on the issue of deep-tank fermentation, more similar to beer production than we ever would have imagined." Laughter all around. "Now then, as you know . . ." He proceeded to give a seemingly full, detailed, and properly scientific report—while holding back, just as the other companies did, on anything truly groundbreaking—and punctuating his remarks with well-planned humor. A few months ago, he hadn't known any of this stuff. Now he sounded like an expert. Correction: he *was* an expert.

"Excellent news," Dr. Bush said when Rutherford finished. "And thank you for your frankness. Next."

The secretary read from her list, and the Lederle man began his report.

Rutherford congratulated himself. He'd done it. His place at the table was secure. A remarkable moment for him. This industry made money by saving lives. Nothing more profitable or more worthwhile (in both the financial and moral sense of the term) than that.

Now he could relax and analyze what the others were saying. None of the esteemed gentlemen here at the table mentioned the cousins. No, they all had their secrets and kept them close. Bush had demanded that all their time be given to penicillin research, but no one followed that edict. Certainly they were working very hard on penicillin production, despite numerous setbacks and problems. The lure of the cousins, however, was too great to ignore. With the cousins you could control the future. You could control the nature of life itself. At Hanover, however, they still didn't have anything. As far as Rutherford knew—and he had spies at all the companies, just as he presumed they had spies at his company—nobody else had anything yet, either. Soon they would, though; he had no doubt. In this business, he felt he was constantly on the edge of his seat, the level of expectation was so high.

On the patent issue, Rutherford predicted that when the first company went to the patent office with a viable, nonpenicillin antibacterial, the company would get a patent—for both the substance itself *and* for the means of mass production. Some excuse would be found to justify the new regulations: "These medications are so complicated to produce that new rules must be put into place to govern them." Something like that. It would be the unspoken quid pro quo to make up for the industry's commercial sacrifices on penicillin. Once upon a time, you couldn't patent natural products. Now you could. Such an elegant solution, accomplished in the background, without a fight, as smooth as could be. Rutherford was just waiting for it to happen.

The meeting was over. The men stubbed out their cigarettes. Gathered their papers. Getting up, they talked in small cliques. Rutherford didn't have any friendships here. Not yet, at least. At the moment, he didn't need any. Let them get used to him being at the table, then he'd start befriending them. Besides, he needed to write down the discussion, both what the others had said and the details that would match the faces with the nameplates. He didn't allow himself to take notes during the meeting. He liked to project an image of someone who had no need of notes. A man who could remember everything—that was Edward Rutherford.

Except the image wasn't the reality. If he wanted to remember the details, he'd have to write them down. He needed to find a secluded corner.

He looked around. Wasn't there a library someplace at the Harvard Club? A gray-haired butler-type guarded the door, an aged retainer, as the saying went. Rutherford approached him.

"Excuse me, young man," Rutherford said in his best making-requests-to-aged-retainers voice, "I need a quiet place to write myself some notes. Old head isn't what it used to be. Any suggestions?"

"Certainly, sir. Follow me."

They went up some stairs—elk, moose, and antelope heads regarding him from lofty perches on the walls—then along a short corridor, through the library, down a few more stairs, and there he was, on a kind of balcony overlooking the meeting room.

"Here you are, sir. Quite private." The fellow was old and black but had a touch of an English accent.

"Perfect," Rutherford said. "Thank you." A tip was in order. Never knew when this gentleman would come in handy for a few tips of a different sort on whatever the high and mighty were discussing in various secret meetings they might conduct here. Rutherford gave him a five, more than generous, which the man slipped into his pocket.

"Good afternoon, sir."

"And to you, my friend."

The man disappeared. Rutherford made himself comfortable despite the two stuffed water buffalo heads now regarding him from the corners of the balcony. He took an unused pad out of his briefcase. Leaving the first page blank, he turned to the second page. Starting his notes with the beginning of the meeting, he methodically made his way through the discoveries reported by the men whom he could now call his colleagues.

Three pages on, he heard a noise. He looked up. Nick Catalano stood before him.

"Sorry to interrupt," Catalano said.

"Not at all." Well, this was a nice surprise. Rutherford stood and simultaneously pushed over the pages of the pad. He never wrote on the top page of any pad because of exactly this type of situation.

"May I intrude on you for a few minutes?" Catalano asked.

"Always happy to talk." Rutherford sat down.

Catalano pulled over a chair. "I'll be brief." He sat straight, as if at military attention.

"Take as long as you like."

"This won't take long."

Catalano was hesitating. Rutherford knew what that meant. Something special at hand. His attention was rapt now. He leaned back to make himself appear relaxed. Crossed his legs. Not a care in the world. He made a pyramid of his hands. Pure patience, that's what he was.

"Uh, well, I'll be frank. A sample has come into my hands. An antibacterial. I don't know what to do with it."

Catalano didn't meet his eyes. Helpfully Rutherford stepped in. "You're wondering if I'd know what to do with it?"

Catalano laughed in relief. "Yes. In fact I'm sure you would know."

"What is it?" asked Rutherford lightheartedly, joining in the amusement to encourage Catalano to let down his guard.

Catalano glanced over the balcony. Rutherford followed his gaze. The room below was deserted except for the elephant. All the humans were at lunch. Nothing like a meeting to get you desperate for a lunchtime martini.

"An antibacterial substance with excellent potential. It might be the miracle drug we've been looking for."

"Ah." This was a surprise. Rutherford kept it light: "Why come to me? Don't you follow the idealistic rules of your idealistic employer, the Rockefeller Institute? Put the recipe into the public domain? No profits, etcetera?"

Catalano turned away. Rutherford regarded his profile. Catalano was handsome, no doubt about that. Dashing. A bad boy who probably had a million girls.

"Idealism doesn't last forever," Catalano finally said.

Rutherford knew that was true.

"I'm thinking about the future. Who knows, might want to get married someday. Buy a house. Have a more comfortable kind of life."

So the issue was money, pure and simple. "Why don't you go to work at one of the drug companies, if you want a higher salary. Come to work for me at Hanover. I'd love to have you."

"After the Rockefeller Institute?"

So, Catalano was proud and condescending, on top of being money hungry (not that there was anything wrong with being money hungry). "Why did you pick me for this opportunity I presume you're selling? Why not one of the big boys?"

Rutherford already knew the answer: he'd planted the seed, over brandy, in front of his own fireplace. Nick trusted him. Rutherford knew there must be something shady about this substance. But it could still be a terrific opportunity. This was business, and this was how business was done. He, certainly, was no idealist.

"Little guys are more creative."

Well, a good answer, Rutherford had to admit. He himself was more creative, that was for sure. That's how little guys got to be big guys.

"I want a million dollars for it."

Rutherford burst out laughing. "I don't know what you've got, but I can tell you, it's not worth that right now. Right now, it's in development. You don't know what's going to come of it. It might be a dud. Has it been tested on humans? It might cause anaphylactic shock." He complimented himself on being able to throw that impressive phrase into the discussion.

"I suppose it could," Catalano conceded.

Now they were getting somewhere. Rutherford wanted the substance, but on his terms. "First of all, you discover this yourself?"

Catalano paused. "Yes."

"Where'd you find it?" Everybody asked this question, even though the answer wasn't important. Once you had the mold or the actinomyces or even the antibacterial bacteria and you could grow it, where you got it from didn't count anymore, except for curiosity's sake. Maybe a certain romanticism was involved, too, in the focus on location: "This sample is from the pine forests of Rome. This one is from the gardens of the Tuileries Palace in Paris. This one from the top of Mont Blanc."

Catalano still hadn't responded. The telling pause, Rutherford thought.

"I found it when I was visiting my parents in Syracuse."

Maybe yes, maybe no, Rutherford thought. "Well, I guess that's as good a place as any."

Catalano laughed more than necessary—it wasn't a joke. Catalano was nervous. He wanted to get rid of this substance, but privately, to conceal his involvement. He felt safer with someone he knew personally. Instinctively Rutherford understood this.

"What makes you so sure it's going to work?" Rutherford pressed. "I'm just supposed to trust you on that?"

"Yes, you're going to have to take my word for it," Catalano said, bold once more.

Oh, a tough one, was he? Catalano thought he was a tough one? Well, Rutherford was tough, too.

"Where is it?"

"Not here. Someplace safe."

"I should hope so. I'll give you fifty thousand dollars and that's the end of it." Fifty thousand dollars was still a fortune. "We'll make it legal. A contract. I'll give you a cashier's check."

"I don't want anything public," Nick said in a rush.

Of course he didn't. "A contract doesn't have to be public." Rutherford had the upper hand, he knew. "I'll have my attorney draw it up. You can stop by the apartment later to sign it. Make it a social call. I realize you may not want to come to my office, what with your position in the penicillin campaign. Shall we say 7:00 PM? My attorney works fast when he has to. You can stay for dinner if you like."

"Your offer's not good enough."

"Well, that's for you to decide."

Catalano said nothing, pondering.

Rutherford had a choice now: to come in strong, or to step back. He wanted the substance, but he'd play through the bluff and pretend it didn't matter to him.

"Look, Nick." He used the first name to draw him in, father to son. "You think things over. Don't decide now. This is a big step. I'll be home at seven, with the check and the contract. I believe you know the address. Stop by or not, it's up to you. No hard feelings if you have second thoughts." He turned back toward the table, ready to resume his work. "Now excuse me, but I've got to write down my notes from the meeting before everything I heard evaporates. Growing old—no fun."

Catalano stood. Picked up his briefcase. Stared into the distance, as if he wanted to say more. Then he left without a thank-you or a good-bye.

Rutherford knew he'd turn up tonight.

As he flipped through his pad to find the page where he'd left off, he wondered where, in fact, Catalano had found whatever it was that he was selling.

Well, in the end that didn't really matter. These drugs were made from natural products, and you might find them outside your own back door. If ownership questions came up later, Rutherford would say exactly that: this particular medication? Why, his grandson had found it in Central Park, across the street from the apartment. This medication had nothing to do with the substance Nick Catalano had sold him.

Anybody could discover anything. That's what it meant to be a natural product—and right now, you couldn't patent them and you couldn't own them. That was sure to change.

This generation of Americans has a rendezvous with destiny. Roosevelt's words at the 1936 Democratic Convention came into his mind. Rutherford was a Republican, but he still listened when the president gave a speech.

Rutherford had a hunch that this might just be his own, personal rendezvous with destiny.

When he got outside, Nick was panting. Sweating. What had he just done? And was it right?

He stopped to get a grip on himself. People bumped into him. He'd interfered with the flow of noontime pedestrians.

Where was he? Where was he going?

West Forty-fourth—that's where he was. Head east, he told himself. Go home. To the Institute. He turned left. The Chrysler Building was before him, so close it was watching him, the metallic gargoyles staring.

The street was packed. The heat was unbearable. The air was thick with humidity. The sky was gray from the heat and the dirt and the soggy moisture in the air. He headed toward Grand Central. He had to get the subway, to go uptown.

The crowd jostled him. The city pressed against him.

He was right to sell the substance to Rutherford. He was right, he was right . . . he repeated this to convince himself. He'd go home, put everything in a shopping bag, and at 7:00 PM he'd give the bag to Rutherford and take his check.

He'd been through his options a hundred times.

Rutherford was Claire's father. Nick knew him and could trust him. Rutherford would protect him.

Nick had to think about the future. What was past was past and couldn't be taken back, or made better, or forgiven.

CHAPTER TWENTY

In the bottom of the fourth inning, the crowd screamed its approval.

"Mom, did you see that?" Charlie turned around to explain. "Billy got to second on an error at first."

Billy was Billy Herman, the hitter. Claire restrained herself from covering her ears to muffle the din.

Friday evening, July 24, at Ebbets Field. The Brooklyn Dodgers versus the Pittsburgh Pirates. They had seats by the railing along the third-base line, which Claire had to admit was somewhat better than being in the bleachers. Charlie and his friend Ben, and her driver, Tony, and his younger brother, Joe, were sitting in the row in front of her. John Smith, of Pfizer, was sitting next to her.

The Dodgers were having a great year, with a seven-game lead over the St. Louis Cardinals, or so Charlie had explained to her. Last year the Yankees had defeated the Dodgers in the World Series, but Charlie was confident the Dodgers would make the series again this year and defeat the Yankees.

"Go—go!" The boys punched each other's shoulders in enthusiasm as Mickey Owen drove in a run and reached second on another error. They stood, jumping and shouting as if they'd run the bases themselves. John Smith also stood to cheer.

Claire did not stand. The heat, the noise, the reek of sauerkraut, the vertiginous angle of the Ebbets Field stands rising around them, exhausted her and gave her a touch of queasiness. She'd never understood the appeal of baseball. This game had started early because of the dimout regulations, and the temperature was still in the high eighties. The humidity was a gel-like sheet pressed over her face. At the beginning of the game, Red Barber, the radio announcer, had urged them to donate blood for the troops. The mention of blood contributed to her queasiness. They were instructed to throw back foul balls, so the balls could be sent to the armed services teams. They stood for the wartime innovation of singing "The Star-Spangled Banner." At that point, Claire had been ready to go home, but she had at least two more hours ahead of her.

Smith rearranged himself in his seat. "I like it out here," he said when the crowd quieted. "I feel relaxed." Dressed in a blue-and-white seersucker suit, tie tight against his neck, perspiration beading on his temples beneath his panama hat, Mr. Smith didn't look relaxed, but Claire took his word for it. He was a large, strong man with gray hair and a granite face. "You feel relaxed, Mrs. Shipley?"

"Yes, very relaxed."

"I'm glad."

The boys were lucky to be using his tickets; she wouldn't offend him by complaining. This week when Claire and Tony had visited Pfizer headquarters, Smith had given them the usual song and dance about Pfizer's lack of success and shown them the usual pristine laboratory. Just as Claire was about to walk down an apparently off-limits corridor, he offered to take her, her family, all her friends and the families of all her friends to a baseball game. He was part owner of the team, so this was no sacrifice for him. At first she'd refused. Then she caught the look on Tony's face—Tony who might someday have his dream fulfilled and become a tank driver—and she thought of Charlie, who would escape the conflict only by the grace of God, and she accepted, provided she could pay for the tickets. Smith insisted he had the seats anyway, but she insisted on paying, and finally he capitulated and let her pay. She wasn't about to start accepting bribes.

So here they were, sweltering in the humidity of a New York summer's evening, Tony's uniform shirt glued to his back with perspiration. Charlie was on his third hot dog, Ben was finishing an astonishing fourth. Joe ignored his hot dog to give his full attention to the game.

"That was inside," Tony shouted.

"Inside," Ben repeated.

"Okay, ball two." Tony provided more details to the boys, and Claire gave up trying to follow. All evening he'd been explaining to them the nuances of each pitch and the special talents of each batter and the histories and statistics of every player back to what sounded like the beginning of time itself. As he spoke to the younger boys, the set of Tony's shoulders was both relaxed and proud.

"Wonderful to see the boys excited," Smith said.

"Yes."

"If you have time after the game, I'll take them to the locker room to meet Leo." Leo Durocher was the manager of the Dodgers. "No women allowed, though." He chuckled. "That all right with you?"

"Yes, of course. A wonderful opportunity for the boys." She tried to sound excited on their behalf.

"I hope they'll have many opportunities to come out here as my guests. With you paying for their tickets, of course."

"You're very kind, Mr. Smith."

"Not at all. The least I can do."

The least you can do for what or whom? Claire wondered.

"Yes, it's nice to come out here to the stadium, isn't it?" he mused. "Out here, everything is free and easy and we can really talk to each other. Not like the office. Too many open ears at the office, eh? That reminds me: I met your father recently."

Claire was taken aback. "You did?"

"Sure. He's involved with Hanover, right?"

"Yes, that's right."

"I saw him at a meeting. At the Harvard Club."

"He doesn't discuss business details with me."

"That's as it should be. I'm the same with my family."

But Claire wondered, How did John Smith know that Edward Rutherford was her father? Were all these pharmaceutical people watching her, just as she was assigned to watch them? She wouldn't let herself become paranoid, but it was disconcerting.

Smith turned puckish. "Forgive me for indulging in a little harmless espionage, Mrs. Shipley: is our setup at Pfizer pretty much the same as the other places you've visited?"

"Pretty nearly identical, Mr. Smith. The part of the setup I'm seeing, I mean. New and never used."

"Good. Glad to hear it. Always good to know that we're keeping up with the Joneses."

"A grand ambition, Mr. Smith, to keep up with the Joneses."

"Absolutely. Tell me something, Mrs. Shipley, this penicillin photography just a job for you, or you have a dog in this fight, too?"

She paused to consider her response. She decided to be honest with him, even though she suspected her honesty would disarm him. "My daughter died of septicemia."

Before them, the three boys and the young man in uniform cheered for another play. But Claire and Smith were suddenly in an intimate conversation.

"She died years ago, though it seems, well, like yesterday. She was only three years old."

"Ah." Smith seemed oddly affected by this, rubbing his knees, his eyes turning bloodshot, but he said nothing more. He turned away from her and watched the game. A hit straight down the center drove in two runs. When Claire moved her feet, she felt as if she were peeling her shoes off the concrete; the soles were sticky from the spilled beer and Coke flowing down from seats behind them.

"Let me tell you some history," Smith finally said. "We at Pfizer were working on penicillin long before Dr. Florey brought his sample over from Oxford. We worked with a group at Columbia University, College of Physicians and Surgeons. A team led by Dr. Dawson, a fine man. We made the stuff, they tested it. Problem was, by the time the penicillin traveled from our manufacturing plant in Brooklyn and to their testing laboratory in Washington Heights, it was useless. Didn't work at all. I told the guys, to keep their spirits up, that the problem was the Williamsburg Bridge. The penicillin didn't like the potholes on the bridge."

He glanced at her. She waited.

"The truth is," he continued, "only God knows what killed it. That's penicillin for you. Completely unpredictable. But when the government decided to move ahead with it, we fell into line. Doing our duty. At Pfizer, we're going from bedpans and milk bottles directly to deep-tank submerged fermentation. This is a secret, by the way, but it's a secret that doesn't matter, because nobody else can do it. Sure they want to do it, they're trying to do it, but they can't. They don't have the know-how. Only Pfizer has the know-how and the experienced, dedicated scientists, from years spent perfecting the deep-tank fermentation methods used to produce citric acid, one of our traditional specialties. We bought an old ice plant on Marcy Avenue, and we're moving in huge fermentors, bigger than railroad cars, over a dozen of them, and we're going forward. We've got one goal: to be the biggest producer of penicillin in the country. Okay, we're not in production yet, but with the team we've got, it's only a matter of time."

"I'd like to get some pictures of those fermentors." She saw the shots in her mind: a row of giant vats in a rhythm of steel, gleaming in the lights she'd set up around them, workmen dwarfed as they walked among them. American industry triumphant. "I'm sure Dr. Bush would, too."

"Yes, I'm sure he would," Smith said. "Mrs. Shipley, I've got men working twenty-four hours a day, catching sleep at the plant when they can. Have we had any success? Can't say that we have. Contamination, that's the problem, over and over. But we will have success, sooner rather than later. In the meantime, we don't need some well-intentioned government flunky like you or James Stanton or Nicholas Catalano coming around and checking up on us. Nothing personal, mind you, and you're always welcome to bring the boys to a baseball game. Anytime." He gestured magnanimously, taking in the field, the terrific seats, the hot dogs. "This has nothing to do with you. It's the principle. We're serving our country and doing our duty, but we're running a business, too. This isn't a Communist state, at least not the last time I checked."

"Of course it's not a Communist state," she said, trying to make herself sound as if she were teasing him, "but I still don't understand why I can't take the pictures. I'll make you look like a hero."

"I don't need to be a hero. You can't take the pictures because this is our business, not yours. Not Vannevar Bush's. It's *our* business. I'm looking ahead to when this war is over. To when penicillin is available to the general public. The government may control the patents, but there'll still be a profit in selling the drug. Do I want George Merck looking at some photos in *Life* magazine and figuring out how I do my work? George Merck is a fine fellow and I wish him success, but I'm not going to hand him the results of my team's hard labor."

He studied her. "Well, I do run on a bit, don't I." It wasn't a question. "You'll have to forgive me." His demeanor conveyed that he wasn't asking for forgiveness. "I still think about poor Lucretia Stanton. I met her once at a conference. Remarkable woman. I offered her a job, but she wouldn't take it. Considered herself above the profit motive. Those people over at the Rockefeller Institute—they think they're better than people trying to do business and make money. But who accomplishes more in the end, eh? We do. Let me give you some advice, Mrs. Shipley. You seem like a nice woman. A good mother. You've got a fine son. Your father's a good man. You know and I know that penicillin isn't the only substance we're working on. Sure, we're trying to save lives, but there's a lot of money at stake here, too. Give up this assignment of yours. Not everybody in this business is as civilized as I am. 'Nice guys finish last'—one of Leo's favorite sayings, as you probably know. An apt motto for many circumstances." He sighed wearily. "It's not for me to tell anyone else how to run his business. But I can confidently speak for myself and my colleagues at Pfizer when I say: we're the experts, let us get on with things. *That* would constitute your personal service to your country. And to yourself and your family."

He didn't speak in anger. He simply communicated facts. Was he threatening her directly, or merely imparting a threat from others? Claire wasn't certain. Yes, he frightened her, but she wouldn't let him suspect it. She shot back, "This just a job for you, Mr. Smith, or you have a dog in this fight, too?"

He surprised her by shuffling in his seat. He stared at home plate for a moment, before turning to her once more. "As a matter of fact, you and I have something in common: my daughter died of bacterial meningitis. Nothing the doctors could do to help her." He stopped, unable to go on. Then, "She loved coming to the ball game. She loved the hot dogs, the ice cream, the peanuts. She was a pretty little thing. Smart as a whip. Penicillin would have saved her—or at least I like to think it would have. We're still waiting for clinical trials on bacterial meningitis. But indulge me: I like to think she'd be alive today, sitting here with us. Talking to the boys. Flirting with Tony. If her doctors had penicillin. Or some other antibacterial. So I'm doing my damnedest to make sure that nobody else's kid dies like that. Meningitis is a horrible death. Septicemia, too. Every death is a horrible death; I'm not running a contest. Mark my words, Mrs. Shipley: Pfizer is going to create an entire nation where kids don't die of infectious diseases. You see, I *am* an idealist—but an idealist who knows that only money, and lots of it, money in the form of patents and profits, can turn my goal into reality. You understand?"

Against all her expectations, his eyes were swollen and watery.

"I do understand, Mr. Smith. Believe me, I do."

Pulling his panama hat down over his forehead, he turned and snapped his fingers at a concessionaire in the next aisle. He ordered a hot dog in a gruff voice. When he received it, covered with sauerkraut and mustard, half-wrapped in a napkin, he cradled it in the palms of his hands without eating it. He stared at the field, the sauerkraut congealing in the summer heat.

The Dodgers won that night, 6–4, their fourth victory in a row.

CHAPTER TWENTY-ONE

⁓

L ate for a staff meeting, Claire slipped into an elevator that was about to close. She didn't notice the lobby porter warning her to hold back. Too late, she realized her mistake.

"Mr. Luce, forgive me."

The rule was that no one, no matter how senior in the company hierarchy, was to break Mr. Luce's morning concentration by riding in the elevator with him. Rumor was that he prayed for God's guidance during his long ride up to the penthouse in the morning. Claire thought this might even be true. The elevator operator, a young blonde whose lush curves burst from her pert uniform, held the door open and waited for Claire to step out. Her nameplate read ROSEMARY.

"Stay, Mrs. Shipley," Luce ordered. "It's all right, Hutton." The lobby porter stepped back, shaking his head, as if signaling his disapproval of Luce's violation of his own standards. Hutton motioned for Rosemary to close the door. Claire lowered her camera bags to the floor. Mr. Luce smelled strongly of cigarettes, the odor filling the Art Deco elevator cab. He was a big man, always taller than she expected from his rotund features. They headed up to the top floor. His floor. How stupid, this trepidation over an elevator ride. He had forced her to violate a sacrosanct rule.

"I'm not supposed to be riding in the elevator with you, Mr. Luce. You like to ride in the elevator by yourself."

A slight smile formed at the corner of his lips. "Just this once. Not making a habit of it."

Whether this meant that *he* wasn't going to be making a habit of it, or *she* wasn't going to be making a habit of it, Claire didn't ask.

"You look distressed, Mrs. Shipley. Not about the elevator, I hope."

She wanted to tell him about her conversation with John Smith, in fact was planning to make an appointment with him today. She couldn't continue with this secret project if it imperiled Charlie, however far-fetched that idea seemed. She was planning to tell Luce that she was stepping aside from this assignment. Somebody else could take it on. She wouldn't tell him here on the elevator, however, with Rosemary undoubtedly alert to every word. Instead she grasped at humor to smooth her way. "I went to a baseball game."

"Why?"

She laughed. "I was invited. By John Smith of Pfizer. The Dodgers. I paid for my ticket. I insisted upon that."

"Good. Baseball. All-American pastime. Have to give it credit. Brings people together. I approve of Roosevelt letting the teams play through the war."

"I'm sure he appreciates your support." In fact the president probably did appreciate Luce's support on the baseball issue.

"Smith owns the Dodgers, doesn't he?" Luce asked.

"Part owner."

"So he's got the seats anyway. Might as well fill them with you, paying or not."

"Thank you," she said, uncertain if this was a compliment.

They reached his floor. "Step out," he told her, and she did. He waited for the elevator door to close. As he stood beside her, she felt his power assailing her, like an aphrodisiac. They were alone. He said, "I heard through a long grapevine that the pharmaceutical companies have been keeping us out."

She appreciated the way he said "us," pulling her in, giving her a sense of belonging and of his protection.

"They do seem to have invested a lot of money building labs they don't use, to conceal their research."

"If there weren't a war on, I'd print your photos of unused labs and test tubes filled with water. Show the American people what these companies have been doing. They're not entitled to treat Time, Incorporated with such disregard. The country doesn't deserve that." He always conflated the good of the country with the good of his company.

"A warning has come my way. A strong suggestion to move along."

"From whom?"

"Pfizer was the conduit, although John Smith seemed to say it had nothing to do with him. He was only expressing the views of less savory elements of the industry."

"Ah." Luce thought this through. "I don't like it, no matter what the exact intentions. It's un-American." He glanced aside for a moment, weighing the options. "Here's my decision: go back to one of the companies. When they don't expect you. At night. On a weekend. Get the real story. Don't go to Merck. George Merck has gotten himself on committees running things for the war, I don't need complaints from him. Go to Hanover. Old man Hanover's never given a dime to China relief, serves him right."

Hanover—that put Claire into an awkward position. There was no reason why Mr. Luce would know that Edward Rutherford had bought the company (which was privately held rather than publicly traded), or that Rutherford was her father. Well, it didn't matter: she was withdrawing from this assignment.

"Mr. Luce, I have my son to protect. And myself, frankly, on my son's behalf. I'm less interested in this assignment than I was. I want you to take me off it."

"Don't be ridiculous. The answer is no. Too much at stake. You're the best one for the job."

"I'm no longer—"

"Mrs. Shipley," he interrupted, "here's what I tell staff traveling to the South, uncovering the truth about Jim Crow. Anyone tries to interfere with you, anyone tries to scare you, you remember this: you are a representative of *Life* magazine. Of Time, Incorporated. You are a representative of *me*."

On the all-important *me*, he turned and walked down the hall toward his office without saying good-bye. Claire was left staring at a large notice on the wall announcing that in the event of a bombing raid, this floor was to be evacuated immediately.

CHAPTER TWENTY-TWO

⌒

Fifteen minutes before midnight, Claire and Tony finally found a parking spot in the crowded lot of Hanover & Company. Crucial war industries were staffed twenty-four hours a day, in three shifts. Judging from the packed lot, the workers here weren't affected by gasoline rationing; or maybe the area lacked public transportation so the workers had no choice but to drive.

Tony and Claire sat in the car and studied the building. The reception area on the main floor was brightly lit, as were the long laboratory wings on each side. The windows, situated high on each floor, offered only a glimpse of the ceilings. Presumably, suburban New Jersey didn't have blackout regulations.

"There's probably a security guy at the front desk, don't you think?" Tony said.

"Must be."

"Sort of guy who'd call his boss if we just turned up there."

"No doubt."

The night was warm, with a fresh breeze sweetened by the scents of thick grass and billowing trees. Bats swept through the starlit sky. Charlie was in Hershey, Pennsylvania, with his grandfather for the chocolate convention, so it was a perfect night for Claire to be on assignment.

"What do we do now?" Tony said.

"Let's sit for a minute and see if we get any ideas."

Claire hoped she'd made the right choice in coming here. She couldn't refuse Mr. Luce's direct instructions. In retrospect, John Smith's warning seemed overblown. As to her father, he'd told her that he didn't manage the day-to-day affairs of the company. She neither hurt him nor helped him by being here.

"Maybe at midnight there'll be a shift change, and we can slip in during the general confusion. Worst case, we'll go to the guard. Probably he wouldn't want to wake up his boss in the middle of the night to deal with the likes of us."

"Yeah, that sounds right," Tony said.

Claire felt herself drifting in the warm summer night, unable to take on the role of leader.

Tony slouched against the seat. "You think there are bears roaming around here at night? Mountain lions?"

"It's possible. In fact, I think I've heard that there are."

He stiffened, city boy that he was.

"In the woods. These aren't real woods." At least she didn't believe this was a real forest. Dark figures moved at the edges of the trees, crouching along the ground. Raccoons, most likely. Lightning bugs burst like sparkles through the air. Had Jamie spent time here at night? Had he watched the play of the lightning bugs? In her next letter, she'd ask him. The sound of the crickets became too loud for comfort.

"Think we can risk listening to the radio?" Tony asked.

"Keep it low."

He turned to WNEW, the big band station. Claire imagined herself at the Rainbow Room in an evening gown, dancing with Jamie in black tie, the revolving dance floor taking them round and round as they moved to the music of Benny Goodman and Artie Shaw, the lights of the city bright outside the windows. He held her tightly, and she pressed her face against his shoulder.

At midnight, the news came on. The Eastern Front was a thousand miles of Russian defeats. The RAF's nightly bombing raids on German cities continued with a firestorm in Düsseldorf that left thousands dead. Good news: thousands dead. Claire imagined the German equivalent of herself and Charlie among the survivors, struggling to endure in the bombed-out city. She couldn't help but imagine a firestorm in New York City, she and Tony watching the red conflagration on the horizon.

Last week Bill Shipley had gone out on an RAF bombing raid and written about it in the *Tribune*. Of the squadron he went with, only three planes came back. The article had disturbed her. If Bill were killed, how would she tell Charlie? Bill was famous enough now that if he were on a plane that didn't come back, his death would warrant a front-page article in his newspaper. The death would be public, part of the war effort. He'd be written about as a hero.

"Hey, get a load of that guy." Tony motioned with his chin.

At the end of the laboratory wing closest to them, a man had exited from the fire door and was lighting a pipe. He was no more than a silhouette against the darkness until his match flashed orange. Government posters on the subway reminded people that during a blackout the lighting of a match could give away your position to the enemy. Here in the midst of the New Jersey forests and pastures, with blackout regulations apparently nonexistent or unenforced, the man had certainly advertised his position to Claire and Tony.

"Guess this is our chance," Claire said. "Let's go."

Tony switched off the engine. He gathered the equipment bags from the backseat, and they approached the man at a slow pace. Claire didn't want to startle him by rushing at him in the dark. As they came closer, she watched him watching them. One army private, one woman, emerging from a big car, not a particularly threatening combination and an unlikely disguise for German spies—Claire felt absurd, but they had to give it a try.

"*Well met by moonlight, proud Titania,*" the man called to them in an English accent.

"What's that supposed to mean?" Tony whispered.

"It's Shakespeare," Claire said.

Tony groaned.

She was heartened that the man had changed the quote from *ill met* to *well met*. "You won't believe this, but I know that guy." She hurried forward. "David Hoskins, how good to see you," she called.

"Indeed." He looked wilted in the summer heat, his forehead beaded with sweat, his hair drooping as if he'd just come from the shower. "Welcome."

When Tony caught up with her, she said, "This is my assistant, Tony Pagliaro."

"Sir," Tony said, shaking hands.

Claire didn't know what to say next.

Hoskins puffed on his pipe, pleasurably filling his time. "So, what brings you two out here, if I may be so bold."

"We're doing a story for *Life* magazine about research into penicillin and other antibacterial medications," Claire said.

"Odd time to do it." Hoskins was amused.

This threw Claire, but Tony stepped in: "Wartime, sir. Midnight, noon—it's all the same to us. We're working twenty-four hours a day. Like you and everybody else."

Claire realized that she adored Tony.

"Absolutely." Hoskins sucked on his pipe.

Claire wished she could wake up. She felt as if the heat had addled her brain.

"We came out here a while back," Tony was saying, "and they showed us the demonstration lab, I guess you'd have to call it. Nice lab, but not what we needed."

"Ah, yes, the public information department does a fine job with the demonstration lab. Completely unrelated to the actual scientific labs, I'm afraid."

"We'd love to see the real labs," Tony said.

For a long moment Hoskins said nothing. "How's our mutual friend James Stanton," he finally asked.

"He's well, thank you," Claire said. "At least I think he is. He's traveling. I haven't seen him in, well, in a while. But he writes."

"The way of the world these days, isn't it? We all have people we miss, I daresay."

"Yes," Claire said, remembering that his family had died in the bombing of Coventry.

"If you don't mind my asking, what was your . . . *game plan*—would that be the proper American phrase?—your *game plan* for this evening?"

"Oh, we're just waiting to see what comes along," Tony said nonchalantly.

"Indeed. I wish you luck."

"So, uh, how do you like working here?" Tony asked.

"No complaints. I rotate from place to place, however. No corporate loyalty for me. I'm lucky enough to be considered an expert in penicillin. I'm an expert valued for my expertise." He laughed softly at this play on words. "Next week, Peoria, Illinois. The United States Department of Agriculture Northern Regional Research Laboratory. That's quite a tongue twister, isn't it?"

"You said it," Tony agreed.

"Well, I've got to get back to work." He retrieved the folded newspaper that he'd used to prop open the door. "In honor of my dear and much-missed colleague Dr. Lucretia Stanton, I will offer you this open door. I can't be responsible for every ne'er-do-well who wanders through it. I'm sure you'll find some very interesting items to photograph."

Tony grabbed the door. Hoskins left them, walking into a deserted hallway and through another door at the opposite end. Claire waited a moment, to let Hoskins distance himself from them, and then she and Tony followed.

This is what Hanover & Company was hiding: a penicillin factory. Fully staffed and fully operational, twenty-four hours a day. Just like the factories for tanks, airplanes, guns, ammunition, and battleships. Except this factory made a weapon designed to save, not destroy, lives. Row upon row of racks ten feet high, filled with milk bottles growing green mold. Portable metal stairs to reach the high shelves. Trays attached to the stairs. Vials and beakers of yellow-brown fluid upon the trays. Dozens of women concealed in sanitary white, including face masks, moving up and down the stairs, harvesting the fluid with pipettes. Not science fiction. Science reality.

Claire finally awoke from the daze of heat. She'd photographed factories many times, and she knew what to do: create a rhythm of geometric abstractions that made otherwise monotonous images riveting. On the far side of the racks were dozens of giant counter-current machines, used to purify the harvested fluid, hundreds of glass vials moving in a visual poetry of machinery, gleaming with reflections.

In the next room, a group of scientists, all men, experimented with fermentation in table-size vats, an apparatus automatically stirring the fluid to keep oxygen moving through it. David Hoskins was working here, making his way from bench to bench, answering questions, offering advice.

Claire saw her cover story for the magazine taking shape. This was what she was truly here for: not fumbling espionage, but the gift she had for creating evocative images. Mr. Luce would be pleased. She'd gotten the story.

Three sharp-eyed MPs patrolled the lab to prevent employees from stealing penicillin for their dying mothers or their suffering children. Penicillin was for the military only. The MPs nodded at Claire, and she nodded in return, establishing an exchange of authority. They were part of Claire's story, too. The MPs must have presumed that Claire and Tony were authorized: otherwise, why would Claire and Tony be here? Tony's uniform must have reassured them, too. The MPs job was to prevent the theft of penicillin, not stop it from being photo-graphed. Claire saw Tony chatting with the MPs. She photographed a small, tough-looking MP observing a scientist withdraw fluid from the fermentation vat for evaluation. Precious penicillin, permitted to save certain lives and not others.

After an hour, Claire was finished.

"Hey," Tony whispered, "how about we leave through the front door, and on our way, we walk right across the reception area to the opposite side? My new friends in the military police say there's some strange stuff going on over there. They haven't bothered to mention it to their superior officers, who don't exactly respect initiative from the guys at the bottom of the totem pole."

"You're terrific, Tony," she said. "You can make even the cops turn a blind eye."

Tony preened. "Well, the guys have orders to guard the penicillin, and that's what they do. Besides, the guys and me, we're on the same side, know what I mean?"

"Yes, I think I do." They packed the equipment, and Tony carried it. "Okay then, let's do a little exploring," Claire said.

"See you around, fellas," Tony called to the MPs.

As Tony predicted, they walked past the guard in the reception area as if they were just part of the scenery. Tony preceded her in the opposite wing and opened the double doors into . . . into Tia's soil lab, only a hundred times bigger. When she reached three dozen, Claire stopped counting the number of scientists at work.

This was the much greater secret, Claire knew: the scientists were investigating nonpenicillin antimicrobials, and they were making progress. She understood this from their steady concentration and from their silence. No idle chatter, no consultation. Cigarettes burned down unsmoked in the ashtrays, leaving perfect, circular lines of ash.

She was shocked that she was here, shocked that no one told her to stop. Claire would report this lab to Vannevar Bush. And she would photograph it, too. The setting was straightforward, and again, she knew exactly what to do. Her work was automatic: the racks of samples; the soil sprinkled onto petri dishes infected with strep or staph. The test tubes coming in and out of the incubator. Tia's lab on a vast scale. This was another cover story. In her mind, she saw the layout spread before her.

Gradually she felt the scientists watching her. One here, another there, looking up from their work, seeing her, consulting with one another. She worked faster. Suddenly she saw, and recognized, the most important work. She put a roll of Kodachrome in the Leica and put the long lens on the camera. She wanted to keep her distance. Here was a fire-engine red fluid being put through its paces. Over there, a carrot-colored fluid. On the far side, a dreadful green. On the other side of a glass partition, a purple fluid was being injected into mice.

One of the scientists was making his way to a desk on the far side of the lab. The desk held a telephone. He picked up the receiver. She had thirty seconds left, no more. Then she and Tony would leave before they were thrown out or arrested.

Her eye was drawn across the room to a transparent blue substance. A clear, flowing, brilliant blue. She concentrated on this. From a distance, she followed the several scientists working with it. One scientist, very tall, with curly black hair and thick glasses, took a small beaker of the medication to the area with the mice. Even from a distance, she was able to capture his injections of the substance into the mice. The color was so beautiful. It stood out. The Kodachrome, she knew, would capture it to perfection. These were the reasons she picked it from among the fire-engine red and the dreadful green: technically, it worked for the color film; and psychologically, readers of the magazine would feel attracted to it and want to learn more about it.

Even as she and Tony hurried away, she continued to imagine this medication—someday, when Düsseldorf wasn't a firestorm, when the

Eastern Front wasn't a thousand miles of Russian defeats—as the subject of a cover story on the penicillin cousins.

Around 5:00 AM, Tony and Claire reached the approach to the access road of the Holland Tunnel. Dawn was breaking behind the New York City skyline, silhouetting the Woolworth Building and the Singer Tower in magenta. The air was cool and sweet, even here, amid the intersecting roads of New Jersey. Claire felt elated, invigorated, after her work through the night.

"Pull over, Tony, would you?" she asked.

"Yes, ma'am, you're the boss."

He pulled to the side, out of the flow of traffic. Claire took her Leica from the backseat and climbed onto the roof of the car. Her city. Her entire life, spent here. And still, on a morning in July, it was to her the most beautiful and exciting place in the world, as she captured the evolving colors of dawn behind and upon the skyscrapers.

They drove the rest of the trip in silence. Through the Holland Tunnel, north on Sixth Avenue, across on Waverly, along the narrow streets of the Village. Striped awnings were unfurled on the town house windows, to keep out the sun and the heat during what would be a sweltering day.

Stars, stars in the windows of town houses and tenements alike, everywhere Claire looked. There was the Castagnaro apartment, with three blue stars. That would be for Harry, Bob, and Bill. She remembered them from stickball games she'd dodged on her way to the grocery store or the subway when she was in college. Over there was the home of the O'Shea family, with one blue star. That would be for Peter, her fifth-grade beau. She'd lost track of him years ago. He must have joined up, too old to be drafted. In the window of a ground-floor tenement, a gold star. Mr. Martowski lived there. A widower. The star had to be for his son Harvey, just nineteen. She remembered Harvey peering into Charlie's perambulator, when she'd come downtown to visit her mother shortly after Emily died. Harvey always seemed to have a penny string of red licorice hanging from his fist. His trousers were patched, his sweater had a hole in the elbow. Harvey Martowski, a boy whose mother had died young. Constance once told her that the other mothers on the block looked after him. Now he, too, was dead.

Tony pulled up to her house, and Claire got out, retrieving the equipment. She had another assignment later, and she was happy to have a few hours to herself, a rare occurrence. With Charlie away, she'd given Maritza time off. She looked forward to a little luxury, a long bath and a lingering breakfast in the garden, cool beneath the thick canopy of trees, sunlight dappling through the shadows. She had thirty-two rolls of film in her bag. Tomorrow she'd take the film to Barnett's fake New York office, which masqueraded as an importing and exporting firm near Union Square. The office wasn't open now, and her next assignment might go late this evening. In the meantime she'd stash the film in her basement darkroom to keep it cool.

She paused at Tony's open window. "Thanks, Tony."

"Yeah, exciting night. Working with you isn't as bad as I thought it would be," he said.

Lack of sleep made her emotional, unable to respond with a light-hearted rejoinder. "Thank you for saying that."

"No, thank *you*." He too seemed moved. She thought of him as a younger brother, or a nephew. She wanted to say more. She wanted to say, come in for a cold drink. But as they looked at each other, she sensed the gap between them, of background, education, and position. What the military called rank, which stopped them both from saying anything more. So they simply said their good-byes.

CHAPTER TWENTY-THREE

⁓

That afternoon, Claire stood on the deck of a navy cruiser docked at the Brooklyn Navy Yard. She was doing a fashion shoot with three models and a stylist to assist. The fashion item in question was a small, round khaki hat with an all-around brim that could be turned up or worn down. The Johnny Jeep hat, it was called, inspired by army hats.

Life was creating a fashion fad. The models who displayed the hat were slender, buxom, and . . . *bold* was probably the word for their poses. In the ninety-five-degree heat, they wore tight thin sweaters that revealed their brassieres beneath. In this context, a visible brassiere, generally considered tasteless, became de rigueur. This fashion story was really about catching the models in cheesecake poses, a favorite combination for Mack and managing editor Billings—who, Mack hinted, was already thinking *cover story* for this cruiser caper. The hat was army-inspired, but the story was being photographed on a ship because stories about the navy sold more copies than stories about the army and also because here in New York City, ships were more readily available than tanks. Claire did wonder about the provocative poses the models might have exhibited on a tank.

"Okay, ladies," Claire instructed Bernice, Martha, and June, "how about you lean over the railing, and I'll lean over the railing, and we'll do these hats justice."

"You got it," Martha said.

The girls knew precisely what was expected of them, and they delivered, with salutes, winks, and over-the-shoulder grins, all performed in their exaggerated, *bold* posture. Come to find out, there were dozens of ways to photograph buxom girls modeling small hats on a navy cruiser. Some shots included the highly evocative skyscrapers of Manhattan in the background. Claire even got several particularly suggestive poses of the girls astraddle the ship's smokestack.

The session broke at five, earlier than Claire expected. Toward the end, her eyelids were starting to get heavy. Staying up all night to work didn't suit her as well as it had ten or fifteen years ago.

By the time she reached home, it was almost six. These long summer days . . . the light was still strong, the humid heat heavy and draining. Her skin was damp.

When Claire put the key in the lock of her front door, she was surprised to find that the door hadn't been bolted. It locked automatically when it closed, but she and Charlie always bolted it for extra protection. She was certain she'd bolted it when she left, but of course she'd missed a night's sleep. Tom, the dog walker, would have been in and out to walk Lucas at three, and he must have forgotten to bolt it.

She entered the front vestibule, slipping the heavy bags off her shoulders and onto the floor. Her arms had a slick of sweat. Gin and tonic, that's what she needed to revive herself.

With the shades down and the windows closed to keep out the summer heat, the house was shadowed. She gazed through the parlor and the dining room to the French doors in the back. The doors opened onto a balcony that overlooked the garden. The soft light of late afternoon filtered through the shades. She felt as if she'd entered a soft-focused photograph by Edward Steichen or Clarence White from early in the century.

The house felt strangely quiet. No one home. And yet someone was home, or should be. She felt a pang of anxiety. No paws were padding upstairs from the kitchen, no wagging tail was thumping the wall in pleasure at her return, no damp muzzle pressing into her palm. Lucas always came to greet her. Early this morning he'd been standing just inside the door when she came in, as if to say, where were you all night?

"Lucas?"

No response.

"Lucas?" She called more loudly.

She went to the French doors and pulled up the shades. The dog door in the laundry room gave him access to the garden. When Lucas slept in the garden in the summer, he stretched out on the cool flagstones beneath the maple tree. But the garden was empty. If Lucas were in the house, he'd stay where it was coolest, which meant the ground-floor kitchen. She walked through the hall to the stairway that led downstairs, glancing into her photo office as she passed.

That's when she realized. The filing cabinets of negatives and contact sheets were open, the contents searched and tossed over the floor. Her mind flew—what work did she have at home? Photos of Charlie and Emily, the portraits she'd done of the neighborhood kids years ago, the newspaper and commercial work she'd done before she went to *Life*. None of this would be valuable to a thief.

Where was the film from the Hanover shoot? The basement darkroom, where it would be cool.

Then she heard the muffled scratching and barking. It came from downstairs, somehow from inside the stone foundations of the house itself. Panicked, she ran down the steps. She slipped on the edge of the carpeting and gripped the banister to stop herself from falling. And she realized: someone could be in the house still. Someone could be waiting for her at the turn of the stairs. But she had to reach Lucas. At the bottom of the stairs, the crying and scraping were louder, coming from behind the cellar door. A chair was pushed against the door to keep it closed. She kept the basement door locked to prevent Charlie from wandering into the darkroom and getting into the darkroom chemicals. A quick glance showed her the marks in the wood where the lock had been forced.

She pushed the chair aside and opened the door. Lucas bounded out and leapt to her with frantic joy. As she held him and rubbed her face into his fur, she smelled the acrid odor of darkroom chemicals. He was wet with them, parts of his fur soaked through. She forced herself to smell his breath and caught the stench of vomit. Vomit mixed with chemicals.

"Lucas, come," she said sharply to make him listen. Gripping the loose skin on the scruff of his neck, she led him through the laundry room, out the back door, and into the garden. She uncoiled the hose and turned it on. She hosed him down. The water was frigid against her palms even through the rubber hose. Lucas loved it—they were playing a game, the best game in the world for him, his gloomy hours in the basement forgotten in the thrill of jumping through the rainbow-reflecting waterfall. He leapt through the stream, pushed his face into the spray, captured the droplets on his tongue.

After he was entirely soaked, she hosed down the flagstones, washing the garden, forcing the chemicals down the drain. She turned off the hose. He shook himself once, twice, water cascading in all directions, a splash from the end of his tail hitting her chin. She didn't get a towel to dry him. She didn't want to take the time, and besides, the damp would keep him cool.

"Lucas, stay." He was rolling on the flagstones, his wet fur making patterns like snow angels. If someone was in the house, he, or she, had most likely used Lucas's bath time to escape.

Claire closed the laundry room door behind her and latched the dog door shut, to keep Lucas in the garden. Turning on the low-wattage overhead light, she went down the shadowy, narrow stairs to the basement. The room opened before her. After the heat outside, she shivered in the basement chill. The enlarger was overturned on the floor. The printer paper, some of it soaked, was emptied from its boxes and strewn across the room. The bottles of chemicals were opened and overturned. She spotted Lucas's vomit in two puddles in the corner. The fix or hypo must taste sweet. He must have lapped it up until it made him sick—luckily made him sick, before he lapped up enough to kill him. The table where she'd left the bag of film from the Hanover shoot—bare.

Of course. She'd been warned by John Smith at the Dodgers game. This was her punishment for ignoring the warning. Thank goodness Charlie wasn't here. Thank goodness she'd given Maritza the day off, and that Tom hadn't stumbled in while this was going on.

She sat down on the basement steps. She tried to catch her breath. She felt foolish. And violated and exposed, as if her body itself had been ransacked. What an easy target she was.

Who could have done this? Who knew she'd been to Hanover, or even who she was? Who was watching? Who had followed her home?

She couldn't let herself think about that now. The possibilities were too upsetting. Instead, she needed to get to work: this mess would take hours to clean up. Best get started. First, though, she should let someone know, to prevent something worse from happening later. Whom to call? Barnett? Luce?

She walked up the stairs to the kitchen, closing the basement door behind her. She'd need to phone the locksmith to repair the lock. She checked on Lucas. The dog had stopped his rolling and was lying stretched out on his back with his four legs spread in the air. She unlatched the dog door, so he could come in when he was ready.

From her purse she retrieved the calling card Barnett had given her after Tia's memorial. She sat at the round table in the corner that held the kitchen telephone. She placed the long-distance call, person-to-person collect, and waited for the call back.

"Carnegie Institution," the receptionist answered.

"Mrs. Claire Shipley from New York for Dr. Andrew Barnett," the long-distance operator said.

"Hold on, please." Several moments pause. "Barnett here."

"Dr. Barnett. Claire Shipley."

"How can I help you, Mrs. Shipley?"

His severe formality put her off. She needed a touch of sympathy to begin telling this story. But she forced herself to plunge in. "Last week, I went to a baseball game with John Smith of Pfizer."

"I know who John Smith is," he said harshly.

She was taken aback. "Yes, of course you do." Did he really think she was passing judgment on his competence? "At any rate . . ." She resumed the story, beginning with the baseball game and ending now, at this moment. He didn't interrupt again. "I assume no one's in the house," she said finally, letting a small part of her anxiety show, even while knowing that she would never get reassurance from Andrew Barnett.

"Well, well," he said. She couldn't be certain across the long-distance line, but he seemed to be amused. "Well, well."

"That's all you can say?"

Indeed, he was laughing. "This is very useful information, Mrs. Shipley."

"How so?"

"Confirmation of what we already suspected and hoped. Greed as the ultimate motivator. Dr. Bush leaves nothing to chance. Things are moving forward on all fronts. Thank you. Thank you very much."

"And my personal risk?"

"All in a day's work, I should think. Beats the Pacific, after all. By the way, if there are any questions, we don't know you. In fact, I don't believe you and I have ever met. Good-bye." He hung up.

He was like a caricature of himself, Claire thought. She couldn't begin to absorb the intricacies of what he'd been trying to tell her. At this moment, her needs were simpler. She was trembling still. She needed to find some way to steady herself. Should she phone Mr. Luce? He was the one who'd sent her to Hanover. It was Saturday. Most likely he wasn't in the office, or if he had been in, to supervise *Life*'s Saturday close, he'd probably left by now. Nonetheless, she was alone, and she needed to hear an understanding voice. The company switchboard put her through to his office. After five rings, he answered his own phone. Gruffly.

"Mr. Luce, it's Claire Shipley."

A pause.

"Good to talk to you, too, Mr. Luce. I'm afraid I have, well, a story to tell you." She related the events of the evening.

"I'll send down a cleaning crew."

"No, that's all right. I can manage."

"You have better things to do with your time. Miss Thrasher will make the arrangements. Thank you for briefing me. Keep on with the good work."

"Mr. Luce, as I mentioned the other day, I don't think—"

"No jumping ship midvoyage, Mrs. Shipley. When Miss Thrasher returns, I'll tell her to phone you back." He hung up without saying good-bye.

The evening loomed before her, hours to fill, without Charlie, without Jamie. She felt lost. Well, she had to fill the evening with something. It was dinnertime. She didn't feel like eating. The quiet of the house pressed against her. Since she was alone, she had to make a new routine for herself. Again her practical side took over: gin and tonic, that's where she'd left off, wasn't it?

As she stood to go to the refrigerator to retrieve the tonic and lime, the telephone rang, startling her. Miss Thrasher, calling back so soon? "Hello?"

"Long-distance," the operator said, sounding as if she was speaking in a static-filled drum. "Hold the line, please." She heard the sounds of the call being put through.

"Mom, it's me, Charlie!"

Charlie? Long-distance? Immediately her heart was pounding. Immediately she feared disaster. "Are you okay, Charlie?"

"'Course I am. It's great here. I wish you were here. I've got two bags of Hershey bars to give you."

This telephone call couldn't be about Hershey bars, could it? "That's wonderful, darling. Thank you. What have you been doing?"

"Well, the first day we slept late and had lunch for breakfast. Then yesterday it was really hot and we went to the swimming pool. I made Grandpa go in the water even though he doesn't swim and he's scared of the water. Guess what: we have chocolate for every meal. At breakfast they put chocolate in the bread. Even my clothes smell of chocolate!"

Charlie sounded so good, so happy. After the initial shock of the call, coming on top of Claire's already jittery nerves, Claire now felt soothed and cheered by Charlie's enthusiasm for these unthreatening activities. Bill Shipley was absent, Jamie was away: thank goodness, Claire thought, Charlie had his grandfather.

"Is Grandpa there?"

"Sure. Want to talk to him?"

"Yes."

"Okay, but I'll talk to you again afterward. Here he is."

The phone was passed.

"Claire, is that you?" Rutherford spoke too loudly, as older people often did on long-distance calls, somehow believing that because of the distance, they had to speak more loudly to be heard.

"Yes, it's me. Everything okay there?"

"Terrific. We're just calling to make sure you're all right."

"You are?"

"Why not?"

"Oh, hearing Charlie's voice surprised me."

"Okay, we have an ulterior motive. The chocolate-covered caramel festival is the day after tomorrow. We're wondering if we can stay an extra day. Wouldn't want to miss that."

Was her father really so wealthy that he telephoned long-distance when anyone else would have sent a less-expensive telegram? "Of course you can stay an extra day."

"Thanks." A pause. "So, everything okay there?"

Should she tell him what had happened? He was away, and he could do nothing to help her. Charlie was right next to him, no doubt listening to every word. "Fine. Everything's fine here."

"You sure? You sound a little, I don't know, tense."

"No, no, I'm fine. Just tired. Too busy. As usual. And the heat is terrible."

"I thought we'd give you a little treat by calling instead of sending a telegram. Glad we found you at home. I was worried you might not be home."

He seemed to be pressing her for something, Claire didn't know what. "I had a late night last night—worked straight through till morning." She made herself sound lighthearted.

"So you're relaxing. Good. You should relax more." Claire heard Charlie's voice. "Charlie has a question, so I'll pass the phone back to him."

"Hi, Mom. How's Lucas?"

"He's fine, honey. I gave him a bath with the garden hose. It's so hot here. The bath cooled him off."

"I want to give him a bath with the garden hose."

"When you get back, we will." She heard her father speaking to Charlie in the background.

"We have to go now, Mom. Hot-chocolate tasting. Don't worry, I'll bring you back some chocolate-covered caramels, too. Grandpa says to tell you bye from him."

"Tell him bye from me, too. Remember that I love you."

"Love you, too."

They hung up. Claire felt more alone than before. All sense of practicality, of forward motion, faded. And yet hearing her son's voice and knowing he was safe and well, hearing her father's voice and knowing that he cared about her . . . she felt consoled for all she did have: her boy, her father, Jamie in the back of her mind, as always.

With a jolt Claire landed on a possibility too disturbing to assimilate: her father owned the Hanover company, and although he'd told her that he wasn't involved with the day-to-day operations, could he in fact have ordered the violation of her home? Was he responsible?

Immediately everything within her rose up to say *No*. Never. That was impossible. He wasn't that kind of man. He'd never do this to her.

Right then Lucas was beside her, pressing his still-damp head against her hand and reminding her that it was time for his dinner.

CHAPTER TWENTY-FOUR

⁓

This was some smarmy guy. Why hadn't he noticed that before? After all, Kreindler had been studying the man's habits for weeks. Kreindler walked along First Avenue in the Sixties, the suspect on the other side of the street doing his usual errands amid the small grocery stores and pharmacies, the Greek shoe repair shop and the Chinese laundry. Old ladies peered out the tenement windows, kids played ball on the side streets. All the typical stuff going on. The summer was almost over, thank God. He'd had enough of the heat. He'd spent August biding his time, following this guy around, waiting to see what was what.

Nothing out of the ordinary, so far. No strange meetings, no suspicious behavior. No visits to Central Park at off hours to put pieces of paper in trees, no doodling with blue chalk to set up meetings. This guy was turning about to be a tremendous bore. Kreindler had three men rotating in the watch (one of them, a young fellow in training for the FBI, was right now twenty feet behind), and they were going out of their heads with the boredom.

Maybe Fritz was wrong about him. It was unlikely, though, that Fritz would even know the man's name if there wasn't something going on. Or maybe Fritz had deliberately given Kreindler incorrect information. Fritz had already (by his own account, confirmed by Kreindler's contacts at the bureau) sent the FBI on a wild goose chase, so possibly he'd do the same to his dear old friend Marcus Kreindler.

At any rate, Kreindler was working with the bureau on this *evolving situation*, as he thought of it. If Kreindler learned anything about Tia Stanton, he would, of course, inform Andrew Barnett. The bureau could take care of everything else: espionage was their job, after all. Kreindler knew how to play the turf game when it suited him.

Sergei Oretsky. The perfect choice, if you were choosing a spy. Fritz knew all about him. A Russian refugee, his family trapped in France. The Germans had imprisoned the family in a camp, their survival dependent on the cooperation of poor Sergei in America. They weren't Jewish, Fritz was very clear about that. Scared shitless, nonetheless— this reflection was accompanied by stentorian laughter, Fritz proving to himself how successful he and his Teutonic compatriots were at terrifying some harmless chump and his family.

Kreindler remembered Fritz at dinner, on his third *Pils* and finally getting to the point. "The thing is, Marcus, the Reich needs the medications. The Reich needs penicillin. It needs whatever else the scientists are finding. These are weapons, Marcus. I know it's hard to believe. But they *are* weapons."

Kreindler did believe him. "So this guy turn anything over to you?"

"Nothing. Back in the spring, he said he was close to something, but poof—it evaporated. We're getting impatient with him. He says he can give us promising sewage, as much as we want, anytime—but that's Russian stuff. It's madness." Fritz shook his head at the monumental stupidity of Russians. "Not the solid results we want. But we're putting the pressure on him. He'll come through."

"And if he doesn't?" Kreindler asked.

To that, Fritz had bellowed with laughter once more. The answer was obvious.

Now, watching Oretsky across the street, Kreindler almost felt sorry for the poor sod, caught up in this business, his life spinning beyond his control. Just another pawn in the great tournament of history. Kreindler wanted to know if Oretsky had been down by the river collecting sewage when Tia Stanton went for a walk along the cliff with a companion.

Kreindler crossed First Avenue and walked behind Oretsky for a block, ignoring the FBI rookie. At the streetlight at the corner of First and Sixty-fourth, Kreindler picked up his pace. "Dr. Oretsky," he said when he was beside him. "You remember me?" Kreindler had interviewed him right after Tia's death. Kreindler automatically took out his identification to make everything official.

Oretsky looked up at him, eyes wide. He was surprised, and frightened. Good. Kreindler had caught him off guard. Kreindler had chosen carefully, not approaching him at work, not at home, but here, on the street, to see if he would run, and to see if anyone else was watching. He planned to walk with him over to the river, take a nice stroll in the cool, late-day breeze on the East River Drive promenade. Nothing like a little visit to the scene of the crime to jostle the nerves.

"Let's go for a walk, shall we?"

Oretsky slowly nodded his head.

CHAPTER TWENTY-FIVE

E dward Rutherford stood beside a laboratory bench at Hanover & Company. Holding a test tube up to the light, he examined the fluid within it. The fluid was the most beautiful blue he'd ever seen. Transparent. Uncanny. He'd waited so long while the scientists did their work. Now it was late-October 1942, although in retrospect the time had passed in a flash.

Didn't scientists say that truth was beautiful? He'd read that mathematicians believed that you knew a proof was true if it was beautiful. He himself had heard many scientists remark on the ugly brownish yellow of penicillin. By contrast his medication had a clarity that gave him faith in it.

Penicillin development was still moving forward in the opposite wing of the lab. The troops would have their penicillin, yes they would; Vannevar Bush would have no cause to threaten Hanover & Company. Even so, the number of military guards in the penicillin lab had been increased because of thefts at other companies. The guards were armed.

No military guards for this medication, however. This belonged to him, and he now had his own reliable and discreet private security force in place. No one was going to steal this, not the substance itself nor any information about it. What happened at Claire's house was unfortunate, to say the least. It could have been handled more neatly: step in when the house is empty, take the materials, the end. But no, the freelance guys he'd been using seemed to think they needed to make a point. Well, he'd made a point, too, and he'd fired them and hired replacements.

Claire had never mentioned the incident (brave girl that she was—his daughter, of course), but sure, she must have been shaken up by it. No lasting harm done, however. And in the end, he was protecting Claire, guaranteeing her future and Charlie's, by taking back those photographs. He absolutely could not let word get out. He could not lose control of this.

He wished he could figure out a way to describe that blue. He'd collected art for decades without really looking at it. He'd only collected it because that's what men like him were supposed to do. You went to a colleague's house, or he came to your house, you looked at the art, you eased your way into conversation by revealing where you got this or that painting and hinting at how much you paid for it (the eternal competition), and before long you were discussing business. The paintings kept your secrets. He'd never, however, talked about what he believed was called the *aesthetics* of the art he collected.

Only now, examining this extraordinary blue, did he understand why a man might devote his life to the study of art. And the best part was, this blue was worth far more than any painting.

The scientists continued to work around him, on this and other substances. They never paid attention to what he was doing. He was the boss, after all. This special medication had a large team working on it, continuing the testing protocols on mice. Experimenting with increasing the yields. So far, the results had surpassed even his own high expectations. The substance worked against every bug they'd thrown at it, gram-positive and gram-negative, even TB. Still another team was trying to synthesize it chemically, so they wouldn't have to worry about growing mold to produce it: synthesis would truly be hitting the jackpot.

He prayed no one was catching up with him. The simultaneously wondrous and dreadful fact about these medications was that you could find the stuff they were made from in anybody's garden. You could think you were onto something special, only to discover that the guy down the block had found it, too, the exact same thing, and was far ahead of you in the testing protocols.

This was the medication that Nick Catalano had brought him. Catalano had been right about its potential. Maybe he really did find it while visiting his parents in Syracuse. Maybe he didn't. He'd paid Catalano off, and so, in the unlikely event it came up, he could rest easy on the competitive question of *provenance*, to borrow a term from art collecting.

Soon his worries about being first would be over. Yesterday he'd filed for patent protection. An underling went to Washington, D.C., with the papers. An official at the patent office took the papers. No one uttered a word of protest. Rutherford purposely sent an underling, to show how routine the submission was. Just dropping off the papers. The development of these medications necessitated complex research and chemical modifications, and thus they should henceforth be considered invented rather than natural—that's what he'd say if anyone challenged the process, but he was confident that no one would, because he'd fully comprehended the game. The troops would get their penicillin, the companies would patent the cousins.

The blue substance was almost ready for human testing, and he needed a name for it. A number wasn't good enough anymore. A number didn't have poetry. The right kind of poetry had the ability to sell products. From his confidential contacts throughout the industry, Rutherford knew the names of other antibacterial medications making their way through the research protocols: Fumigacin, Clavacin, Patulin, Flavacidin. Absurd names. Who would ever want to say to his wife, "I'm heading over to the pharmacy to buy some Patulin"? It sounded like a laxative.

He wanted to name his medication after Charlie. He also wanted to include some reference to the color. He believed that an old-fashioned name would inspire confidence. For a small fee, he was consulting with a classics professor up at Columbia. Betty, Rutherford's secretary, had made the original contact. The professor turned out to be an obsessive who'd been sending Rutherford letters about medical linguistic precedent and about the etymology of *penicillin*, how the word came from the Greek for *mushroom* or *fungus* and the *pen* part meant *fan* and the . . . a trove of useless information.

Rutherford did, however, learn from his professor that Latin had a word specifically for the blue of the sky: *caeruleus*. *Cerulean*, in English. Rutherford praised the wisdom of a language that had a word specifically for sky blue. Furthermore, *Carolus* was the medieval Latin for *Charles*, which was the English name borrowed from the French, which came from the Latin . . . the professor could write a book about this, and it would sell one copy. To himself.

Caeruleus and *Carolus*. Similar in appearance and sound. He'd have to add the required *-mycin*, or *-illin* or plain old *-in* at the end. Apparently a scientific reason determined each particular ending, but Rutherford wouldn't let that guide him. He found an unused pad, turned over the first page, and played around with some combinations. Finally he landed on it: *Ceruleamycin*.

It was a little odd, but people would get used to it. Five years ago, who'd ever heard the word *penicillin*? Only a bunch of scientists. Ten years ago, who'd ever heard of sulfanilamide or sulfathiazole?

Rutherford wanted people to think of the sky whenever they heard the name Ceruleamycin. Penicillin was a hideous brownish yellow, so you could promote it only on its effectiveness. Rutherford grasped his advantage: his medication had beauty *and* effectiveness, and now a marvelous name. The advertising plan took shape in his mind: *Think blue*. Once the medication caught on, he'd use some of the profits to set up a foundation for medical research, just like old man Rockefeller. He knew that would make Claire happy.

Okay, he still had some problems to deal with. The medication had never been tested on humans. It could cause an allergic reaction, severe side effects, anemia, cancer, death. All his hopes might come to nothing. But at least his scientists were confident that the medication was ready for human testing. The next step was to find people to test it on. He needed to do mass trials, on many diseases, in a contained population. He'd heard rumors of imprisoned criminals volunteering for various types of medical tests, to do their part in the war effort. He'd also heard rumors of conscientious objectors to the war doing the same. And there were rumors of clinical trials being done at insane asylums or homes for the retarded; to Rutherford, this was going too far: he wouldn't sully his medication by testing it on the retarded or the insane. In due course, he'd find the right group of critically ill patients to test it on.

Staring at the test tubes filled with liquid blue, Rutherford felt a deep stirring within him, as if he were gazing into a crystal ball that showed him the secret of life itself.

And when his secret was ready, he was going to sell it.

CHAPTER TWENTY-SIX

~

North Africa. November 1942. The surgeon needed only to speak in code. "Iliac," said Pete Mueller.

They saw the bleeding artery in the bloody mess of the wounded soldier's abdomen, and Jamie clamped it while Mueller went to the next problem, the perforated intestine.

Jamie was in North Africa to conduct clinical trials on penicillin. Nick wasn't with him: Nick was needed to monitor continuing research developments at home, and if Jamie were killed in the war zone, Nick would be able to carry the project forward.

Jamie wasn't a surgeon, but a shortage of doctors on the North African front meant that whenever needed, a physician assisted at surgery. Their operating room was in the basement kitchen of a French colonial school turned hospital, somewhere in the province of Relizane, Algeria, Jamie didn't know exactly where, and he was so tired he no longer cared. Officially the Allied invasion the week before had been met with only light resistance. *Light resistance*: that was no consolation for the patient on the table before them. Jamie hoped he never had to witness *heavy resistance*.

Now that the blood flow from the artery had been stopped, Jamie could examine the wound. Was there a gash in the stomach? Part of the liver gone? How had this poor kid lived long enough to get here? Well, he *was* here, and Mueller was sewing him up. The electricity started flickering on and off and then went off altogether. All in a day's work at the North African front. One of the orderlies held up a flashlight to light the incision. After an hour or two or three of surgery, the boy was still alive, his pulse and blood pressure approaching normal. He might survive after all.

Was it the middle of the night? The afternoon? Jamie had lost track. He worked when the patients came in. He felt as though he were sleepwalking. Sometimes he worked all night and all day, as time disappeared into endless action.

Jamie had the penicillin waiting: the soaked pads like the kind he'd worked with in New York, to place upon the sewn-up incision after surgery; the fluid for the injections. Back in Newport News, Virginia, the troop staging area, he'd been told to prepare for an invasion task force of nearly 40,000 men. He had penicillin stocks for maybe a hundred men, if he was lucky. Yes, progress was being made in mass production, but the demand for the medication remained far greater than the supply.

On the ship, he'd worked every day in the sick bay, because even among men being ferried to battle there were all the usual colds and influenzas, pneumonias and strep throats. Not to mention flare-ups of the ubiquitous syphilis and gonorrhea from congenial evenings in Newport News. But his penicillin was reserved for battle wounds.

Reserved for this poor boy before him: Matthew Johnston, Chicago, Illinois, eighteen years old. Nurse Nichols, standing next to Jamie and holding the suction, always asked the boys where they were from before they went under anesthesia. *Where are you from, I bet you've got a million girls chasing you there. You'll be back up and at 'em before you know it.*

Jamie felt two warring emotions inside himself: to remember this boy with massive abdominal wounds, and to *not* remember this boy, so that he could just do his job and take his notes, be a professional without emotional concerns distracting him.

The ground vibrated. That meant a bombing raid somewhere

nearby. Mueller paused in midstitch, waiting for the rumbling to pass. The Allied airfields were grass, and the grass had turned to mud in the horrendous rains that started a few days ago, preventing the Allied planes from taking off. By contrast the German airfields were paved, and so the German bombers were still able to strafe and destroy at will.

"Okay, let's wrap this up," Mueller said.

Nurse Nichols stepped forward to assist. When they were ready, Jamie placed the waiting penicillin pad over the closed incision.

Mueller and Jamie changed out of their bloodstained surgical gowns and gloves in a pantry.

"I'm going to take a nap." Mueller was a Texan, with a big Texas boom of a voice. He was a terrific surgeon, and Jamie was filled with admiration for him. "Wake me if we're under attack. I don't want to sleep through my own demise."

"Will do." Jamie enjoyed Mueller's gallows humor, the dash and devil-may-care attitude, an aspect of the military professionalism Jamie was still reaching for: joking about your own death.

Mueller wore a wedding ring. Advertised his marriage. He'd showed Jamie snapshots of his wife and three children. A family, a goal Jamie still hoped to attain.

Dodging the orderlies who mopped the floors, Jamie and Mueller walked up the wide staircase with its intricately carved stone banisters. Green and blue tiles with geometric designs covered the walls.

"Hey, doctor, how about a cup of coffee at the corner café?"

They turned. Nurse Nichols was coming up the stairs behind them. Everywhere Jamie went, nurses. Nothing shy about them. They were a self-selected group, these frontline nurses. You needed a lot of courage and a tough stomach. Nurse Nichols was in her late twenties and quite a bit more experienced in the ways of the world than he was, Jamie sensed. Even in her standard-issue uniform, she was the most attractive nurse he'd seen among the many nurses of the U.S. Army Central Task Force fighting its way east across North Africa. She looked worthy of a pinup shot, the tossing mane of light brown hair, the wide face, the ample breasts pressing against her regulation shirt. He'd witnessed her walk through a ward and bring happiness to every wounded soldier simply by swaying her hips.

"I don't think she's talking to me," Mueller said under his breath.

"No, I don't think so."

"Let me know how the coffee is in this town."

"Absolutely." They shared a laugh. Mueller, whose billet was on the second floor, continued up another flight of steps while Jamie waited for Nurse Nichols. This school building was the height of nineteenth-century French colonial grandeur, with inlaid tiles, vaulted ceilings, the works. Jamie felt as if he'd entered an art history class, the foreignness of it all was so startling to him. The main entry gallery was wide and high, like the ceremonial entryway of a museum or a train station. The Central Task Force used the entry gallery as an open ward for the wounded. Not his wounded, though. The penicillin patients had their own ward, a cordoned-off portion of the gymnasium in the rear of the school.

"You ready to go?" Nurse Nichols asked, joining him. She was from Oklahoma, "never left till now, but for one trip to Austin, Texas," she sometimes told the soldiers, in her lilting Oklahoma accent, while prepping them for surgery.

His watch said eleven. The rain had stopped, and sunlight was angling through the latticework over the windows. Therefore, it was morning. Time for a cup of coffee.

"Yes," Jamie said.

They went through the monumental front doorway and into the town. Once again, the French colonial influence, brought onto Muslim North Africa. You had to admire it, the architecture of this town. The whitewashed buildings, the filigree decoration. Here in a war zone, with buildings bombed, kids running around wild, and orphanages overflowing, a café was up and running, tables outside, coffee or at least imitation coffee being served, cigarettes smoked. The important things in life, taken care of: you could count on the French influence for that. A story was being circulated to much laughter in the mess hall about a unit of American troops who surrounded and conquered an enemy encampment, only to discover it was a café, filled with locals who welcomed the newcomers with wine and women. As Jamie glanced at a group of young American recruits unloading a supply truck, again he thought, It's all so foreign; what are we doing here, so far from home?

At the café, Nurse Nichols sat across from him. They ordered coffee. It came with hard cookies.

"They call these biscotti," Nurse Nichols said. She dunked one into her coffee with a flair that made her look as if she'd been dining in French cafés all her life instead of languishing in Oklahoma. "These cookies are Italian, but they serve them here anyway."

"Ah." Jamie imitated her. He tasted hazelnut. Where did the locals get these things, the rich coffee, the cream, the cookies, the china cups? But he said nothing. Snow-covered mountains rose in the distance. Normally Jamie would want to know the name of that mountain range, but at the moment, he couldn't muster the energy to care.

"Doris—she's one of my nurses—says this town has beautiful olive trees in the central square."

Clearly Jamie was supposed to say, let's go for a walk when we finish our coffee, let's look at the olive trees. He didn't feel like looking at olive trees.

"And there's acres and acres of orange trees outside of town. Doris says it's just gorgeous."

He didn't want to be rude, but he didn't have the strength to discuss orange trees. The paradox was, he wasn't tired when he was in surgery or doing rounds in the penicillin ward; then he was awake. When he wasn't working, though, his energy drained away.

She must have understood this, because she lit a cigarette and stared into the distance. Jamie watched her. Lipstick on the side of her coffee cup, lipstick on her cigarette. She wore a short-sleeved uniform blouse, her regulation jacket over her shoulders. Strong shoulders, an alluring hint of cleavage giving promise of more . . . there were rules about fraternization, although he couldn't remember exactly what they were, and besides, he was navy, she was army, and as long as it was kept discreet, who'd be the wiser.

Really, he should say something. She didn't deserve silence. "I'm tired," he said.

She smiled in relief. "Me, too," she said.

She was available to him, he knew. All he had to do was ask. No, he didn't even have to ask. He simply had to nod his head. Touch one finger upon her hand. She shared a classroom with five other nurses, five cots in a row with sheets hung between them. But his cot was in the assistant principal's office. He had the entire office to himself. They finished the coffee. He paid. The breeze picked up, bringing the smell of burned flesh and gunpowder.

She waited for him to give a sign. "I need to visit my patients," he said.

"And I've got to supervise my nurses," she replied, promptly covering any chagrin she might have felt while simultaneously reminding him that she, too, had power here. She was in charge of fifteen junior nurses. She had more power than he did. She'd chosen him, he realized. But he wasn't prepared to accept. He pictured the cherished snapshot of Claire on his bedside table.

Back at the ward, Jamie went from patient to patient, giving injections, changing bandages, making detailed notes. To protect himself, he slipped into the usual physician's shortcut of remembering them in terms of their ailments, not their names. The perforated stomach. The third-degree burns. The double amputee. The chest wounds. Matthew Johnston wasn't here yet; he was probably still in the surgical recovery area.

After finding Johnston and confirming that he was stabilizing, Jamie returned to his assistant principal's office on the first floor. He lay down on the cot and let himself fall into a chasm of sleep.

Banging on the door woke him, he didn't know how much later. He opened his eyes. Raining again.

"Lieutenant, wounded in." The voice of his medic, Harry Lofgren, from Green Bay, Wisconsin. Lofgren worked only with penicillin testing. He didn't assist at surgery.

"I'll be right there," Jamie called. He sat up. He ran a hand through his hair.

He opened the door into chaos, stretchers covering the floors, medics and nurses hurrying from patient to patient. Where had these boys come from? A battle in the hills, who knew where, even forty or fifty miles away. They were patched up by medics at the front, then brought here by truck.

The men called to him as he walked among them. They were delirious with pain, most of them, calling to the shadow that was him as he moved through their line of vision. No, he couldn't stop to help them. He walked right through the chaos and downstairs to the pantry to prepare for surgery, as he'd been doing day after day. He went through the rituals of sterilization, maintaining necessary standards.

Mueller was already there, changing. "Hey, Stanton," he said, "enjoyable cup of coffee?"

"Just coffee, no more nor less. I guess it was espresso. Actually it was good. Cream, too. I don't know how these French colonials do it."

"Well, however they do it, we can count on them to keep doing it, so you'll have plenty of time for more coffee later."

"We'll see. Anything interesting this evening?"

"Amputation. They've got him ready."

"Ah." Jamie hated amputations.

"Let's at it, then." Mueller's mouth and nose were covered with a mask, as was Jamie's. But the eyes showed. Professional. A busy evening ahead. An amputation, he called it—he didn't call it a boy from Iowa or Michigan or Colorado who might not see his family again.

Nurse Nichols was already there, standing beside the patient along with the requisite assistants. Everybody worked without talking, saving their energy. Except for Nurse Nichols.

"What's your name, soldier?" she asked.

"Billy Baines, ma'am."

"Where you from?"

"Kansas City, Missouri, ma'am." He spoke boldly through what must have been excruciating pain. His left leg was mangled beyond repair, a black, bloody, filthy mess. His foot was already gone. He looked about fifteen. Jamie felt compelled to ponder: a good case for testing penicillin as a preventative for gangrene. "Not Kansas City, Kansas. Kansas City, Missouri."

"That's an important distinction and I'm glad you told me. I won't forget. I bet you've got a million girls there, chasing you, soldier. We're going to have you back at it in no time. Because this is your lucky day, Billy Baines: you've got the best surgeon in the United States Army right here with nothing else to do tonight but fix you up."

But Billy was already under the anesthesia and couldn't respond.

And there Billy was, the next day, as Jamie treated him in the penicillin ward. He was laughing at some wisecrack made by the boy in the bed on the opposite side, a boy with a chest wound, a perforated lung, and five broken ribs. Laughing was painful with five broken ribs, but he was joking around anyway.

First, Jamie checked in with Matthew Johnston. He was doing well. Then, the abdominal patient, the shrapnel wound, and the others from previous days. Jamie had twenty-two patients on the penicillin ward. Seeing them joking together, he did begin to learn their names. He followed his ritual of four-hour intramuscular injections. He changed the penicillin-soaked bandages. Lofgren took over when Jamie was in surgery. Lofgren was also responsible for collecting the urine of the patients and extracting penicillin from it in their make-shift lab. Surprisingly, penicillin was excreted by the body, and because they had so little, they retrieved whatever they could.

Sulfa drugs weren't suited to desert climates, British studies had shown that. The men were dehydrated from the heat, and in conditions of dehydration, sulfa drugs caused kidney damage. But the penicillin was working fine, Jamie was pleased to see. No side effects, no allergic reactions, everything going according to plan.

"Good job," Jamie told Lofgren when they finished rounds. He'd trained his medic in everything, the tacit reality being that if anything happened to Jamie, someone else, i.e., Harry Lofgren, had to be able to carry on.

Days passed. Awake, asleep, awake. As long as he did his job, Jamie understood his place and everything was clear. When he stopped doing his job, he was disoriented.

One morning he went directly from the operating room to the penicillin ward.

"Now, what's your girl's name, soldier?" A nurse was sitting at the bedside of a boy who'd lost his right arm. She was writing a letter for him.

"Her name's Betsy."

"Okay. *Dear Betsy*, that's a good way to start, isn't it?" the nurse asked. "What's next?"

The boy looked confused and didn't respond. Jamie put himself in the boy's place: how could he even begin to explain to Betsy back home? The minarets and palm trees. The whitewashed buildings. The desert scrub. The tanks and bombs and strafings. And the right arm, gone.

Have I written any letters? Jamie asked himself. He actually couldn't remember. Everything except the tasks directly in front of him became a fog. He hoped he had written to Claire. Probably he hadn't. He should. What would he say? I'm here, I'm alive. Nothing to worry about. He wouldn't write anything more than that, because no words could explain the truth of what was going on here, and the truth wouldn't get by the censors anyway.

One day he saw a calendar. A requisitions officer came around to check on their supplies, and this guy had a calendar. Only two weeks had passed since Jamie came ashore here. Two weeks. If asked, he'd have figured that two months had passed at least. Two years. The kid with half his abdomen burned away, the kid with his left leg blown off, the kid missing half his face. Penicillin could stop infection from setting in—that's what he had to keep his focus on. Not whether or how the patient would go back home, would live and function at home, without a leg or a face. Saving the life was what mattered. Stopping the infections. Fulfilling the protocols of the clinical trial. Getting the boys who could return to battle out to the front lines: penicillin, a weapon of war.

Then one day, he saw a suppurating thigh wound, with the telltale red marks up and down the leg. This wound had seemed like nothing when the patient came in. Shrapnel in the thigh—that was next to nothing. But now Jamie was looking at gangrene.

He pointed it out to Lofgren. They nodded but said nothing. Didn't want the boy to know. Penicillin was supposed to work for gangrene, right? Jamie doubled the dose. He felt as if everything had slowed down inside himself. If penicillin turned out *not* to work against gangrene, well, that would be a blow. He took this personally now. He sat down and wrote every single detail in the chart. If the gangrene became worse, the boy's leg would have to be amputated.

Jamie recalled a colleague at the Institute who'd been a field doctor in the Great War. Told him that he'd kept two dogs at his field hospital in France to lick and purify the wounds. Canine saliva had antibacterial qualities. Did a dog's saliva work better than penicillin? Could a dog stop gangrene? Lucas Shipley would have made a good companion here.

Another visit to the café, after lunch at the hospital canteen. Nurse Nichols across the table from him.

While they drank their coffee in what had become a companionable silence, a truck came in from the front. The wounded on stretchers. And then another truck arrived, for the dead, the bodies laid out, covered.

He thought back to when he and Tia were young, how he'd turned her head away from the bodies piled in the horse-drawn cart. Now he and Nurse Nichols watched. His life passed before his eyes, the way people said it happened during the unfolding of a serious accident. His own life would end here, he knew suddenly and without doubt. He tried to make his peace with it. So much unfinished. His love for Claire. The family he, they, might have had. The hard truth of Tia's death. Whether penicillin and the cousins would change the world. All this, unknown to him.

He studied Nurse Nichols, who studied the nurses and orderlies organizing the wounded. She was off duty today. Her first name was Alice, although he'd never called her that. He'd never see Claire again. The young soldiers, the eighteen- and nineteen-year-olds, they believed nothing bad could ever happen to them. A good thing, when you're ordered to rise out of a dugout and walk into machine-gun fire. Jamie was old enough to know otherwise.

And different rules applied when so many were approaching death's door. Mueller was also off duty this afternoon, so there'd be no calls for Jamie to go to surgery. The hospital had four surgical teams, and Jamie worked only with Mueller. The penicillin research put Jamie on duty every day, but he didn't have to return to the ward for two hours at least.

He reached out his hand. With his index finger, he caressed the side of her left hand from her thumb to her wrist. Alice. She turned her head slowly to look at him. She nodded, an eighth of an inch, no more. That was all she needed to do, to whisper *yes*.

It was easy, comfortable, and good, like the passing flings he used to have with married women back home. Afterward, he couldn't let himself fall asleep or even rest. He had to get to the ward. Alice was asleep, her long, thick hair spread across the pillow. Even naked in her sleep, she looked like a pinup. Rita Hayworth. She hadn't disappointed him. He'd quietly put Claire's photo under some papers when they came in. Alice had pretended not to notice. Probably she had someone at home, or in some distant war zone, too.

The sun was out. The sun enveloped her. He didn't feel anything for her but a stirring appreciation of her beauty. He had no idea what she felt for him. He hoped it wasn't much. He wanted them to be only what they'd been before. At the same time he desperately wanted to fuck her again and again, to keep himself alive.

It was the next day. Or the next week. He'd lost track. He'd been trying to gauge the passage of time by how often Alice came to his room, but even that he couldn't keep track of. Her visits were like a massage that stayed with him through nights or days.

When they weren't together, she'd pretend she didn't know him. No more tête-à-têtes at the café, no more hints about walks among the olive trees. Good. They wanted the same from each other. He wished he could ask her, though, if she felt the same frisson through the day and night that he did after their times together, but they never talked about the personal or the intimate. If they did talk, they talked about the patients. Or rather, she talked about the patients and he listened. Strange, to be most intimate, and yet never speak of anything that mattered to themselves, to their lives at home, or their thoughts and hopes and wishes. Nothing.

Mueller was on duty today. First case, an ugly abdominal wound. Of every type of military surgery—head wounds, shrapnel in the neck, arms blown off, amputations—Jamie hated abdominal surgery most. Even after all these days, abdominal surgery still made him queasy, though he managed to hide it. Maybe Mueller was queasy, too. Even Alice. They were all doing what they needed to do, pushing themselves through.

"Where you from, soldier?"

The soldier, Keith Powers, drifted in and out of consciousness. He didn't respond.

"I'm from Oklahoma." Alice had told Jamie that she was certain the boys could hear her whether they were able to respond or not, so she kept up the conversation. "You don't know what hot is like until you've been to Oklahoma in the summertime. Don't you worry, soldier. With our Dr. Mueller, you've got the best surgeon in the entire United States Army devoting himself to you today."

Perforated intestines, bullet hole in the stomach, blood pouring everywhere. . . . Good Lord.

And now, right in the middle of their work, literally adding insult to injury, bombs started falling. The screech, the explosion, the rumble in the earth, the electricity flickering.

"God damn it," Mueller said as the table shook.

The electricity went out.

"Fucking hell," Mueller added for good measure.

An orderly turned on the flashlight. The planes were getting closer, what sounded like a battalion of them (even though planes didn't fly in battalions), almost overhead. These abdominal surgeries took a long time and always seemed to coincide with electrical problems and bombing raids. The planes were now on top of them.

Jamie felt like he was being sucked into a vacuum, the oxygen suddenly exhausted around him. With great clarity he thought, I've heard about this, this void, from friends who've survived raids.

And then he experienced exactly what had been described to him: the vacuum, the power of the blast overwhelming him, lifting him, rendering him weightless. The deafening sound of the explosion, and then the eerie, dark silence.

~

CHAPTER TWENTY-SEVEN

T his way to the remains," a bulky police office shouted to the group waiting in line.

Remains was a better word than *bodies*, Claire thought, following the group into the stone-vaulted, makeshift mortuary. Men in rubber aprons lined up the charred bodies in rows of fifty or more, covering the floor. The workmen left pathways between the rows of corpses. Stopping, staring, stepping onward, stopping, staring, stepping onward, the living walked up and down the rows and searched for the bodies of their loved ones. The Allies had invaded North Africa three weeks earlier. Claire felt she was witnessing the aftermath of war right here.

Boston, Massachusetts, Sunday, November 29, 1942. The day after the Cocoanut Grove nightclub fire. On Saturday night, the club had been packed with a raucous crowd, rumored to be a thousand strong, celebrating the upset victory of the Holy Cross football team over Boston College. A busboy holding a match for guidance while changing a lightbulb had set an artificial palm tree aflame. At least that was the story the newspapers were giving. The fire spread with astounding speed, and in the panic, dozens were trampled. Bodies were piled six feet high behind the blocked entrances. Hundreds were dead, hundreds more injured.

The camera was Claire's shield. Most of the dead no longer looked human. They looked like ancient, blackened tree branches fallen in a forest. Or like heaps of misshapen, molten metal. You spotted two parallel shapes with dark bands at one end and realized that you were looking at legs, and that the bands were the tops of stockings. Or you noticed a twig covered with a curling imprint and realized you were looking at a hand and forearm clad in a long lace glove. In this forest of the fallen Claire suddenly came upon a body that was perfect, a pale young woman who might have been asleep, lipstick in place, blond hair brushed. She was like a blessed saint amid the wreckage.

Seeing Claire pause, a mortuary attendant offered gruffly, "Asphyxia." The attendant was muscular and ruddy. The rubber apron barely concealed his broad chest. "Smoke eats lungs," he added. In the space beside the saint, he arranged a heap of charred fabric into a shape that could almost pass for human.

Claire first learned about the fire at six that morning, when she answered the phone at home and heard Mack's voice. "You're going to Boston. Stop at the office for what you need, then get to the airfield." Along the way, she read the newspapers with the first reports.

By the time she reached Boston, in a torrential rain, the area around the nightclub was under martial law. The civil defense authorities were using the incident as a dress rehearsal for dealing with a German bombing attack. She showed her ID and gained access to the cordoned-off blocks teeming with fire trucks, ambulances, and police cars. She showed her ID again to get into the ruined, smoldering club. Volunteers were still bringing out the dead, piling up bodies in the backs of trucks and in empty storefronts. Ambulances came and went in a blaring stream, taking survivors to hospitals. The reek of smoke and ash filled the air, choking her. She wrapped her scarf around her nose and mouth as a filter. Inside, firefighters searched the wreckage, tossing chairs and tables into a corner. On the bar, clean glasses stood at the ready, waiting for avid patrons to sidle through the Saturday-night crowd to order a drink. The scene became disconnected, like a dream. Shoot it like a disconnected dream, Claire told herself, an image here, an image there, because if you try to take in the entire scene, the horror will be overpowering and the reader will turn away. A *Life* writer was with her, but she stayed out of his way and he stayed out of hers. Claire took her own captions.

In the afternoon she had come to this makeshift mortuary. The real mortuary had been overwhelmed by the bodies. She knelt down to the level of the dead to photograph the faces of the living as they searched for their loved ones. One small token of identification, that's what the families looked for. A gold bracelet. A diamond ring. An emerald brooch. A St. Christopher's medal. Military ID tags. Any distinctive item that hadn't melted or been disfigured by the flames. The stench was overpowering. The living covered their mouths and noses with handkerchiefs. At first the stench had made Claire gag. But she got used it. She didn't know which was worse, the gagging or the getting used to it.

After five hours, she felt she was going blind, no longer able to focus the camera. She had to take a break, smoke a cigarette, drink a cup of coffee—anything to escape. On her way out, in a corner of the mortuary's vaulted entrance hall, she saw one more shot: a four-foot-high pile of hats. ALL HATS FOUND AT THE SCENE, a handwritten note read. Gray felt with a black band. Naval dress. Coast Guard. Magenta velvet with black face veil. Red felt with a sweeping gray feather charred at the tip.

Hats without owners, reeking of blood and smoke and burned flesh.

She sent the day's take back to New York with the writer. Mack instructed her to stay in Boston to await developments. On Tuesday, a bellhop knocked at the door of her hotel room after dinner with a telegram from Andrew Barnett. "Proceed to Massachusetts General Hospital, meet Catalano."

Hearing from Barnett reminded her of their last conversation. After the ransacking of her home, Claire had gone on with her work, but she'd felt vulnerable, especially now, when she was traveling and Charlie and Maritza were home without her. Whenever she put her key in the front door, she felt a flash of hesitation. Her home had always been her refuge. The place where she felt safest. Now she had doubts. Her only choice, however, was to move forward, and that's what she did.

So Nick was covering for Jamie. She'd been doing a good job, she thought, of not worrying about Jamie. She hadn't heard from him in weeks. She assumed . . . well, she had to assume that he was doing his job. She hoped he was in North Africa, part of Operation Torch, rather than Guadalcanal or New Guinea. Either way, he wouldn't be at the front lines. Clinical testing for a new medication would take place *behind* the front lines—wouldn't it? In a secure place where patients and doctors could be safe, day after day. Wasn't that right?

She didn't know. The front lines could be fluid, moving back and forth as different groups, different commands, made progress or retreated. She refused to allow herself to worry. Obviously he didn't have time to write. Or the mail wasn't working properly. But Nick's taking Jamie's place brought her up short, making Jamie's absence more immediate and more frightening.

When she arrived at the hospital, Claire discovered that no one at the front desk knew Nick Catalano's name. No one had a record of Claire's name, either. She was barred from going upstairs to the burn ward. She was already on edge, and this roadblock made her angry. "I'm here under official orders."

"Sorry, ma'am," explained the well-dressed receptionist, her white hair in a stylish perm. "I don't know what to tell you." She was probably a volunteer, Claire realized.

"Call the hospital director."

"I have my rules."

"I need to speak with your supervisor." Was there another entrance, on the other side of the building?

A slight, round-faced man in a bow tie approached her. "Is it Mrs. Shipley, by chance?"

"Yes." She didn't make herself polite.

"Ah, good. I was told to be on the lookout for you. I'm Dr. Chester Keefer."

He put out his hand. Claire had no choice but to shake it. She'd heard his name in meetings with Barnett. Keefer was in charge of the national clinical testing program for penicillin, under the auspices of Vannevar Bush's operation. He was a prominent physician here in Boston. He carried himself with a studied diffidence that made him look more like a professor than a clinician.

"The medication is arriving by ambulance," he said, overly composed. He turned to the receptionist. "It's all right," he said to her. "Mrs. Shipley is with me. I'll vouch for her."

"Thank you, sir," the woman said.

Claire took a deep breath. She calmed herself. Had she sounded so angry with the receptionist that Dr. Keefer now felt a need to pacify her? Apparently so.

"Shall we wait for the medication together?" he asked.

"Certainly." She forced her voice to match his tone. "Thank you for asking."

"Don't mention it."

She felt they were in a pantomime of politesse. In the grungy waiting room, they sat side by side.

"Did you know that the medication is being brought from the Merck Company in Rahway, New Jersey?" Keefer asked. "Thirty-two liters, in a metal container. The ambulance is traveling with a police escort on the Boston Post Road. And through this driving rain. How difficult for the drivers. Terrible. Who knows if the medication will be efficacious when it finally arrives? Of course flying would have been even more risky, no doubt about that."

"You're right."

"Well, tonight we'll see if our medication can help burn victims. I do hope so. The medication has never been tested on burn victims. Staphylococcal infection. That's what we need to protect our patients from."

He never used the word *penicillin*, she realized. Always he used a code word.

"In military attacks," he explained, "burn victims are everywhere. At Pearl Harbor . . . well, I have trouble bringing myself to speak of the hundreds, the thousands, of burn victims after the Japanese attack on Pearl Harbor . . ."

As he spoke on, without waiting for her response, Claire comprehended that for all his diffidence, and despite his unfalteringly kind-hearted and soothing demeanor, he was filled with worry. He expressed the worry by talking. Talking and talking, as if he were in a lecture hall, or a confessional.

"Burns . . . if the patient survived the initial event, infection was the killer," he said. You had to seal the skin immediately. *Staphylococcus aureus* was the most common culprit. Tannic acid was the treatment. Pouring tannic acid across gaping flesh. Horrifically painful. You gave the patient morphine before you started. A good deal of morphine. You needed several trained assistants for each patient. To hold the patient still. Because of the pain. If the patient survived the treatment, the burned area formed a thick protective coating.

They had to find something better than tannic acid. Maybe this medication would be the answer.

He turned to Claire, a peculiar expression on his face. His everyday mask of teacher and physician was gone. "Have you heard that I'm in charge of clinical trials for this medication? For the entire nation?"

"Yes, I have heard."

"But do you know what that means?" He didn't wait for her to guess. "It means I have to decide who receives the medication and who doesn't. Every day telegrams come to me. Dozens of telegrams.

Every day. From physicians across the country. Begging me for access to this medication. Telling me about this patient or that patient, this mother or son or husband who will die without it. Life stories, in telegrams." He stopped. He studied the floor. Rubbed his forehead. When he spoke again, his tone was slower. Quieter. "But there's so little medication to go around, Mrs. Shipley. Whatever we have, it's not enough. And it's supposed to be for the military only. But at the same time, it needs to be tested, on a variety of diseases. More diseases than we can locate in the military at any given time. We have to test it on civilians who have the particular conditions we're interested in, to find out if it will work. Mrs. Shipley, the system is set up so that I have to decide who will receive the medication and who won't. I, Chester Keefer, have to decide who will live and who will die."

"I'm sorry," Claire replied. What else could she say? It was 3:00 AM. She felt herself swaying from lack of sleep. He, too, must be reeling from fatigue. His defenses were gone.

"How can they expect me to play God?"

He seemed to want an answer from her.

"I don't know," she said.

"Will God forgive me?"

She wasn't a confessor. How could she offer him absolution? In her middle-of-the-night daze, she, too, felt God's judgment upon him.

He turned away. He was silent for a long time. Then, "I wish James Stanton were with us. He would help me with this."

Of course he would, thought Claire.

"On a few occasions over the past months, when I couldn't be reached, he was the one who had to play God."

"Tell me about him." She wanted to see Jamie through Keefer's eyes.

"A great man," Keefer said. "One of the great unsung heroes of the war. Well, someday this will all come out. A tragedy. When I heard—"

"What tragedy?" she interrupted.

Keefer gazed at her in confusion. Slowly the confusion turned to comprehension. "Oh, my dear, of course you had no way of knowing. Were you and Dr. Stanton acquainted?"

What was he trying to say? "Yes, we were. We are. We're close."

"Oh. I'm so sorry." He stopped, clearly thrown and unable to go on. "I . . ." He put his hand on her shoulder, offering his sympathy.

Was he saying that Jamie was *dead*? It wasn't possible. She would have sensed it, felt it, inside herself. She would have known. She didn't believe it. "What are you talking about?" she asked softly.

He stared at her, seeming to question whether he should go on. Then, soothingly: "As far as we've been able to find out, it was a bombing raid on a hospital. Communications have been intermittent since then. My understanding is that there were no survivors."

No survivors. That didn't refer to Jamie. *No survivors* was never a phrase that would apply to Jamie. "It's not possible. I don't believe you." And she had her proof: "I never received a telegram."

Gently, Keefer said, "Are you listed as his next of kin?"

Was she? She didn't know. She couldn't say. Who would he have put down as next of kin, if not her?

"Maybe officially he's listed as missing in action," Dr. Keefer said.

But if a man was missing in action, a telegram arrived from the War Department saying so.

"His journey was considered secret, that's probably why . . ."

"You're wrong about this, Dr. Keefer. Your information is incorrect," she said firmly, making herself believe it. Keefer didn't know what he was talking about.

Work. She had work to do. She was a soldier, too, and she had to keep on, she had to do her work. That's what Jamie would want, and that's what she was going to do. This discussion was interfering with her work. 3:15 AM. Where was the ambulance with the medication? She would get through her assignment and later, much later, she would learn the truth and believe it. Or not.

"Yes, yes," Dr. Keefer said. "I'm sure you're right. The rumors that go around, the false reports, it's outrageous. So," he said, as if they were beginning an entirely new discussion, "do you know Dr. Nicholas Catalano?"

"Yes." She would place herself in this conversation and nowhere else. This was what Jamie would want. Her thoughts would focus right here, and nowhere else.

"Dr. Catalano's the one who'll be here to test the medication. That's why he stayed behind, when Dr. Stanton went to the front. For just such an eventuality. He's traveling in the ambulance with the medication. I've never met him. I've heard only the best. They needed someone objective, to supervise the test. You understand what I mean, objective?"

"Yes."

"Someone who doesn't work for the commercial companies," he explained anyway. "Someone who's not beholden. I realize his expertise is in vaccines, but green mold was never my specialty, either. Green mold makes for strange bedfellows, eh?" He smiled wanly. "I'm glad you're here with me tonight," he added. "Makes the hours of waiting go by more quickly."

"Yes." He was feeling sorry for her, Claire sensed. She didn't want his pity.

At 4:25 AM, the ambulance arrived. Police lights filled the waiting room. The scene turned into chaos. No one noticed Claire Shipley. She worked unencumbered, and she didn't stop working, because to stop working was to be overcome with fear. She let the chaos envelop her, her camera freezing it shot by shot. The metal container of penicillin was wheeled in, strapped to a gurney. It was covered by a navy and green plaid blanket. Black watch, Claire thought—that was the name of the plaid. She thought about the plaid to stop herself from thinking about Jamie. A thick wool blanket, to keep the penicillin warm through the cold, wet night. Nick Catalano was looking older, his blond hair going gray at the temples. He kept one hand on the container as the orderlies pushed the gurney down the corridor, the protective touch of possession, like a father safeguarding a child. He glanced in Claire's direction, but he didn't seem to register her presence.

Crowding into the outsize elevator, an elevator big enough for two or three stretchers side by side, they went upstairs. At the proper floor, they pushed themselves out, rushed down a hallway, the director of the hospital raising his arm like a beacon and leading the way.

They turned: the burn ward. The beds stretched into the distance. In each bed was a survivor of the Cocoanut Grove fire: men at one end of the ward, women at the other, a makeshift barrier separating them. The resident doctors strode forward to greet Nick and Dr. Keefer. The residents reported that the patients had been given fluids, had been stabilized as much as possible. The residents began to present their plan for penicillin testing. Nick interrupted and presented his plan: 5,000 units injected intramuscularly every four hours. The residents protested; they had worked out a plan, this was their hospital, the testing would follow their plan. Playing God, Dr. Chester Keefer interrupted and announced that they would proceed with Nick's plan.

The stench of the burn ward. The patients swathed in bandages, even their eyes and ears covered. The congealed black mass of whatever skin wasn't bandaged. The intravenous fluid tubes stuck into the odd patches that weren't black or red or oozing. Many patients were unconscious. Of those who were conscious, not all could speak. Some charts listed only numbers, not names.

Claire greeted the patients before she photographed them. Most didn't respond. But she refused to photograph them as if they were living corpses. She wanted to offer comfort, although she didn't know where to touch them, or if she was even allowed to touch them. She didn't know what to say to them. She certainly couldn't ask them to sign permission forms; she'd let Mack or Andrew Barnett worry about that later. So all she could say was, "Hello, Mr. Daniels," to a patient who might lose his legs. Or, "Good morning," to a woman, number 37 according to her chart, whose face was swaddled in bandages.

At the hour when the dressings were changed, the moans were heartrending. The doctors and nurses wore face masks, which unfortunately muffled any words of comfort they might be offering. Claire turned her camera away from the unbandaged limbs, the mass of red and black and the white where bone shone through. She wasn't a doctor. She wasn't taking photos for a medical textbook. She wouldn't take pictures that were too lurid to be printed in the magazine.

As the hours passed, some of the patients began to call her "nurse," those with bandaged eyes able only to sense her, not see her. "Nurse, nurse." At first she tried to explain and then she gave up trying. How did you explain to someone who was immobilized and blinded and calling out in agony?

Mr. Brady, Mrs. O'Toole, Miss Flynn—"Oh, Miss Flynn, you have the most beautiful red hair." Spread across the pillow, her red hair was like a halo around her face. Miss Flynn was twenty years old. Miss Flynn's face was covered with bandages. Her eyes were covered with bandages. Only her hair showed. Only her hair hadn't burned. How was that possible?

"You're lucky, Miss Flynn," said Nurse O'Brien, sturdy, steady, no matter what she saw, "you've been chosen to receive a new drug. It's called penicillin. It will stop infections from the burns. It will save your life."

Penicillin will save your life, but never cure your scars, Miss Flynn, Claire thought. Never make you beautiful again. Twenty years old, Miss Flynn.

"Nurse, nurse, I need you, nurse, water," someone called from several beds down the row. A few sips of water through a straw, a few reassuring words from a young nurse. The soft, kind words.

Claire didn't know whether to pray that penicillin would save poor

Miss Flynn or pray that it wouldn't. At the other end of the ward, a young, nameless man who didn't look more than sixteen stared at Claire but didn't speak. When Nick examined his wounds and rebandaged them, he needed to be so very gentle that Claire had to turn away.

Nurse O'Brien, forced to step around Claire for the third time, confronted her by the window. "Doesn't it bother you, to be taking pictures of them and never helping them? Aren't you ashamed of yourself?" she asked, the lovely Irish lilt in her voice turned to anger.

Before Claire could answer, the nurse turned away, responding to a patient crying in pain, promising and bringing him an injection of morphine. Claire thought, *Was* she ashamed of herself? She had to believe that she was helping these people, if only by creating empathy in those who read their stories. Maybe inspiring others to help them. If she didn't believe this, she couldn't go on.

She returned to work. The next time she took a break, it was dark outside. Deep night. A day had passed. She checked her watch. Close to 2:30 AM. Too late, most likely, to find a taxi back to her hotel.

Nurse O'Brien came to her once more. No preamble, no apology. Pushed a kit bag into her hand. "You can use the on-call room at the end of the hall." She pointed. "There's a bed, a chair. The door says STAFF ONLY. You can lock it from the inside."

"Thank you." With the image of a bed conjured in her mind, Claire suddenly felt exhausted.

"You can wash up in the room marked NURSES ONLY. That's our shower. You'll find clean robes behind the door. A toothbrush and toothpaste in the kit. A few other things. Here's the key."

Nurse O'Brien thrust out a key hanging from an unpainted slab of wood.

"Thank you. You're very kind."

The nurse turned away with a sniff, mixing judgment with her charity.

Claire took a shower. The shower head was narrow, and the water pressure was strong. Instead of a soothing glide, the stream of hot water felt like tiny blades cutting her skin. Several days after her visit to the nightclub, her hair still reeked of smoke. She washed her hair twice, scrubbing with her palms, trying to get rid of the stench of smoke and burnt flesh.

Was Dr. Keefer right? Was Jamie dead? *No*, it wasn't possible. *Yes*, it was possible. *No*, it wasn't. *Yes*, it was. Jamie was dead. He'd abandoned her. She felt a terrible and irrational anger against him for deserting her, for letting himself be killed. The anger consumed her.

She had work to do in the morning, she had to sleep. She turned off the shower. She put on the clean terry cloth robe hanging behind the door. She wrapped her head in a towel to dry her hair. She came out of the shower room with her clothes in a jumble pressed against her chest.

As she walked down the hall to her room, Nick came out of his own shower, terry cloth robe tied at the waist. His hair was wet, with the look of having been combed by fingers. He opened the door to an on-call room across the hallway from hers. She glimpsed a narrow, metal bed stand, an old-fashioned wooden bureau, a bit of rug, lace curtains too feminine for the tiny, otherwise masculine room.

Nick looked at her. All day, he'd sensed her presence at the periphery of his vision. She was the remaining link to his dead friend. His dead friends, Jamie and Tia both. He could burst into tears in Claire's arms.

But that's not the way he interacted with women. He'd tried with Tia to learn a different way, and he and Tia were friends to start with at least, so it was easier. But that was over before it had a chance to unfold. His vaunted experience was useless when it came to figuring out how he could have Claire Shipley wrap him in her arms and comfort him. He understood only one way to become physically close to a woman. He said, "Why don't you spend the night with me."

It wasn't a question or even a suggestion; it was more like an insufficiently guarded thought. He was naked beneath the robe. She, too, was naked beneath her robe. His body was lithe and firm and strong. As was hers.

Death was all around them. Miss Flynn might have died in the time it took Claire to shower, shampoo, and comb her hair. Jamie had forsaken her. Everywhere was death. Here, overseas, the earth itself was consumed by welling streams of death. She felt desire. The desire to be close to one person, before she and everyone else was swept away. She imagined herself walking toward him. Jamie was dead, and for this one night she would grasp at being alive, fearing she might regret it but not knowing how much time she might have remaining for regrets, the smell of burning flesh lingering in her memory. She imagined the entire scene in an instant.

And then she did it. She walked through the door. Nick followed. He closed the door behind him. He wanted something different, more meaningful, not this. But he didn't know how to ask for it, or how to create the circumstances for it. And this must be what she wanted and expected of him. After all, she'd accepted his invitation. She'd walked through the door. She'd think he was weak if he didn't follow through. He was supposed to be strong. His friend was dead, so he wasn't betraying him. Just as Tia was dead when he took possession of the medication, so he wasn't betraying her: this is what he told himself. He couldn't understand his own life. He needed, wanted, someone, a woman, Claire Shipley; he needed to touch someone, embrace someone, be close, somehow, to someone.

Claire switched off the light. The room was dimly illuminated by other lights, the wards across the airshaft, the lights from the stairway windows. Jamie was dead, so he would never know. In the dark Nick could be anyone. In the dark he could be Jamie. She didn't know Nick, didn't understand him, didn't recognize his smell or touch, felt no connection to him beyond the link of death. He placed his hands upon her shoulders, pulled her close. Kissed her, hard and blunt. She sensed in him and in herself an anger and despair, a quick, brutal desire.

When she woke up, she was alone. She reached for the clock on the bedside table and shifted it until she could pick up some light from the window and see the time. 6:15 AM. Nick's clothes were gone from the chair where he'd tossed them, the robe left in their place. He must be back at work. That's the proper attitude, she thought. The attitude of a man. Get up and leave without a word, without offering anything of yourself apart from what happened in the semidarkness, satisfied simply with the release of passion.

She showered once more, trying to wash off Nick's smell along with the stench of the dead and dying. Returning to her own room, she got dressed. She put on yesterday's clothes. They felt heavy with sweat and grime. She needed to return to the hotel, where she'd bathe yet again and change into a suit: This morning at ten, she was covering the official hearing into the cause of the Cocoanut Grove fire.

When she left her room, camera bags over her shoulders, the cleaning staff was changing the bed linens in Nick's room.

A bed made clean in the early morning, the occupants having vanished without a trace.

CHAPTER TWENTY-EIGHT

O n a gray afternoon just before Christmas, Detective Marcus Kreindler got himself assigned to a new case. A double homicide, in Chinatown. He decided to walk to Chinatown. Get a little exercise, God knew he needed it. Since he was already at police headquarters, on Centre Street between Grand and Broome, the distance wasn't all that impressive.

When he crossed Grand Street, he turned to look back at the headquarters building, a gigantic stone palace in the style of something called French Baroque, his department secretary, of all people, had once explained to him. He never got tired of it, the gaudy decoration, the magnificent central cupola. He loved the contrast between the glitzy outside and what actually went on in the inside, criminals paraded through lineups, interviews going on, the whole business. There were contrasts outside, too, between the French palace and the surrounding dives where reporters hung out, waiting for hot tips.

He might have a hot tip for the reporters later. Had to get to work, though, to find out. Quickening his steps, he walked east on Grand to Mott Street. At Mott, he turned south. Walking through Little Italy, he felt completely at ease. Maybe on his way back he'd stop for a cup of coffee at Ferrara, have a piece of *sfogliatella*. He loved the flaky pastry with its sweet cheese. Now that he thought of it, he'd have one in the shop and two for the road, so that he could share with Agnes tonight. She'd like that, and like even more that he was thinking of her.

The Christmas decorations in this part of town were really something. In fact he'd noticed this year that everywhere he went, the decorations were extravagant, as if they were designed in inverse proportion to how tough everybody's lives had gotten. *Fuck you, Krauts and Japs*, was what the decorations seemed to say. (In Little Italy everybody conveniently forgot that Italy itself was part of the Axis.) Kreindler realized something: bombing cities to smithereens was supposed to break people's will, but instead, it made their will to resist stronger.

He crossed Canal Street, trying not to get run over in the multiple lanes of traffic. He entered the narrow, teeming streets of Chinatown. Right away, he was in a foreign country. He was glad he'd decided to walk, as the roads were clogged. In the gutters, accumulated muck reeked even in the December cold. Urine (human, canine, feline) mixed with chicken bones, feces, motor oil, gasoline, and maybe a few fetid egg salad sandwiches to top it off. At sidewalk markets, whole fish, their silvery skin mottled and shiny, were arranged on outdoor tables that abutted battered metal garbage cans overflowing with a week's refuse. The windows of the vegetable markets displayed produce he didn't recognize, big-leafed and pale green.

Newspaper offices posted war bulletins in their windows and on adjoining walls, Chinese characters printed in red on orange paper. Crowds of men gathered to read. Walking at a slow but steady pace, Kreindler looked the men over. They wore their suits and hats, and their wool topcoats, with a studied formality, as if they'd decided this was what they were supposed to look like in New York City, although they didn't exactly understand why, or what or where it was going to get them. Maybe they just thought the suits and ties would make the cops look the other way, and probably they were right.

A huckster placed himself next to Kreindler and matched his stride step by step. "Girls. I've got girls for you," he whispered. "All clean. Doctors look at them every day. Beautiful girls, any kind you want. White, black, oriental. Big tits. Biggest you ever saw."

Kreindler walked on, pretending not to notice. Prostitution wasn't his beat.

He crossed Bayard. When he reached Pell Street, he saw his destination: down the block, three squad cars were parked at a tenement at the corner of Pell and Doyers. An ambulance brought up the end of the line.

Doyers Street. Fifty years ago, it was famous for gang wars. Back then, it was a street flowing with blood, or so the legend went. The only place Kreindler ever saw a street flowing with blood was in a village in France, during the last war.

Here's what happened early this morning on Doyers Street: the neighbors reported a mutt whining, growling, pawing at the outside entrance to the basement of that particular tenement. Dogs could smell blood a mile away, Kreindler swore. One thing led to another, the cops got called in, and what did they find? Two guys shot dead with one bullet each to the back of the head, very efficient. Done by someone who knew what he, or she, was doing. Since the victims were Chinese, this was no big deal at headquarters. It didn't even make the late editions of the English-language newspapers. But the story was all over the Chinese papers, according to an acquaintance of Kreindler's in the community, a contact cultivated over long years of dim sum (or whatever the hell they called it), just as he'd cultivated Fritz uptown.

Apparently the Chinese papers went into a lot of detail about the basement being full of green mold growing in milk bottles. The Chinese reporters seemed to think this was a little strange. The first cops at the scene were willing to ignore the green stuff—after all, just a couple of Chinks, doing what Chinks do and getting killed for it, as the first detective assigned to the case so aptly described the situation to Kreindler.

But when Kreindler heard about the mold in milk bottles, everything started making sense to him. He pulled seniority and got himself assigned to the case. He telephoned his contact, who went by the name "Sam" because Kreindler couldn't pronounce his real name. The Chinese language sounded like gibberish to him, a fact that didn't make Kreindler proud, but there it was. Anyway, Kreindler asked Sam if there were any other deaths that morning. Twenty minutes later, Sam called back and reported the death of a woman, wife of a local big shot. Sick with some kind of female complaint that sounded to Kreindler like the clap, doubtless caught from her husband. Gave herself a shot of yellow medicine and dropped dead.

Before he left the office, Kreindler made a long-distance call on the police department nickel to Washington, to let Andrew Barnett in on the story. Turned out Barnett was in New York anyway for some kind of science meeting at the University Club; only the best places for Dr. Andrew Barnett. Kreindler tracked him down there. Barnett was now on his way to Chinatown to take a look at the basement in question. Kreindler wanted to pass some news on to Barnett, too. After months of questioning, Sergei Oretsky had finally revealed some useful information relating to the death of Lucretia Stanton.

Outside the tenement, a half-dozen officers and ambulance attendants lounged against the cars, smoking and awaiting Kreindler's instructions. The medical and forensic reports had already been taken care of, organized by the previous detective. These fellows were ready to wrap up here. A rookie stood guard at the entrance to the basement. The kid was thin, with bad skin. Kreindler introduced himself, nodded to the senior guys lounging against the cars. He recognized most of them.

A black dog was tied to an iron railing at the top of the steep staircase that led down to the basement. It was a short-haired mutt, touch of white under the chin. Its ribs were showing. The dog pulled at the leash. A stray, by the look of him. The dog pressed its nose against Kreindler's trousers, no doubt hoping for a rescuer.

"Untie the dog," Kreindler said. The rookie obeyed. Kreindler wasn't about to call the dogcatcher and condemn the creature to death.

Kreindler had already seen enough death to last a lifetime. The dog looked up at Kreindler hopefully. "Not today, boy," Kreindler said. Just as if the dog understood English, it took off into the crowd. Anybody watching would have thought it had someplace to go.

Kreindler added his own half-smoked cigarette to the gutter muck and went down the stairs. The basement was dank, moisture seeping through the walls. It smelled like sewage, or like some long-forgotten underground stream. It also smelled like blood, and like dead bodies lying around too long. A bare bulb dangled from a wire stretched across the ceiling. The wattage was weak. Twenty-dollar bills were scattered across the floor. The remains of more than one meal filled the garbage bucket next to the sink. Pieces of sandwich wrapping paper with holes eaten through and strips of leftover lettuce had been pulled to the floor—rats, unmistakably. Shelves of stoppered milk bottles lined the walls. In the corner was a contraption of tubes that reminded him of a device he'd seen at Lucretia Stanton's laboratory. The table in the middle was covered with scientific stuff, vials, test tubes, petri dishes, syringes.

Two contorted shapes, covered with tarps, lay next to the chairs. Only the shoes, sticking out from the end of the tarps, showed that the shapes were humans. Blood puddled on the floor, still sticky and coagulating.

Of course growing green mold in a basement wasn't illegal. Now that he thought about it, Kreindler was surprised more people weren't doing it.

"Detective Kreindler." Andrew Barnett was hurrying down the stairs, striding across the room, all good spirits, bow tie in place, coming to shake his hand. "Good to see you again."

Kreindler couldn't stand this guy. "Wonderful to see you, too." They shook hands on their mutual admiration.

"So, what have we got here?" Barnett said, as cheery as if they were out at Belmont for an afternoon at the races.

"As you see."

Barnett looked around, and then he did see. His right foot, clad in a well-polished leather shoe, was one inch away from a puddle of blood. He stared at the tarps. He realized what was under them. He registered the garbage and the evidence of rats and the green mold in milk bottles in racks along the walls. His face fell. Kreindler had sometimes wondered what that phrase meant; now he saw it happen right in front of him, cheeks down, lips down, eyelids drooping.

"I'm thinking black market," Kreindler said jovially, allowing himself a moment to enjoy Barnett's distress. "You agree?"

No response.

"So what's your best guess about what this stuff is selling for on the black market?"

Still no response. Well, he didn't want the guy to pass out. That wouldn't do anyone any good.

Abruptly Barnett was in the corner with the dry heaves. Kreindler prayed he wouldn't actually throw up.

While Barnett tried to get control of himself, Kreindler briefed him on the story, as a way of pretending he didn't notice what a hard time Barnett was having. "Here's what we've got . . ." He went through the entire thing, right through to the strongman's dead wife, because that's how long it took Barnett to come out of the corner.

"A hundred dollars," Barnett said, wiping his forehead with his handkerchief. The guy was in a cold sweat, but otherwise he seemed okay. "To the best of our knowledge, penicillin is selling on the black market at a hundred dollars per dose. I've heard about these . . . facilities, but this is the first one I've seen."

"Well, I've seen about enough. You?"

Barnett nodded.

"I'll give the men upstairs the go-ahead to start taking out the bodies. You and I can go somewhere to get a cup of coffee or green tea or whatever they serve in this neighborhood."

Barnett blanched at the mention of coffee. "I need to catch a train back to D.C."

"Then I'll walk you to the subway." Kreindler figured Barnett was a taxi kind of guy and couldn't resist needling him.

"What's the best place to get a taxi?" Barnett asked.

Just as he thought. "Probably the Bowery. I'll walk you over there." They'd have a few minutes, at least, to talk, and that was all that Kreindler needed.

Upstairs, Kreindler's orders were sharp and quick. The men got to work.

As Kreindler and Barnett walked across Pell Street toward the Bowery, Barnett was uncharacteristically quiet. Kreindler wished he knew what this guy was thinking. But, none of his business and just as well.

However, he had to go forward: "I've got some news for you, Dr. Barnett."

"What kind of news?"

Good, Barnett must be feeling better. He sounded more like his usual arrogant self. "I identified a German spy at the Rockefeller Institute and informed the FBI. They're running him now as a double agent. Probably you know him. He studies sewage. Sergei Oretsky."

Barnett looked at him sharply. He was caught off guard, clearly. Took him a minute to catch up. Then he looked relieved. "Oretsky's got nothing to do with my projects. Completely different department. Outside my jurisdiction."

"Glad to hear it." Kreindler said nothing more, making Barnett work for the next piece of news.

"Anything else?" Barnett finally asked.

"Yes. We've been questioning Oretsky a good deal, and pretty much getting nothing but nonsense. Then a few days ago, out of the blue, he starts telling a story." Why a suspect would sit on information for a month or two or three and then blurt it out, Kreindler never understood, but sometimes it went that way.

"What kind of story?"

"Well, as you may know, Sergei Oretsky spends a lot of time at the waterfront, collecting samples, I think he calls them, from the sewage outlets. He told us that on one of the days last May when he was out doing his collecting, he happened to see Dr. Nicholas Catalano walking on the path along the cliff with Lucretia Stanton. Resumed going about his business, then when he looked back, Lucretia Stanton was at the bottom of the cliff and Catalano was nowhere to be seen."

Barnett stopped walking and turned to Kreindler. He waited for a handful of teenage girls in school uniforms to amble past. Then he spoke in a harsh whisper, his rage barely controlled. "You're using the confession of a suspected German spy to accuse a man at the forefront of the government's program in—well, in one of the most important programs the government is running? Is that what you're doing? Be careful, Detective, be very careful, before you start making accusations that you can't prove against Dr. Cat—against a man like that."

"I'm ready to bring Catalano in for questioning."

"You do that and you will lose your job. You're not on this case—remember? I'll handle this."

Abruptly, Barnett strode ahead to the Bowery. Lots of taxis, traffic not too bad, Kreindler noted. "Good day to you," Barnett said over his shoulder as he stepped into the street to hail a cab.

"And to you." Kreindler watched Barnett get in the taxi and take off in the wrong direction for Penn Station, proving either that he didn't know any better or that he was eager to escape.

So, Kreindler was back to watching, and waiting. He had plenty of time. The war couldn't last forever. When the war was over, Kreindler would still be here, but Andrew Barnett would be back teaching economics at Stanford. There was no statute of limitations on murder.

I n the taxi, Barnett leaned his head back against the seat, filthy as it probably was. He opened the window and let the city sounds wash over him. The driver turned on Worth, heading to the West Side, making a zigzag uptown, trying to avoid the worst of the traffic.

He'd handled the conversation with Kreindler pretty well, Barnett complimented himself—the part of the conversation regarding Nick Catalano, that is. The basement, okay, Barnett couldn't be expected to do better with that, he'd never been to a murder scene. The existence of the black market was no surprise to him. After the success in Boston following the Cocoanut Grove fire, penicillin was out of the bag. Black market manufacturing sites were popping up all over. Dr. Bush had decided against trying to control them. The civil health authorities would have to deal with the problem. After all, penicillin wasn't Dr. Bush's only project, and it wasn't Andrew Barnett's only project, either. All scientific endeavors in the interest of the war came under Bush's jurisdiction. Penicillin was important, but it was second to their most important project, which was the atomic bomb. In the context of the bomb, this business in Chinatown was nothing but a distraction.

Still, Barnett couldn't help but wonder: Nick Catalano. Could Sergei Oretsky's accusation possibly be true? It was awful, of course, and Barnett hated to think he might be working with a murderer who could strike again. But if word about Catalano started going around, how was Barnett supposed to deal with that? Dr. Bush wouldn't appreciate Catalano as the solution to the problem of Lucretia Stanton's murder. Dr. Bush might be so unhappy about it that he'd shoot the messenger, as it were, and send Barnett to follow in his brother's footsteps in the Pacific.

On the penicillin front, things had been going so well recently. From all reports, the penicillin trials in North Africa were a great success. The companies were developing penicillin without patents for the military, while researching other substances in the background: Claire Shipley had proven this, although in retrospect Barnett wished he hadn't revealed quite so much satisfaction about it when she called to tell him. Dr. Bush's approach was brilliant, Barnett had to give him that.

The taxi approached West Thirty-first Street. In the winter's early dusk, Pennsylvania Station loomed before them with its shadowed monumentality.

Nick Catalano, accused of murder. No, no, that could never be allowed. Catalano's work was essential to the war effort, especially with Stanton out of the picture. A pity about him. A real loss.

A murderer to be brought to justice in the winter of 1942/1943? The entire undertaking was ridiculous.

CHAPTER TWENTY-NINE

⌒

C laire." Should he have referred to her as *Mrs. Shipley*? Nick wondered. The exigencies of address still confused him sometimes. They'd been intimate: that entitled him to use her first name, didn't it? "It's Nick Catalano."

Silence. So, his call was unwelcome.

Finally: "Nick, hi."

Not even a *how are you?* Or, *good to hear from you*. She was more stalwart than he thought. More stalwart than he was. Tougher. Well, he'd put himself forward this far, he might as well continue: "I'm in New York for a few days. I thought we could have"—he'd intended to ask her to dinner, but in view of her reaction—"coffee together. This afternoon, maybe?"

The call surprised her. But, she thought, how could she *not* agree to see him? She wasn't cruel; she certainly didn't think of herself as cruel. And she'd made love with him, after all, although it had counted as nothing. Did that make her cruel? Or just mean that she lived her life the way, well, the way the typical man lived? The shock would be if that night had actually meant something to Nick, Nick with his presumably well-earned reputation for enjoying, so to speak, the company of many women.

Still . . . he was Jamie's best friend. Maybe she misjudged this call. Maybe he needed comfort as much as she did.

In the weeks and then months that had passed since the Cocoanut Grove fire, when she'd learned that Jamie was dead, she'd forced herself to live from day to day. One day, then the next day, then the next. Christmas came, and she and Charlie were with her father. They were among the most fortunate people in the world, she knew as they gathered around the tree on Christmas Eve: it was December 1942, and they were together. A family. Then on New Year's, she thought the same: January 1, 1943, and we're together. What else could she do or think? She couldn't let Charlie see her collapse in grief.

Nick was waiting for her response. "Yes, Nick, we should have coffee." She thought through the options. "How about the café at the Hotel Lafayette, at University and Ninth?" That was a good choice, popular and bustling—and several blocks from home.

"In an hour, say?" He tried to be lighthearted about it. He didn't want to sound desperate. He felt immensely needy. He sensed a great emptiness inside himself, and he didn't know how he would ever fill it. He couldn't help but feel the sting, that Claire had deftly arranged for them to meet at the café instead of inviting him to her home.

"Well," she hesitated, running Charlie's schedule through her mind. He and Ben were at the movies with Ben's older brother, so she had a few hours free. "Yes, in an hour would be good."

"I'll see you then."

They hung up. The day was cold but sunny, and she'd enjoy a brisk walk over to Ninth and University. She could do some chores on the way back.

He had reached the café before she did. When she walked in, he was already at a table against the wall. The café's well-dressed patrons, almost all smoking, were reading newspapers, playing chess, or arguing about one philosophical or political point or another. The café at the Hotel Lafayette was known as a gathering place for *intellectuals*, a term that Claire always thought of in italics, the same way she thought of *artists*, remnants of the old, self-conscious Bohemianism of the Village. Seeing Nick there, watching a chess match at the next table, she thought he looked forlorn. She regretted the instinctive desire she'd felt to avoid him, to push him away. He was probably suffering as she was. Doubly so, on account of Tia and Jamie both.

She slipped into the seat opposite him. "Hello, Nick. Good to see you."

He stared at her for a moment. He thought, Jesus, this woman, so easy on the eyes, *and* so intelligent . . . had Jamie truly known how much he had?

The waitress came over. "Just coffee," Claire said.

"The same," Nick said.

Once the waitress had left, Claire leaned toward Nick. "I wonder what kind of coffee it will be," she whispered with a touch of mischief. Rationing continued to make good coffee almost impossible to find. "Moderately real? Just barely real?" Maybe this way, with banter, she could find a felicitous connection with him. Allow him, somehow, into her heart. Maybe she owed that to Jamie's memory.

Nick laughed at this, but he couldn't think of any appropriate response. He'd once had a good deal of banter at his command. He could recall charming many a girl at many a bar. But Claire Shipley wasn't a girl.

The coffee arrived. Claire sipped it. "It's truly terrible." She sipped it again. "I'm going to give it the award for worst coffee in New York City."

"That sounds a little extreme." Nick took a sip, then another. "No, you're too charitable. I'd have to give it the award for worst coffee in history." There, he'd managed it: he was bantering. Claire, with a slight smile, sat back in her chair, as if suggesting that she was, after all, pleased to be with him.

"Charlie went to the movies." She didn't know why she forged on with this tangent. Talk of children was an easy gambit with other parents—parents were always able, if not eager, to talk about their own and other people's children—but Nick wasn't a parent. Now that she'd begun, though, she had to finish. "*Der Fuehrer's Face*, starring Donald Duck. Last Sunday we went together to see *To Be or Not to Be*. We liked that. It's very funny. Have you seen it?"

Nick felt totally thrown by this woman. Haltingly, he murmured, "Look, Claire, I want to say—" That was as far as he got. He couldn't go on.

She reached across the table and placed her hand around his. "What is it, Nick?"

She was concerned for him, he could see that. Her lovely eyes upon him, her expression taking him in, all of him, not just the surface.

He wasn't in love with her. He just wanted to say that he couldn't rule it out for the future. They had so much in common. Dead friends, that was what they had in common, but even so. They'd made love to each other, so they also had that, although he realized it wasn't exactly love they had made.

"Claire, I was thinking we should get to know each other better." There it was, presented in the most innocuous way he could muster.

She let go of his hand and leaned back in her chair. Her look was more sad than angry. Her look was certainly not encouraging.

"I'm sorry, Nick. I'm so sorry." And she was sorry. She could offer him so little. She'd given everything to Jamie. But she couldn't hurt Nick. No, she would never set out to hurt someone. "It's too soon, for me. To think about getting to know any man better."

"But we've already been close," he said, a touch of anger, or perhaps simply indignation or disbelief, slipping into his voice.

She didn't need to defend herself, and she wouldn't. "Those were terrible circumstances."

"Maybe we got off to a bad start."

She smiled at this, and he smiled also.

"We can start over," he said, his tone lighter. Soon he would be leaving for the Pacific, to continue the clinical trials for penicillin. But he didn't tell her this. He didn't want her to agree to see him out of a sense of duty.

"I wish we could, Nick. Maybe someday." They sat for a time in silence, sipping the awful coffee and abstractedly watching the chess game at the next table. "I have to go," Claire said abruptly after glancing at her watch. "Charlie will be home soon." She opened her purse to pay for the coffee.

"My treat," Nick said.

"Okay, thank you. You're going to stay?"

"Yes. I'm thinking of taking up chess." They both knew it was just a pleasantry, but at least it let them part amicably.

Out on the street, Claire's sadness mixed with an unexpected sense of well-being. The sun was shining, Charlie would be home soon, they'd have a quiet dinner, just the two of them, and take Lucas for a walk. On her way home, she bought some groceries. A good day, all told. She could be happy with a string of such days.

CHAPTER THIRTY

⁓

How are you?" asked Dr. Knowles, the neurologist.
The man opened his eyes. He tried to focus on Dr. Knowles, round and balding, a volunteer, like so many aging physicians at the front. This was a real hospital, albeit one taken over by the American military. He had a vague memory of someone, sometime, saying this hospital was in Algiers. Maybe it was. When he looked out the window he saw palm trees.

"I've got a headache. As usual."

The doctor laughed at him. That's what came from being a wounded doctor: the other physicians found their entertainment in you. The patient tried to be good-natured about it, even though they were constantly accusing him of being demanding, high-handed, and overly sure of himself. No matter what he said, they accused him of giving them instructions instead of waiting for them to dispense their better wisdom. All this was part of a long tradition, and he didn't object.

Some time ago, before the patient could really comprehend, Dr. Knowles told him that he'd come through the attack with a bad concussion. Only one bomb had hit the hospital, and the damage, relatively speaking, was slight. Miraculously, the blast had thrown him under a steel surgery table, and the table protected him. Superficial cuts and bruises, an insignificant shrapnel wound in the shoulder. But he must have hit the floor hard, because his memory was gone for a while. His hearing was still weak from the force of the blast. He had trouble concentrating. Reading was almost impossible.

"Get yourself up and dressed, why don't you, Stanton. No malingering, now." Knowles said this with a grin. The infectious disease expert malingering: that was the latest twist in the ongoing drama of his recovery. "You've got a visitor waiting to see you. Very exciting. It's"—a pause for effect, and a slight inflection, as if to indicate the visitor was a girl—"your medic."

"You've decided to let me go back to work?"

The grin turned sly. "Guess we can risk it for a half hour."

Slowly Jamie got dressed, not in his uniform, but in the loose clothing the hospital provided for those patients who were up and about. The ensemble included felt slippers with cardboard soles. Jamie's roommate, Fred Paston, was in fairly bad shape, his head entirely wrapped in bandages, including his eyes. Only his mouth and nose were visible. Paston seldom spoke. Following the example of Nurse Nichols, Jamie often spoke to him.

"I'll be back," he said as he left the room. Slowly he made his way down the hall to the visiting area. He stood close to the wall, his left hand palm outward, so he could steady himself against the wall if he needed to. When he lifted his arm this way, his shoulder ached a bit from the shrapnel wound; he'd check in with the hospital's physical therapist about this.

Like the school in Relizane province, this hospital was French colonial, with archways, carved latticework, and multicolored tiles, blues, greens, reds covering the walls. Everything was clean and open, with warm breezes blowing through wide windows on all sides. It was nothing like the hospitals of Philadelphia, or New York.

"Boy, am I glad to see you!" Lofgren exclaimed. And he did look glad. Jamie had forgotten how young Lofgren was, just twenty.

They sat down on army-issue metal chairs just inside a narrow balcony filled with pots of geraniums. Jamie looked out at the hospital gardens, glimmering in the sunlight—pure whites, bright greens, dazzling yellows, exaggerated and precise. Too precise. The clarity and precision hurt his eyes. Probably some neurological damage, he self-diagnosed. The garden had a fountain, and the fountain worked, tossing water through the air.

"How's the work going?" Jamie asked. He spoke against a background of falling water.

"I've got the report right here." Lofgren undid the clasps on his pack and found the report. "I've been doing exactly what you taught me. The results have been really good. I mean, I hope you think so. I made this copy for you, sir. You can keep it."

Jamie assumed this was a nice way of saying that the original had been sent to Washington for Dr. Bush, and for Nick and Chester Keefer. Jamie took the report and leafed through it. It was long, and carefully done. Impressive. He didn't want Lofgren to know that he couldn't focus on reading it. "This is terrific, Lofgren. I'll study it later. In the meantime, let me ask you something. I've been a little confused. Anybody else make it out that day?"

Lofgren glanced away. "The patient, sir."

"The patient?" Jamie wasn't following this.

"Yes, sir. Keith Powers. No one knows how he made it, he was in real bad shape by the time the . . . the new team got to him, but they patched him up and now he's doing good."

"The new team?" Jamie pushed slowly forward. "What happened to Dr. Mueller?"

"He didn't make it."

"Nurse Nichols?"

Lofgren stared out the window. "No. That entire surgical team was wiped out. Except for you, I mean."

"Me and the patient?"

"Yes, sir. Like I said." Lofgren covered his awkwardness with excitement. "Keith Powers—he's on the penicillin ward. You can meet him. You'll read about him in the report, too."

"Ah." Jamie felt his energy flow out of him. He was using all his strength just to stay upright. Alice, gone. Pete, gone. But he, Jamie, was sitting here alive in the visiting room of a French colonial hospital with arched windows and a vaulted ceiling in Algiers, enjoying the morning breeze off the Mediterranean. How could he account for that?

"And remember that gangrene patient? Shrapnel in the thigh, a minor wound that turned into gangrene?" Lofgren was saying, filling the silence. "Fully recovered! He's back at the front. He was awarded a Bronze Star! Your decision to double the dose, that's what saved him, sir."

"Thank you, Lofgren. You took care of him, too. In fact, you must have seen him through the worst of it, after the bombing raid."

Lofgren blinked in a kind of embarrassed gratitude. "You coming back to work soon?" Lofgren looked suddenly crestfallen, like he might cry. He was no more than a boy, far from home, and Jamie was old enough to be his father.

"I'll be back soon. As soon as I can. Can't be spending my time lounging around here." He stood. He swayed, and Lofgren reached for his arm. Jamie pushed him off. With that, Lofgren looked hurt. Jamie was filled with regret but made a joke of it.

"Got to get used to my own two feet, eh, Lofgren? Got to build up my strength, to get back sooner."

"Yes, sir." Lofgren was happy again.

"You've done a great job. I'll make sure the commanders know that you're the one who carried this forward while I was recovering."

"Thank you, sir. Well, I've got to get back. Almost time for the next round of shots. We moved to a different location, just a half hour from here."

"Tell me something, Lofgren, before you go. What's the date?"

"The date?"

"The neurologists keep asking me to tell them the date—it must be on their checklist for making sure I haven't lost my mind. But since they never tell me what the date is, I never know the correct answer."

"January fifth."

A long time had passed. "So I missed Christmas."

"Guess you did, sir. We'll have another celebration in the ward when you get back."

"Thanks. I'll be counting on it."

"Good-bye, then, sir."

"Good-bye for now."

Jamie watched Lofgren go. Then he walked slowly to his room.

"I'm back," he said to Paston, immobile on his bed. Jamie stood at the window and stared out at the palm trees and at the Mediterranean beyond.

Chance—that's all it was. Governing who lived and who died. He wouldn't let himself think about Alice, or about Pete. Instead he'd think about returning to work. He'd have time enough to think about the dead when he returned to America.

Home. All at once he knew he'd make it, just as surely as a few months ago he'd known he wouldn't. Why? He had no idea. A conversion inside himself. Inexplicable.

January 1943. He'd missed Christmas and New Year's both. He needed to write a letter to Claire. Surely he could manage a few sentences. The prospect of this task gave him more energy than he'd had in a long while.

CHAPTER THIRTY-ONE

~

Claire and Charlie spent their Saturday afternoon doing chores around the neighborhood. They went to Bigelow on Sixth Avenue between Eighth and Ninth for a few pharmacy items. Using their hoarded ration allotment, they bought new shoes for Charlie, who'd outgrown his old ones, at the kids' shoe store on Eighth Street. They went to Wanamaker's on Broadway at Ninth, where Claire bought a new lipstick. On their way back, they made a stop at the Marshall Chess Club on West Tenth Street to pick up a schedule of classes for children. Charlie wanted to learn to play, and his grandfather was considering signing up for the kids' class, so they could learn together. As always on Saturday, Claire and Charlie went to Zito's on Bleecker Street to buy bread, a long, crispy loaf whose yeasty aroma wafted up from its wrapper. Bleecker between Sixth and Seventh was lined with pushcart vendors selling vegetables. Not too much variety at this time of year, but Claire stocked up on onions and potatoes. Crossing Seventh, they continued down Barrow, a quiet, tree-lined street with narrow sidewalks. They stopped beneath the windows of the Greenwich House Music School to listen to a violin class for children.

"Would you like to learn to play the violin?" Claire asked.

"No!" Charlie said adamantly. Horrified, he turned and walked away, as if the merest hint of an interest in music would condemn him to years of lessons. Claire loved him so.

When they reached the corner of Bedford, they turned right. A perfect afternoon, Claire thought as they continued along past the town houses and small tenements. The bright sun melted the snow at the curbs, creating a dirty gray slush—but a thin coating of clear water flowed from beneath the curbside slush and seeped over the street to make it shimmer and glow.

Seeing the light upon the street made her want to set up her darkroom again, to create prints that captured that shimmer of sunlight. After the ransacking of her home, the cleaning crew sent by Miss Thrasher had done a terrific job, but a cleaning crew couldn't put everything back to the way it had been. Now, finally, she was feeling ready to make things whole again.

Claire and Charlie reached the corner of Grove Street and turned onto their block.

Charlie saw him first.

J amie had a key, but he didn't feel he had a right simply to unlock the door and let himself in. He'd been out of the country for almost three months. He hadn't seen Claire in six months. He'd had an affair with a woman who died beside him. He'd seen things he could never bring himself to recount. He didn't doubt for a moment that Claire waited for him. And yet, he felt he needed to be invited in. He knocked on the door. He heard Lucas barking within, in greeting or warning, he couldn't tell.

No one answered his knock. So he sat down on the cleanly shoveled front stoop. Dirty snow was piled along the sidewalk. It was the weekend. Maybe she'd turn up. Even if she didn't, he was content to stay here for a while and get his bearings. There wasn't really anywhere else he wanted to go. His residence rooms awaited at the Institute, so he had a place to sleep, making him luckier than most, in view of where he'd come from. The day was cold, but he wore the army-issue winter coat he'd worn through North Africa, where the days were hot and the nights frigidly cold. So he was lucky on that score, too: he had a warm winter coat.

The clinical trials in North Africa were complete, because the penicillin supply was used up. Rather than send more, Dr. Bush had opted for the next trials to take place in the Pacific, under conditions of jungle warfare. Nick would be in charge. Jamie would consult with Nick for the next several weeks, then Nick would travel to San Francisco and ship out to the battle islands of the Pacific. As Jamie was packing up in North Africa, his main concern had been for Lofgren. He'd tried to get him into a training program for physical therapy, or at least into a supervisory position, but North Africa was seeing fierce fighting now and medics were needed at the front, so that's where Lofgren was sent. Jamie had given the young man his address and asked him to be in touch, in that probably far distant day when the war would be over.

Jamie had written to Claire a half-dozen times, although he didn't know if she'd received the letters. He'd received none in return, which might mean only that the military mail service hadn't been able to find him.

Maybe if he'd been in North Africa longer, he would have become accustomed to broken bodies that had once been filled with the strength and glory of life. Recently, he'd been having memory flashes of the bombing raid. He wished he still had amnesia, a lesser evil than the memories: the screaming, the begging, the moaning, maybe his own. The rusty smell of blood. The taste of explosives.

He propped his duffel against the wrought-iron banister and rested his head against it. At least his headaches were gone. His hearing seemed normal. His ability to concentrate was gradually returning. Sometimes his shoulder ached, especially when he carried his duffel. He couldn't believe how tired he still was, even after all the sleeping he did on the boat. He didn't even go up to the deck when he heard the others cheering at their first sight of the New York skyline and the Statue of Liberty.

Lucas had stopped barking. The dog was probably curled up asleep just inside the door. Waiting for Claire, just as he was.

Claire stood where she was, immobile. In the past months, she'd learned to let the events of the world wash over her. Amid the chaos and confusion, she could control so little beyond herself and Charlie. Her dear Jamie . . . the shock of understanding that he must be dead. The shock of the first letter showing he was alive. His presence now. One shock after another, even as she knew this was the story of families all through the neighborhood and the city and the nation. Still, these were her shocks. She'd received two letters from him, each of which she answered. Then, nothing. Now he was sitting on her front stoop. This was the way it was, this had been written about in the newspapers: moms and girlfriends and wives looked up from their cooking or reading or sewing, or returned home from their war jobs in the factories, and there, standing before them, were the men they loved.

She moved slowly toward him.

Charlie was prodding Jamie to get up. "Why are you sitting outside in the cold, Uncle Jamie? Where's Lucas? Don't you have a key? I thought you had a key." Charlie didn't stop for answers to these questions. "Did you lose your key? *I* have a key! My mom told me you weren't dead anymore."

Now the door was open, and Lucas burst out, jumping on Jamie.

"What ship were you on, Uncle Jamie? Where were you in Africa exactly? Will you show me on the map? Did you see my father? What kind of planes did you see? Did you see *Germans*?"

Now Claire stood at the bottom of the front stoop. Jamie, Charlie, and Lucas were on top of the stoop, five steps above her. Claire was grateful for Charlie's hundred questions: the grilling filled the space between herself and Jamie, letting her gradually take him in, feel his presence, understand and sense him once more, before they were alone together.

Jamie turned to her. "Hello, Claire." He thought she looked older. Worn down. Her eyes not as bright as he remembered. He didn't want to think about how he looked; he was certain he looked awful. "Did you receive my letters?"

"Two letters." He looked too thin. His skin was gray.

"I wrote a lot more than that."

"I'm sure they'll turn up eventually." She gave him a tentative, encouraging smile.

Charlie had an overnight birthday party to attend at his friend Joey's, over on Bank Street. Claire and Jamie walked with him to the party at 6:00 PM, along Grove to Bleecker, and Bleecker to Bank. Jamie was glad to be among the oddly intersecting streets, the small cafés and bookshops, the cobblestones, and hundred-year-old town houses.

"Bye, Mom. Bye, Uncle Jamie."

Charlie bounded up the steps to the vestibule of the building where Joey and his family lived, a tenement on Bank Street between Waverly and West Fourth. Joey and Ben waited at the doorway, the steep, dimly lit stairway up to Joey's fifth-floor apartment visible behind them.

"See you tomorrow," Claire called.

"Have fun," Jamie said.

"My Uncle Jamie just came home from North Africa!" they heard Charlie telling his friends. "He was bombed by the *Germans*!" Suitably impressed, Joey and Ben peered out the doorway at Jamie.

Claire took Jamie's arm. "I thought we'd have dinner tonight at the Charles," she said. "Over on Sixth between Tenth and Eleventh. That's the elegant French restaurant that just happens to share its name with my son. My treat. In honor of your return."

She pressed to go out for dinner before he could ask to stay home, because she felt nervous to be alone with him. She wanted to talk to him, but she didn't know what to say or where to begin. After imagining this moment so many times, she was now at a loss. Nothing seemed adequate. Her everyday concerns seemed petty compared to what he must have seen and experienced. And what about Nick? She had resolved to keep that from him. But what if Nick himself said something to Jamie about what had happened in Boston? That would be worse.

For his part, Jamie felt months of tension slowly ease in her presence. They walked on Bank toward Greenwich Avenue. He relived the walk they'd taken through these Village streets on the night of their first dinner together, over a year ago. Already then, he was in love with her. Now, as they crossed Seventh and walked east on Eleventh Street, the slush turned slippery at the crosswalks. The temperature was dropping. How could he ever tell her about Alice, and Pete? About Harry Lofgren? Or his patients? About the white-washed colonial buildings and the palm trees and the breezes from the Mediterranean? He couldn't tell her. He couldn't tell anyone. The memories were too painful. Best to start afresh, telling nothing. Asking nothing. Simply grateful to have made it back, to pick up where they'd left off.

Turning right on Sixth Avenue, Claire looked up at Jamie with a measure of anxiety and found him scrutinizing her. He stopped walking. He kissed her on the lips.

The future would take care of itself, she decided, returning his kiss. No confessions were needed. For tonight, at least, the future would take care of itself.

1:00 AM. At home. Claire drifted in and out of sleep. They lay pressed together with their faces so close that she felt the warmth of his exhalations on her chin. She breathed the very air that he breathed. As she felt herself settle deeper into sleep, she turned. She faced away from him, his arms wrapped around her, their legs intertwined. Having him here, she felt safer than she had in months. She positioned his hand on her breast. He rested his face on the back of her head.

He cradled her against his body, his chest against her back, the now-soft part of him pressed against her flank, legs against legs.

This was love, he thought as his body and his usually teeming mind eased into sleep. The thought seemed like a revelation to him. Here was love.

CHAPTER THIRTY-TWO

⁓

At 3:10 PM on the third Thursday in February 1943, Charlie was on his way home from school when he felt a catch in his throat. The week had been strangely warm, a February thaw, his grandfather called it. Charlie decided to take the long route home, via Christopher Street, with its small shops and groceries. He had some change in his pocket, but he didn't have enough for the candy at Li-Lac. Li-Lac was expensive. He stood at the window, peering in at the candies he would have bought if he'd had a few more pennies, and then he turned toward home.

On Bedford Street, purple crocuses were pushing out from the dirty snow in one of the window boxes. The houses on this block of Bedford were older than his house, almost as old as the Revolutionary War, and their sidewalks and front stoops tilted at odd angles. Halfway down the block, a black-capped chickadee poked around in a flower pot amid the curled and dried remains of a geranium. The chickadee found a treat and flew off happy, with a sharp beat of its wings. Then without warning Charlie felt the catch in his throat. He expected to feel pain, but he didn't. *Catch* exactly described what he felt.

At dinner, he had trouble swallowing. He concentrated on the mashed potatoes. His mother was away, doing a story in Vermont about cows. She'd be home in a few days. Uncle Jamie arrived in time for dessert, homemade applesauce with raisins. After dinner, they played chess. Because of Uncle Jamie being with him, Charlie completely forgot that he was having trouble swallowing. But later, when he was lying in bed after turning off his light, it came back to him. He realized also that his eyes and nose were watery, and his muscles ached. He had a headache behind his eyes.

He didn't want to tell Maritza that he was sick. If he did, she'd put hot mustard plasters on his chest and make him go to school wearing garlic or a ball of camphor in a bag around his neck. Even though he wasn't the only sick kid at school with garlic or camphor, and although maybe it even helped, he hated it. When he had scarlet fever, she put onions on the windowsill. Thank goodness no one had been allowed to visit him.

The next morning, his head felt too heavy to lift from the pillow. When he didn't go down to breakfast, Maritza came upstairs to find him.

"Where are you, Charlie?" As usual, she wore a flower-printed skirt and blouse with patterns that didn't match. She made all her clothes, and some of his, in her sewing room downstairs. She filled the doorway. Her white hair was covered with a blue scarf, and the blue matched her eyes. Her face was round and wrinkled, her voice gentle. "Still in your bed?"

He nodded. She pressed the back of her wrist against his forehead and made a noise like "stzaw." She kissed his forehead to confirm her findings. "Poor baby."

He didn't like being called a baby, but when he was ill, he did enjoy being treated like one, so he felt resentment and appreciation simultaneously.

"Stay." She left him. Sometimes she spoke to him as if he were Lucas. Today he didn't object.

Soon he heard Jamie's step on the stairs. When he arrived at Charlie's door, his hair was still wet from his shower. He was dressed in his uniform. He carried the medical bag he stored, locked (as Charlie and

Ben had discovered one afternoon when they tried to open it), in the corner of Charlie's mother's bedroom closet. "So, young man. Maritza tells me you have a fever. How do you feel?"

"My legs ache. And my back. My nose is stuffed up. My eyes are watery. And I can't lift my head."

"Interesting." Jamie examined him. Charlie noticed that Jamie blew on the stethoscope to make it warm before listening to his heart. Dr. Crawford never did that, and the stethoscope got icy cold in the winter. "Do you have a headache?"

"Sort of. Behind my eyes."

"Sore throat?"

"Mmm . . . no, I guess not."

"Details, please."

"Kind of uncomfortable. But not sore."

Jamie examined his throat, felt for swollen glands, looked in his ears. He took his temperature. "It's 103.2. Impressive." He cleaned the thermometer, put everything away, snapped his black bag shut. "Well, my Charlie, you have influenza. Not much to be done about that, except spend the week in bed. Think you can manage to get through a week in bed?"

Charlie considered this. He'd miss shop, which he really liked, especially now that his class was making models of German and Japanese planes for the air force recruits to study. But he had a spelling test on Monday and this would be a good excuse to get out of it. "Okay."

"Good." Jamie gave him a long slow smile that said, don't worry, everything's going to be all right, being sick can be fun if you approach it the right way. "I'll tell Maritza to look after you."

"Tell her no mustard plasters or garlic." The strength of his protest brought Charlie up to sitting. "And no camphor." He fell back from the effort. "Please, no camphor."

"Maritza has her own tried-and-true way of doing things, and far be it from me to interfere. Where she grew up, they didn't have doctors or proper medicines. Apparently garlic, hot mustard, and camphor did just as well. A fact I try to bear in mind every day."

Claire returned from Vermont on Saturday to find Charlie still running a fever above 103. She told Mack that she needed to take some time off to stay home with her son. Reading aloud to Charlie, playing card games with him . . . the days passed quickly. Jamie was in Washington, hoping to return soon. Maritza brought Charlie juice and made him soup.

At first, his illness followed the expected pattern. For two days he felt worse, then for one day he felt truly terrible, and then gradually he began to improve. His fever receded. Claire consented to the removal of the mustard plaster and the bag of garlic. She'd already gotten rid of the camphor, which, she'd told him secretly, she didn't like, either. Soon he could sit up in bed and focus his eyes. He regretted admitting this when Claire had him start the homework his teacher had dropped off.

On the following Saturday at 10:20 AM, the expected pattern fell away. Claire always remembered that moment, the dividing line between before and after, although there must have been signs, if only she'd recognized them. Looking forward to a midmorning cup of tea, she happened to glance at the clock on Charlie's bedside table. 10:20 AM. Charlie began to cough, a raw, brutal cough that sounded like it would burst open his insides. When the cough finally calmed, he wheezed to catch his breath.

Within a few hours, his fever spiked to 104. With Jamie still in Washington, Claire phoned Dr. Crawford. At six, he arrived. Dr. Crawford's appearance always surprised Claire. He was built like a jockey, small, thin, soft-spoken, with a hard edge of determination. Dr. Crawford had announced his retirement last year, but with younger doctors heading to the war zones, he kept up his practice in their absence. Dr. Crawford had always been generous to Claire and Charlie, and Claire regretted the three flights of stairs he had to climb to reach her son.

Dr. Crawford listened to Charlie's chest, asking him to breathe in and out, in and out, until another coughing fit interfered. Claire wished she could plug her ears to block out the sound of his coughing. Stethoscope held upright, Dr. Crawford waited patiently. When the coughing stopped, he continued the examination. He tapped between Charlie's ribs and listened carefully for reverberations. He pressed the side of his hand against Charlie's ribs and asked Charlie to breathe. He was testing for fluid in the lungs.

"Step into the hall with me for a minute, would you, Mrs. Shipley," Dr. Crawford said calmly, as if nothing were amiss. He walked as far as the guest room, and she followed. He took a deep breath, and gave a long exhalation. "Pneumonia," he said. "In both lungs."

The word hit Claire like a punch. Pneumonia could be fatal. Often it was. The Old Man's Friend, it was called, because it brought death. It was never called the Young Man's Friend. Never the Child's Friend. "Should we take him to the hospital?" Claire asked.

"We can take good care of him here," Dr. Crawford reassured her. "Better, in fact."

That's what Emily's doctor had said. Those words exactly. *We can take good care of her here. Better, in fact.*

"I'll arrange for a nurse. I assume that's all right? Mrs. Shipley? Claire?" He demanded her attention, when her daughter filled her thoughts: Emily's eyes, hair, cheeks, Emily running, jumping, sleeping, all of this pressing into Claire's mind.

"Yes. A nurse. Yes." Claire wouldn't ask questions about details and cost. If Dr. Crawford wanted Charlie to have a nurse, he would have one. Claire would ask her father to pay. She wouldn't stand on pride now. Her mother had paid for Emily's nurse.

For the next days, Claire entered a kind of suspended animation as

Charlie's condition became worse and worse. He became the beginning and end of her world. Everything else dropped away.

Dr. Crawford treated Charlie with sulfapyridine, but days passed, and it had no effect. He drew a blood sample, took it to St. Vincent's Hospital for testing, and returned the next day with a serum treatment.

The serum, too, had no effect.

Claire tried to reach Jamie, but Vannevar Bush's secretary said he was visiting research labs in the South. She didn't know his exact schedule, but would try to get a message to him.

Claire sent a telegram to her father, who was in Cincinnati on a business trip. *Charlie has pneumonia*, the telegram said. Rutherford cut short his trip and returned home. He was shocked when he saw Claire on the stairs, her hair uncombed, her clothes unkempt. He was even more shocked when he saw Charlie. He'd visited just six days before, when Charlie had appeared to be on the mend. They'd played tic-tac-toe. Now Charlie was lying upon three pillows, propped up to keep fluid from accumulating in his lungs. His skin was white. Deathly white, as the saying went. His fingernails were a strange bluish black. Rutherford glanced sharply at Claire and was about to ask her if she'd noticed the color, but she looked dazed.

"You should lie down, Claire," he said.

"I've been telling her to lie down all day," said the officious nurse, coming into the room with warm washcloths to bathe Charlie. "I'll need to ask you to leave now, so I can wash the patient."

"What is your name, nurse?"

This question seemed to offend her. "My name, sir, is Cynthia Burns, but you may call me Nurse Burns."

"Very good, Nurse Burns. You can bathe my grandson later," Rutherford ordered.

"I beg your pardon—"

"Later." He dismissed her with a wave of his hand.

With an exaggerated sniff and toss of her head, as if making a record of her displeasure in case her abilities were ever challenged, the nurse left them.

Rutherford turned to his daughter. "Claire, I want you to lie down."

Claire dutifully followed her father's instruction, acquiescing without a word, retreating to her bedroom on the second floor.

Rutherford watched her go. How had the situation reached this awful state, he wondered. Someone needed to take charge here. And yet, as he sat in the rocking chair at the foot of Charlie's bed and watched the boy thrashing and twitching, as he listened to Charlie's wheezy, rattling breathing that came so very fast, Rutherford understood that this course of events was beyond anyone's control. No one could take charge, because no one could control what was unfolding within Charlie's body.

But it was impossible that his grandson would die. Rutherford wouldn't allow it.

He placed his hand on Charlie's ankle. He rubbed the boy's foot.

Without speaking, Charlie moved his foot toward Rutherford's hand, to tell him he liked it, to ask him to keep doing it. Rutherford felt tears coming. He fought against them, because he wouldn't allow Charlie to see or hear him cry.

Penicillin. Obviously. It wouldn't have worked against the influenza (caused by a virus, not bacteria), but against the pneumonia that had now set in, it *would* work. Rutherford should have thought of this the moment he received Claire's telegram. His fears had overwhelmed him. And he wasn't accustomed to this option. Who was? Certainly not old Dr. Crawford. Penicillin was new, but it was there waiting, and it would cure Charlie.

Bursting with his idea, he called to the nurse, who'd been sitting in the guest room reading the *Daily News*. "Watch the boy." He went

downstairs, and found the phone extension in Claire's study. He sank
into her desk chair with a weary thud. Stanton, wherever he was, still
hadn't been in touch with Claire, so Rutherford had to act on his own.
First he called his office, demanded of his secretary a list of phone
numbers that he then wrote down in his meticulous print on the small
pad he always kept in his jacket pocket.

"What are you doing?" Claire said behind him. She swayed on her
feet. She'd been in a deep sleep and had been woken by her father's
voice on the phone.

"Saving Charlie." His first call was to his own company, Hanover.
He asked for the chief penicillin researcher: "Get me Dr. Bryant," he
said to the switchboard operator.

"May I ask who's calling?" she said.

"Edward Rutherford. His boss."

"I'll connect you, sir."

Rutherford waited what seemed like a long time. Finally: "Bryant
here."

"Dr. Bryant, my grandson has pneumonia." Hit him hard and fast,
Rutherford decided, before doubts set in. "I need you to pack up some
penicillin for him. I'll send a messenger for it in an hour."

A pause. Then Bryant spoke in a whisper: "I don't have any stockpiled, Mr. Rutherford. Only enough for the current experiments." He
stopped. "I'm talking from the phone in the lab, sir. The MPs are
patrolling." Pause. Rutherford could imagine the scene, which he'd
witnessed often enough: the young MPs following their orders and
standing over the penicillin scientists one by one. "Okay, they're on
the other side. Look, I could start putting something aside. A small
amount tonight, a little more tomorrow. Maybe by the end of the week
there'd be enough to start treatment . . ."

"That's too goddamned—" Rutherford stopped himself from
shouting. The poor man was only doing his duty. "Thank you." He
hung up. He turned to Claire. "You know some of these people at

the other companies, the bigger companies, don't you, Claire? And in Washington?" He showed her the list on the pad.

She nodded.

"You can telephone them, can't you, Claire?"

She nodded but couldn't find the strength to move.

"I've got the phone numbers. It's better coming from you. You're his mother. You have priority over everyone else."

Again she nodded.

"Come here, darling. I know you can do it."

He helped her to the chair, got her settled. She might have been sleepwalking. He struggled to hold himself back, not to pressure her with the urgency he felt. If she broke down, then for certain Charlie would not be helped. He explained to her what to say. "Here's the first number, sweetheart."

And so she placed the calls. Although each call was different, each was the same. George Merck, John Smith, Vannevar Bush . . . she actually reached them, that was the first miracle, but they would not, could not, help her. Bush's secretary was still trying to track down Jamie. Ask Chester Keefer, everyone said. Call Chester Keefer—he's the one who controls distribution. If *he* says so. . . . Maybe, maybe, maybe . . . the guards are watching, armed guards, the permission must be official.

Gradually the problem dawned on Claire: by now, clinical trials had shown that penicillin cured pneumonia. In fact, penicillin was the best possible cure for pneumonia. This was proven scientific fact. And that was the terrible irony: if Charlie had contracted a more unusual disease, he might have had penicillin immediately. To see if it worked. Its use on an unusual disease fell under the category of scientific investigation, gaining knowledge applicable to military needs. Penicillin was made available for that. But for pneumonia, even Chester Keefer would be hard-pressed to release it. Not that they didn't *want* to give their penicillin to Charlie.

"I'd like to help him," said John Smith at Pfizer. "Truly, I would. But I can't."

Chester Keefer was unavailable, his secretary said. Twice Claire called, between other calls. Still unavailable. Maybe later. Maybe. Fifteen minutes later, she placed the call to Boston once more. The operator phoned her back when the call went through.

Finally, suddenly, she reached him. "Hold on, please," his secretary said.

"Mrs. Shipley. I'm so sorry I missed your calls."

Claire was almost struck dumb. She wished she had the strength to push and prod and order him, but she didn't. She had barely the strength to stay polite. Barely the strength to explain her predicament. But she did explain it. She did ask. On hearing the answer she expected, she graciously thanked him and hung up the phone.

"What did he say?" her father asked her.

"He said, 'Please, don't ask me to play God.'"

"'Don't ask me to play God'? What sort of a goddamned thing is that for him to say?" Rutherford howled, losing his otherwise staunchly guarded control.

"I don't know." Claire would cry now for certain. She'd held back from crying, for better or worse, all through the telephone calls. But now, her father yelling at her, she too would lose control. "I don't know."

Seeing what he had done, Rutherford withheld what he was going to say next. He put his hand, ever so lightly, upon her shoulder. He tried, ever so haltingly, to console her. Not only her, but also himself.

Another idea came to Rutherford. An idea he wouldn't have risked, except his grandson's life was at stake, and this was the only idea he had left.

D*on't ask me to play God.* Upstairs, Charlie didn't have the energy to open his eyes or to speak, but he did hear his grandfather shouting. *Don't ask me to play God.* In the yearly Christmas pageant at school, someone always played an angel, and often a real baby played the infant Jesus, but no one ever played God. Maybe it wasn't allowed. How would you play God, if someday it was allowed? Charlie tried to conjure an image in his mind, a white beard, and white hair, but that ended up looking like Santa Claus, and he didn't think God looked like Santa Claus. He tried again. God. A tall man, he thought. But why? God could be medium-size. More common. Charlie's father was medium-size, he remembered that; his father was just about the same height as his mother. And after all, God created man in His own image. But that could simply be a metaphor, a word he'd learned this year in school. Maybe God could look like anything He wanted to. Charlie imagined that all the beautiful creatures he'd ever seen in the world were actually God in a different form. He saw a scarlet tanager, brilliant red, flitting through green leaves. Then he himself was a scarlet tanager, taking flight, rising above the tree line, Central Park spread far beneath him as he flew toward heaven.

W hat kind of human patient did you conduct an experiment on? Someone who'd run out of options. Someone like Charlie.

Jamie returned to town that afternoon and took a taxi directly to Grove Street. Vannevar Bush's secretary had finally tracked Jamie down in Louisiana. He'd had a long trip back. When he arrived at the house, Rutherford took him aside, motioning him into the small room on the parlor floor that Claire used as a photo office.

"Look here, Stanton, you know very well that a while back I bought the Hanover company. They've—we've—got a new antibacterial drug. We've been looking for a place to conduct clinical trials. It's one of the cousins. I'm sure you understand. So let's just jump over all the rigmarole and get this job done." Keep steady, Rutherford told himself. Hold on long enough to get through this. To save Charlie. If it wasn't too late.

Jamie heard him out. In the office, one of the windows was open a few inches, and the long diaphanous curtains billowed on a breeze. The winter sun poured in. "I understand," Jamie said. He'd heard the rumors. He knew the score, as the saying went. He also knew that only Dr. Keefer could release penicillin to civilians.

"Can you tell Claire? Can you explain to her? I don't think I can."

Jamie heard the break in the old man's throat. "Of course." Jamie thought this through. "I'd want to take Charlie to the Institute," he said, thinking of the practical procedures they should follow. "That's the best hospital for supervising an experiment. We'd have to keep records of everything."

"That's fine with me," Rutherford said. "Whatever you think is best." He felt himself at the mercy of this man, almost thirty years his junior and so much more knowledgeable than he was.

Claire came into the house, returning from taking Lucas for a walk. The dog bounded over to greet Jamie, jumping up to lick his chin. Jamie pushed him down but pressed the dog's head against his leg, to capture his warmth and affection. Claire walked down the hall to join Jamie and her father.

"Jamie, I'm so glad you're back." Why were they standing in the photo office? she wondered. Did they need something? A photo of Charlie? She still hadn't had time to fully reorganize the files after the ransacking; she couldn't let a clean-up crew do that. She'd just piled everything up. The office was a mess.

Jamie thought she looked awful. Her hair was wild. She wasn't even wearing lipstick. Letting go of Lucas, he reached to embrace her.

Rutherford felt a spasm of fear: would Claire finally realize that he himself had ordered the theft of her Hanover photographs? Would she finally, now, confront him? He stared at her. She was in no condition to be putting two and two together. Charlie was the beginning and end of her concerns.

"Claire," Rutherford said, "Jamie needs to discuss something with you."

Jamie pulled back from their embrace. "Yes, Claire. Yes, I do." And so Jamie spelled out the situation to her. A new medicine. A human trial. "Charlie would be a good candidate," Jamie said, putting on a strong, confident voice. His doctor's voice. Not a father's voice. Not a grandfather's voice.

As he spelled it out, Claire struggled to take in what he said. *Candidate* was a good word, she thought. *Candidate* had a connotation that was both truthful and hopeful. *Candidate* didn't suggest death as a possible outcome. Outside, the sun had set. What happened to the day?

"Let me ask you something, Doctor," Rutherford said, summoning up a tone of objectivity. "What are his chances without it?"

Jamie knew how to be objective. Objectivity was a game, and he could play it. "Based on my experience of children this age, at this stage of the disease process, less than five percent."

"It's your decision, sweetheart," her father said. He put his hand on her shoulder for the second time that day. Or maybe it was already the next day, and the next day's sun had set. She couldn't tell. His hand was trembling. She saw it tremble as he brought it toward her, and she felt it trembling upon her shoulder.

She had to say something. They waited for her to say something. It was her decision. Her choice. She remembered the afternoon when she'd gone to Charlie at the end of his nap and discovered that he'd turned himself over for the first time. He'd giggled impishly when he saw her. She remembered the moment he first pulled himself to standing, holding on to the edge of the bookcase. Less than 5 percent. Her decision. What were they talking about?

"I'm not a doctor," she said. *Don't make me play God.* The phrase came into her mind unbidden. She may have said it aloud, but she wasn't sure. She felt a knife inside her that entered at her collarbone and went through to the small of her back. She looked at Jamie. The man she loved. He waited. She trusted him to know the proper course. "Whatever you think is best," she said to him.

"Yes," he said.

Jamie carried Charlie to the backseat of Rutherford's Lincoln-Zephyr. Rutherford drove. During the journey uptown in the big car, smoothly driven, Claire found herself thinking about Tony Pagliaro. His wish had been granted, and he'd been transferred to the war months ago. Years or decades ago, it felt like to her now. He'd assisted her for those fleeting weeks, and then he was gone. He, too, was sent to North Africa. He, too, put in the way of death. As of course they all were, at each moment of each day. She'd called the bakery and spoken to his mother. She'd asked his mother to phone her, if ever there was news. *News* somehow implied bad news, although Claire didn't intend it that way. So far his mother hadn't phoned, and Claire hoped with the cliché, no news was good news. She missed Tony. She wished he were here to take Charlie to the hospital. Charlie would be safely distracted during the ride with Tony. They'd discuss baseball—or at least Tony would talk about baseball; Charlie looked too weak to respond—and Charlie would assume that everything was going to be fine. If Charlie looked at his mother or grandfather or Uncle Jamie right now, he'd realize that everything probably wasn't going to be fine.

Because the hospital was filled with naval patients, not appropriate company for a child, Nurse Brockett authorized Charlie to use the Rockefeller family quarters, which were empty at the moment. The family quarters were on the top floor and reached through a plain but highly polished wooden door. Once inside, Claire found herself in the equivalent of a private home, Persian carpets on the floors, tapestries and paintings on the walls, upholstered furniture. The rooms were aired out, dusted, prepared and ready for any emergency.

Dr. Lind was waiting for them. He did everything he could to get Charlie settled. He was like a teddy bear himself, the perfect doctor for a child, Claire thought. Claire felt grateful for the heart murmur that kept Dr. Lind out of the military. Had Charlie remained conscious, he would have enjoyed meeting Dr. Lind. Instead Charlie's head swayed, as if he were in the deepest dream.

Then the men disappeared, and Claire was alone with her son.

Claire didn't know, could never have imagined it: the men were gathered downstairs in the lab. Tia's lab, which Lind now used when he had time. Nick Catalano, too, had joined them, from the vaccine lab down the hall, where he assisted when he was in town and had the opportunity. His trip to the Pacific had been delayed due to lack of sufficient supplies of penicillin. They waited for the chief researcher from Hanover to arrive from New Jersey with the new medication, the penicillin cousin.

Jamie looked around. Everything was the same and yet miniature. He'd imagined the lab bigger while he was away. Almost ten months since his sister died. Here in the lab, her home in the truest sense, she was a palpable void. His acute awareness of her absence created her felt presence. Maybe because he'd never had a chance to mourn her, her absence from the lab hit him hard. But he didn't have time to dwell on his feelings.

Hanover himself arrived, instead of the chief researcher. An assistant accompanied him, carrying a canvas bag. Youthful, pale, the assistant took the medication from the bag. The container was wrapped in a white towel.

"We'll bring more in a few days," Hanover said. "This was all we had today."

Impassively Jamie watched the assistant place the beaker on the table and unwrap the towel to reveal a tightly sealed glass jar, quart size.

It was the color that told Jamie. The astonishing clarity. The pure, bright blue. In an instant, he was sitting outside on a bench with Tia, the sun warming their backs. *It's the most beautiful blue*, she said.

He studied it for a long moment, trying to piece together the past months, piece together the truth of what was on the table before him. Rationalizations came into his mind: someone else could have found the same substance. No doubt it was everywhere. A waste product of mold. Mold was everywhere. Or so he tried to convince himself. He glanced at the man he already thought of as his father-in-law. Rutherford was watching him. Not with any particular emotion, just watching. Waiting.

Charlie was upstairs. Jamie couldn't pursue this now.

The dose. He had to put the question of the proper dose foremost in his mind. "How far along are you on human testing?"

Hanover looked confused. He glanced at Rutherford. The confusion between them told Jamie what he needed to know even before the assistant piped up to explain:

"Well, we, uh, we have the protocols almost in place for human testing. But no human being has yet received the medication."

"What's the dosage you've been using for mice?"

This the assistant could answer. He stepped forward, took notebooks out of the briefcase, presented Jamie with the test results.

Jamie had no choice, he knew. Since the medicine had never been given to a human being before, they didn't know whether humans might be allergic to it. It could cause anaphylactic shock. In the hope of saving Charlie, Jamie wouldn't kill him by mistake. Jamie would test the medicine on himself first. He did the math in his head. The average albino mouse weighed about 28 grams, or one ounce. He weighed 185 pounds, give or take (more likely a little less since his months in North Africa). With 16 ounces to the pound, he weighed approximately 2,960 ounces. He had to grin: he was nearly 3,000 times the weight of a mouse. With some quick reckoning, he worked out the dose.

"All right. Dr. Lind, find a syringe, would you. I'm going to give myself a shot of this stuff. Just to make sure it doesn't kill me."

"You can't do that," Lind said.

"I won't risk the patient having an allergic reaction."

"Give me the shot," Lind said. "I'm the one who should have the shot."

There was the doubt again, distracting him: which of Tia's colleagues had betrayed her? Jamie saw precisely how the plan must have progressed: Rutherford employed a spy here, a situation common enough and no surprise. Tia trusted her colleagues. Most likely her killer was someone close. Was it Jake Lind? Was it Nick? Could it have been David Hoskins, her closest colleague? Nowadays Hoskins went from one commercial lab to the next, using his penicillin expertise to assist with mass production. He'd cycled through the Hanover company, too.

When Tia's killer had the substance and her notes, he took them to Rutherford and in exchange Rutherford gave him—what? This was the point that held Jamie up. Most likely money. Jamie couldn't imagine himself killing for money. Another scenario went through his mind: could the medication have been stolen right after she died? You didn't need to kill her to steal the medication. So maybe she wasn't murdered. But in that case, why was she walking along the cliff?

"Since I can't serve in the military," Lind was saying, "let me do this."

"Don't be ridiculous, Jake. The heart murmur could skew the results. You know that."

Lind stared at the floor. Jamie turned to Nick. Nick said nothing. Offered nothing. Did this make him more, or less, likely to be Tia's killer? Or did it simply mean that Nick agreed with Jamie's decision and saw the necessity of it?

Hanover and the assistant were also silent.

"I'll take the shot," Rutherford said.

Jamie watched Rutherford take off his jacket, roll up his sleeve. "I'm closer to seventy than to sixty. My last will and testament are in order. I'm ready to go. Let's get on with it."

Was this justice? Jamie wondered. Rutherford would redeem what he'd done by sacrificing himself? Rutherford would take responsibility now, at last? Jamie was tempted to do as Rutherford suggested.

But he refused. First, do no harm. The physician's code. He'd harm himself before he'd harm another.

"I appreciate the offer, but no. Dr. Lind, the syringe?" Jamie took refuge now in formalities. "And kindly write everything down, if you would."

"I'm telling you once more: you shouldn't do this," Lind said, even as he found a syringe.

"I've noted your opinion."

"You should have a full physical before you do this. At least let me do the pulse and blood pressure, take your temperature."

Lind was right about the vital signs. Jamie paused for these necessities. Then he opened the blue vial. Filled the syringe. Suddenly, unexpectedly, like a knife in his stomach, he felt fear. He'd given injections to untold numbers of mice and rabbits and guinea pigs and dogs and human beings, but he'd never administered a shot to himself. Well, the technique couldn't be all that different. In fact the technique was the same. The important part was not to think about the fact that it could kill him. He had to jab the needle in properly. He couldn't allow one of his colleagues to give the injection, because if the medication did kill him, he didn't want his colleague to be responsible.

What would he miss most, if he died in the next thirty seconds? Claire, of course. But he couldn't live with himself, couldn't ever look Claire in the eye, if he went upstairs and gave this shot to Charlie and the boy went into anaphylactic shock and died. Now Jamie knew what it meant, that old clichéd phrase about giving your life for someone you loved.

He took a deep breath and jabbed the needle into the muscle of his upper arm. Steadily and slowly he pushed down on the plunger until the beautiful, clear blue liquid had disappeared. He removed the needle, gave the syringe to Lind, took the ball of alcohol-soaked cotton wool that Lind had prepared, and pressed it against the injection site.

A sensation of stinging spread in a widening circle around the injection site. He gripped the edge of the table. He focused on his breathing. Slow, deep breaths.

"The stinging is fairly bad," Jamie said. "Write that down, Lind."

The younger man stared at him without moving.

"Come on now," Jamie said, "don't give out on me. Write it down."

Lind made the note.

Jamie began counting to himself, to try to get a grip on the stinging. One, two, three, four . . .

When he reached eighteen, the stinging flowed away. The medication was being absorbed and dispersed. "Write down that the stinging stopped after approximately twenty seconds. Let's repeat the pulse and blood pressure."

Lind did so. "Slightly elevated."

"From sheer terror," Jamie said, forcing himself to laugh to set the others at ease. They looked terrible. Much worse than he looked, he was certain. They appeared shocked and were immobile. "You'd better take my temperature, too, in case there's rigor."

His temperature remained normal.

Jamie rolled down his sleeve, replaced his cuff link. "Well," he said jauntily, for the benefit of those around him, any one of whom could have murdered his sister. "The medication didn't kill me. Good to know."

F*or what is your life? It is even a vapour, that appeareth for a little time, and then vanisheth away.* The echoes from the King James Bible of her childhood reverberated in Claire's mind.

Hour after hour, day after day, Claire sat beside Charlie's bed, watching him. She barely noticed the turn outside the windows from darkness to light to darkness. She had stepped outside time. Sometimes Jamie was with her, sometimes not. She lost track of his explanations and stopped listening to them, simply trusting that he would be back when he could. The war couldn't wait for a child to survive or to die. She pushed away the meals placed in front of her, drank sweet tea with milk when her father handed her a cup, registering only that the tea was hot and flush with sugar. She hadn't tasted so much sugar for a year or more. She didn't even stop to wonder where it came from as she greedily swallowed it.

Charlie seemed to dream through the shots given by Dr. Lind every four hours. Through the blood tests. Through the fever, fluctuating between 105 and 106. Through the anguish and confusion around him when the medicine didn't work. Through the raising of the dose by 25 percent and then by another 25 percent. Claire pushed back his hair and placed a warm, damp cloth upon his forehead to cool him, because Dr. Lind said a warm cloth was better for cooling a fever than a cold cloth.

Claire felt disconnected from herself, watching herself watch her son. He looked more frail each day, as if he were turning into vapor before her eyes.

On the fifth night, she reached for a fresh cloth and abruptly, without explanation, she no longer felt disconnected. Instead, she was utterly within herself, and within this moment. She understood that Charlie would die. She was about to weep. But she wouldn't weep beside him. She wouldn't let him hear her crying. She pushed herself up from the chair. Her legs ached. She had the legs of an old woman.

Stiffly she made her way to the shadows by the corner of the room. A tapestry hung on the wall before her. A tapestry of leaves and birds, in the style of the unicorn tapestries owned by the Rockefeller family. She studied this tapestry. As she studied it, it became three-dimensional. The leaves swayed in the breeze. The birds flew out from it. The birds were twittering around her. The smallest landed on her shoulder. Pecked gently at her ear.

Am I hallucinating? she wondered. Ever so slowly, not wanting to startle it, she lifted her hand to pet the head of the tiny bird on her shoulder. She wished Charlie were awake, so he could tell her what type of bird it was. The bird was so beautiful, so perfect, as it studied her. Ever so softly she placed her index finger on the back of the bird's head. Her finger went right through it.

She *was* hallucinating. She was terrified. For Charlie. For herself. She began to cry.

Her father was beside her. She didn't know where he'd come from. He turned her around. Suddenly she was leaning against her father's chest, and he was holding her. Protecting her. He caressed her hair and she sobbed against his chest. She was his little girl again; she'd been lost and afraid and he'd rescued her. He began to speak to her, in what sounded like a foreign language. He spoke several sentences before she realized that the language was English.

"I'm sorry," he was saying. Over and over. "I'm sorry. Do you hear me, sweetheart? Everything I've done, everything that's happened."

She didn't respond.

"Do you hear me, Claire?" He pushed her away slightly, so he could see her face. She nodded. She heard him. She understood him, he knew. "I looked at things differently then. I never would have"—he gasped for breath—"I never should have given you up. I didn't know what it meant, to give you up. All those years without you. Thirty years, like a lifetime. Without you. Never met Emily. A whole life. Gone. I'm sorry."

She pressed her face against his shoulder. She wished she could pull his jacket around her, to keep her warm and safe. She breathed deeply the cigar smoke on his jacket.

"You can trust me now." He caressed her hair as if she were a child, as if they could—they would—start over and live together through the years that they had lost. "I'll never leave you again. I'll never leave you. Do you forgive me?" He needed to hear her say it. He couldn't simply sense it, he needed to hear it, so he could remember her words when she was no longer in his arms, when she was home with her new husband in her own house, as she should be, and her father was home alone in his study, and he would hear her words echoing over and over, and her words would console him forever.

For Claire, all the years of pain and misunderstanding slipped away. She was left with the truth, stark and wondrous. He was her father, and they understood each other, and they loved each other. "I do, I forgive you."

"I love you, my sweet little daughter."

"I love you, Daddy."

When Charlie woke up, he heard birds singing. He lay still to listen. The sound was beautiful. He wished he could coax out each bird's separate song and follow its line. What was the month? February. What birds sing in the last days of winter, the earliest days of spring? Sparrows. Of the many types of sparrows, the song sparrow was his favorite. He heard the song sparrow in the concert.

He remembered now. He'd been ill. He wondered if he'd died and was hearing birds singing in heaven. If he were hearing the song of God. He opened his eyes, looked around. He was in a room he didn't recognize. The room had paintings, wood paneling, and pictures made from cloth. His legs felt heavy, and he didn't try to move them. His shoulders felt heavy, too. Too heavy to lift. He turned his head. His neck ached. His grandfather was asleep in a big chair. His mom, wrapped in a blanket, was asleep in a chair pushed against his grandfather's. She was curled on her side, her head resting on the armrest. Grandpa's hand was on her shoulder.

So he knew he wasn't dead. He looked past his family to the long windows. The city, too, was asleep in the gray half-light.

He was too tired to call out. Instead he lay still, looking at his city. While he watched, the skyscrapers of Manhattan turned lavender. It was dawn.

CHAPTER THIRTY-THREE

~

L ook, Orion," Claire said. Gripping Jamie's hand still more tightly, she pointed with her other hand through the bare tree branches toward the constellation.

Three nights after Charlie's fever broke, Claire was leaving him for the first time. She and Jamie were going out to dinner and then to her house for the night while her father stayed with Charlie. As they walked along the paths to the Institute's main gate, Claire sensed the life coursing through her. She hadn't been outside in over a week. She felt as if she were rediscovering the world after a long absence; that she, too, like Charlie, had returned from near death. She was alert to the sharp chill against her cheeks, the crunch of late-winter snow beneath their feet, the shimmering of the stars in the dim-out.

For his part, Jamie didn't want to shatter Claire's well-earned happiness by telling her his suspicions about where the medication came from. He needed proof first, and he didn't know where to find the evidence. In the meantime, all he had was the color, that beautiful blue. He wouldn't force Claire to choose between her father and her fiancé based on nothing but the arrival of a rare and beautiful blue. So Jamie was watching and waiting. Reviewing the words and actions of his supposed friends to try to piece together the truth.

Claire sensed he was preoccupied. Often he was, these days. She suspected he recalled incidents from the war that he didn't want to share with her. She didn't want to imagine that he'd learned about her and Nick in Boston and was hiding his anger and pain. Whatever the cause, she had to work to keep Jamie's attention, which she'd never had to do before. She was self-conscious around him, as she'd been when they first met. "Charlie once told me that Orion has three of the brightest stars in the sky," she said, more to fill the silence than from an interest in the stars. "Naturally he knew their names, but the only one I remember is Rigel," she chattered on. "Part of the left foot. See?" Jamie didn't respond. She studied his face. His thoughts were far from her.

Nick came down a side path from the administration building. "Hey, Jamie," he called.

"Hi, Nick. Heading out?"

"As usual."

"Good for you."

Did Claire hear envy in Jamie's voice, that Nick was heading to a party or a bar, whereas Jamie was committed to her for the evening?

"Last gasp before heading to the Pacific," Nick said.

Claire had heard that Nick's orders had finally come; he'd be leaving New York for San Francisco in a few days.

"I'm sure you'll need it," Jamie joked.

"I don't doubt it." Nick seemed his old self, Claire thought, or at least he was putting on a better front than he had that afternoon at the Hotel Lafayette. "I heard Charlie's doing better," Nick said to Claire.

"Yes."

"I'm glad."

"Thank you."

This exchange seemed innocuous enough to Claire. When she looked at Jamie, he was staring toward the gates, as if he hadn't heard.

A crowd of about twenty had gathered. An unexpected sight. When Jamie had arrived from Penn Station in the late afternoon, he'd noticed only six or seven milling at the gate, and he'd paid them no attention. Now, as he observed them from the top of the path, they looked like a crowd with a purpose. The guard was trying to keep them out. He'd already closed the gates to the driveway and was now closing the sidewalk gates.

When they reached the guard, gray-haired Mr. Hodges, he was as imperturbable as ever.

"What's the trouble here?" Jamie asked.

"They're wanting the medicine, sir. The penicillin. They think we have it."

"We don't have any. We couldn't give it away even if we wanted to. It's illegal to give it away."

"I told them we're not a pharmacy, sir, but that wasn't what they wanted to be hearing. The big crowd of them came over here from New York Hospital about ten minutes ago. With Dr. Rivers away, I'm not sure what to do."

In the light from the streetlamps, Claire had trouble making out their individual faces. But the impression from their clothes was poverty. Loose coats, patched sleeves, rain-swollen shoes with cracked leather. A Depression that had never ended.

After the Cocoanut Grove fire, everyone seemed to know about the miracle drug. Andrew Barnett had told Jamie that crowds gathered outside hospitals all across the country, every day, desperate for it. Meanwhile the hurdles to mass production remained. Chemical synthesis was going nowhere. But the family members gathered here couldn't wait for mass production or chemical synthesis. They needed penicillin *now*, just as Charlie had desperately needed it—before he was lucky enough to be given the secret, blue cousin.

"Poor souls," Nick said. "Well, I'll just wait till later. Or tomorrow night—pack tonight and go out tomorrow."

They said their good nights, and Nick went back the way they'd come.

"All right, Hodges," Jamie said calmly. "We'll push on through.

You can close the gate again behind us. I'm sure they'll go home after a while."

"Yes, sir." Mr. Hodges opened the gate. "Let them through now, folks," he said. "Come on then, make a path."

Jamie and Claire's presence at the open gate galvanized the crowd. "Look, that's one of them," a man said.

"My baby is sick," a woman said. Her scarf had fallen back to reveal a white streak through her hair. She grabbed the lapel of Jamie's coat. "My Jenny." The crowd pushed forward. "Sarah, Tommy, Rebecca, Joey," suddenly they were all shouting names—disembodied names to Claire, but startling and frightening when someone shouted "Charlie." Then "mother, brother, wife, husband" in a shrill keen.

Jamie struggled to recall where he'd heard such shouts before. Then he remembered. Years ago. Outside the hospital where his father died of pneumonia brought on by influenza. His mother had sent him there to find his father, or at least find information about his father. But when he arrived, Jamie saw the cause was hopeless. The hospital was packed with patients, the ill everywhere, the dead and the dying mixed together, their lips blue, their hands blue, some of them coughing up black blood, half the staff ill, no one left to take care of the mothers and fathers dying on the floors. Nonetheless he'd pushed his way through the crowd, got inside, walked the corridors searching. He never found his father. In retrospect, it was astonishing that he hadn't become ill, too. Instead he had lived to help wrap his mother in a shroud and take his sister to their grandparents. To identify Tia's lifeless body. To fall in love with Claire and be a father to Charlie.

Without particularly registering what was happening, Jamie was swept into the center of the crowd. Claire was ignored.

"I'll call the police," Mr. Hodges said, hurrying to his booth.

"Where is it?" a husky teenage boy said, thrusting his hand into Jamie's coat pocket. The boy was crying. He was too old to be crying in public. "My mother. Where is it?"

"Try the other pocket," a man shouted.

Claire felt anguished. Powerless. Jamie . . . she couldn't help him. He was so precious to her. She felt his vulnerability. She could lose him in an instant. The human body was so frail. She knew his body so well. Every detail, most intimate, she knew so well, and these desperate people could, would, injure him so easily and readily.

"I have nothing," he said, raising his arms to make their task simpler. He spoke gently. Soothingly. "Search as much as you want. I have nothing." He unbuttoned his topcoat. He behaved as if he routinely encountered all of this.

And the truth was, none of it disturbed him. He'd seen too much already. He'd been an infectious disease expert for years; he couldn't even remember how many patients he'd lost. His sister was dead, his buddy blown up beside him in North Africa. Poor people begging on the street for penicillin didn't bother him. Rather, he felt an overwhelming sympathy for them. These poor, poor people, bereft in every way, and here he was, a physician, in fact a prominent and successful physician, with no method or plan or knowledge or power to help them. He wanted to comfort the people around him, and yet he knew comfort wasn't going to help them, either. So instead he served them by allowing himself to be the target of their despair.

Claire watched the man she loved transform what could have been a humiliation into a moment of profoundest empathy.

You must, his lungs, her stomach, my baby's eye, a fever, a blister, you must, won't heal, help me, help her, help him, a cacophony of desperate pleas.

A police siren sounded, far away. Slowly it became louder. The people in the crowd took note. Looked around in all directions. Became cautious. The siren became louder still. They released their grip on Jamie's coat. The revolving red lights of a police car were reflected on the windows of the buildings along York Avenue. The lights reached them sooner than the car itself. They couldn't risk arrest. Who would take care of their loved ones then? The crowd dispersed into the darkness.

When they were gone, Jamie adjusted his hat. He reached his arm toward Claire, his hand beckoning for hers. She emerged from the shadows near the gate. She put her arms around him. They embraced until the police arrived to question them.

The following morning, just before noon, Claire returned to the Institute, having seen Jamie off at Grand Central. At least today she had a general idea of where he was going: according to the schedule board, his train was headed to New Haven. At the Institute, two police officers guarded the gate. No crowd would gather now. Mr. Hodges cleared her through.

As she walked up the hill toward the hospital, through a cool, early-spring breeze, she felt weak, as if she'd survived an illness herself. She needed time to regain her strength. She felt the warmth of the sun on her face, beginning to heal her.

Recovering sailors, bundled in coats and hats, smoking, were lounging upon the benches under the bare trees. Jamie had told her that most of the sailors were suffering from streptococcal infections, endemic in the military.

"Hey, nurse," one of the sailors shouted at Claire. He was dark-haired, his eyes bloodshot. Like his colleagues, he was well shaven; apparently Nurse Brockett insisted on that. "Come on over here. I want to introduce you to my friends."

Much laughter from his fellow sailors on the benches.

"Sorry guys, I'm not a nurse."

"Even better."

As soon as they were healthy, no doubt they'd be sent back to their ships. They'd end up in the Pacific, most of them. The Solomon Islands, New Guinea . . . How many would return?

"Much better, as a matter of fact."

"Watch yourself, sailor."

"He is watching himself," a buddy said, to guffaws.

"I wish I could stop to visit, but I'm here to see my son. He's waiting for me."

"Maybe we know him."

"I don't think so. He's only ten."

"Ten? Probably not. Hope he's okay."

"He's on the mend, thanks. Good luck to you all."

"And to you, lady," he said.

Claire stood outside the hospital for several minutes to let the sunlight seep through her. She still felt the pressure of Jamie's hands upon her. At home last night, his preoccupations had seemed to dissipate, and he'd been himself again. This morning the combination of the sun's warmth and the memory of his hands assured her that all would be well between them.

When she arrived at Charlie's room, he was sitting in a chair playing checkers with Dr. Lind. The board was on the hospital table between them. At the moment, Charlie found checkers easier to focus on than chess. Checkers was also easier for him to win. Charlie looked thin and very pale, as if all his blood had left him. Dark circles rimmed his eyes. He had little stamina and became tired after the smallest effort. But his smile, and his spirit, were back to normal. He was still receiving the medication to make certain that the infection didn't return. A container of it arrived from New Jersey every few days.

"I won the first three games," Charlie said when he saw her.

"But I'm close to winning this one," Dr. Lind said.

"Don't count on it." Within four moves, Charlie had scored another victory.

"Oh, brother," Dr. Lind said, shaking his head. "Now that your mom is here, I'm going to take a break. I need one. I hope I'm a better doctor than I am a checkers player. I'm going to visit my other patients with what I've still got of my self-respect." Lind left them.

"How do you feel this morning?" Claire rubbed her knuckles against his arm.

Now that he was feeling better, he didn't like her to be obvious in her affections, and he moved away. "I feel good. I feel perfect. But Dr. Lind said I have to keep getting shots of that awful blue medicine for another week and stay here for at least a week after that. Maybe longer. The shots really sting. And Nurse B keeps taking my blood for all kinds of tests, and that hurts, too. Why can't I go home?"

"You were very ill, don't you remember?"

"Not really." He glanced at her mischievously. "Could you bring me some doughnuts? Nurse B says I can only have broth. And maybe rice pudding."

"I'll try to get you a doughnut for dessert tonight."

"With chocolate frosting. Please. Guess what? Tomorrow, if Nurse B allows it, Dr. Lind's going to take me to see the Audubon bird pictures in the hospital hallways. He says I have to go in a wheelchair, though. And not complain about it."

"Not complaining is good, especially when Dr. Lind is giving you a treat."

"I want to walk."

"When Dr. Lind says you can."

"Oh, I forgot. Grandpa said to tell you, he went home to take a shower and change his clothes. He was getting smelly. But I didn't tell him that!"

"Not telling him was a good idea."

"Mommy?" He frowned and tapped his left ear. "My ears feel funny."

"What do you mean?"

He tapped his right ear. "It's like I've got earplugs or something. Or like I've got water in my ears. Like after swimming."

"Did you tell Dr. Lind?"

"No, we were too busy playing checkers."

"You can tell him later, then."

"Okay." He rested his head against the back of the chair. "I'm tired."

"That doesn't surprise me. Why don't you take a nap. I'll help you back to bed."

He didn't object, so Claire knew how tired he must be. After he snuggled into the covers, he said, "Can Lucas come to visit?"

"I'll ask. They'll probably say no. I don't think dogs are allowed in hospitals."

"Lucas isn't a dog. I mean, he isn't *just* a dog."

"I'll try my best."

Charlie fell asleep, and Claire kept watch over him.

By dinnertime, he was deaf.

⟶

CHAPTER THIRTY-FOUR

On the upper floor of her father's Fifth Avenue apartment, Claire stood at the windows overlooking the park and shivered in the damp March chill. On account of rationing, even this building, home to the wealthy few, had been forced to cut back on heating fuel. She pulled up the collar of her sweater, even though she wasn't supposed to move.

Charlie was drawing a portrait of her. He sat in bed with the pad propped on his bent legs. In turn, Miss Blake, his drawing teacher, did a portrait of Charlie while he worked. Miss Blake was an earnest young woman who, in her flowing skirt and embroidered blouse, seemed to brim with artistic enthusiasm. Charlie was Miss Blake's first deaf pupil, and her way of dealing with him was to explain her lessons in a slow, soothing voice, which, of course, Charlie couldn't hear. Instead he intuited her meaning from her gestures and examples. Miss Blake visited three times a week. Rutherford had already purchased an easel so that when Charlie became stronger, he could paint in oils on the terrace.

Claire's father had received his wish: when Charlie was discharged from the hospital, he and Claire came here to live. Even Lucas joined them. Claire felt she had no choice. Everything was easier to manage at her father's. The recovery time for double pneumonia was months in the best of circumstances. Now with the deafness, most likely Charlie couldn't return to his old school. Rutherford had hired a sign-language teacher, math and English teachers, and a science teacher. Nurses were on duty twenty-four hours a day, although mercifully Charlie was almost well enough to dispense with them. Specialists had been brought in from up and down the East Coast to evaluate the feeble hearing he still had and to recommend treatment. Some of these specialists hazarded a guess that gradually a portion of his hearing would return, while insisting that this was something the family could only hope for, not plan for.

Claire and her father were united. She felt as if she'd grown up all over again while Charlie was hospitalized. Her anger toward her father had dissolved. Most nights after Charlie fell asleep, Claire and her father had an after-dinner drink in the library. They talked quietly of Charlie's hardships as well as his hard-won victories. They discussed his teachers' goals for the next day. They read for an hour or so before bed and listened to the news on the radio. In the war, the tide had begun to turn, according to the commentators.

The war seemed far away. Irrelevant, even, to their concerns. Claire and her father enjoyed a simple routine, and it was enough. No grand gestures were necessary in their day-to-day companionship. They were united by their love for Charlie and their belated love and understanding for each other. Most families Claire knew had been decimated by war and illness; her family had finally come together.

MaryLee took care of running the house. Due to rationing, merely shopping for food consumed hours each day. Charlie had lost so much weight that he looked skeletal. MaryLee knew the black marketeers in food on the Upper East Side. She knew how to find the best cuts of beef, the ones the butchers kept behind the counter for people like her. Owing to MaryLee, Charlie had steak every night for dinner. He enjoyed the most delicious cakes and cookies, because MaryLee knew where to buy sugar and cocoa. She brought home canned fruits and vegetables and even real butter in abundance. She made Charlie cheese omelets and bacon every morning for breakfast. Up and down Madison Avenue, up and down Lexington Avenue, MaryLee conducted her searches, buying only the best, regardless of price controls or ration points. Mr. Black (as everyone called the black market) was at her beck and call.

Rutherford told MaryLee to take all the time she needed, to spend whatever was necessary, as she traveled the paths of Mr. Black. For once Claire didn't pass judgment on the privileges of wealth. Charlie couldn't get penicillin when he needed it, in this he was equal with others, but now that he was among the wounded, she wanted him to have filet mignon and fudge cake all of his days.

Claire turned her head and studied her son. Did he still hear in his dreams? Did he remember the sound of her voice? She was afraid to ask him. All his life, she'd tried so hard to protect him, and Emily, too. But in the end, she'd failed them both.

Since Charlie's deafness, Claire found herself increasingly attuned to the everyday sounds around them, the sounds Charlie could no longer hear. The call of the newspaper boys on the avenues. The honking of car horns. The neighing of horses as they pulled the early-morning milk carts. These common sounds, which she'd barely registered before, pounded into her ears now because Charlie couldn't hear them. Some sounds she feared: What if Charlie were alone when an air raid siren alerted the city to an attack? What if he were alone when someone screamed a warning of "fire"? How would he survive?

"You moved!" Charlie said. "You're not supposed to move."

She looked out the window again, the park a blur from the tears that too often filled her eyes. His voice still sounded like himself. How fortunate this difficulty came relatively late in his childhood, after he could speak fluently and already knew how to read. So said the chief audiologist, Dr. Greene, by way of consolation.

"Just a few more minutes," Charlie said. He made an effort to be disciplined, even though he sometimes thought he was going to explode with impatience. He wanted to go outside and play stickball.

He wanted to take Lucas to the park. But Dr. Lind said he wasn't well enough.

In the month since his hearing left him, Charlie's other senses had become more acute, as if doors were opening in his mind. The scent his grandfather gave off, of cigars and a spicy aftershave. The light, flowery perfume that told him his mom was nearby. The aroma and taste of food. Bacon and warm chocolate pudding were more luscious than he'd ever experienced. At night he could see better in the dark. The softness of Lucas's undercoat upon his fingertips, the scratchiness of the wool blanket. These sensations were like a mystery unraveling. Sign language was like magic, secrets expressed in the turns of his hands and in the shapes of his fingers.

All this was more than he could share with the grown-ups around him. Not when they stared at him with sad and frowning looks of worry, thinking he didn't notice. Or when they seemed to take a deep breath at his door and put on a special smile just to get the courage to talk to him.

"You can see the picture in three minutes," he told his mother. "Not one second sooner."

While Claire posed for Charlie's drawing lesson, Jamie left the hospital and made his way down the path beneath the trees toward the gate of the Rockefeller Institute. He planned to walk to Edward Rutherford's apartment. It was a long walk, and he wanted the time alone to think.

Months ago, as he'd arranged, Tia's friends had gone through her apartment and dealt with the bureaucracies of death for him. Beth had sent him three boxes of items she thought worth saving. Tia's life, reduced to three cardboard boxes. Not surprisingly he'd put off opening them. But now that he was in New York for a few weeks, he'd decided to go through them. Beth had mentioned that the boxes included some scientific mementoes. *Memento* wasn't the word he would have chosen for Tia's scientific work, but of course Beth was trying to be kind.

The mementoes turned out to be notations on the chemistry of the blue substance that was obsessing Tia before she died, the one she'd told him about the final time they'd seen each other. Why Tia had kept these notes at home, Jamie didn't know. Sometimes his sister was an enigma to him. At any rate, this morning he'd completed a chemical analysis comparing the medication Charlie had received with the substance his sister had discovered. The two were identical.

Chance, or theft? Theft or—and—murder? He couldn't put off confronting Rutherford about the origins of the medication any longer. Nevertheless, he was filled with misgivings. He wished he could pass off the job of confronting Rutherford to someone else. Maybe Andrew Barnett could finally prove his worth and step in to figure out the truth. Or Marcus Kreindler.

He wasn't about to start accusing others of murder, least of all Claire's father. Obviously Rutherford had not murdered Tia, not by his own hand, at least. And yet . . . Jamie had been learning a lot recently about the business of medicine. The companies were developing penicillin for the government, but soon the cousins would be for sale. For reasons Jamie couldn't quite follow, these natural products—the cousins—would have full commercial patent protection, a sleight of hand he'd realized long ago was useless to resist. The medications would sell for whatever price the market would bear—and the market would bear a lot. Who wouldn't give everything they owned to save their husband or wife or son or daughter?

Jamie paused at the top of the path leading to the main gate. He looked around at the Institute, his home. The research buildings, the hospital, the opulent gardens. Spring was at hand. The half-frozen soil smelled rich and fertile. Crocuses perked up here and there, miniature shocks of white and purple.

He and Tia had blinded themselves to the truth directly before them: here they were, congratulating themselves on working at the Rockefeller Institute, where altruism reigned. But what funded the Rockefeller Institute? The ill-gotten gains of the Standard Oil Trust. Its exploitative tactics, its threats, and the execution of those threats.

Jamie remembered an occasion when old John D. Rockefeller himself visited the Institute a few years before his death. Rockefeller was a gaunt old man who handed out small change and grinned with a leer at the pretty young nurses. The staff welcomed him, vied for the opportunity to get near him, this renowned multimillionaire who made their jobs possible. No one mentioned how he'd made the money that made the jobs possible, no battle too small, no upstart too insignificant to crush. Rumor was that he'd stop at nothing, literally nothing, to get what he wanted. But he always made certain his own hands were clean.

And Rockefeller wasn't the only one. How easily the robber barons had turned themselves into paragons of beneficence. In a few generations, their names had gone from being feared and reviled to being lauded. Meanwhile, they were married, had children, lived amid their families, who apparently loved and admired them despite their business reputations.

Was Rutherford's sense of competition as fierce as old man Rockefeller's had been? Did he have spies at every research center around the country, on the lookout for the next breakthrough? Someone at the bottom of this chain could have pushed Tia, with Rutherford learning about it only later, if at all. In that case, Rutherford had done nothing but set the tone.

Jamie greeted Mr. Hodges at the gate and turned north on York Avenue. Charlie's deafness added another layer of complexity to Jamie's concerns. He couldn't shake the idea, irrational, he knew, that he and Tia bore responsibility for Charlie's deafness. This was like a knife in him. It made him dread facing Claire. And yet Charlie would be dead now if he hadn't received the medication. Choices no one should have to confront. Surely he could have stolen penicillin from somewhere, and Charlie would still be able to hear. Could have, should have, if only . . . untaken alternatives beset him.

He hadn't told Claire that he was in town. If he arrived and she was out, that was fine. He'd visit Charlie. He hadn't seen them since Charlie was released from the hospital.

Here he was. Eighty-first Street and Fifth Avenue. Across the street was the Metropolitan Museum. He hadn't been to the museum in years. Maybe he should go now. What was the current exhibition? He should have checked the newspaper this morning. The doorman announced him.

"Who answered the call?" Jamie asked.

The doorman hesitated. Clearly this wasn't a question he was usually asked. Maybe he heard some connotation Jamie hadn't intended.

"The housekeeper," the doorman replied. "But they're all at home."

"Thanks, I appreciate it." So, everyone there. Everyone to greet, and with what? His suspicions, his regrets, his love.

The elevator operator took him upstairs, and let him out in the Gothic hallway lined with tapestries. He stood for a moment, getting his bearings. Trying to remember where to turn.

"Dr. Stanton!"

Edward Rutherford approached him from the dining room, a coffee mug in his hand. Jamie knew that Rutherford used the honorific of *doctor* out of respect and appreciation. He heard both in Rutherford's voice, and this made Jamie feel simultaneously unworthy and wary.

"Welcome!"

Business papers were arrayed on the dining room table; Claire had written that her father was often working at home these days.

"What a wonderful surprise. Does Claire know you're in town? Wait until you see the progress Charlie's making. You'll be amazed and impressed."

Jamie found himself shaking hands heartily with this man who stood to profit, and handsomely, from the death of his sister, whether he'd ordered her death or not.

"I think Claire is upstairs posing for a drawing lesson. I did my part yesterday. Go on up, no need to waste your time with me."

Jamie felt Rutherford's charm. He sensed no guilt or despondency, only security and optimism.

"I want you to know that you have my sympathy, for, for"—Jamie suddenly felt at a loss, stumbling over his words—"for the unforeseen side effects."

"Don't be ridiculous." Rutherford brushed the idea aside.

"No, no, I don't understand—" Jamie stopped, uncertain of what he didn't understand. Or rather, he understood so little, doubted so much, that he didn't know how to begin to express himself.

"You're not blaming yourself, are you?" As Rutherford studied Stanton's tone and expression, he was taken aback. He realized that Stanton must be doing exactly that: blaming himself. Stanton looked terrible. Well, he'd never really had a chance to recover from his war wounds. He looked beyond exhausted. Dark circles under his eyes. He'd lost even more weight. His skin still had a grayish cast. He must have been torturing himself about Charlie's deafness for weeks. Rutherford and Claire had been living with Charlie and witnessing his progress every day. They'd had time to get some perspective. That was Stanton's problem. He hadn't had any opportunity to gain perspective. Once he did, he'd realize that there was no need for pity, not for themselves and not for Charlie. For now, Rutherford saw that his duty was to reassure Stanton.

"Charlie is alive and getting better. That's all I care about. Believe me." This was a situation Rutherford forced himself to view in black and white.

Jamie wasn't listening. "You've got to go back and have your scientists search for impurities," Jamie said. "The side effect could very well be the result of impurities. Lind told me he needed to raise the dose. The higher dose could have been too much for a child. A contaminant." Jamie's thoughts, and his words, were jumping from here to there and back as he tried to cover the suspicions gnawing at him and threatening to overpower him. He hadn't gotten enough sleep in weeks. In months. He was losing control of himself. "The medication itself may be fine. You've got to test for contaminants. How will you test it, though, without imperiling other children? That's the question you have to answer first. On the other hand, this medication might be a dead end. You have got to accept the fact that it might be a dead end. But you have to test it first."

Jamie talked on and on, barely able himself to follow the logic of his words. He was trying to stop himself from saying other words, words that couldn't be taken back, words like, someone in your employ murdered my sister. And, for what? For a medication that makes you a fortune? A medication that causes children to go deaf?

"We're working on it," Rutherford said slowly. He stopped, thinking. He was worried about Stanton. The man must be under a great deal of stress. Maybe he was still suffering pain from his wounds in North Africa. Psychological pain wounded just as much. What horrors had Stanton seen? Rutherford wanted to find a means to soothe him. "Believe me, we're working on it." Stanton must be terribly pressed, about a million things, to think they weren't. Maybe there was some bad news from the front. Some secret penicillin test that Stanton couldn't talk about, and it had gone very badly. No matter the cause, Rutherford had to help Stanton get back on track. Probably he needed a drink. And not coffee.

"Maybe this side effect presents itself only in children. Next time, find a patient who's older. Elderly, even," Stanton was saying.

But no, Rutherford realized as Stanton talked on obsessively, the problem really was that he hadn't seen Charlie yet. He didn't know how well the boy was doing. That explained everything. The gift of

Charlie's life: that was the only thing that mattered. The deafness didn't count. Any parent would agree.

Rutherford broke into Stanton's barrage of words. "Listen to me," he said sharply. "Listen." Rutherford closed his eyes to focus his words, as if better-focused words would make Stanton hear and understand him better. "Listen to me." Finally he had Stanton's attention. "This medication saved my grandson's life. When I was in that hospital room, those nights, I thought I'd lost him. I didn't know how I'd walk out of that hospital without him. I felt like an old, old man. Like my life was over. I was ready to die. Then all of a sudden the boy's sitting up in bed asking for doughnuts. Now he's upstairs having drawing lessons. Nothing stops him. Nothing."

Rutherford opened his eyes and his eyes filled with tears. He tried to stop the tears, but he couldn't. Tears were pouring down his cheeks. "It was a miracle. A miracle, Dr. Stanton." He couldn't stop weeping. He and Stanton were both struggling to function, right at the edge. He turned away from Stanton. He pressed his palms against his eyes. He breathed deeply. He had to get a grip on himself. He had to talk about something else, get himself back in control. Get himself back to business. Yes, business. Again he took a deep breath. Slowly his sense of self-possession returned. He was coping, yes, he was.

"I'll tell you something, Stanton." He took out his handkerchief, blew his nose, pretended he had a cold. "Claire doesn't know this yet. But once the drug is ready and we're marketing it, I'm going to turn over 50 percent of the profits to a foundation. Name it after Charlie. A medical foundation. Like the Rockefeller Institute, only smaller. Although who knows what could happen, once this medication takes off. Maybe we could create a foundation to compete with the big guns."

In Rutherford's still-damp eyes, Jamie saw a glint at the prospect.

"You'll be on the board of directors, I'm hoping. I'm asking. Begging you. Help me with this. I'll need your help, figuring out how to distribute the money, what diseases to target. I'm doing this as a gift for Claire. To make up for, well, to make up for things in the past, a lot of things, even though some of them couldn't be helped."

Stanton stared at him. Rutherford was virtually confessing to him: he wanted to be just like Rockefeller and Carnegie and all the rest. Do whatever it takes, wresting what you want from the world, then redeem your conscience by giving back a half that still leaves half behind, still leaving you a millionaire many times over.

"You should go upstairs and visit my grandson. You'll get a happy surprise, I can assure you. He's doing great. No feeling sorry for himself, not that boy. He's like his mother, and his grandfather: not just making the best of whatever comes his way, but bending it to his own will. I'm proud of him."

"Let me ask you something," Jamie said. "Where did the medication come from?"

"What do you mean?" Rutherford was puzzled by the non sequitur.

"The question is simple enough. Your prized product, isn't it? Guaranteed of success, no matter what the side effects? Ceruleamycin, that's what you're calling it, right?"

Jamie watched Rutherford staring at him in confusion. Was it possible that Rutherford had no idea of where the medication came from? Jamie wondered. "You must know where it came from. That's the sort of fact a man like you would know without having to look it up."

"Where it came from? It came from the lab."

"Before it was in the lab. What was its history before it was in the lab?"

"I suppose there are records that say. I can ask someone to investigate." The Harvard Club. Water buffaloes staring at him. A decrepit stuffed elephant. Nick Catalano, offering Rutherford the discovery of a lifetime—from Syracuse, the city of his birth. None of this was James Stanton's business.

"Where was it collected?"

"There must be two thousand soil samples in that lab."

"Two thousand samples—but this is the one that works. Maybe the only one that works. Is it from Central Park? From Claire's backyard? Or maybe it's from my sister's lab. From a sample she collected when she was visiting our childhood home."

"You know very well that these substances can come from anywhere. You can find the same thing in a million different places."

"I happen to know that Ceruleamycin has the same chemical structure as a substance my sister was working on before she died."

"That doesn't mean a thing. Somebody else could have discovered it, too."

Jamie knew this was true. But he was compelled to push on: "My sister wasn't suicidal, and she wasn't the sort of person who has accidents."

Slowly Rutherford said, "Anyone can have an accident." He paused. He thought back. The coroner had ruled that Tia Stanton had an accident. Rutherford recalled speculation about suicide, but the ruling was accidental death. "Your sister's death was a tragedy," he said. "But an accident." Was Stanton denying the report? If he didn't believe it, why hadn't he challenged the report months ago?

Rutherford put himself back to last summer. He'd had a dozen irons in the fire, a finger in every pie, as he always said, and he wasn't missing dessert, not ever. And the pie that excited him most then was the same one that excited him the most now: antibacterials from soil. His staff was collecting samples from around the world. Nick Catalano was selling, Rutherford was buying. Privately, to be sure, but so what?

Slowly Rutherford put the facts together for a theory. He had a rule to live by: always remember, in your secret heart, that two plus two equals four. Even when businessmen, politicians, and adulterous husbands all around you add two plus two and proclaim they're getting five. True enough, you too might, now and then, find yourself publicly proclaiming that two and two makes five. But you could allow yourself that luxury only if, in your heart of hearts, you recognized and accepted the truth. Had Nick Catalano murdered Tia Stanton for this medication? Was there proof? Rutherford put Stanton off. "Accidents can happen. Anywhere. Without warning. That's what makes it an accident."

Jamie could hold back no longer. Within himself he'd lost the battle of resistance, and now that the barricades were down, he couldn't control the force within him. "Your people killed my sister," he shouted in anger. He couldn't remember the last time he'd shouted in anger.

"Of course 'my people' didn't kill your sister!" Rutherford couldn't help shouting, too, even though he knew, and warned himself, that generally a voice so quick to express anger was masking guilt. "That's ridiculous!" He couldn't stop himself from shouting because this was more than business. What Stanton was saying would ruin everything he'd built, including and especially his newfound relationship with Claire. He would never allow his bond with Claire to be broken. Nothing would be allowed to come between them now.

"Then tell me where the medication came from." Jamie's family, gone. His sister's legacy, her greatest accomplishment, gone. And for what? For a millionaire to become even richer and then give half the money away, as if that would make everything better? As if that would bring Tia back? What was the use of her life? Of any of their lives? His parents, dead of influenza, his sister, his patients, young men in the military forces of every nation, dead. This was the only meaning he could grasp at: his sister had discovered a substance that could ease the anguish of others, and it had been stolen from her. "It's a simple question. Give me a simple answer."

"You need to go home and get some sleep," Rutherford said, struggling to make his voice calm. "Take Claire out for lunch and then go home and get some sleep."

The months of frustration, the months and years of rigorous self-discipline—all Jamie's facades crumbled. He didn't have the strength to hold himself in check. "Did you hire someone? Or were you just waiting with the fee after it was over? Who was it that you paid?"

"This is my business, let me deal with it." He should have seen this coming, Rutherford chastised himself. He should have thought of this possibility long ago. He'd let his enthusiasm carry him away.

"That's your justification?"

"Stop! Be quiet! Don't shout."

They turned. Claire stood on the stairs, gripping the handrail. She was distraught, eyes bleary from crying, hair wild. "You'll upset Charlie with your fighting." The sun was pouring through the stained glass window at the landing behind her. It glinted off the gold leaf on the Renaissance paintings of the Holy Family along the wall. "What's he supposed to think when he hears you two like this?"

The men were struck silent by her mistake. For a long moment, they said nothing. They had to be delicate now. How fragile she was. How would she react when she realized what she'd said? Jamie wanted to console her. He took three steps toward her, but he couldn't take the ten more that would get him to the staircase and into her arms.

"Sweetheart," Rutherford said. "We're sorry. We didn't mean to raise our voices." How much had she heard? "Of course we have to stay calm for Charlie's sake." He wouldn't correct her. Never. "We forgot. We'll be more careful from now on. We won't upset Charlie, not ever."

"What were you arguing about?" she asked.

Okay, maybe she didn't hear much or even anything, Rutherford hoped. Maybe she heard the tone without registering the words. He had to be steady now. "Business, the war, so many problems we're trying to deal with."

Jamie studied this woman, the love of his life, standing before him. He felt her anguish. Ten steps, to reach her. He pictured his sister in his memory, saw her happy, laughing at some joke in the lab. Saw her body laid out in the morgue, a different kind of lab. He watched himself, as if he were separate from himself, identifying her body. Her face was perfect, her body broken.

Here was his terrible dilemma: to deny his own family and a possible ugly truth in order to be with Claire, or to ask Claire to credit a possible ugly truth and deny her family to be with him. "Your father ordered my sister's death, did you know?"

"What?" she asked blankly.

"If he didn't directly order it, he set up the circumstances that led to it. Created an atmosphere that condoned it. And he's going to profit from it. Hugely."

"I don't understand." Frowning, she looked from one to the other. "What do you mean? That doesn't make sense."

"Ask him to explain it to you."

She glanced at her father but said nothing.

"Go ahead, Claire. Ask him." He regretted this as soon as he said it—his baiting of her. How could he do this, to the woman he loved? But how could he take it back?

Father and daughter looked at each other. Claire's beloved face, filled with confusion. She was innocent. Of that Jamie had no doubt. He'd wounded an innocent.

Jamie couldn't tolerate her pain. Without conscious thought, he turned and walked to the elevator. Pressed the call button. The elevator seemed to take an hour to arrive. He sensed Claire staring at his back. Finally the elevator door opened. He stepped in. He greeted the elevator operator. He was lost. He didn't know where he would go or what he would do, once the elevator reached the ground floor. He didn't turn around to see his almost-family watch him go.

After Jamie left, after the elevator door closed behind him, Claire didn't move. She stared at the elevator door. What had just happened? She couldn't understand. What had he been talking about?

She'd seen him, she'd heard his words, but she couldn't figure out what he'd meant. She sat down on the stairs and wrapped her arms around her legs. She rested her head upon her knees.

Now her father was beside her, easing himself, with a sigh at the effort, to sit on the staircase, one step down from her. She was concerned for her father. He needed to get some exercise, if he was so stiff that he could barely manage to lower himself to the steps. When he was ready to get up, she'd offer him her arm to help him, offer it in some imperceptible way, so he wouldn't realize that she'd noticed his weakness.

"Ah, I'm sorry, sweetheart," he said.

"Did you understand what he was talking about?" she asked.

"He thinks my medical company had something to do with his sister's death." He kept his voice calm. No denial. No defense. No outrage. "He believes his sister was murdered and that I may have caused or condoned her death."

"He couldn't have said that."

"He did say it, sweetheart." Keep it simple. As if she were a little girl. A child, younger than Charlie.

"But that's not true."

"I know, darling."

They sat without speaking. Claire imagined Jamie leaving the building. In her imagination, she followed him along the street. Where was he going? Along Eighty-first Street, a line of town houses, returning to the Institute? Or had he crossed Fifth Avenue to the museum, where she could find him amid the Rembrandts and Vermeers? They would pretend that nothing had been said, pretend that she hadn't seen him in many days and now they were simply happy to be together, looking at their favorite paintings. She'd take him to see *Woman with a Pink*. The woman's husband was portrayed in the companion painting which hung beside her. This painting was called *Man with a Magnifying Glass*. Perhaps the husband was a scientist, like Jamie. The pink carnation: the symbol of marriage and love. Of love within marriage.

"He's been in the war," Rutherford said. "Who knows what he saw there. Things you and I can never imagine. He was wounded. That might have mixed his mind up a little. He's not himself yet. He still needs time to recover."

She didn't respond.

"Don't worry, honey, I'll find out what he was talking about. It can't be true. After all, the police said his sister had an accident."

She nodded.

Rutherford patted Claire's hand, trying to reassure her, to slow her down to the here and now, the moment by moment—that was the way to get through this. Meanwhile his own mind was racing, putting the pieces together, identifying the questions, searching for answers, planning his next move.

Minutes passed, and still they sat together. Claire felt safe here. Her father was right: it was the war. Jamie had been wounded, probably more badly than he ever let on. Slowly, amid her father's paintings by Giotto and Cimabue, amid the angels and the golden-haloed saints, she realized that the man she knew and loved might have died in North Africa after all.

CHAPTER THIRTY-FIVE

C laire hung up the phone. It was 8:30 AM. Each day for a week she'd tried to reach Jamie, leaving a message with the switchboard operator at the Institute. Each day he never phoned back. She knew she wasn't missing any return calls: here at her father's, someone was always home to answer. She couldn't go to the Institute and wait at the gates until she saw him. Or was that exactly what she should do? He was the love of her life—or so she'd thought. What was the proper way to fight for him? Maybe she had no means to fight for him. He had to return by choice, not battle.

From her upstairs bedroom at her father's apartment, she looked out the window to Central Park. The trees showed the pale green of spring. She imagined him, wherever he was, waking up, showering, shaving, putting on his naval uniform, beginning his day.

She couldn't keep leaving telephone messages for a man who wasn't going to reply. His silence was his clear response anyway. Gradually Charlie was getting better. Soon he'd be well enough for Claire to return to work. She'd resume her life as if it had never been interrupted by a man named James Stanton. She slipped off the emerald ring he'd given her and put it in the back corner of her bureau.

And so the days passed, and then weeks, and months. The war dragged on, with steps forward, here and there, for the Allies. Admiral Yamamoto, commander of Japan's navy, was killed in an Allied ambush. The Axis powers were defeated in North Africa. German

U-boats no longer destroyed Allied shipping in the North Atlantic. But the Germans still controlled Europe, and Americans were fighting island by island across the Pacific.

And still Claire had no word from Jamie. Her father was right: Jamie had been wounded in the war, in more ways than they knew. Eventually she stopped noticing how much time had passed since he'd left her. As Charlie grew stronger, Claire returned to work part-time. Rutherford resumed his usual schedule, traveling and scouting business opportunities. The family rebuilt itself on new terms, like so many other families that had been torn apart by the war.

When summer came, Charlie was well enough to go to a sleep-away camp in the Adirondacks. Reports of running races and tennis matches filled his first letter home. Claire missed him even as she felt relieved by his happiness at camp. In his letter, he told her to say hi for him to Uncle Jamie. So many dads and step-dads and uncles and brothers were far away; for now she wouldn't have to explain to Charlie that she no longer saw Jamie.

With Charlie at camp, her father left New York on an extended business trip to the West. MaryLee and Maritza took their yearly vacations. Rather than stay on alone in the rambling Fifth Avenue apartment, Claire moved back to her own home on Grove Street.

And that's where she was on a warm day in July 1943, soon after the Allied landings in Sicily, when Claire answered the door at four in the afternoon and found Dr. Jake Lind standing on the front stoop with a Japanese man.

Although Dr. Lind had warned her about the visitor on the telephone, Claire wasn't prepared. The man was about five-foot-five and carefully dressed in a threadbare, shiny suit with vest and a panama hat, the straw frayed. His wide face was somber. Claire hesitated without even realizing that she was hesitating. She'd never been introduced to a Japanese person. She'd never been to a Japanese restaurant. On Hudson Street, a Japanese man owned a lapidary shop, but Claire had never been inside.

Wartime propaganda portrayed the Japanese as monsters. After Pearl Harbor, *Life* magazine had run a picture essay comparing in detail the racial characteristics of the Chinese, our friends, and the Japs, our enemies, so Americans wouldn't confuse them.

The man standing next to Dr. Lind, hat in hand now in a gesture of politeness, didn't look like a monster. Yet for the first time in her life Claire found herself wondering what the neighbors would think.

"May we come in?" Dr. Lind asked. He'd said on the phone that he felt some sympathy for this man because the man's daughter had a link to Tia. Because of this link, he couldn't bring himself to send the man away. Maybe Claire would be able to help the man.

"Do come in, of course." Claire remembered what she needed to do. The duties of hospitality. "Welcome." She stepped back to let them pass.

"This is Dr. Isiguri Ito," Dr. Lind said when they were safely in the front hall.

"How nice to meet you," Claire said, automatically shaking hands with Dr. Ito. Claire found herself slipping into her mother's demeanor of absolute politesse. "It's a lovely evening, why don't we sit in the garden." Claire led the way downstairs.

When Dr. Lind phoned to ask to stop by, she'd wondered if she'd feel awkward around him. He must occasionally see Jamie. She was glad to realize that she didn't feel awkward—not about that aspect of Dr. Lind's visit, at least. She'd succeeded in making herself numb to Jamie. Dr. Lind had been good to Charlie, and by now he'd come to belong to their world as well as Jamie's.

But as they walked through the house to the garden, Claire caught herself watching Dr. Ito's hands, wanting to know at every moment the location of his hands. Not because he might steal something, but because he could use those large, strong, smooth hands to strangle her and Dr. Lind. Irrational, she knew. But this was the enemy, in a way that the German and Italian moms and dads of Charlie's classmates—

Karl's father or Maria's mother—could never be. Racism. Unwittingly she, too, had been infected by the war propaganda. The Japs, as they were called in common parlance, were the enemy. This was a Jap.

They sat down in the garden, cool in the breezes, peaceful with the birdsong of the late afternoon.

"Dr. Ito is a physician," Dr. Lind said. He sensed that Claire Shipley was ill at ease. He never would have expected it from her. Surely her work would have made her more cosmopolitan and tolerant. On the other hand, maybe she was ill at ease over seeing not Dr. Ito, but *him*. Lind knew that she and Jamie had had a falling-out of some kind, but he didn't know the details. In any event, Dr. Lind was not ill at ease about Dr. Ito. He had been raised to believe that all people were the same, regardless of their physical appearance. As a scientist and physician he knew this to be true. The same blood, the same bones, the same sinews. Only the outer surface was different. A superficiality, literally.

Claire didn't offer them anything to drink, then she remembered her manners. This was her mother's house, too, and she'd been raised to welcome visitors, friend or foe.

"Would you like some tea?" Claire asked, glad to hear herself sounding hospitable.

"Thank you, how kind of you, Mrs. Shipley," Dr. Ito said without a trace of accent. He could pass for a cultivated, highly educated American.

While she boiled the water and organized the teapot and cups, Dr. Ito sat at the edge of his chair, as if prepared to stand and bow at the slightest provocation.

After the tea was served, Claire said, "Have you had a long journey, Dr. Ito?" Her mother had often used this as an opening gambit with strangers. *Have you had a long journey?* And, *Where are you from originally?* Then, depending on the response, *I understand the scenery is lovely there*, wherever *there* happened to be. Thus her mother set strangers at ease.

"I am from Seattle, Washington," he said, as gracious as any gentleman of her mother's acquaintance. "Born and raised."

That, at least, explained his lack of an accent.

"I've been fortunate enough to travel to Seattle," Claire said. "The scenery is lovely there."

"Yes, it is. Quite lovely. Recently, however, I have been living in the western mountains. In the State of Idaho. With others of my community. Beautiful countryside. Except in the winter, when it's below zero. And the summer, when it's above a hundred. The spring provides deep mud and the autumn provides dust, but apart from all of that, the setting is lovely." A wry smile played at the edges of his lips, and with that bit of banter, Claire knew: he was among the tens of thousands of Japanese Americans sent to internment camps in the western states after a presidential order in February 1942.

"And what brings you to New York City?" she asked, ignoring, as her mother surely would have ignored, any reference to his recent difficulties.

"I am in transit. I have been called to join a Nisei regiment preparing for the European theater. As Dr. Lind has so kindly explained, I am a physician. I will be permitted to treat the wounded and ill of my own kind of Americans, not the Caucasian kind." He gave a bitter laugh.

"And I understand from Dr. Lind that your daughter was acquainted with Dr. Lucretia Stanton?" Claire asked, pretending she hadn't heard the edge in his laughter.

He smiled warmly now, with an unexpected generosity and affection. "Yes, yes, that is correct."

"How so?"

"My daughter is, or rather was, before our current situation, a Girl Scout. Her troop was asked to send soil samples to a Dr. Lucretia Stanton at the Rockefeller Institute in New York as one part of a science badge. Akiko went about this with great concentration, collecting in forests and along the banks of streams and in our own garden. Dr. Stanton sent her a letter of commendation, reporting that although none of the samples progressed from the first testing stage, there was an impressive variety in the mold. That letter, with its Rockefeller Institute letterhead, is tacked to the wall above my daughter's bed in our new . . . home."

"Your daughter must be unusually gifted," Claire said.

"Thank you. Perhaps she will be inspired to become a scientist. That would be an honor to our family." He bowed to them, slightly, at the thought of this possibility.

"Pray do continue, Dr. Ito."

"Recently, in our current situation, I had cause to remember these efforts of my daughter. I wrote a letter to Dr. Lucretia Stanton, and I'm grateful to say that this letter was forwarded to Dr. Lind."

"Indeed." Claire had learned this language literally at her mother's knee. *Indeed, pray do continue*—her mother was from the era and background of Henry James and Edith Wharton.

"In February of 1942, my family, among other members of our community, was instructed by the authorities to leave our homes and our businesses. This was a time of sadness and confusion. After a brief stay at a somewhat unpleasant relocation center, we were sent to what became our current home, if you will, Camp Minidoka. Under difficult circumstances, we organized schools, a camp government, a fire brigade, and various committees for food, clothing, and entertainment." He spoke matter-of-factly, without self-pity. "I was among the lucky ones, in that my profession is useful anywhere. I was permitted to serve as camp physician-in-chief. Our camp has hosted upward of thirteen thousand people, served by a medical support staff rather hastily scrambled together. You can well imagine the rates of infectious disease among people crowded into unheated barracks under such conditions.

"Several months ago, a group of medical personnel arrived at the camp. I don't know if they were physicians, although they tried to create the impression that they were. Certainly they needed some type of security clearance to be allowed in. We were, and are, considered enemy aliens, so undoubtedly certain standards must be met by those who wish to interact with us. At any rate, they came to us to test a new medication. They needed my cooperation. They didn't ask for my cooperation, they assumed it, then ordered it when I requested more detailed information.

"At first they seemed to be doing some good, so I went along without learning the details. We had many infectious conditions at the camp, streptococcal infections of the usual types, pneumonia, tuberculosis, several cases of meningitis, anything and everything that gains a foothold among thousands of people bunking together at close quarters. And this drug helped my patients. However, it was even given to those with relatively minor symptoms, patients who might very well have recovered without it. I assumed it must be penicillin or a variant of penicillin, but no, these medical men informed me, penicillin was restricted to the military and what did I know of penicillin anyway—as if I must be a spy simply for knowing the name of the medication, when anyone could already read about it in the newspaper before the war. Thus they attempted to threaten me for being aware of what was common knowledge." He paused, shaking his head.

"One of them, a pleasant young man who gave his name only as 'Pete'"—Dr. Ito pronounced the name "Pete" as if he assumed it was false—"admitted to me in an unguarded moment that this drug was similar to penicillin in that it was also made from mold. Thus I thought back on the work Akiko had so carefully undertaken, collecting soil samples in those days when we were still allowed to live in our proper homes."

He paused, seeming lost in his memories.

"And?" Claire said.

"Ah, yes. As time passed, I began to notice a mysterious set of

side effects developing from the use of this medication. Granted, my
patients would recover, some rather quickly. I saw several cures which
I consider remarkable, if not miraculous. No one died from the medication. In fact many would have died *without* the medication. Obviously my community has no access to penicillin, and supplies of sulfa
medications are limited. So perhaps some might consider us lucky. But
side effects began to set in, as I say. Deafness, blindness, permanent
tingling or lack of feeling in the extremities. The men conducting the
tests found nothing amiss in these side effects. They had cured the patients of the disease at hand, the rest was meaningless. To them. One
evening when I was nursing a patient with heart trouble, I was able
to glance at their record book when one of then stepped away. Their
records were meticulous. Miss J, age nineteen, suffering from scarlet
fever, was listed as having fully recovered, but she is now blind. Mr.
M, age thirty-six, suffering from pneumonia, was also listed as having
fully recovered, but he is now deaf. And so on.

"I began to comprehend the outrage perpetrated against us. Soon
my patients and their families made the link, too. Most of us are citizens of the United States. I know we are a people without a voice,
without rights; let us be frank, a people who are reviled. But surely this
is not justice. As a medical professional myself, I know you have to tell
people the possible side effects in advance, so they and their families
can weigh the risk."

Claire leaned forward in her chair. "Did you try to do anything
about this?"

"What recourse do we have? I managed to secure some information from the Food and Drug Administration in Washington, but
apparently they have no jurisdiction. Or aren't willing to accept jurisdiction. I took the situation to the director of the camp, a military
man, who listened with great sincerity and concern and promised to
look into the matter. Two weeks later, I received orders to report to a
Nisei unit on its way to the front. Forgive me for possibly sounding

over-dramatic, but in my travels here from Idaho, I have sensed that I am being watched.

"What makes an American? That's what I wonder. I am an American citizen, born and raised in America. My parents are American citizens, born and raised in America. My grandparents were immigrants. Does being an American mean you have the opportunity to fight for your country? To aid the soldiers fighting for your country? If so, that is what I shall do. Tomorrow I go to Governor's Island to be processed. My wife and children will stay at the camp in Idaho. I will be sent to Europe, not to the Pacific, where I would face the Japanese enemy and—the authorities fear—be tempted to turn traitor. I do not consider myself an enemy, but apparently I look like the enemy. Appearances can be deceiving, however, as we tell our children." He stopped. For a moment he stared at her without blinking. Then he looked away. "In any event, I am grateful to have an opportunity to stop in New York City and share this information with you and Dr. Lind."

"Do you have any proof of your—" Claire almost said *accusations*, but caught herself. "Your concerns?"

He took a sealed envelope from the inside pocket of his suit jacket. "I copied this from their record book. Not everyone suffers the side effects. Only a few. Perhaps that is their excuse. And I reiterate, no deaths can be traced to the medication. But I must also reiterate that some of these patients were only mildly ill and might very well have recovered without the medication. Once I overheard several of these so-called medical men discussing their expectation that this drug will receive full patent protection and be available for sale to the public within a year or two."

Claire didn't know what to say. Dr. Ito put down his teacup and sat with his hands flat upon his thighs.

"I wish I could have brought you a sample. I watched, I tried. I am sorry that I have failed in this regard. They were very careful. The used syringes were cleaned promptly. The medication was kept in a locked refrigerator. They were alert to spies. They didn't want this miraculous medication to make its way to the Empire of the Sun."

Dr. Lind said, "The reason we came to see you, Mrs. Shipley, is that I thought you might be able to convince your magazine to cover this. It's outrageous, probably against the Geneva Conventions, to conduct medical experiments on prisoners."

"Do you have any idea what company was making the drug?" Claire could take this information to her father. He was in a position to discover more. She would also alert Andrew Barnett and Vannevar Bush.

"I tried to find out, but the vials were unlabeled."

"What did it look like?"

"Ah, yes. I neglected to mention this to Dr. Lind. Its appearance was astonishing. Worthy of a haiku. A color like the brightest mountain lake. Like the sky on a cold winter morning. A color I have seen created by humans only in the finest watercolor paintings. An extraordinary shade of pure, transparent blue."

CHAPTER THIRTY-SIX

H ow's your son?" Mr. Luce asked Claire. His penthouse office was hushed, as usual.

"As well as can be expected."

"Does he need anything?"

"Things are stable now. Thank you for asking. He's at a summer camp for deaf children. He's enjoying himself."

"Who's paying the fees?"

"My father."

"Good. Let me know if Charles does need anything. If either of you needs anything. No time to be shy."

"Thank you. And thank you for giving me so much time off to care for him."

He shrugged off her thanks. "You made this appointment for?"

"An injustice has been brought to my attention. A story the magazine should investigate."

She explained what Dr. Ito had told her, made her case. Luce listened without interrupting.

She didn't reveal that she suspected this was the drug that had made Charlie deaf, or that when Dr. Ito described its color, she had gasped. She didn't tell Luce that she hoped against hope that someone else had stumbled upon the medication, that some other company, not her father's company, was testing it at Camp Minidoka. Anyone could have found that mold. She wanted to know the truth before she confronted her father. She felt as if she'd had a veil across her eyes, and now the veil had fallen away: a logical conclusion was that her father was indeed responsible for the ransacking of her home and possibly even implicated in Tia's death. Nonetheless, she couldn't reconcile her image of such a man with the loving father and grandfather she knew. Her motivations for agreeing to pursue Dr. Ito's story were deeply personal—although she would never share that fact with Mr. Luce. With Luce, she'd be strictly professional.

After Dr. Ito had gone, she'd tried to contact Andrew Barnett. When he didn't respond, she'd tried to reach Dr. Bush. Neither one had returned her telephone calls. She'd been cut off without an explanation. With Bush and Barnett apparently stonewalling her, Mr. Luce was now her only recourse.

She gave Mr. Luce the list of names with test results and the side effects Dr. Ito had noted.

Luce examined the list and gave it back to her. "What do you propose I do with this information?"

"You should send me to Idaho with a writer to unravel this story. Find out the name of the company. Put a stop to testing this drug on innocent people who are essentially prisoners of war."

He said nothing.

"In addition, you should brief your wife on the situation and ask her to hold congressional hearings about conducting medical experiments on internees." Claire Boothe Luce had been elected to Congress from Connecticut the year before.

"You ask for a lot, Mrs. Shipley." Luce paused. "You may not know that a while ago, Mack sent a team to one of those internment camps in the desert. What did the photographer come back with? The Japs have organized themselves into music groups and dance studios and foreign-language classes. They've created their own newspapers and baseball teams. They're acting as if they're perfectly normal Americans under duress.

"Mrs. Shipley, I take seriously the power of the photographic essay, its power to move men's minds and hearts more deeply even than words. I have a responsibility to the nation. The people in that camp who became ill might well be dead now without this medication. From your description, the problem was that they weren't told in advance. And some, you say, had mild symptoms. We both know that mild symptoms can turn serious, even fatal. As things turned out, these patients didn't die. They received a free and unmerited gift, many would say."

"Mr. Luce, the drug causes a variety of severe side effects in a number of patients, and those people might not have become ill in the first place if it weren't for the camp conditions."

Luce had the power to change the world with his influence, with his ability to bring problems to the attention of the nation. He wielded that power every day.

"And I must tell you that in the"—she reached for the proper word—"in the private work Vannevar Bush asked me to do, this was one of the issues he raised: companies devoting themselves to antibacterial medications other than penicillin."

"I don't want to know the details of any private arrangements you may or may not have with government officials. You should brief them on the situation, not me."

"I have attempted to do so. Dr. Bush has not responded to these attempts."

"Ah, well. That tells us a good deal, doesn't it." He wasn't asking a question.

"Mr. Luce—"

"Not a good time for muckraking, my dear," he said gently. "The troops need penicillin. I'm in favor of whatever Vannevar Bush needs to do to get it to them as soon as possible. Maybe someday, when the war is over, we'll have the luxury to debate whether potentially lifesaving medications should or shouldn't be tested on internees without their knowledge and consent."

She stared at him. He picked up a pencil and began to work on his page proofs, as if she were no longer there. She stood up and left.

The Rockefeller Center promenade was crowded in the noontime rush. Usually the opulent gardens and towering skyscrapers glinting in the sunlight invigorated Claire. Today, as she mulled over her options, their glory was a rebuke.

She made a mental checklist of colleagues at other publications who might be able to take the story, but she didn't get far. Most likely their editors wouldn't be interested in muckraking during a war, either.

Claire looked around. A naval officer squeezed the hand of the young brunette he walked with, and he placed her hand against his heart. She moved against him, and they walked shoulder to shoulder, the woman's light summer dress pressed against her body by the breeze as they made their way along the Channel Gardens. Claire thought of herself and Jamie. The ache in her chest was staggering.

A black man pushed a bass in a white case that was taller than he was, no doubt heading to one of the jazz clubs on West Fifty-second Street. An elegant woman in a well-cut suit checked her makeup surreptitiously in her compact mirror before entering the RCA Building to meet her husband or boyfriend or lover. Or to do a job interview. A sailor kissed a girl in a doorway. Would any of these servicemen be alive a year from now?

Cornstalks filled the Channel Gardens. Rockefeller Center had its own victory garden. Wafting in the breeze in the middle of Manhattan, the thickly planted cornstalks conjured an image of prairies far away.

Distracted, Claire wasn't looking where she was going, and she bumped into a bulky figure. "Excuse me," she said, quickly pulling away. "I'm so sorry." She looked at him, taking in the stocky frame, bullish demeanor, and thick dark hair. With a shock she realized who it was. "Bill? . . . Bill Shipley?"

"Oh." He stepped back, an expression of unwelcome surprise on his face. "Claire Lukins." Not a question, nor an especially happy statement. She hadn't heard her maiden name in a long time. He didn't make a move to give her a hug or shake her hand. Then Claire noticed the woman standing beside him. She was Claire's age at least, most likely older, with reddish blond hair and a round face—soft features, soft body, that peachy English look that was so generally praised. Claire was glad to be wearing her Henry Luce outfit, complete with high heels and a new hat. "This is Pamela Thompson. Pammy, this is . . ." He couldn't bring himself to say it.

"The first Mrs. Shipley," Claire said, stepping forward to offer her hand.

Pammy flushed and glanced at Bill with a wide, wounded expression that told Claire he'd never quite gotten around to telling her about the first Mrs. Shipley. She did not reach out her hand to meet Claire's.

"Would you give us a moment, Miss Thompson?" Claire asked.

Pammy looked at Bill, who nodded without meeting her eye. She went off toward a shop window. As she turned, Claire saw her wedding band. Was she married to Bill, or to someone else? Bill wasn't wearing a ring, but he hadn't worn one when he was married to Claire, either. Most men didn't advertise the fact that they were married by wearing wedding bands. Claire never understood why women didn't do the same, in protest. Once she'd wondered whether Jamie would wear a wedding band, a ring that she would give him. Well, at least they'd never had to confront that problem.

"So, Bill." Where to begin with him? Best to be frank. "What are you doing here?"

He was watching Pammy as she stood at the windows of the Librairie de France. But he returned his attention to Claire. "Three weeks R and R. First vacation since before the war. Doing some sightseeing. Boston, New York, Washington. Giving some talks on the overseas situation. Taking Pammy to meet my sister in Nebraska. Pammy's a reporter with the *Guardian*." Claire heard the pride in his voice. "She'll be doing some pieces along the way. Everyday life in wartime America."

"Sounds wonderful," she said, and it came out kindly, like a compliment. Because of Charlie's worship of him, Bill had grown taller and straighter in her imagination, but here, in the flesh, he was brought down to size. His hair was streaked with gray. He'd put on a good deal of weight. Weren't there food shortages in Britain? Maybe he was drinking too much. She was astonished that she'd ever loved him, or been intimidated by him. Her life had moved far beyond him, to a place where he was irrelevant. He'd proven himself a coward by not writing, by disappearing after he'd found someone new. Luckily, because of her father, she no longer had to worry about Bill supporting his son. Claire could afford to be generous. "You want to see Charlie while you're in the States? He's away at camp, but maybe after your Nebraska visit . . ."

She asked without even thinking to mention Charlie's deafness, a natural part of him now. She expected Bill would say no, anyway.

"Oh." Bill looked surprised once more, presented with an option he hadn't planned for. "You think that's a good idea? I don't want to give him any false hopes."

"False hopes about what?"

"That we, well, you know what I mean."

"No, I don't. What do you mean?" She wasn't going to help him.

"That we might be getting back together."

"I don't think he has any false hopes about that. I'm sure he'd enjoy seeing you, though. He reads your dispatches. Religiously, I'd have to say. Clips them and pastes them into a scrapbook."

"He does?" This seemed to make Bill happy, although whether for Charlie's sake or his own, she couldn't tell. "He reads well enough for that?"

"He's older now. You'd be impressed by how mature he is." That was a gratuitous dig, and she retreated from it. "Yes, he reads well enough."

"I remember him, well, younger."

"He's enjoys bird-watching and drawing. He's learning to play chess. He gets good grades in school." No, she wouldn't say that he almost died of pneumonia and was deaf. Bill had relinquished his right to know the whole story. "But it's true, we don't want to get his hopes up."

"I'm only in New York for, well, less than a week."

"And Miss Thompson would be left on her own for a few hours. She might start to wonder. Especially if she wasn't previously aware of the existence of a son."

She expected him to argue with her, or even laugh, but instead he blushed. He was never one to gainsay embarrassing truths. She realized the sad fact: Bill was doing to Charlie exactly what Edward Rutherford had done to her. How much would Bill regret this later? He'd have to find out for himself.

"I wish I could give you something for him, but I hadn't thought . . ." He held out his empty hands, as if to say, with so many burdens he'd been under—the war was the least of his trials—he couldn't be expected to be carrying a gift right here in the middle of Rockefeller Center on a warm summer's day.

"Don't even think about that. He wants for nothing. I've got a much better job than I did the last time I saw you."

"I've seen your stories. Your covers. Brava! Beautiful work. That Christmas Rockette!"

The Christmas Rockette would wind up as her epitaph. "Oh, the same for the *Herald Tribune*, I assure you. Everyone values your analysis."

Then Claire knew what she had to do. Time, Inc. wasn't going to take Dr. Ito's story. She despised Bill, but he was tenacious. He could push through any muckraking story he got his hands on. If she couldn't get the information she needed herself, she'd get it indirectly through him. "I've got a great story for you, Bill. In case you have the time and inclination. You and Miss Thompson can look into it together."

The daily *Tribune* didn't compete with the weekly news magazines. Bill really was the best person to take the story. Plus, she didn't think Bill knew that Edward Rutherford was her father. She hadn't been in touch with her father during her marriage, and she couldn't recall giving Bill any details about him. She'd tell Bill about Hanover & Company and her suspicions, while she clung to the idea that maybe, possibly, some other company had found and developed the medication used at Camp Minidoka. Not her father's company. Not her father.

"What puts you in the mood for sharing?"

"Don't quote me, but my boss doesn't want the story. You'll understand why when I tell you what it is. It has to do with a new medication . . ." She told him what she knew.

"Ah. I can see why the old man doesn't want it," he said when she finished. He licked his lips, as if hungry for it. "Not a particularly uplifting tale." He pondered the possibilities. "Well, thank you, Claire. I'll talk to my editor this afternoon. Experimenting on prisoners. The fact that the prisoners are Japs will make it a tougher sell, but I'll pitch it as a business story. The business of medicine, a great tag. I expect I can get approval."

"I'm counting on it."

When he smiled at her, he almost looked attractive. "Nothing like a little crime and corruption to liven up the day."

"*Your* day, at least. Anyway, I knew you'd like it. There's something else." She hesitated. "There might be a murder involved, too."

"All the better."

"Not in this case. I met the ill-fated woman. Did a story with her. The police said it was an accident, but it hit home, given that we were acquainted." Choosing her words carefully, she gave him an account of the death of Lucretia Stanton. "Just remember, Bill, you didn't hear any of this from me."

He laughed warmly. "I don't even know you, Claire Lukins."

She joined in his laughter, and yet the wisecrack was true. Her laughter turned cheerless. Years of marriage, two children, and he didn't even know her.

⟋

CHAPTER THIRTY-SEVEN

About a week later, on a Tuesday morning a little after 7:00 AM, Claire answered the phone at home. The long-distance operator put through Andrew Barnett.

"Mrs. Shipley, at last."

"Let's see, how long has it taken you to return my calls?"

"Sorry, sorry, couldn't be helped. One thing after another here." He didn't return her calls because she wasn't important enough to take priority over other matters he had to attend to. Did she think penicillin was Dr. Bush's only project? Barnett had been in Los Alamos when she left her messages. Penicillin and the atomic bomb: two weapons of war. "How are you?"

"Well enough."

"Glad to hear it." Barnett sounded falsely exuberant even to himself. A few days before, Barnett had learned that his brother had died in the Pacific. During a strafing, he'd received a shrapnel wound in the right calf. He'd been recovering. Then gangrene set in. The doctors amputated above the knee, but it was too late. Penicillin cured gangrene. But Mark's ship didn't have penicillin. No ships had any. Progress was never fast enough.

"Why are you calling me now?" Claire took a tip from Mr. Luce on handling unwelcome conversations. With Bill helping her, she didn't need Barnett.

He was brought up short by her brusqueness. He wouldn't tell her about Mark. Everybody had family members at risk. He didn't need sympathy from her. Besides, Claire Shipley's usefulness was wearing thin. "I'll get right to the point. Tell me, are you ever in touch with your highly esteemed former husband, William aka Bill Shipley?"

"As little as possible. He hasn't had anything to do with me in years. And vice versa. I think he may have remarried, although I'm not positive."

"I can confirm the remarriage."

"Thank you. That certainly makes me feel better."

"He's been nosing around Washington and through the verdant meadows of New Jersey in a way that certain people are beginning to dislike."

"If you had returned my calls in a timely manner, maybe he wouldn't be."

"Let's deal with facts rather than hypotheticals, shall we?" Barnett turned nasty, and Claire had a sudden vision of him as a viper. "You have any influence over him? If so, perhaps you could do us both a favor and call him off."

"I have no influence over him whatsoever. I don't even like him, truth be told. But I never say anything bad about him, and I never allow anyone else to say anything bad about him, because he's the father of my children." She caught herself. "The father of my son. Please remember that."

Barnett knew all about the death of Emily Shipley. "Yes, I promise to remember that he's the father of your children—out of my own self-interest, hoping as I always do to remain in your good graces." There—his sense of his own charm and competence was safely restored; he could manage to do his job no matter what he faced in his personal life. In fact, doing his job well was the greatest gift he could give Mark's memory. "The point is," he said before she could assert, if she were so inclined, that he wasn't in her good graces, "he's giving the impression of a bull terrier that never lets go."

"A bull terrier?"

"I thought you'd appreciate a dog metaphor. Don't you have a dog?"

"I suppose he is like a bull terrier." Bill hadn't changed, and he was doggedly carrying out the job she expected him to do. A job she needed him to do before she could confront her father.

Barnett went on, "I'm fielding complaints from a variety of places. Why people think they should complain to me, I don't know."

"Just one of the many crosses you have to bear, Mr. Barnett."

"Precisely."

"Besides, what's it to you, if he goes about his business?"

"In case you haven't noticed, he's a famous reporter for the *Herald Tribune*."

"You manage to find time to read the newspapers in your line of work?"

"Every now and again. Anyway, when I met Bill Shipley several days ago, I told him to step back, or words to that effect. Alas, I'm learning from subsequent reports that my admonitions served only to make him more determined."

That was typical of Bill.

"He's getting a little too close to home plate." Barnett waited for her to grasp what he was trying to tell her. He couldn't come right out and say, I can't be held responsible for what happens to him. "Frankly, I can't say I liked Bill Shipley."

"Now, now, didn't I warn you about speaking against him?"

"Luckily he won't be around much longer." That was saying too much. Barnett backtracked. "He's due in Nebraska next week to visit family and then he returns to England, if my sources are correct, and they almost always are."

"That makes me feel better, too."

"Glad to be of service." Despite their banter, Barnett hoped she understood that nothing about their discussion was comical. Bill

Shipley was clearly determined to find and reveal information that could damage the project of supplying penicillin to the troops. He appeared set on revealing the patent compromises regarding the cousins. No doubt he'd talk to Detective Marcus Kreindler, who might reveal to him that Dr. Nicholas Catalano—one of the leaders of the penicillin program, now risking his life to conduct clinical trials under battlefield conditions in the Pacific—had been accused of murdering a colleague.

In the Solomon Islands, horrific battles were taking place. American boys were fighting and dying each day under the most brutal circumstances. Who was Bill Shipley, compared to those boys? Barnett didn't need to secure permission from anyone to do what was necessary; he knew what was expected of him. He tried once more with Claire. The last time. "In a war there's no morality."

"What's that supposed to mean?"

Victories are never morally clean, Barnett thought. No matter who was doing the fighting. He let a long silence fall between them. "Well," he said finally, "if you don't know what that means by now, I can't explain it."

That evening, Claire returned home exhausted from a long day's work, covering a casting call to replace chorines on the hit Broadway musical *Oklahoma!*. Mack wanted to find one girl—one particular all-American girl, confident yet vulnerable, a kind of Every-girl—to follow from casting call through rehearsals and costume fittings, to her first performance. Claire may have found her in Estella Gant, a twenty-year-old from Raleigh, North Carolina, who came onstage for her audition and got the job. Tomorrow Mack would look at the contact sheets and decide if indeed Estella was the one.

Before Claire could start dinner, the telephone rang. "Hold for long-distance," the operator said, and put the caller through.

"Claire." It was Bill. "Finally. I've been trying your number all day."

His tone indicated that any reasonable person would have waited at home on the off chance that he would call.

"You missed the story. Missed the entire thing." He said this with smug pleasure. "Incredible—you missed it all."

She felt tears smarting in her eyes. This was how Bill always spoke to her, whether discussing work or laundry or breakfast oatmeal for Emily. Forever elaborating on her incompetence. It still hurt. After she ran into him at Rockefeller Center, she'd fooled herself into thinking that she'd escaped this power he had over her. Obviously she hadn't. With Bill, she must never, ever let down her defenses. She struggled now to push those defenses back into place.

"Okay, this is the real story: patent protection on natural products. The blue medicine is the first one to get it, and now the drug's going to make a fortune. One rumor I'm hearing is that it was stolen from that poor woman in New York who slipped or jumped or got herself pushed off a cliff. One of the government's top guys may be involved. The other rumor I'm hearing is that it was found in Syracuse, of all places. That's something I've got to figure out. The clinical testing in Wyoming or Idaho or wherever it was—that just involves a bunch of Japs, let's face it. They're irrelevant."

"Bill," she protested, her outrage bringing back her confidence, "they're internees. Entire families, experimented on and put at risk."

"Oh, Claire, you are so naive. Really, your naivete amazes me." With him, every disagreement was personal. She didn't have the strength or the simple energy required to fight back. "Nobody cares about the well-being of a bunch of Japs. Nobody. Aren't you reading about what they're doing every day in the Pacific? What they've *been* doing for years? The brutality? Anyway, I'll be in New York in a few days. Got some interviews set up. Detective Marcus Kreindler, you know him?"

"I've heard the name," she said softly, feeling chastised in spite of her attempt to keep up her defenses.

"Then there's the tycoon behind the blue stuff. Edward Rutherford. You know him?"

"Yes." She hesitated. "Yes, I do. I have to tell you, he—"

"Looks like he's behind the whole thing. Maybe ordered the murder, too. To get his hands on the medication. Can't prove it yet, but I'm working on that assumption. He's exactly the type. They're all the same, these so-called captains of industry."

"Bill, I need to tell you—"

But Bill wasn't listening. She could hear Pammy's voice, and Bill's responses. They were making plans to leave for a cocktail party and then a formal dinner. He had to change. *Now.* They were already running late. Simultaneously he was adjusting the radio to the 7:00 PM news reports and commentary. He was everywhere at once, everywhere except with Claire. Finally: "Listen, Claire, you still there? I'll be in touch." He hung up without saying good-bye.

She sat at the telephone table for a long time. So long that Lucas came and stretched out beside her on the floor. She might have no choice but to accept her father's complicity. And yet . . . mixed with her anger and disappointment in Edward Rutherford was love, and an urge to protect him. Her father. The two warring impulses—to warn him, to denounce him—left her paralyzed.

CHAPTER THIRTY-EIGHT

B ill Shipley liked to smoke in the open air and watch the night unfold. That predilection would be the death of him. Literally, thought Andrew Barnett.

They were on the late train from Washington to New York. Shipley hadn't spotted him. Barnett kept his distance. Barnett also wore the uniform of an army private. Anyone looking closely would see that he was a little old to be a private, but this was the best Barnett could do at short notice. When they boarded the train, Barnett hadn't had an exact plan. Shipley was making things easy.

He'd watched Shipley go outside onto the back—observation deck? Barnett couldn't for the life of him remember what that narrow, gated place at the back of a train was called. The place where politicians stood during campaigns to wave to the passing crowds. Barnett didn't usually have trouble retrieving words from his memory. He must be tired. Well, who wouldn't be, with his job? Anyway, Barnett hoped, prayed, that Shipley wouldn't decide to come back inside too soon . . . no, he stood there at the railing, smoking.

The last car of the train was packed, mostly with military boys, and it was hot. The breeze coming in the open windows only made the train hotter. Early August 1943: boys returning from leave, boys going on leave, new recruits heading toward training, trained soldiers and marines and sailors heading toward the ships in the giant port of New York—the ships that would take them to fight in the Solomon Islands or in Sicily.

Walking down the aisle, Barnett had to make an effort not to trip over the soldiers' duffel bags. He also made his way around the soldiers' arms and legs, which seemed strewn all over, as the soldiers fit themselves into whatever space they could find to sleep. With his brother dead, Barnett was more patient with these boys than he used to be. They had an extravagant youthfulness. They were like puppies who played until they were exhausted and then collapsed into sleep wherever they happened to be. Boys, being sent into the maw of hell.

He had his own cigarette going. He'd just be smoking outside, too. That was his plan. His excuse for appearing at the back of the train.

He opened the door. Went out. "Evening," he said to Shipley. Politely, the way well-brought-up people were expected to behave.

"Evening," Bill Shipley said in return, not recognizing him, not even looking at him, probably annoyed that someone had interrupted his meditations, especially an enlisted man, at the bottom of the heap. Shipley turned away, leaned against the far railing, indicating that he didn't want company.

Good. It was after midnight. There was no moon. Darkness was all around them. A minute passed, and two guys, also in military uniform, joined them. Now the platform was crowded, which would discourage others from coming outside. The two newcomers were with Barnett, and they knew what to do. He left the timing to them.

They waited. They smoked. What were they waiting for? Barnett had been assured that they knew their jobs. That they were the best. Still they waited. Of course he couldn't ask them any questions. He could only wait with them. He positioned himself so that he blocked the door leading into the train.

In the end, the issue of timing took care of itself. A freight train was suddenly storming past next to them in the opposite direction. Shipley was already leaning toward it. Barnett couldn't see what happened, but it was over in a second. No shouting. No screaming. Nothing. Both trains careened onward in the dark.

The guys continued to smoke and chat. The freight train disappeared into the distance. The track was black and empty. Except for the rumbling of the passenger train, silence filled the night. Barnett smoked another cigarette, too. Out here, at least, the breeze was cool.

Then he made his way back to his seat, three cars from the back. Perfectly calm, that's what he was. As he walked back, nobody paid attention to him. Almost everybody was asleep, anyway. He found his seat. His seatmate was a sailor, slumbering with his head against the windowpane.

Barnett sat down. He checked his watch. He'd been away from his seat ten, fifteen minutes. Now he started shaking. Sweating. The scene replayed itself in his mind. Over and over, he saw the whole thing play out. The shock of the freight train beside them. The guys making their move.

He lit another cigarette. He steadied his breathing. He calmed himself. In a war there's no morality, he assured himself.

But maybe that notion wasn't quite right. Maybe a war made its *own* morality. Barnett's brother was dead, and Barnett would damned well do whatever he needed to do, to make certain that nothing and no one interfered with this boy, sleeping soundly in the seat next to him, getting what his brother hadn't had: penicillin, the weapon of war.

A day later, Detective Marcus Kreindler sat at his desk reading the morning papers. It was 7:45 AM, and the office was still mercifully quiet. He'd made good time on his morning commute. Too good, in fact. He hadn't meant to get here so early. But he couldn't sleep. Last night they'd received news about their nephew Greg: Kreindler and Agnes happened to be having dinner at her sister's. Right before dessert, the Western Union kid arrived on his bicycle. What a job to give a kid, delivering telegrams telling parents that their children were missing in action. On his way to work, Kreindler dropped off Agnes at her sister's.

Now he had over an hour to drink his coffee and give the papers more than the usual front-page once-over. He had a meeting at 9:00 AM with William Shipley, reporter. Shipley wanted to discuss with him a secret medical project and its link to the death of Lucretia Stanton.

Hearing her name on the phone several days earlier had given Kreindler a jolt. He pictured that beautiful face once more. Evidently Andrew Barnett had done nothing with the information about Nicholas Catalano that Kreindler had so generously provided him. Well, Kreindler couldn't spend his time worrying about what Barnett might or might not do. Catalano was in the Pacific, doing his extremely important government work. When and if Catalano returned to New York, Kreindler (with the approval of his boss, Barnett be damned) was planning a little welcoming party for him.

Kreindler put aside the *Daily News*, picked up the *Tribune*. Agnes stuck with the *News*, but he tried at least to look at them all, because you never knew when a newspaper story would shed light on a case, the way the local papers in Chinatown had opened up the black market murder case. Besides, it was a good idea to give the *Tribune* a read on a day when he was meeting a *Trib* reporter. He could offer Shipley a little flattery, if appropriate.

But even hardened Detective Kreindler got a shock this morning. On the front page, beneath reports on the Allies fighting their way across Sicily, was the headline: WAR CORRESPONDENT KILLED IN RAIL ACCIDENT. WILLIAM SHIPLEY DEAD AT 39. There was a picture of him, labeled as taken in 1935. Shipley looked handsome enough in a jacket and tie. A little severe. It was a professional studio shot.

The article continued on the inside. It took up a full column. Kreindler read slowly. The truth was, he wasn't what teachers called a smooth reader. He had to go slowly if he wanted to catch the nuances. Enjoying a brief holiday leave, Shipley was traveling through America with his wife, a star reporter for the British newspaper *The Guardian*. There was no mention of Claire or Claire's son. Guess Shipley didn't list them on his *Tribune* CV. People were sensitive about divorce, of course. A train accident in Delaware the night before. Body not discovered until the following morning, by which time, multiple fractures, head injuries, loss of blood . . . the words gave a hint of the gruesome reality that Kreindler could imagine only too well. The death was being treated as an accident. Speculation was that he'd gone out for a smoke and fell asleep on his feet, exhausted from his labors. A tragedy.

Kreindler put down the paper. Yet another *accidental* death. He wondered what Andrew Barnett would think about the coincidence. Actually, Kreindler figured, Andrew Barnett had probably arranged the coincidence.

I n Greenwich Village, Claire sat in her garden with the newspapers. She was still dressed in her nightgown and robe. Later the day would be warm and humid, but now, beneath the trees, the air was cool, weightless, and fresh. The ersatz coffee was hot at least, coaxing her awake. Lucas settled himself under the garden table, rubbing his nose against her bare ankles.

She'd been up late, doing a story at the Stage Door Canteen at Times Square. Actress Dorothy McGuire had been there, dancing with the servicemen. Claire was glad to be back at work full-time, even if the stories Mack gave her were fluff.

By chance the *Trib* was on top. Fierce fighting in Sicily. Naples bombed. She turned over the paper, for the stories beneath the fold, as newspaper parlance went. And there she saw the picture, and skimmed the report on a man she didn't exactly recognize. Was it—her *husband*? This was perplexing. She looked again to verify her first impression. Yes, William Shipley. She felt . . . nothing. She took another sip of coffee.

Then the reality pushed in on her. She read the inside portion. To her relief, she and Charlie weren't mentioned.

She cradled her coffee mug, still warm, in both her hands. The sunlight filtered through the trees. Bill Shipley. The father of her children. Barnett had warned her. He'd virtually told her that this would happen. By putting Bill on this story, had *she* sent him to his death?

Thank God Charlie wasn't here today, with his scissors and his scrapbook. What was the best way to tell him the news? Should she go to his camp upstate, or could the news wait until he returned home? She'd discuss this with her father. He'd know what to do.

Her father. *Your people killed my sister*, Jamie's words rushed through her mind. Was her father responsible for Bill Shipley's death, too?

No, it wasn't possible. She wouldn't believe it. And yet . . . her father was ever present.

In a war, there's no morality. Who was it, who'd told her that bit of wisdom? Ah, yes: Andrew Barnett, economist turned philosopher.

Suddenly, sitting there beneath the trees, with the soft morning sunlight filtering around her, Claire wondered if the late Bill Shipley was right, and she was indeed most naive.

CHAPTER THIRTY-NINE

❧

W hy his thoughts went to Tia Stanton at the end, Nick didn't have the energy to figure out. He was bleeding to death, slowly, and there wouldn't be any rescue. The ship was sinking. A clearly marked hospital ship, attacked from the air. For a while, he'd been conducting his clinical trials on the ground, at a field hospital just back from the front lines, hidden in the jungle. That location had quickly proven too dangerous. The ship was supposed to be safer. Probably the pilot of the plane was returning from an island raid, spotted the hospital ship, and, having a few bombs left, just couldn't resist.

When Nick was a student and a young physician, he often wondered what dying felt like. Now he was finding out. He didn't feel pain. Instead he felt a pleasant drifting. As though he were floating. He was dimly aware of activity around him, the uninjured fleeing, struggling to escape. Their struggles had nothing to do with him.

Those months after Tia's death—could he have done something else, made some other decision? He didn't see how. Nonetheless he played the events through in his mind once more. By chance he was in town, and he was free for lunch. He'd gone to her lab, hoping to persuade her to have lunch with him. The lab was open, but no one was there. Nonetheless, he went in; Tia always made everyone welcome. In the cousins' room, her work was laid out. He sat at her bench, in her place, and read through her notes. Out of boredom.

Out of interest. As a way to fill the time. Nothing more. Nothing less.

He was shocked. Yes, yes, she'd mentioned now and again that she was on to something. Told him she was excited. But he never would have dreamed how far along she was, how spectacular the results were.

So peaceful. He hadn't envisioned that death would be so peaceful. This type of death, at least. He felt weaker and weaker. He wished he could write down his reactions, for the benefit of those after him. Where was Margot, his nurse? She might be interested. She could write it down for him. Too many women, he'd had. Even Claire Shipley. He couldn't bring himself to look his best friend in the eye after that rousing episode. After Jamie returned from the dead, he seemed to suspect something. Did Claire confess? Here was the kicker: Jamie came home after all, and he, Nick, would not.

The story of that afternoon, running through his brain like a movie, resumed. He read Tia's notes. Examined the petri dishes, beakers, and test tubes relating to the substance. Saw the mice receiving the medication and the mice acting as the control group. Number 642, she called it. He recognized what she had done: she had made a remarkable discovery. He would congratulate her when she returned to the lab. He continued reading, following the story lines of other, less successful substances.

He heard footsteps. Someone had come into the lab, walking quickly toward him. "Tia?" he called out, so she wouldn't be startled to see him.

But instead of Tia, Sergei Oretsky was at the doorway. Oretsky looked shocked to see Nick there, and he paused, as if thinking through what he should do or say. "She's dead," Oretsky finally shouted, like a taunt. He was red-faced. Sweating and panting in such a way that his clothes looked too small for him.

"Who's dead?"

"Mademoiselle Stanton. Mademoiselle Stanton is dead."

"What? That can't be right."

"I am right."

Nick couldn't fathom this. "Calm down, Oretsky. You're not making sense."

"She's fallen from the cliff. An accident."

Nick heard police sirens in the distance.

"Go see for yourself, if you don't believe me."

The sirens were louder now. Closer. Oretsky glanced toward the windows, as if he could see the sound of the sirens.

Nick stood. He wondered where to go, to find out what was going on. The sirens were very loud now. And then he realized, the last place *he* would go, to find out what was going on, was here, to the lab. What was Oretsky doing here? What did Oretsky want? Oretsky was shifting from foot to foot, nervously swaying, as if waiting, desperately, for Nick to leave.

The truth was, Nick had never really trusted Oretsky: Oretsky was Russian, after all. So foolish, these prejudices, Nick realized. Often enough, people had mistrusted Nick because his family was Italian. Often enough, he'd felt the sting of that mistrust. Because his family was Italian, and poor, he'd always had to be ten times as smart as the others, work ten times as hard, to be allowed into their schools. To date their daughters. To achieve the pinnacle of his field: a position at the Rockefeller Institute.

But despite the prejudice Nick himself had experienced, there it was: Nick didn't trust the Russian Oretsky. Besides, Oretsky didn't really belong at the Institute. He'd come here on a one-year fellowship, and in an act of charity, Dr. Rivers had allowed him to remain when the war broke out. Whereas Nick had been on the staff of the Institute for over a decade now.

Nick wouldn't leave the Russian interloper Oretsky alone in Tia's lab.

Oretsky gave Nick a peculiar look, as if he wanted something from Nick but was reluctant to ask. "Go. Go see for yourself," Oretsky said softly. Nick could barely hear him for the shrieking of the police sirens down below, in front of the hospital and also, presumably, at the bottom of the cliff. Abruptly, the sirens stopped. The police cars had arrived. "She is there. By the cliff. I am right."

The two men stared at each other.

Nick was determined: he would never leave Oretsky alone here.

"All right, you two, that way. Jenkins, you come with me . . ." The urgent, raised voices of the police officers in front of the hospital reached the two men.

Abruptly, Oretsky turned and left. In fact, he ran, although Nick couldn't imagine what he was running away from, or what he was running toward. These Russians, so emotional and unpredictable.

Nick looked down at Tia's work on the table before him. No matter what had happened to her, he couldn't leave her work here, for anyone who happened by to stumble upon. Oretsky could come back. Anyone could come in here. Nick didn't have a key to the lab, so he couldn't lock the door behind him. Jamie was out of town. Jamie would want Nick to protect his sister's work.

Nick felt a surge of energy. Quickly he searched. In a lower cabinet, he found a Bergdorf Goodman shopping bag in the shape of a shoe box. Methodically, he gathered all the materials relating to number 642 and placed them in the shopping bag. In the desk drawer, he found a razor blade, and he cut the pages from Tia's notebook. Taking the back stairs, he brought the bag to his residence rooms. Placed the bag under the bed, for safekeeping.

Then he went to the hospital cafeteria, a general gathering place, to find out what was going on. His colleagues were there already, talking in tight clutches. The police were there, too. Oretsky was with his phage research group, looking through some notes, his earlier upset seemingly forgotten.

Nick learned that Lucretia Stanton was, indeed, dead at the bottom of the cliff, just as Sergei Oretsky said.

Drifting . . . how long did it take, to bleed to death? Well, that depended on the type of injury. Nick felt no pain, and he wasn't precisely certain where he'd been wounded. The shoulder, maybe. His left shoulder felt pleasantly warm, perhaps from blood. He was so tired now. Soon, he would fall asleep.

After Tia's memorial, when he found Jamie in the lab, he'd almost said to him, I have Tia's great discovery upstairs in my rooms. I kept it safe for you. The Institute will develop it now, for the good of humankind. That was the Institute's motto, after all.

But Nick found he couldn't say anything to Jamie. Tia was dead. He, Nick, was alive. Jamie had been raised in wealth. Nick had not. The things he could do with the money he'd make from selling the substance . . . not simply for himself but for his family. For his parents. For the children he might himself someday have. There was no reason to say anything to Jamie about the substance. No reason at all.

Tia was dead, and she couldn't be brought back to life.

For some reason, Nick's grandmother came into his mind. His mother's mother. She took care of him when he was young and his parents were at work. In the image that came into his mind, she gave him that secret smile of hers that said, now we're going to do something that your mother would disapprove of. Like buying ice cream cones on a regular afternoon instead of saving the ice cream money for a birthday or a holiday. Sometimes they'd spend even more money to take the trolley to Syracuse's lake. They'd buy their ice cream cones by the lake (he, chocolate; she, strawberry), and they'd sit on a bench at the lakeshore and enjoy their ice cream.

His grandmother was from a small village in the Dolomite mountains of Northern Italy. When Nick was very young, three or four, she still kept a loaf of stale bread on the kitchen counter, as her own mother had, as everyone in their village had. The bread was moldy—

he had told Tia about this when he was trying to court her. The story made her happy. When anyone in the family had a cut or scrape, his grandmother would slice off the end of the bread, press the moldy side against the wound, and wrap a bandage around to hold the bread in place for a few days. No one in their family ever developed a wound infection. The mold was *Penicillium*. But this was old-country medicine, and, until recently, scientists never took it seriously.

Eventually Nick's mother got rid of the stale bread, calling it a disgusting holdover from the country they were never going back to, good riddance.

Nick saw his grandmother once more, saw her smile, as if she were coming to staunch the wounds he now suffered.

Silence, all around him. He was floating. Life, death . . . he was floating in between. Again he wished he could tell someone how peaceful he felt. But no one was nearby to listen.

CHAPTER FORTY

⁓

E dward Rutherford stood at the window of his office, high up in the tower of 20 Exchange Place. You could see a long way from here. Feel like you were on top of the world. The window faced north, and he could see all the way to the Empire State Building.

He'd returned to town this morning, on the sleeper from Chicago. The train was overcrowded and arrived two hours late. That was the war. He didn't even have time to go home to change. He had a new project: two guys with revolutionary ideas about semiconductors. Nothing might come of the project—or their ideas might change the world. Rutherford was going to support them for a few years and see what happened.

Betty, his secretary, buzzed him. He went to his desk and pressed the intercom button. "Your daughter to see you, sir." Before he could respond, Claire had walked in the door.

Rutherford understood the instant he saw her. She was dressed up, high heels, tailored suit, full makeup and a perfect hat. She was ready to do battle. This was probably what she called her Henry Luce outfit.

"Sweetheart, what a surprise! You look terrific!"

She didn't respond. Not a good sign.

"I'm just back from Chicago. Sit down, sit down." He ushered her into a chair, one of four surrounding a coffee table in the corner. The office was designed in the Art Deco style, very sleek, to match the building. "How's everything? What are you up to?"

"Nothing much."

Nothing much. He knew that phrase from months past, when they were first getting to know each other. *Nothing much* covered everything that she didn't want to tell him. Everything that mattered in her life. He wasn't happy to hear it, and it told him how upset she must be. "Shall I tell Betty to bring some coffee?"

"No, thank you."

"Well, then." He smiled at her. He put on an eager, probably fatuous look that said, I'm ready to hear absolutely anything you have to say.

She seemed to need a moment to compose herself. Then:

"James Stanton was right, wasn't he? You did order the murder of his sister."

"*What*, young lady?"

No, *no*. He mustn't take this tack. He must not. He knew how to conduct this battle. He had to state the facts as he knew them, without pushing or prodding, without overpleading or pressing his case in any way. "No," he said calmly, "I did not order the murder of Lucretia Stanton."

"I don't believe you."

"Whether you believe me or not is irrelevant. Your accusation is false."

"So how did your company just happen to have her discovery to develop?"

"That's very simple. Nicholas Catalano sold it to me. He said he found it in his hometown. Whether this is true or not, I don't know."

"And since he's dead anyway, you can't ask him." Jake Lind had sent Claire a note about Nick.

Rutherford had no answer to this.

"You also colluded in the death of Bill Shipley."

He just barely stopped himself from laughing. "For your sake, I might have been tempted to get rid of him, but no. The word on the street, as they say, is that government security did the job."

Barnett: just as she thought. Part of her wanted to believe everything her father said. To walk out with him to lunch, uptown at the Cloud Club, the businessmen's club in the spire of the Chrysler Building. They'd discuss Charlie's latest letters. Plans for Charlie's schooling in the autumn. They'd discuss how to break to Charlie the news of his father's death.

No, she didn't want to fight with Edward Rutherford. But she made herself press on. "You knowingly injured innocent Japanese prisoners by authorizing the testing of your new drug in the camps in the West."

"My staff worked hard to find the best place to conduct clinical trials." He made the tactical move of meeting her halfway: "I suppose that reasonable people might differ on this, but I truly believe that we did those people a great deal of good and only trivial harm."

She didn't know what to say to this. Was deafness trivial harm?

Now she'd arrived at the ransacking of her home. She paused.

He misinterpreted her silence as a partial victory. He made a step toward her: "I know I could have done better, darling. All these years. Everything we talked about when Charlie was in the hospital. But I'm not a murderer. My people aren't murderers." He was about to compare himself favorably in this regard to certain other robber barons and their ilk, but he restrained himself. "Like anyone, I have regrets."

"Did you order my home ransacked?"

"The men went overboard, I found out later. They got carried away. They were stupid, and they were fired. But that photo shoot of yours was a security breach, and I had no choice but to get the film back as soon as possible. I needed to protect my property. The government didn't have the right to see those photos. I phoned you as soon as I heard, remember? To make certain you were all right."

Had she heard him correctly? She was astonished. Apparently he could rationalize anything, in the name of business.

She looked at him for a moment. Then she stood up and walked out, slamming the office door behind her.

Rutherford stared at the door for a long while. Then he listlessly returned to the window to look out at the city. . . . Thunderstorms were coming on, fat gray clouds behind the skyscrapers to the north. The clouds made the skyscrapers glow silver. How beautiful this city was. By definition, man-made. Skyscraper technology was incredible. What was the next step in skyscraper technology? What did you need, to allow structures to be built higher and higher yet? New types of flame retardant, maybe. Stronger glass. New types of steel? If buildings were constructed of glass and steel instead of stone, they would be lighter. Lighter meant higher. He'd do some research. Someday this war would end. A new age of glass and steel skyscrapers would begin. Looking out the window, he imagined the skyline transformed. When the time came, he would be ready.

He let Claire back into his mind. He wanted his family to be together. That was truly what mattered most. He already had more money than he could ever use. He'd figure something out. He'd make this up to her and gain her forgiveness.

Nothing much. He never, ever, wanted to hear that phrase from her again. Not ever.

CHAPTER FORTY-ONE

～

A nother day, another German restaurant in Yorkville. Kreindler
was getting sick of thirty-foot murals of Bavaria. Today, the
Original Maxl's. This restaurant boasted singing waiters. Mercifully,
Kreindler and Fritz were dining early, 4:00 PM, and no waiters had
started their damned yodeling just yet. Incredibly, the restaurant was
crowded, jam-packed with German-prating geezers.

Kreindler was having *Kassler Rippchen* with *Kartoffelsalat* and
sauerkraut. Fritz was digging into the wurst platter with fried potatoes
and red cabbage.

This would be Fritz's last wurst platter for a while. Today was the
day. At least one federal agent sat in the room. The FBI was round-
ing up the Yorkville ring. Kreindler's job was to keep Fritz here, nice
and safe over his bratwurst and *Weisswurst* until everybody else was
downtown. That included Sergei Oretsky. The double agent would
be taken in along with the rest of them. Well, he'd saved himself
from the electric chair with his cooperation, but he'd be sent away a
long time.

Kreindler was feeling nostalgic and couldn't resist a few digs at
Fritz. "Things aren't going too well on the Russian front," he said,
feigning disappointment. "We're getting pushed back everywhere."

"Don't believe the propaganda you read in the papers," Fritz assured him. A piece of red cabbage hung from his lip, and he slurped it
in. He cut off another piece of sausage, so big Kreindler was sure he'd

choke on it, but no, it went down smooth as silk. Well, you had to admire a guy who enjoyed his food. Fritz took a swig of beer.

"Don't you worry, Marcus," Fritz assured him. Inwardly Kreindler flinched at the use of his first name, but he held himself steady. "I've got some news for you. This is a secret, so don't go passing it around: we've got a weapon in reserve. A big weapon. The biggest. The Führer is just waiting for the right time to use it. Getting everything into position, so it'll do the most good when it's really needed. Once the Führer uses the weapon, the enemy will be forced to surrender. We'll be in charge. You thinking of yourself as New York City police commissioner under the new order, Marcus? I can see you there. After we send away the cretins and the Jews in charge now."

"That would be very nice, Fritz. Something to look forward to." Fritz was tone-deaf to irony. "Thanks for letting me in on the secret." He'd have to tell the FBI about this weapon business. Andrew Barnett, too.

Fritz waved his hand magnanimously. "Of course. You're a friend, Marcus. We're loyal to our friends."

"Thank you for that," Kreindler said.

"Anytime."

With Lucretia Stanton on his mind, Kreindler turned the conversation to her. What the hell, he figured. He'd read in the paper that Nick Catalano was dead in the Pacific, along with three hundred of his shipmates. The Japs had bombed a clearly marked hospital ship. "Hey, Fritz, remember a while back we were talking about the scientist you fellas have over at that place on York Avenue—"

"Yeah, yeah, the Russian. He's a dud. He's never gotten us anything useful. Almost a year ago, he even started sending us stuff that didn't work—and he must have known it didn't work."

Kreindler put the timing together, to when the FBI had made Oretsky into a double agent.

"We were ready to cut the tie," Fritz was saying, "when he started telling us how devoted he was, he even murdered some girl there, in his devoted efforts to help us. So we kept him on, what the hell."

"What?" Kreindler couldn't help it, his astonishment got the better of him.

"Yeah, yeah, remember, a year and a half ago or so, an accident on a cliff? That was our guy," Fritz related with some pride. "Apparently she was on to him. Found him snooping around her lab. He convinced her to take a walk so he could give the sob story about his wife and children kept as prisoners in the Reich. Wandered onto the path along the cliff, looking at the scenery, and he gives her a push. Thinks he'll get everything that way, but in the end, he gets nothing. Can't get back into the lab, or so he said. A washout." Fritz licked his lips, catching the last of the succulent combination of cabbage, sausage, and spiced mustard.

"You know what's so great about the whole story with him? I only found this out recently—this is incredible: the family he was trying to protect in France? They were already dead! The whole story was just a ruse to draw him in! Got to admire them, the people I work for."

"What do you mean?"

"Exactly what I said. The wife, the kids, the old mother—they got sent east at the beginning. They were Russians, what do you expect—they got picked up right after we moved in, and *poof*, no more family." Fritz snapped his fingers. "The poor bastard is falling all over himself trying to protect people who died years ago. That's brilliant, isn't it?" Fritz said. "Wish I'd thought of it myself."

"Yes." Kreindler nodded slowly. "Brilliant."

Fritz turned to order another beer. Kreindler used that moment to glance at Olsen across the room. Olsen had his eye on the front door, which was behind Kreindler. Olsen nodded. Kreindler heard the men coming in.

"Sorry, Fritz," Kreindler said as four guys came up to Fritz. Boy, the guys were big, 250 pounds at least, and tall. "You don't have time to finish that beer."

That was it. Surrounded by the four guys, Fritz was gone in a few moments, no fuss, no muss, nobody in the restaurant, apparently, even bothering to look up from their schnitzel and sauerbraten.

Kreindler sat for a while. Sure, he needed to get downtown, but the feds were in charge, so there wasn't much for him to do now.

Even though he was officially on duty, he ordered a *Pharisäer*. Nobody looking at the coffee mug would think it held a good deal of spirits along with the hot coffee. He needed the shot of rum. It was good for his heart anyway, right?

A guy like Oretsky would tell a lie a minute to get what he needed. He'd have a different untruth for every occasion as he desperately tried to hold on to his family. Kreindler should have realized this. He'd believed Oretsky when he said he'd seen Catalano and Tia Stanton walking along the cliff. It gave Kreindler a witness, it solved his problem. It made perfect sense.

On the other hand, when Oretsky told Fritz that he himself was guilty of Tia Stanton's murder, this may well have been a move calculated to endear him to Fritz, so who knew if it was true. It might be true, it might not be. And why did Oretsky want Fritz to love him? To protect his family in Europe. The family that was already murdered.

What was Kreindler supposed to do, tell the feds to charge Sergei Oretsky with Tia Stanton's murder? On what proof, exactly? On the word of Nazi Fritz, saying that Oretsky confessed the whole thing to him? Yeah, yeah. Sure, sure.

Nicholas Catalano. Sergei Oretsky. One was already dead. The other would be going to prison anyway. So it didn't even matter. William Shipley's death was mixed up in there, too, but no sense trying to make that public: the government wagons would circle round to protect Barnett.

A plague on both your houses. He felt like a character at the end of a Shakespeare play. The stage was covered with dead bodies, and he was the last man standing. Germans worshipped Shakespeare, read and performed in German translation. Kreindler's mother read Schlegel's Shakespeare to him in an effort to teach him German. He'd snuggled against her, her hair and clothes smelling of chocolate from the shop, as she read *Hamlet* and *Romeo and Juliet* and *Julius Caesar* (his mother liked the tragedies) aloud in German while he followed the text. That must be sixty years ago.

Was this how his career was supposed to end, on a stage covered with dead bodies? With murderers never convicted?

Well, the war wasn't over yet. He wouldn't be retiring until it was. Until the young guys came home from the battlefields. In the meantime, his city still had a lot of surprises to offer him. He was sure of that.

He called for the check. When the waitress came over, he told her to pack up two orders of *Apfelstrudel*. A consoling little bedtime snack for him and Agnes.

CHAPTER FORTY-TWO

I t was raining. Claire sat at the breakfast table with her toast and coffee, the newspapers spread around her as usual. This afternoon, Charlie was coming home from camp. She was meeting him at the station. Again she tried to figure out what to say to him: how to tell him that his father was dead. And to break the news that they wouldn't be spending time with his grandfather anymore. She'd refuse to explain why—just as Claire's mother had refused to explain why she'd left her husband, Claire's father.

Exasperated and despairing, she turned to the *Times*. She spotted this headline: Hanover & Company Announces Powerful Antibacterial Drug. The secondary headline beneath read, New Drug Promises to Surpass Penicillin in Effectiveness and Applications.

She read the story.

> At the company's New Jersey laboratories, Mr. Edward Rutherford, chief executive officer, and Mr. Keith Hanover, president of operations, yesterday announced the development of a powerful new antibacterial drug made from mold, Ceruleamycin. According to sources at the Office of Scientific Research and Development, Committee on Medical Research, no military restrictions will be placed on the new drug. Unlike penicillin, which remains under military control, Ceruleamycin will

be available to the general public at commercial prices. It has proven effective against gram-positive and gram-negative bacteria, including tuberculosis.

Mr. Rutherford said, "Initial clinical trials have shown great success, with no side effects whatsoever in the majority of patients. As with any medication, a few patients suffer some mild side effects. Clinical trials and refinements are continuing. I expect the drug to be available for purchase within the next year or eighteen months. In the meantime, we're telling the nation to 'think blue'—that's how to remember the name. Ceruleamycin. It looks like the sky."

The *Times* also reported that Rutherford was releasing the drug in honor of his grandson, who'd been rescued from a life-threatening case of pneumonia by taking the medication.

The article continued on the inside for a half page. Hanover was a privately held company standing to earn millions from this drug, the first commercially available, systemic antibacterial, but in an act of profound and extraordinary civic generosity on the part of Edward Rutherford, all profits after expenses would be donated to a foundation for medical research.

An accompanying article was titled A PHILANTHROPIST IS BORN. This was a profile of Edward Rutherford from his youth in Allentown to his creation of the foundation that would put him, or so the paper claimed, in the same league as John D. Rockefeller, Andrew Carnegie, and all the rest. Praise was pouring in from around the country, duly quoted. FDR himself lauded the "fine example" Rutherford provided of innovative business leadership working for the good of the nation and humanity itself.

Ceruleamycin. *Worthy of a haiku*, Dr. Ito had said. *A color like the brightest mountain lake.* All profits after expenses to be used for the creation of a foundation for medical research.

Her father knew that she would read the paper. Claire remembered how Charlie used to read the *Trib* and think that Bill Shipley's articles were filled with messages for him. The BBC was famous for broadcasting coded messages to agents in France.

This was her father's message to her. He was doing all he possibly could to make amends: For Tia Stanton dying young, no matter who was responsible. For the Japanese who'd endured the clinical trials. For the violation of Claire's home. Maybe, too, for the departure of James Stanton.

Fleetingly she wondered if Jamie had read this news, wherever he was.

And gradually she saw the truth, starkly. They lived in history, not ideals. This afternoon she would tell Charlie that his father was dead— dead in the war, she would explain in sign language, which was true, in its way. Charlie would want, would *need*, to see his beloved grandfather. She could imagine the evening playing out: They'd have dinner uptown, and maybe decide to spend the night there. Charlie and his grandfather would play chess. Charlie's father was dead. The man who might have been his stepfather was gone, too. He needed his grandfather. Claire had no choice. She wouldn't break apart her son's only family.

She went to the telephone and called her father's office. She wasn't ready to speak to him, but she'd leave a message with his secretary.

"Mr. Rutherford's office."

It was Betty.

"Hi, Betty, it's Claire. Is he in town?"

"Yes, Claire, he is."

"Could you tell him that Charlie's train is arriving at Grand Central this afternoon at 3:45? I'm sure it will be late." They'd shared a touch of knowing laughter. "But tell him I'll be at the station at, oh, 3:30, just to be on the safe side. I'll meet him by the information booth."

They said good-bye.

Claire felt herself awash in shades of gray.

EPILOGUE

⁓

James Stanton watched a crane take Claire Shipley from view to view. He saw her climb out of the crane platform and clamber onto the wide factory beams, fearless, to take photos of the giant vats below. How astonishing she was. He'd never met anyone like her. He wanted to be up there with her, to embrace her. To do more than embrace her. He hadn't seen her in over a year, and she still affected him the way she had the first time he ever saw her.

He tried to visualize the factory complex through her eyes. The gleaming steel vats holding 20,000 gallons each of fermentation broth. The row of silver scrubbing towers five stories high to clean the air used to aerate the broth. The maze of pipes leading a quarter mile in every direction. Giant tubes and filters hanging from the beams. Above all, the sky, the blue prairie sky with its floating strings of clouds. This factory was in the middle of a cornfield, ten miles south of Terre Haute, Indiana, on the Wabash River. Construction, research, and production went on simultaneously, with a Triple-A work priority, the highest possible. The factory had only a partial roof. A roof wasn't essential for the work, so roof construction came last.

Up on the beams, lying on her stomach, Claire saw the figure of a military man walking amid the fermentation vats. She photographed him to give some perspective on size. The vats towered over him. He walked into a patch of sunlight, the break in the factory roof.

And then she realized. It was him. Jamie. Her heart beat fast, and she felt light-headed. She rested the camera on the beam. She wouldn't risk moving to another place, not yet, not until she caught hold of herself. The beam itself was quite safe (she wasn't suicidal), despite what anyone might think who was watching from below—despite what *he* might think. The beam was three feet wide, thick, and stable. Even so, she couldn't let herself become distracted while she was up here. And he'd distracted her.

In the past year or so since she'd last seen him, she'd built a front of anger over her anguish. But now, spotting him there, she felt a jolt, and a powerful yearning for him, filled with desire. As strong a desire, and as much love, as she'd felt when they were together. To her it was as if the argument at her father's apartment was only yesterday. Suddenly she was as weak and vulnerable as she'd been at that moment, the strength draining from her limbs.

He couldn't see the details of what she did up above. He didn't know that she'd spotted him. Didn't know that she stayed in that one place because after seeing him, she didn't trust herself to move. He continued to wander the factory, imagining it through her eyes. The scene was like a movie set for a futuristic thriller. And the purpose of it wasn't to destroy lives but to save them. His work was complete. When the Allies had invaded France a few weeks before, every American medic carried Pfizer-made penicillin in his kit. Jamie had witnessed, and in his own way assisted, a technological and medical breakthrough of astounding proportions . . . corn steep liquor, *Penicillium chrysogenum* from a rotten cantaloupe, deep tank submerged fermentation: these were the ingredients. The battle for penicillin was won.

Jamie knew he'd been a fool, and a coward. Kreindler had told him about Sergei Oretsky's confession, suspect as it was, coming through the Nazi Geckmann. As to Nick, and the theft of Tia's discovery . . .

well, Edward Rutherford had, in fact, set up a foundation with the profits: he'd tried to make amends. Jamie had no right to blame Claire for what had been done by Nick, or by her father.

Shades of gray, everywhere Jamie turned. For the past months, Jamie had internally debated how to arrange a rendezvous with Claire. He'd never returned her phone calls, and so he didn't feel he could simply pick up the phone and call her now, a year later. Or maybe he was simply too cowardly still to approach her that way; she could hang up on him, after all, and he couldn't face that. He wanted, needed, to see her in person. Meeting here, as if by chance, was the best he could do. When Vannevar Bush mentioned that she was visiting the Terre Haute plant, Jamie scheduled his final tour of inspection to coincide with her visit.

All right, she thought. Her heart rate had slowed. She could manage now. She brought herself to kneeling. Yes, she was fine. She returned to the crane platform, and she waved to Bob, the crane operator, to take her to the next spot. She was almost finished for today anyway. A few more shots, especially that spot by the far wall—she indicated to Bob what she wanted—because from there she could gain a high perspective of both the fermentation vats and the prairie clouds above the factory.

After her father set up the foundation, Claire had hoped that Jamie would be in touch with her. For days she listened for the phone. Grabbed at the mail. Every time she returned from a trip, she willed that a message from him would be waiting for her. But no message, or letter, or phone call ever came. Even now, the pain of the memory made tears smart in her eyes.

At the far wall, she went on with her shoot. She made it last longer than it had to, putting off as long as possible the moment when she would be forced to greet Jamie. But she couldn't put off the moment forever. She gave a signal to Bob, and he lowered her to the factory floor.

Jamie approached her. "Hello, Claire."

His tone itself was an apology. She heard this and recognized the awkwardness, at the least, that he must be feeling.

"What are you doing here?" she said, masking her pain with anger. She wished she could walk into his arms and hold him while he held her in return.

Well, not exactly the greeting he'd hoped for, Jamie thought, but under the circumstances he didn't feel he could rightly protest. "I'm on a tour of inspection. I arrived this afternoon."

She said nothing.

He tried to ignore her shocked and angry look by making a wisecrack. "I know what *you're* doing here, so I don't have to ask."

She disregarded the attempt at humor. "I'm finished for today. In fact, I'm leaving Terre Haute tonight." In his presence, after these months of silence, she tried to harden herself against him once more. How dare he turn up without warning, expecting her to be ready to laugh and to forgive?

"I've got a car and driver, can I give you a lift back to town?"

This placed her in a quandary: she had to ask the factory's military security detail for a ride whenever she needed one, a real burden for them, and so she didn't feel she could reject Jamie's offer.

In silence they walked to his car. She carried her equipment, taking a step away from him when he offered to help.

The driver saluted when they came up. He opened and closed the doors in strict military demeanor, all by the book. Not like Tony. Tony's mother had telephoned five months ago. The moment she identified herself, Claire knew what had happened. Tony had died, in Italy, a few days before Christmas. Since he'd stopped working with her, Claire had received two letters from him, lighthearted, chatty. She sent these letters to his mother after he died. The Allies were advancing in France. In Asia, the Allied assault against the Mariana Islands had begun. In Claire's small neighborhood of Greenwich Village, the blue-star banners of service were turning more and more often into the silver-star banners of the wounded, and the gold-star banners of death. Increased casualties were the sacrifice required for victory.

As the military car drove along the barbed-wire fence that cordoned off the extensive acreage of what was supposed to be a secret site, Jamie made a stab at conversation. "Watching you up there on the beams, I got the feeling that, well"—he knew he was sounding foolish, but it was the best he could do—"you must enjoy photographing factories."

She was sitting as far from him as she could. Even so, she was alert to every movement of his body. Alert to the bending of his legs, to the way he kept his forearm against the top of the open window to catch the breeze. "Yes," she said forcing her gaze on the scenery, flat and fertile. "I do." Over the years she'd done some of her best work at industrial sites. The steel mills of Gary, Indiana. The hydropower dam system of the Tennessee Valley Authority. Any industrial project could be transformed into art. These past days at the penicillin plant, she'd felt a surging sense of optimism, for herself, for Charlie, for the country, the darkness and despair of the past months ebbing away from her. But these feelings weren't something she could share easily, least of all with the man next to her. She would share them with her father when she returned to New York. She and her father had uncertainly reconciled, each trying to do better at understanding the other, trying to find a common ground between her idealism and his harnessing of the ways of the world.

When they reached her hotel in Terre Haute, where she would retrieve her suitcase before the train, the early evening sunlight was raking over the buildings.

"I remember from my last visit that there's a park along the river," Jamie said. He wanted so much to touch her face. "If you feel like a walk."

She considered this.

"I'd like to take a walk with you," he said. "I'd like us to have a chance to talk." There. He was trying. He was inching forward. "I heard from Marcus Kreindler . . ." He let the implication fall away.

"I'm not interested in true confessions." That was mean, she realized. In fact she was interested in learning what the detective had said to Jamie.

"No, of course not. But I'll tell you anyway: he exonerated your father of, well, of what I accused him of."

Ah. That made her happy indeed. But she wouldn't share her happiness with the man beside her. She also realized: Jamie had learned the truth, but he hadn't contacted her to let her know.

"Will you walk with me?" he asked.

With the light so bright and clear, and with some, at least, of her spirit lifted by the triumphs of her workday, she really did feel like a walk.

She left her equipment with the bellman in the lobby.

Jamie led the way to a path along a tributary of the Wabash River. The path was framed by weeping willow trees.

"How's Charlie?" he asked.

"He's doing well." She offered no details. He'd have to work harder than this, for details. Charlie was finishing his first year at a boarding school for the deaf. He enjoyed it. Some of his hearing was returning. Last week, he'd written to tell her that he'd heard the call of a goose over the lake behind his school.

"I read about his father's death."

"Yes."

"Please give Charlie my best."

"I'm not sure that's a good idea." She hated to say this, but it was true. Charlie had had enough upheaval in his life; he didn't need James Stanton disappearing and appearing at whim.

They came to a rustic bridge. They stared down at the lazy river water, filled with the pale green reflections from the foliage on either side. This was the man she'd loved, Claire thought. The love of her life. Once upon a time. She stared at a tiny whirlpool in the river, a turning kaleidoscope of green leaves and brown branches. A leaf drifted onto the water and was carried gently, tilting this way and that, down the stream.

"How about you?" Jamie said. "How are you?" The question came out as a demand, startling him. He loved her so.

"Well enough."

He put his hand on her shoulder, and she stepped away from him. Not abruptly, simply in a natural way of starting to walk again, so that his arm fell to his side.

They continued along the path. Claire concentrated on the light, the gorgeous, raking, orange sunset light. The reflections upon the river and upon the riverbank, shimmering and shining. All around her, the world had turned to a fierce radiance, giving her a sense of immediacy and perfection.

"After what happened—" No, that wasn't the way to start. "I'm sorry." That didn't seem adequate, either. "I was a coward."

"You did what you thought was right," was the best she could come up with.

After a prolonged silence, Jamie continued, "My work is finished on the penicillin project. I know Dr. Bush would like me to keep touring factories indefinitely, because it would make his job a lot easier, but I've realized my real work is passing me by. That evening in front of the Institute, when all those people were begging for penicillin, do you remember?"

"Yes." It seemed like years ago.

"I've volunteered to be a physician at the front. I've been accepted."

"What?" She couldn't take it in. She stopped. She turned to face him. Her defenses against him collapsed in an instant. The yellow light of sunset glowed around him and upon him. She wanted to grasp him and hold on to him forever. She fisted her hands, pressing her nails into her palms.

He regarded her with a half smile.

"You're going to Italy?" she asked, making an automatic link to Tony.

"No, no, I'm with the navy. I have to be in San Diego on Monday, ready to ship out, as they say."

"Monday?"

"Yes."

Just like Tony. She felt lost. She realized how much energy she'd been exerting, for months, to resist the anguish Jamie had caused her, defending herself against missing him. She wished she could summon the strength to ask him straight out: Why didn't you return to me, once you learned the truth? But that felt like begging, and she wouldn't beg him to come back to her. She was ready to cry.

"None of that now." He touched her cheek with his fingertips, let his hand fall. "Have to wear a smile when saying good-bye to the valiant troops."

She thought about the normal questions people asked when getting such news, and she asked one: "You have any idea where you'll be sent?"

"Somewhere in the Pacific. An island hospital. A hospital ship. With the landing parties. I don't know." He had no illusions. He knew it would be terrible. He'd read enough in the newspapers about the horrors of Saipan and New Guinea, to know that much. Still, it was his duty. He'd made the only choice he could make, if he wanted to live with himself after the war—if he survived the war. "I don't care, so long as I'm far away from mold. Green, blue, red, whatever color you pick."

"What about the research you've done?"

"I'm a physician, I have a responsibility to do more than push paper around and arrange compromises among business interests. That's what I began to realize that night, in that crowd of desperate people outside the Institute." Amputations, abdominal wounds. Sending nineteen-year-old boys home without their legs. Without a hand, without an arm. Military medicine, saving lives. Relieving pain. Stopping infections with the new weapon of war.

"Maybe I could write to you." He managed to keep his tone even. "Look you up when I get back."

Claire knew that a woman never said no to a man going to the front. If a man was going to the war zones and he thought he needed you, if he wanted to imagine your face when he fell asleep at night, you gave him permission whether you liked him or not, even if you secretly wished you would never see him again. You gave him a hope to come back for. You might not be waiting for him when he got back, but at least you would have helped him to survive.

"Yes, of course, Jamie," she replied automatically. And because he was leaving for the front on Monday, because he might die there and she would never see him again, she felt an urge to reach up, slide her arms around him, and kiss him good-bye. Yet it was a futile urge, after all that had happened between them, and she fought against it.

Jamie waited for her. He would never press her. He'd gotten this one concession, and it felt like a blessing: he would look her up when he returned.

They circled back to town. Collected her possessions at the hotel. He accompanied her to the train station and waited with her on the platform. The platform became crowded. Boys in uniform, mothers in fine dresses and high heels, fathers in suits and ties: You dressed up to see your serviceman son off at the station. After all, you might never see him again. The sisters and mothers cried. The fathers and brothers pretended not to.

The train arrived too soon, even though it was twenty minutes late. Now it was beside them, waiting.

"All aboard," the conductor called.

Jamie took her shoulders and pulled her close. He hugged her as tightly as he could, and kissed her on the lips. He felt her lips open to his, felt her kissing him in return, felt her pushing her body against him.

The train whistle blew. Claire knew she had to pull away from him. She didn't want to. They pulled away together. With him beside her, she waited her turn to board the train. She climbed the steps, and he handed up her case and her equipment bags. Others followed, so she had no choice but to go in.

Feeling still the memory, the imprint, of his hands upon her back and shoulders, the moisture of his lips upon her cheeks, she hurried to the window. She joined the newly boarded passengers leaning toward the glass. The passengers knocked on the windows, to get the attention of those outside searching for them. The train began to move. One last look, one last wave . . . that might have to last a lifetime. She saw him. How handsome he was. The love of her life. He was searching for her but couldn't see her. The lowering sun was reflecting off the windowpanes, into his eyes. The train speeded up. He was lost to her view.

HISTORICAL NOTE

To write *A Fierce Radiance*, I spent many months reviewing books, newspapers, and periodicals dating from the World War II era. Although penicillin and other antibiotics are essential to our daily lives, the history of how they came into existence is little known. I felt compelled to explore this story.

After the British scientist Alexander Fleming discovered penicillin in 1928, he struggled without success to develop it into a viable medication. Penicillin was virtually forgotten until the Second World War broke out in Europe in 1939. Under the pressure of the war, British scientists looked at penicillin once more. Because of advances in technology, they had better luck than Fleming, although production remained heartrendingly difficult. As the Blitz intensified and Britain faced increasing hardships, penicillin research shifted to the United States. When America entered the war after the attack on Pearl Harbor in December of 1941, the mass production of penicillin came under the jurisdiction of the same government organization that would supervise the development of the atomic bomb. At D-Day, in June 1944, every medic going ashore in France carried penicillin in his pack. So successful were the pharmaceutical companies in mass producing penicillin that within five years after the end of the war, penicillin was worth less than the packaging it was sold in.

In the early days, penicillin was harvested and purified in small labs and tested on patients waiting nearby. Although the FDA existed, it did not have the regulatory authority that it now holds. Estimates are that roughly a million doses of penicillin were given before a patient suffered an allergic reaction; if the first patient to receive penicillin had experienced an allergic reaction, the drug may well have been abandoned. Antibiotics do produce a variety of side effects, however. For example, the first antibiotic to treat tuberculosis, streptomycin, discovered in 1943, can cause deafness.

As I pursued my research, I was struck by the fact that penicillin, a natural product, did not receive commercial patent protection, whereas the antibiotics that followed did, even though they, too, were natural products. This change intrigued me. *A Fierce Radiance* combines fact and fiction to create, I hope, an authentic portrait of a moment in time. The Hanover company is fictional, and therefore its prized antibacterial medication, Ceruleamycin, is also fictional, but Merck, Pfizer, and the other pharmaceutical companies mentioned are very much real and several are still prominent today. Many of the antibiotics (which I call "the cousins") that followed penicillin, including Aureomycin and Erythromycin, were developed in the same way as Ceruleamycin, beginning with researchers collecting soil samples from around the world.

The main characters in *A Fierce Radiance* are fictional, but several of the secondary characters are real, including Henry Luce, Clare Boothe Luce, Vannevar Bush, Dr. Chester Keefer, John Smith of Pfizer, and Dr. Thomas Rivers of the Rockefeller Institute. Anne Miller was indeed the first American to be rescued from death by penicillin. In each case, I have portrayed these individuals as accurately as possible. The events of the influenza epidemic of 1918 in Philadelphia took place as described, including the death carts that churches sent through the city streets to collect the bodies of their parishioners. Penicillin was in fact tested on burn victims after the Cocoanut Grove Fire. The Rockefeller Institute, now called the Rockefeller University, still has the humanitarian goals described in the novel. I have, however, simplified the various levels of government bureaucracy involved with penicillin development, and occasionally I have compressed time.

Claire Shipley's work as a photojournalist was inspired by, and in some cases based on, actual stories that ran in *Life* magazine during the war years. For example, the stories about the Johnny Jeep hat, and about taking care of pets during bombing raids, did indeed run in *Life*.

For readers who would like to learn more about the development of antibiotics, I recommend: *Penicillin: Meeting the Challenge* by Gladys L. Hobby; *The Enchanted Ring* by John C. Sheehan; and *The Forgotten Plague* by Frank Ryan, MD. For the history of *Life* magazine and the work of women journalists during World War II: *The Women Who Wrote the War* by Nancy Caldwell Sorel; Life *Photographers, What They Saw* by John Loengard; and *Margaret Bourke-White* by Vicki Goldberg. For life on the home front during World War II: *Don't You Know There's a War On?* by Richard R. Lingeman and *No Ordinary Time* by Doris Kearns Goodwin. And for New York in the 1940s: *The WPA Guide to New York City* and *Greenwich Village, Today & Yesterday* by Berenice Abbott and Henry W. Lanier.

Penicillin and the antibiotics that followed have changed the lives of virtually every human being in the past seventy years. Bacterial resistance to antibiotics developed from the beginning, however. Today, resistance is a major medical problem. Unless antibiotic use is curtailed, or new drugs are developed, humanity could easily return to the era when otherwise healthy adults died from a scratch on the knee.

ACKNOWLEDGMENTS

I give special thanks to Marnie Imhoff for welcoming me to the Rockefeller University, and to Carol Moberg for so generously sharing her extensive knowledge of the history of the Rockefeller Institute and of antibiotic research. Alfred Jaretzki III, MD, provided his insights into medicine and medical history, answering a million questions with the care, good humor, and encouragement that for many years have made him a dear friend as well as advisor. Professor Gil Rose of Swarthmore College assisted with the Latin. Bella Bankoff offered her memories of New York during the 1940s. Hannah Isles kindly shared her personal reflections on some of the issues raised in the novel. The librarians at the Rockefeller University, the New York Society Library, and the New York Public Library were unfailingly patient and helpful. Any inaccuracies are, of course, my own.

With her clear-sighted wisdom and discernment, Claire Wachtel, my brilliant editor, made this novel possible. She has my profound and eternal gratitude. Maya Ziv, perceptive, discerning, and delightful, guided the paperback into publication. Michael Morrison, Jonathan Burnham, and the staff of HarperCollins gave *A Fierce Radiance* their utmost attention. I thank Julia Novitch for her kindness, knowledge, and precision. The evocative cover was designed by Vaughn Andrews. For their many talents and generosity, I also thank Diane Aronson, Shelly Perron, William Ruoto, Eric Levy, and Anne Weiss. On the publicity side, Heather Drucker was a master and a miracle worker. Jocelyn Kelley brimmed with ideas and energy. At ICM, Tina Wexler and Elizabeth Perrella smoothed my way with their bright spirits. My deep appreciation goes to my marvelous agent, and friend, Lisa Bankoff, who not only stood by me during the years I wrote this novel, but also reviewed the manuscript with her remarkable literary acumen.

I have been blessed by wonderful friends who've inspired me with their support, encouragement, and affection. For wise, warm counsel and much-needed laughter, I thank Alexandra Isles, and Ann Darby, Roxanne Donovan, Cornelia Dopkins, Dick Dopkins, Beth Gutcheon, Cindy Halpern, John Hargraves, Marnie Imhoff, Grace Ledbetter, Nancy Newcomb, Ida Nicolaisen, Heidi Rotterdam, Jeff Scheuer, Laura Scheuer, Carol Shapiro, Elisa Shokoff, the late Robin Magavern, and of course, Richard Osterweil. I'm especially grateful to Beth Gutcheon for her extraordinary generosity and understanding, as well as her eagle eye.

Above all, I thank Michael Marissen. He knows the reasons why.

About the author

Insights,
Interviews
& More . . .

How I Became a Writer

WHEN I WAS SIX YEARS OLD, I decided to become a writer. I can't explain why. The conviction swept over me one day while I was walking to school and never left me. During my early writing years, I penned short stories about magical pets and warrior princesses who ruled their kingdoms wisely and rode into battle on white horses. I'm happy to report that by high school I'd put aside pets and princesses and turned my attention to other literary pursuits. With the guidance of my terrific teachers, I sent my poems to magazines around the country. I collected rejection letters from all the best places. Some of them included a word or two of polite thanks for the submission, which I interpreted as encouragement.

Once I was out of college, I focused on writing fiction, but I also faced the pesky problem of earning a living. So I got up early and wrote for an hour before leaving for work. I held a variety of jobs: a paralegal at a law firm, an assistant photo editor at a newspaper, a researcher at an art gallery, an associate producer on documentary films, and a fact-checker at magazines. In retrospect, I realize that having a wide variety of jobs is terrific training for a fiction writer, because it teaches you about professions you can lend to your characters. But in those days I was just happy to be able to pay the rent.

The first short story I ever published was rejected forty-two times before it found an editor who loved it. I experienced much better success with my second story: it was rejected only twenty-seven times before it

66 In retrospect, I realize that having a wide variety of jobs is terrific for a fiction writer, because it teaches you about professions you can lend to your characters. 99

found an editor who loved it. Twenty-seven rejections, let alone forty-two, take years. Having my short stories rejected became part of my job—printing fresh copies, sending them out, having them rejected, printing more copies, sending them out, having them rejected, and so on.

Then one day, a letter arrived from the editor of a prestigious literary journal. The editor wrote that he had been moved by the story I'd sent him. He wanted to publish it. Reading this letter felt peculiar; I wasn't prepared for it. I quickly concluded that the editor was mistaken. He had confused my story with another, one that belonged to someone else. But no, the envelope included a contract to sign and return, and the contract listed the title of my story. I accepted before he could change his mind, but the acceptance took a while to integrate into my routine: what was I supposed to do with my list of editors who hadn't yet had the opportunity to reject this particular story? Well, luckily those editors got their chance with future stories.

Often I'm asked if I have any advice for aspiring writers. My first piece of advice, distilled into one word, is this: persistence. Forty-two rejections of one story may seem like a lot, but without them my story never would have reached the editor who published it.

My second piece of advice goes against the common wisdom of "write what you know." What you know is the given, the default background of everything you write, because it's an inescapable part of who you are. Instead, write what you don't know but want to learn about—whether it's a warrior princess riding into battle on a white horse, or a photojournalist ▶

> **" I quickly concluded that the editor was mistaken. He had confused my story with another, one that belonged to someone else. "**

How I Became a Writer *(continued)*

covering the development of antibiotics during the Second World War. I believe that the urge to discover gives immediacy and passion to writing. Readers sense this energy and become caught up in the writer's voyage, and when this happens, the reader will follow you anywhere. ❧

An Interview with Lauren Belfer

How did you get the idea for A Fierce Radiance?

At its heart, *A Fierce Radiance* is a story about my own family. For all the years that I knew her, my elderly aunt kept a photo on her bureau of her brother in the 1920s, when he was nine or ten years old: a blond boy paddling a canoe with his father, both of them laughing and in high spirits. This was the last picture my aunt had of her brother. He died at age eleven from a fast-moving infection contracted after a Fourth of July celebration. Antibiotics probably would have saved his life. That is, if antibiotics had existed.

Sixty years after his death, my aunt still mourned him. She told me that the light and happiness went out of her parents' spirits after he died, and that she grew up in a home filled with sadness.

When I spoke with friends about this story, they often responded by telling me stories of their own: about a loved one who had died from a sore throat, from the scratch of a rose thorn, or from a blister caused by new shoes. All stories of beloved family members who died from an infection because antibiotics didn't exist.

These stories compelled me to write *A Fierce Radiance*. I wanted to learn how penicillin and other antibiotics were developed, and how the momentous transformation they brought to humanity was experienced by individuals living the change in their daily lives. ▶

> 66 I wanted to learn how penicillin and other antibiotics were developed, and how the momentous transformation they brought to humanity was experienced by individuals living the change in their daily lives. 99

An Interview with Lauren Belfer *(continued)*

Do you have a background in science and medicine?

When I started, I knew next to nothing about antibiotics, and apart from required courses in high school and college, I'd never studied science or medicine. So I set out to learn what I needed to know to write the novel. I read medical histories, as well as the memoirs of scientists and researchers who'd made discoveries during the 1930s and 1940s. A friend introduced me to the scientists at the Rockefeller University in New York, where some of the early antibiotic investigations were conducted. Drawn into the idealistic atmosphere of that center for medical research, I reviewed the pioneering work of René Dubos and other scientists, and I pored over photographs of old laboratories. I began to feel my way into the world of scientific and medical research, a process that took years and felt like learning a foreign language.

Even as I became conversant in the language of science, however, I kept in mind that I didn't want to write a textbook or a treatise. I wanted to write a novel, a close portrayal of people and their emotions, dreams, and struggles. I knew that the scientific material in the novel would only be compelling to my readers if it was reflected through the passions of my characters, and so, from the beginning, I tried to view the science through their eyes.

Why did you make the main character a photojournalist?

> I knew that the scientific material in the novel would only be compelling to my readers if it was reflected through the passions of my characters, and so, from the beginning, I tried to view the science through their eyes.

In addition to taking photography courses in high school and college, I once worked as an assistant photo editor at a newspaper. I knew my way around the darkroom, and I was intrigued by photojournalism. So creating Claire Shipley was a way to imagine an alternate future for myself.

I also realized that a photojournalist would be an ideal narrator. Claire is an outsider looking in at the world of scientific research—just as I was when I began to research the novel. Claire feels a profound, indeed heartrending interest in the development of antibiotics because of its importance to her own family, and she learns about science and medicine as she pursues her work—just as I did.

Claire's profession gives her a unique perspective on the issues of her day, a perspective invaluable to me as I shaped the novel. A fearless pioneer, Claire resembles Margaret Bourke-White, the renowned *Life* magazine photojournalist and one of the first female war correspondents ever to work in combat zones.

Why did you choose the World War II era for A Fierce Radiance?

Most of the research that led to the mass production of antibiotics took place in America under the pressure of the Second World War, so the time period chose itself.

You bring a vivid sense of immediacy to the American home front during World War II. How did you do that? ▶

In portraying the nation at war, I tried to forget everything I knew about the actual course of history and imagine what those months and years must have been like for people experiencing them moment by moment, unsure of what the future would bring. For example, from our perspective in 2010, we know very well that New York City and other American cities were never bombed during World War II. But, as I discovered in my research, people living in those days assumed that American cities *would* be bombed. They were horrified by the devastating bombings of London and Rotterdam, and they expected the same to happen in America. I tried to capture their fears, their hopes, and their desperate plans to take care of their families if their homes were destroyed and the nation invaded. I put myself into their shoes, asking myself: how would I feel if enemy soldiers were marching down my street? Would food and fresh water be available? Would electricity and plumbing be functioning? What would I need to do, and how far would I be willing to go, to help my family survive?

What was your research process for the novel?

I read every issue of *Life* magazine from 1939, when the war began in Europe, through 1945, when the war ended. I read years of the *New York Times* on microfilm. The *Times* archive is available online, but microfilm was much better for my purposes, because it showed me the advertisements as well as the short announcements and articles that often

66 How would I feel if enemy soldiers were marching down my street? Would food and fresh water be available? Would electricity and plumbing be functioning? 99

appeared at the top and bottom of the pages and contained a wealth of information.

By systematically reading *Life* and the *New York Times*, I discovered a home front I'd never known about. I read article after article on how to prepare your family and your home for bombing raids. These touching stories included the smallest details of daily life. For example, since pets were forbidden in air-raid shelters, *Life* ran a photo essay on how to prepare dogs and cats for air attacks. While families went to the air-raid shelters, dogs were supposed to be leashed to the foot of the bathtub, or to the bathtub faucet, and left with a chew toy and a bowl of water. Cats were to be put in boxes or crates next to the dogs and also given a toy and a bowl of water. I was forced to imagine what I would tell my young son if we had to leave our beloved golden retriever leashed to the bathtub while we went to an air-raid shelter.

Did you make any unexpected discoveries during your research?

I'd never known that during the first winter after America's entry into the war, invasion was considered not just possible, but likely. *Life* predicted that the enemy would take a three-pronged approach: Japanese forces would move through Alaska and into the Pacific Northwest, while the Germans would simultaneously attack New York City and New Orleans, moving north along the Mississippi River valley to divide the nation. Americans were told to sabotage infrastructure facilities to prevent them ▶

> " While families went to the air-raid shelters, dogs were supposed to be leashed to the foot of the bathtub, or to the bathtub faucet, and left with a chew toy and a bowl of water. "

from falling to the enemy. Reading advice on how Americans should blow up their own bridges and rail lines to keep them out of enemy hands truly brought the war home to me.

You mention advertisements. What role did they play in your research?

I took great pleasure in reading the advertisements in *Life* and in the *New York Times*. I learned the popular styles in everything from clothes and alcoholic beverages, to automobiles and kitchen appliances. In the *Times* I learned what was on sale at Macy's, so if Claire Shipley needed new shoes, say, she could buy them at a good price. Of course I could have invented such details, but using the reality whenever possible made the scenes more immediate for me and also, I hope, for my readers.

One advertisement in particular still haunts me: an ad in the *New York Times*, placed by Bonwit Teller, for cashmere sweaters imported from Scotland. The ad said the sweaters had survived the Battle of the North Atlantic to get to Bonwit's and that we Americans had a responsibility to help our British allies by buying these sweaters. Nowadays we tend to be cynical about advertising, but that ad brought tears to my eyes. I wanted to go straight to Bonwit's and help Britain by buying a sweater!

New York City is like a character in the novel—how did you conjure up the wartime city?

> **66** The ad said the sweaters had survived the Battle of the North Atlantic to get to Bonwit's and that we Americans had a responsibility to help our British allies by buying these sweaters. **99**

In addition to reading about the city during the war in the *New York Times*, I sought out collections of photographs from the 1930s and 1940s, so I could study exactly how the city looked—what people wore on the streets, what goods were displayed in the shop windows, and what cars were popular. I spent hours walking the streets of Greenwich Village to get a feel for the places that Claire Shipley walked, to put myself in her shoes and imagine what her life was like: shopping for groceries, going to a café, or walking her dog. The Village is my favorite part of New York, the most intriguing and haunting to me—its centuries-old homes, its narrow, cobblestone streets, and its tradition of Bohemianism and political and artistic rebellion. I pictured Claire and her family as part of their neighborhood's tumultuous history.

In the novel, a fictional pharmaceutical company tests a new (fictional) antibiotic on Japanese-American prisoners held at an internment camp in the West. Did anything like that really happen?

I have no evidence that new medications were tested on the Japanese Americans held at internment camps during World War II. However, all through the 1940s, medications were indeed tested on prisoners and on the disabled, so my fictionalization of the testing is entirely plausible. Recently, the U.S. government apologized for infecting prisoners and others in Guatemala with venereal ▶

diseases in the years immediately after World War II to test whether penicillin could cure them.

What draws you to historical fiction?

When I read for pleasure, I almost always choose a work of historical fiction. I'm fascinated by how people lived in earlier eras, and by the passions and struggles that motivated them. By its very nature, historical fiction is about individuals struggling with the choices that their societies give them. Reading historical fiction is the closest we can come to experiencing what it actually felt like, in a visceral way, to live in a different time and place. It can also give unique insight into our own family histories.

In addition, I suspect that deep down I have an emotional reason for my attraction: my father taught history and my mother taught art—and is still an artist—so history and creativity have always been part of the fabric of my life. From discussing history with my father throughout my childhood, I learned to place myself in different historical eras and to imagine what it would have felt like to live in those times. As I developed as a writer, I wanted to use my knowledge of history to portray how the events of the wider world affect daily life.

How is the story of A Fierce Radiance *relevant to our lives today?*

After it was published, many strangers came up to me at book events to tell me that their families had stories like the

66 Reading historical fiction is the closest we can come to experiencing what it actually felt like, in a visceral way, to live in a different time and place. 99

novel's. They told me about grandparents, parents, aunts, and uncles who died because penicillin and other antibiotics didn't exist—just as friends had told me such stories when they heard about my aunt's brother. These stories reverberate through generations of families.

In the approximately sixty years since antibiotics became widely available, the medications have been so successful that they've simply become a given, always there when we need them. In the process, they've changed the way we look at life. Because of antibiotics, we now presume our children will survive into adulthood and that adults generally will survive into old age.

As I learned during my research, however, this presumption is false. The story told in *A Fierce Radiance* has a frightening relevance to our world today. Due to overuse, more and more antibiotics don't work. Infectious bacteria are becoming increasingly resistant to these medications. Even methicillin and vancomycin, two of the most powerful antibiotics, have been weakened by resistance. An entire class of bacteria has now been labeled MRSA, for methicillin-resistant *Staphlococcus aureus.* Another is called VRE, for vancomycin-resistant *Enterococcus faecium.* What these complex phrases mean—as I learned from my research—is that the people we care about most are once again dying from infections that were curable just a few years ago. For the first time in decades, human beings are once again dying from scratches on the knee. ∽

> " Due to overuse, more and more antibiotics don't work. Infectious bacteria are becoming increasingly resistant to these medications. "

Surprising Facts
I Learned During
My Research

1. Penicillin, and many other antibiotics,
   are made from common molds and
   mold products. Nowadays we take these
   medications so much for granted that
   until I wrote the novel I had never
   stopped to think about where they
   came from. But once I did I almost
   didn't believe it: *antibiotics? mold?*
   The idea seemed outlandish. *Penicillium*,
   for example, is the mold that makes
   blue cheese blue and that grows on
   stale bread. The molds used to make
   antibiotics were, and still are, discovered
   through trial and error. In the 1940s,
   pharmaceutical companies asked people
   around the world to collect and submit
   soil samples to their laboratories for
   testing. These soil samples came from
   mountaintops and riverbanks, from
   backyards and garbage dumps. One type
   of antibiotic, cephalosporin, was found
   in a sewage outlet in Sardinia.

2. Before modern medicine, people in
   parts of eastern Europe traditionally
   kept a loaf of stale, moldy bread in their
   kitchens. When a family member had a
   skin injury, people cut off the moldy end
   of the bread and bandaged it upon the
   wound to prevent infection. Although
   people didn't know this, they were
   harnessing the power of what we would
   come to call penicillin. I do wonder,
   though, who first had the idea to wrap
   moldy bread on skin wounds?

“ One type
of antibiotic,
cephalosporin,
was found in a
sewage outlet in
Sardinia. ”

3. Briton Hadden, who co-founded *Time* magazine with Henry Luce, died at the age of thirty-one from blood poisoning brought on by a scratch from a pet cat.

4. I found it an essential—and little known—fact of Henry Luce's character that he grew up in China, the son of American missionaries. I believe that because of his outsider's perspective, he developed an idealized and idealistic view of America and of what America could and should be. This view came to be reflected in his magazines.

5. The German American Nazi group, the Bund, was more active before World War II than I ever imagined. The Bund held mass rallies in New York City and ran youth camps around the country.

6. In any war before antibiotics, more troops died from infection than from actual wounds on the battlefield. The desire to reverse this horrifying statistic was a prime motivator in the development of penicillin.

7. During the worldwide influenza epidemic of 1918, the number of deaths was so overwhelming that in Philadelphia, for example, "death carts" from the churches and synagogues went through the streets to collect the bodies of parishioners for burials in mass graves. The epidemic traumatized American families. Newspapers didn't report on it honestly, however. World War I was still raging in Europe, and newspapers didn't want to appear unpatriotic by reporting on mass ▶

❝ In any war before antibiotics, more troops died from infection than from actual wounds on the battlefield. ❞

Surprising Facts I Learned During My Research *(continued)*

graves at home. In America today, we've essentially forgotten the trauma of the influenza epidemic of 1918, even though it touched almost every family.

8. New York City's FDR Drive, originally called the East River Drive, was built on rubble from the bombed-out city of Bristol, England, that was brought to New York as ballast on merchant ships.

9. Nowadays, we often hear about people being allergic to penicillin, but approximately a million doses of the medication were given before a patient suffered an allergic reaction. If the first patient to receive penicillin had had an allergic reaction, most likely research on the medication would have been abandoned, and antibiotics might never have been developed. ∾

Don't miss the next book by your favorite author. Sign up now for AuthorTracker by visiting www.AuthorTracker.com.